CUP OF THE SHINING SUN

cup
OF THE
Shining Sun

DYAN DUBOIS

LUMINARE PRESS
WWW.LUMINAREPRESS.COM

CUP OF THE SHINING SUN

Printed in the United States of America

Cover Design by

Luminare Press
442 Charnelton St.
Eugene, OR 97401
www.luminarepress.com

LCCN: 2020916636
ISBN: 978-1-64388-441-7

For Sarah,
the inspired traveler

Table of Contents

Acknowledgements

Creating may be solitary, but refining requires a team. My deepest thanks to those who supported this effort with their invaluable editing advice and encouragement: Rajinder Gill, Anthea Guinness, Jan Weir, Peggy Meyer, Janet Switzer, and Rentia Humphries.

Chapter One

The Oracle

A shadow blocked the Aegean sun. Askara shifted her position on the stone wall and waited for the darkness in her vision to turn orange, aware the spasm in her back from the cramped economy seat had slowly released. Relief seeped into her like warm honey. She inhaled the fresh air of the Oracle of Delphi, but the shadow remained. Shielding her brow, Askara opened her eyes and shuddered. A man stood only three feet away. Askara bolted upright.

He apologized for startling her, saying he wanted to read the plaque covered by her foot. Askara forced a weak smile, pushed the hair back from her face, and assured him she had dozed off momentarily and didn't know about the plaque. She glanced at the bronze rectangle: *Tholos of Delphi, circular temple, sacred Temple of Athena Pronaia, center of the world. Please do not climb on sacred stones.*

She stood, grasping her backpack. "I'm the one in the way. Sorry."

"Please, stay. I'm leaving. You were here first." He leaned forward to rub dust from the bronze plaque. "That much I knew...center of the world."

Askara smiled. "Well, you're ahead of me. How is this the center of the world?"

"Zeus declared it. He released two eagles to cross the world in opposite directions, and they met here; therefore, it's the center of the world. I hope you don't think this forward, but you look like a woman I knew years ago, at school in India, but you sound American."

"I'm American. And Indian. My dad's from the Punjab, mom's American. I wasn't educated in India." Usually, Askara would have scoffed at such a weak lead-in. But this man seemed genuinely embarrassed and polite. "I look like her? Funny, Californians mistake me for Mexican, but you nailed Indian right away. Where's your home?"

"Bombay." He extended his hand. "I'm Darian Dalal."

"Askara Timlen. Delphi feels special. Think the prophetess is still here?"

Darian looked at her quizzically and grinned, revealing a narrow gap between his front teeth. "Not since the 4th century A.D. You know how it goes, nothing like tourists to ruin a marvelous thing."

Askara laughed, "Yep, especially Americans who sleep on hallowed ground. No respect. What brings you to Greece, pleasure, or work?"

"Both. I am on a business trip. My family firm in Bombay runs an import/export company, industrial products, rubber, metal parts, that sort of thing. I travel often, so I make a point of visiting cultural sites. Makes work trips more enjoyable. You?"

"Work trip. Antiques buyer. I work for a man in San Francisco, importer of carpets, jewelry, art, you know, high-end things. He sends me to finish deals—mostly verify authenticity. I do the sign-offs. I'm like a white-glove service. Pay's fair; travel's great."

"You must be good at what you do."

"I've nailed two big sales for Mr. Ramsey, one in Africa, so he sent me back again. I'm en route to Kenya to handle an Ethiopian heirloom jewelry purchase.

"Selassie's selling off jewels?" Darian said in disbelief.

"Not the Emperor, someone else, probably a distant cousin. Ramsey is super interested in this deal. I thought he'd go himself, but his wife is pregnant. He needs to stay close to home, so here I am."

"You handle everything? You will travel home with jewels?"

"Ramsey has a friend Mr. Reh who will help me. He'll introduce me to the person representing the family. I'll re-evaluate the piece—not hard—since Ramsey saw the jewelry himself a year ago. I need to verify it's not a facsimile. Ramsey's friend will help me with the tax forms, everything on the up-and-up. Mr. Ramsey's fastidious about legal issues. He has a great reputation in San Francisco. That means a lot to him, a whole lot. Mr. Reh'll escort me to the airport, help with declarations paperwork, and I'll fly home to San Francisco.

Askara read the surprise on Darian's face and something else…admiration. That felt good. She noticed he had checked out her hands, no wedding ring, just as she had his. No wedding ring. He implied a transaction like that could put her in jeopardy. But Askara assured him Ramsey was thorough. What she omitted—that she questioned Ramsey's loyalty, based on the café waitress Mimi he daily visited when he went for Turkish coffee—made her feel sorry for his wife.

"I have business in Nairobi in two days. Do you stay in Nairobi?"

"Mombasa," Askara said.

"Oh. Would you want to meet for a one-day safari? It would be pleasant to have company."

"Sure. That sounds fun. Contact the Whispering Palms Hotel. I don't have the number on me." When the sun slipped to touch the olive trees, Askara realized she should hurry. "Oops, my bus for Athens leaves at four. I want to look around more first." Askara felt her face redden as she said, "Have time in Athens for dinner some night?"

"Yes. I have no set plans. I completed my work yesterday. Tomorrow I will see the Acropolis and downtown sites. Interested in walking the Acropolis in the afternoon? We could have dinner if that works for you."

"Sounds great." Askara looked around. "Wow, wonderful view from here. I thought the walk from the gate was good but look down the mountain. It's even more impressive. Want to walk around a few minutes?"

They circled the central platform of the Tholos ruins and heard a guide answer a tourist's question. Askara grimaced at the American man's pronunciation. He asked if *Playdoh* came to the Oracle for advice. The guide politely told him he suspected so. All the leaders consulted the Oracle before they made decisions.

Darian whispered to Askara, "This was a hotbed for intellectual dissertation. Plato certainly would have been here."

"Yeah, the priestess must have been amazing. Talk about power. Based on her prophecies, men made war or peace. Too bad the temple's gone." Swinging wide around the three remaining columns, she stepped into the center of the circle. The sunbaked stones tickled her feet. Her legs went weak like electrical circuits cutting out, sputtering, turning numb, she heard a whisper from the earth, a woman's voice. She turned to Darian and grabbed his forearm to balance.

"Did you hear that? Someone whispered."

"No, want to sit? You're tired. Probably the breeze, maybe that tourist over there. Sound travels. Great acoustics here. From the amphitheater's top rung, you can hear a pin drop center stage. I saw a guide demonstrate that."

"No, the sound came up from the earth."

Darian smiled. "Yes, I read that in the brochure. The Oracle speaks like a whisper from the earth. Guess you read that too."

Askara realized she sounded absurd. She smirked. "Yep." But Askara felt something she could not explain. Her head throbbed when she looked at the broken columns in front of her; they swayed. She shut her eyes and slumped like a rag doll.

Darian steadied her before she hit the ground. Easing her into a sitting position, he told her to bend her head over her knees and breathe. He grabbed a bottle of water from his bag. "Here, drink this. You've gotten too much sun, probably dehydrated."

Askara reached for the bottle and sipped. Minutes passed. Darian sat next to her, wrapped his arm around her shoulders to brace her.

"Sorry, don't know what's happening. I suddenly felt so dizzy. Things aren't moving now. I'm okay." When she tried to stand, she collapsed on her haunches. Had she felt better, she would have laughed; instead, she mumbled, "Wow," in a weak voice.

"Pardon. This sounds brash, but are you pregnant?"

Askara thought, not unless it's the immaculate conception. "No," she said in a thready voice. "Think I'm low blood sugar. Have anything to eat?"

Darian pulled a candy bar from his bag and ripped the foil. Askara gummed the sticky chocolate slowly. She sat still. "That helped, thanks. I need to catch the bus back to Athens." She stood and found her feet under her this time. "I've got to go. It's a long walk down."

"I have a car and driver. Can I give you a lift?"

"That would be better, thank you," she said and looked at Darian, his eyebrows a rippled arch over his eyes. "Don't worry. I'm fine."

"Sit here. I will find my driver. He's sleeping in the olive grove down there. He'll bring the car to the gate."

Askara wanted to look up at Darian, but the sun's angle made her eyes sting. Instead, she looked at her knees and nodded *yes*. Hearing his loafers crunch the dry grass as he trotted away, Askara sat against the stone wall in the shade of a column and waited. When the queasiness left her stomach, she heard a woman's voice whisper: *Beware of men with gold and eyes that see.* Askara whipped around. No one was there. In the distance, she saw a small Darian descending the hill. When the guard approached and ordered her off the wall, she asked if he had heard a woman speaking. The man waved her toward the exit gate. She slowly moved away and trudged down the path. Darian met her and led her to the car. During the two-hour drive to Athens, Askara slept.

SINCE THAT DAY, ASKARA HAD PLENTY OF TIME TO THINK about how she and Darian had met at the Oracle and their two nights of passion in Athens. And the irony of it. No woman could have maneuvered to lure a man any better, yet she had no intention to do so. On a business trip to land her largest-to-date assignment, hoping to become her boss' number one purchasing agent, wasn't particularly a girl meets boy in paradise scenario. How did she, a woman who had given up on love, run smack into it when she wasn't looking?

Askara assumed their reunion in Mombasa would be sublimely passionate. Her luck had shifted: love could be hers. She walked to the window to lift the wooden blind with a finger. Bright sun on sand and water made her eyes squint at the thin line where sea and sky merge. She wondered, where is he? Her thoughts raced back to Darian on that sunny December afternoon at the Oracle of Delphi. She saw him standing in the center of the ruin, three feet from her. His simple—didn't mean to startle you—changed everything.

Askara kicked her sandal across the tile floor. A gecko scurried up the wall to the ceiling; the lizard's pale pink body melded with the dull plaster. She wiped her face with a limp handkerchief. His words their last night in Athens—let's see where this leads—reverberated in her head. Askara, feeling foolish, remembered how eagerly she had replied *yes*. Famous last words. Now Darian's a no-show.

Her thoughts escalated when she heard someone outside. She yanked open the moisture-swollen door. The estate gardener at the Whispering Palms Resort nodded with an enormous smile. Askara's excitement crackled like old porcelain. Her disappointment matched the rising heat. She nodded kindly and said *Jambo* before slamming the door.

She knew the only way to shake off the blues was to swim. She plied the pool's length multiple times, catching glimpses of life above the waterline. Women in bright dresses raced across her goggles: affluent Africans, Asians, and Europeans. She spotted a Kikuyu woman in a traditional print dress, yellow and brown geometrics, with a matching headscarf, encircled by men and women jockeying to get close. From billboards in Nairobi, Askara guessed she was Margaret Kenyatta, the mayor of Nairobi, President Jomo Kenyatta's daughter. She heard a baritone voice from the outdoor piano bar singing *Moon River*. She gulped air, flipped a turn, and started back, stopping mid-lane hearing her name. A man in a khaki safari suit motioned to her. She swam to the edge.

"Madam Timlen? Bungalow 5?"

"Yes."

"There's a caller for you at the front desk."

Askara jumped out, threw a beach dress on, and followed the man to the lobby. Still trying to untangle her braid, she spotted Darian.

"You came!" She extended her dripping hand. He enveloped hers in both of his. Askara felt the warmth of his grasp against the coldness of hers.

"As soon as I could."

Askara smiled. She led the way through the lobby, across the pool patio, and down the rose-and-jasmine garden path to her bungalow. When they reached the door, she pushed the door open with her body.

"Why didn't you call?"

"Didn't think I needed to. You knew I was coming as soon as I could when I finished."

Askara felt relieved but put in her place. She worried she sounded like an angry housewife. She didn't *know* he would come; she hoped he would come. Heat rose in her face. "Good to see you, Darian. I had hoped to see you two days ago when I had more free time. Unfortunately, I have a big negotiation tonight, the business dinner party thing I'd mentioned. Here, rest on the cot in the front room. You must be tired. Turn on the ceiling fan. Relax. There's cold beer in the fridge. I've got to get ready for tonight."

Darian set his suitcase down by the door. "Would you rather I booked another room?"

"Do you want to?"

"I don't want to inconvenience you. I hoped to escort you to that dinner, if agreeable. Have things changed, Askara?"

Askara tried to pull herself together. Darian's not contacting her to say he would be late, hurt her, and made her question him. After all, they had only spent two days together. Hard to know someone in such a short time, she knew. But he had come, even if he had not bothered to let her know when. "Sure, come if you'd like. Might be very boring. Mr. Reh's driver comes for me at seven o'clock. I have to get ready." Askara walked into her bedroom and yanked the door so hard it shook in the frame when she closed it.

Darian opened a cold Tusker and slumped in the chair on the porch, under the whirring fan. "Askara," Darian called out, "may I speak to you?"

Askara heard him but turned on the shower to wash away her chlorine tears and pretended she couldn't. She dried off and stood at the mirror, applying kohl to her eyelids. No need for blush, she thought. She slipped into a saffron-colored *salwar kameez* suit and began weaving her damp hair into a French braid when she heard Darian's muffled voice.

"I'll be out in a minute." Dousing herself with tuberose oil, she finished her braid and slipped into heeled sandals that boosted her height. But she lingered in the bathroom, feeling embarrassed, unsure of how to proceed.

Darian spoke loudly through the closed door. "Askara, I offended you. I promised to meet you. I should have wired when I had to delay. Please, accept my apology. I, in no way, meant to hurt you."

Relieved, Askara opened the door. She gave him a wry smile. "Thank you, but you don't owe me. I made assumptions. We haven't known one another very long."

He lifted her chin to lock her gaze. "You think we hardly know each other. Is that how you *feel*?"

Askara cast her eyes down. "Well, we met a week ago. Two dates in Athens. That's not much time to know each other."

Darian laughed. "We've known each for ages. At least, that's how I feel. When I saw you at the Oracle, I recognized you. I wanted to know you again. I walked to you."

Askara shifted and studied her fancy, gold sandals. "Sorry. We need to go. Let's resume this talk when we get home. Duty calls. I'm so nervous, Darian. Thank you for coming. My contact, Mr. Reh, has arranged a meeting tonight with a Mr. Nagali from Uganda. He's only in Mombasa this evening; then, he returns to Kampala. So much rides on me pulling off this deal."

"Understood. I'm quite happy to escort you, and I know how these things work. I'll be your silent business partner at dinner."

"Mr. Nagali is President Idi Amin's soothsayer."

"What? A witch doctor is selling gems. Must be black market. Why would he have access to Ethiopian heirloom jewelry? Askara, we might find a dead chicken tacked to your bungalow door when we return."

Askara laughed. "Legitimate. My boss sees to that. I can't mess it up."

A knock rattled the door. Askara jumped and rushed to open it. A thin African man wearing a safari suit, straw hat in hand, said, "*Jambo, Mama*. Mr. Reh sent me to collect you.

I wait there." He pointed to a black Citroën parked under a palm tree on the white gravel drive. He turned and walked toward the car, leaned against the bumper, and lit a cigarette.

THE DRIVER SKIRTED THE INDIAN OCEAN BEFORE TURNING inland on a small road edged by field after field of sisal plants, pale green against red Kenyan dirt. In thirty minutes, they arrived at the entrance to Mr. Reh's compound. Pink, purple, and white bougainvillea flanked the driveway that ended at a massive English Tudor-style house.

"Vestige of colonial days," Askara whispered to Darian.

"Independence hasn't hurt Mr. Reh," Darian replied.

Askara fidgeted with stray tendrils of her hair and straightened her tunic. She hoped to make a great first impression. The unspoken seconds before a deal make all the difference, she knew. And this deal meant a lot to her, her most expensive purchase, an important one. Mr. Ramsey wanted heirloom jewelry to be a significant entry in his upcoming book, and he expected Askara to buy a fantastic piece on this trip, one he could credit as his own. She understood that meant he trusted her judgment and her ability to land an outstanding deal on an international scale. That would make or break her career, in his eyes, she knew. He might even have her direct the jewelry side of his business someday. He asked her to help him produce his book on jewelry, saying he preferred antiques and carpets. Plus, with two young sons, and another child on the way, Mr. Ramsey told her he no longer liked international buying trips. Europe, yes, but Africa and Asia, no. Askara knew she could build her niche and grow the business. She had always wanted to be in charge. This purchase would be the start.

Mr. Reh's driver stopped. Before Askara could gather her things, he sprinted around the car, opened her door with a white-gloved hand, and stepped back into a ramrod salute as she stepped out.

"Thank you," she said before the man vaulted back into the driver's seat to move his car out of the way of a large, black Mercedes full of Europeans.

"Busy chap," Darian whispered to Askara.

Darian and Askara walked the flagstone path lined with roses to a patio crowded with cocktail-in-hand guests conversing in English and Swahili: African men in traditional and Western garb, African women in popular silkscreened prints, Indian women in saris and 24-carat gold jewelry, and their men in Western suits. The British stood out as much for their pale skin as their lack of style with women in pearl jewelry and pastel floral dresses and men in dark suits. Askara sighed, British colonial understatement at its best.

A man stuffed into a tuxedo cinched by a tight cummerbund dashed across the well-manicured lawn to greet them. He extended his hand. "Miss Timlen?"

"Yes."

"Mr. Reh here. Wonderful to meet you. Your boss, my dear friend Mr. Seth Ramsey, praises you highly, says you have a keen eye for jewelry. And how is he keeping?"

"He's fine. Busy as ever, working on a book, the history of jewelry."

"Is that so? How nice for him. Such a learned man." Mr. Reh turned to Darian and extended his hand. "Nadir Reh, here."

"Mr. Reh, this is my friend, Darian Dalal."

"How good of you to come to my humble gathering," he said, glancing over at the Europeans pouring from the newly arrived Mercedes. "Now, if you will excuse me, I must greet my guests. I shall look forward to conversing with you at dinner. Please, my house is yours. I shall advise you, Miss Timlen, when Mr. Nagali arrives. I take my leave now." With a slight bow that crimped his girth, forcing him to straighten abruptly, he excused himself.

Darian caught Askara's hand in his, grinned, and led her to a seat by the fountain where water splashed from menacing gargoyle faces into a large pond of goldfish and pink lotus flowers.

"Perfect place for guest-watching," he said before a waiter in a stiff white suit and a large red turban, rushed over to offer them drinks and hors d'oeuvres.

"What about your contact?" Darian asked, dipping an Indian Ocean prawn's broad pink-and-white stripes into a spicy sauce.

"Mr. Nagali? Don't know much about him. He's Zambian, lives in Kampala, Uganda, and works for the government. Ramsey met him through Mr. Reh. I think Mr. Reh's cousin Haroon works for Nagali in a Mercedes import business."

Darian perked up. "Hmm, I wonder if I would know anyone Nagali works with?"

"You deal with African countries?"

"No, not yet. Our business focuses on Asia. Africa's an up-and-coming market if politics do not get in the way. That's why I came here to negotiate a contract with the Kenyan government. African Ugandans are bitter toward Asian Ugandans—after all, the Asians control the country's economy—but until the Africans can manage as well, far better for everyone to have a flourishing market than not. Here in Kenya, the prejudice isn't strong."

"That's not such a popular topic."

"No, I suppose not, but these affluent Kenyans largely control their country now."

Askara felt herself enjoying Darian's company, as she had when they first met in Athens. What seemed aloofness, his formal way of expressing himself must be cultural, a carryover from British rule, an imprint of his upper-class education, she figured.

As the evening light faded, they strolled indoors to listen to a band play European pop music. Some guests danced. They sat and watched. Darian had told her he didn't know how to dance. Rather than offering to teach him, Askara nodded and said she preferred talking. It took her mind off the task at hand.

By the time dinner was served at midnight, many had drunk their dinner in the previous hours, making their conversations animated, verging on incoherent, political discussions. The guests embroiled in ideology drifted out to the veranda with their drinks and cigarettes, while Askara and Darian sat with other hungry guests at the long table. Hardly anyone spoke. Separated by crystal vases brimming with eye-level bird-of-paradise flowers, they waited as servants brought dish after dish to them. The smell of curries wafted on the warm night air, provoking havoc with guard dogs tethered at the far end of Reh's lawn.

Mr. Reh, at the head of the table, thanked his guests for coming and commanded them to enjoy the excellent Kenyan coffee from his brother's estate, served with desserts out on the veranda, before departing. As Mr. Reh approached, Askara felt an immediate revulsion to the man walking beside him. She knew he was Mr. Nagali. Mr. Reh introduced them quickly and excused himself to talk to other guests.

Mr. Nagali, a short man, barely topping five feet, possessed a commanding, resonant voice that reverberated in the night air, his proper Queen's English rising to an eloquent roar. He made pleasant conversation, directing his interest entirely toward Askara.

"Miss Askara, I come from a long line of influential people in Zambia."

"That's nice, I mean Zambia, what's it like?"

"Beautiful, high plateaus, rivers. I come from Lusaka, the capital, in the Copperbelt, our major export, until recently. You know Zambia was a British colony. We're the only country to enter the Olympics as one country and exit as another. That was in 1964 when we became independent. Independence happened the same day as the closing ceremony."

She started to reply but watched Nagali methodically block Darian from the conversation, turn, and step away to ignore him purposely. Darian seemed aware of the tactic but remained pleasant. Nagali's rudeness irritated her. Askara appreciated Darian being there, especially because something about Nagali unnerved her. Maybe his eyes? She thought. Askara wanted to forego the dinner, complete the deal, and leave Reh's pretentious party to have private time with Darian.

"You see," Mr. Nagali said, looking only at Askara, staring into her eyes, making her feel like a bug under glass, "I am a particularly important man in Uganda. People come to me for all manner of services, the least of which is jewelry. Yes, I deal in gems, from time to time, but my number one profession is advisor to President Idi Amin Dada, Uganda's most impressive ruler."

Askara replied, feigning interest, "You're with the government? Oh, no one told me."

"I am not *with the government*, madam. I *am* the government. I advise and clarify the government. I am President Amin's dream interpreter, his soothsayer."

Askara's eyes lifted slightly. Darian, standing behind Mr. Nagali, smiled at her with sardonic amusement. Mr. Nagali wheeled around and glared at him.

Darian offered, "How interesting, Mr. Nagali, do go on," in a lackluster voice.

Nagali turned back to Askara, fixing her with a wide-eyed stare, black eyes surrounded by arcs of white above and below the iris, made brighter by his ebony complexion, and said in a murmur, "See this." He held up a large necklace ornament. "This sacred amulet given to my father by his father contains the power of divination bequeathed to my family by the greatest soothsayer to have ever lived in Zambia. With this, he could control the seasons and the simple minds of people. Now it is mine. I divine God's messages for Uganda's illustrious president."

Askara felt more uncomfortable. Nagali looked at her as he spoke, his enormous eyes traveling her torso, resting on the curve of her breasts, dropping to her clenched hands that felt cold despite the warm night air, and landing on her stomach. She wanted to push away from him, to escape, but they had not yet spoken of the proposed jewelry purchase. She broke away from his stare to study the gold amulet around his neck, a large cylindrical antique with an embossed design of interlocking forms, some human, some animal.

"Do you know the power in this amulet?" Mr. Nagali continued. "With it, I decide who lives, who dies, who gets rich, and who makes successful business deals." Askara's stomach rolled. A cold spasm shot up her back; goosebumps formed on her forearms.

She replied lightly, "Well then, you must be a busy man. Can we get to Mr. Ramsey's business now, the Ethiopian jewelry?" A desperate feeling closed in on her. She wanted to rush out of the room. Thank God, Darian's here with me, she thought.

"First, you should know what you came to purchase," Nagali said in a hushed tone. "It came from Emperor Haile Selassie's grandmother's family. Since the Emperor traces his lineage back to the Queen of Sheba herself, this royal jewelry would be a curator's prize—if real. Of course, I believe it is, but you are the expert. You must decide for yourself when you see the set. My amulet will give you clarity of vision."

Askara reminded herself landing a significant heirloom jewelry purchase would bring her a promotion, at least that was her hope, and more foreign assignments. But now, meeting this Zambian soothsayer, Askara surmised if the jewelry were real, the purchase price had been extremely dear, probably involving foul play.

"You want to hurry, madam? I have quite a prize for you, a collector's find, one Seth Ramsey will appreciate."

"Yes," Askara replied unenthusiastically, feeling the energy drain out of her. "I believe he saw it before."

"Follow me. I've locked it in my guarded car parked outback, for security reasons."

She reached over to tap Darian's shoulder so that he would accompany her. As she did, Mr. Nagali positioned himself between them, took her by the arm, wheeled her around, and led her to the rear door of the main hall. Askara, too exhausted to resist, called Darian in a weak voice, but he didn't answer. Mr. Nagali rushed, pulling her forcibly by the hand, toward his parked car shrouded in shadows, leaving Darian behind.

Askara wrenched her arm from his grip. "Please, don't lead me like a child! I don't want to see the jewelry tonight. The light's not good. I'll contact you tomorrow." His grip clamped down mercilessly on her hand. She turned to look for Darian but could not see him in the shadows.

With nostrils fanned out like an angry cobra's head, Nagali turned her around to face him. He hissed in a deep voice, "Look here at my amulet."

Askara heard a whisper: *Beware of men with gold and eyes that see.* Askara avoided looking at the amulet, but a force dragged her eyes back to the figures that moved, at first in small undulations, then more extensive sweeps. A grotesque half-man, half-animal slithered down the shaft of the amulet, making a sharp turn toward Askara. Blue light emitted from its eyes. Askara felt her body become weightless. Everything around her faded into shadow; only the beckoning creature remained, luring her closer with its gyrating form, its bumpy purple-gray tongue flicking to devour unseen flies. With each thrust, she heard a low, guttural sound, a throaty hum layering on itself, rising to a complicated tone. Louder and louder. An alluring rhythm of distant African drums drew closer, drowning cricket and bullfrog night sounds. Even the guard dogs fell silent under the oppressive hum—*muh, muta, muh, thuma, uma, muh*. The sounds beat in her chest, radiated in her pulse, roiled her stomach, and turned her world black.

Darian's voice yelled, "Askara. Stop!"

Her chest heaved and convulsed. She jackknifed forward. The icy chill left her with white-hot anger burning in her veins. Askara straightened up to face Nagali.

"You bastard!"

Darian's hand wrenched her wrist from Nagali's grip. He shoved Askara behind him, out of Nagali's line of vision, and slammed his fist down on Nagali's chest, breaking the amulet's clasp. It fell to the gravel with a slight clink. Darian grabbed Nagali's shirt, jerked him close, and shouted into his bulging eyes. "I should whip you. Get the bloody hell out of here before I tear you apart."

Nagali straightened up, yanked his dress shirt from Darian's grip, and growled in a voice tight with rage: "You, sir, are out of line. You have no idea whom you have just offended. The cost is dear. You will find out. Step away from my car." He lifted the amulet from the gravel, opened the car's rear door, jumped in, and shouted at the driver. "Go!"

Darian wheeled around to see Askara huddled behind him, "Did he hurt you? What happened?"

"I'll tell you later," she said in a weak voice and burst into tears. Askara spotted the gawking crowd gathered on the distant veranda as Nagali's Mercedes sped down the long drive toward the gate, spraying gravel. She leaned into Darian and hung onto him like a scared child.

"One moment, you were in the room with me. I don't remember what happened. It's like lost time. The next, you were across the parking lot with that odious man. What did he do to you?"

"Nothing physical, but I feel violated. Nagali touched my arm, grabbed my hand, but my mind…he poisoned my mind."

Darian gently brushed the hair back from Askara's damp face. They stood for several minutes for her to steady herself, Darian pressing Askara to his chest. "We should go now, Askara, people are staring."

As they walked back toward the parked cars, Mr. Reh accosted them. "Miss Timlen, Mr. Dalal, I missed you after dessert. Please, pardon me. With so many guests, it is difficult for a host, you understand. Madam, did you have a chance to discuss with Mr. Nagali the heirloom jewelry?"

"Yes," Askara whispered.

"Is it what Mr. Ramsey had in mind?"

"No, Mr. Reh, not really."

"No deal, then, eh?"

"No...but thank you for arranging the meeting. The dinner was lovely," Askara said and feebly shook his hand with a frigid grasp. "Pardon me, I feel sick, a relapse of malaria, I think. Could your driver take us back to the Whispering Palms right now?"

"Most certainly. My pleasure. I shall call on you again. And you, Mr. Dalal."

"Thank you for the invitation, Mr. Reh. The dinner was lovely. Sir, how do you know Mr. Nagali?"

"I met him through my cousin Haroon in Kampala. Haroon imported Mercedes that Nagali purchased for President Amin. Unfortunately, my cousin died in an accident on Lake Victoria. A tragic loss for the family. Nagali took over the Mercedes company. We have stayed in touch since. Amiable chap."

"My condolences, Mr. Reh."

MR. REH'S DRIVER GLIDED ALONG THE BLACK SERPENTINE route to the Whispering Palms bungalow. Askara, nestled in Darian's chest, slept. When the driver stopped at the resort, Darian stepped out first and helped Askara, pressed a tip into the man's hand, and dismissed him. A slight ocean breeze rustled the palm fronds, adding rhythm to the night music of chirping crickets. Gentle waves breaking shone silver under the full moon. A sweet floral scent wafted in the humid air.

Walking hand in hand, Darian guided Askara to the patio, assuring her, "Fresh air will do you good, Askara." They sat on a chair swing. Darian pulled Askara close. Rocking back and forth, he could feel fear and anxiety, sticky like the humid air, clinging to her. She shivered. He wrapped his arm tighter around her shoulder. "You're safe. I've got you. Relax. You will never see that creep again, I promise. I don't know what trick he was up to, but forget him and his stupid big-eyed look, and that cheap amulet. All of it. I can assure you any jewelry that man had to sell was fake."

"I can still feel his wild demonic eyes boring into me."

"Well, look into my eyes then. What do you see?"

Askara looked up at Darian. "Moonlight on water."

"What else?"

"Comfort. Tenderness. Safety."

"Good. You're safe, focus on that."

"Darian, I, um, I'm sorry I was rude to you when you arrived."

"I'm not. If I were the sort of man to make a false promise, I hope you would be rude. But I am not. You don't understand me...yet."

Askara fell into silence for a few minutes thinking about his words, then cleared her throat. "Do you smell that sweet scent?"

"Yes. Lady—or Queen—of the Night, the white jasmine flower planted in those beds over there. It grows in India too. That scent brings back fond memories of my grandmother, who lived with us. She was a great storyteller. She told one about that flower."

"I'd like to hear a story."

"Don't know if this is the right time, or if that story is the right story."

"Let me decide."

"As you wish," Darian said, and began his grandmother's story:

> Once there was a beautiful girl from a village who sat under the moonlight dreaming of the man she would marry. She had long black hair flowing in soft waves to her waist, large dark eyes like a doe, and the voice of a songbird. She would sing softly, accompanied by crickets, songs she had written about a young, strong warrior who would one day make her his wife. The delicate sound of her voice awakened the sleeping blooms of the tiny white jasmine flower. It would open and sway with her hypnotic melody, releasing its sweet aroma into the night air.
>
> Miles away, in the dark forest, a demon lived underground, surrounded by roots and grubs and skeletons of people he had consumed. He only climbed above ground at night, so he could hunt unseen and then return to his dirty lair by daybreak. Many young girls had disappeared from the nearby villages never to be found, yet no one suspected him. He could see with the eyes of a nocturnal animal, move with the stealth of a tiger, and strike with the vengeance of a cobra. The young girls he took for slaves lived forever underground, serving him until he consumed them.
>
> One night while he rustled through the underbrush, he heard a faint sound, a hypnotic melody

that seemed to float on a heavenly flower scent. As the moon was full and knowing that villagers dare not roam in the light of a full moon, being fearful of specters, he made his way, nose raised in the air, and followed the scent far from his forest liar. He quietly stole through rice paddies and trotted past vegetable fields and small villages, following the ever-stronger scent. The delicate melody became a young girl's voice full of longing for her love. He followed her song to the stone wall that encircled a group of small, mud-waddle huts. A candle lit only one; all others remained dark. He crouched and slithered closer into the compound, stealing from hut to hut, until he could see the girl clearly in the moonlight. She, an apparition of loveliness, a delicate form graced by silver light, sat next to white blossoms which, as she sang, opened into starbursts. The grotesque forest demon knew she would never accept him, ugly as he was. Wanting her desperately, he transformed himself into a handsome young man clad as royalty. He cast a sleeping spell over the villagers and approached the young maiden.

At first, she startled, seeing a stranger in the lonely night, and said, "Who comes into our garden unannounced? Name yourself." She shouted an alarm to her sleeping father, but the forest demon quickly replied, "Have no fear. I am a traveler from the Maharajah's household, who is lost. I seek direction. Where am I, good lady?" He had transformed his voice into a steady, resonant caress, his clothes to that of royalty, his manner to courtly grace, and his appearance to that described in the young maiden's song.

"Step closer so that I may better see you," she said, eased by his manner. Her heart expanded with surprise upon seeing the man of her longing standing in front of her. She looked down in girlish modesty. "My lord, you have wandered far from the main road. You must be fatigued. Let me get you some water and something to eat."

"Thank you, good lady, but your sweet song has quenched my thirst and satiated my hunger. I ask only that I might sit here and listen to you."

The young maiden laughed nervously and bid him a seat on the steps next to her. As she sang, she realized with dismay that the crickets—which always chirped with her—had grown quiet. Her voice still enchanted the night air, but the melody waned. She apologized to the gentleman, who hadn't noticed at all, and continued as he requested. To her, he appeared the embodiment of her heart's song, strong and tall with broad shoulders and an angular face. Only his eyes differed. His were impossible to see beneath the prominent brow, as if set in permanent shadow, hidden from the brilliant moon above. As she sang, she noticed the white blossoms, which had opened on this full moon night had shriveled, their tarnished petals gripped tightly around the central stem. Their hypnotic scent ceased to waft through the air.

A sense of dread crept over the maiden. Once again, she called her father, who lay on his *charpoy*, certainly close enough to hear. She faltered, but the demon commanded her to continue. She perceived the aggression in his voice and trembled. In a thin, scratchy voice, she resumed her song.

Although her father slept, he knew his daughter's danger and implored the gods to come to her aid. Praying silently and urgently, he evoked an answer to his prayer.

The demon grew agitated as the maiden's singing waned. His form decayed to its usual hunched, grotesque animal-like appearance. The maiden tried to scream, but he covered her mouth with a hairy, dirty hand, nearly choking her. She felt the life drain from her as he squeezed her delicate body in a rough embrace. She slumped down on the stone steps, unable to move. Circling her body like a wild cat, he lunged.

Suddenly the night sky ripped apart, sending stars flinging to distant mountains. From a blinding light, a woman descended, full of fire, with eyes like a million torches.

"Touch not that maiden!" she shouted. A thousand arms expanded from her swirling form, each with a fiery sword in hand. She began a mesmerizing dance piercing and burning the demon with every turn. He writhed and begged for forgiveness, prostrating himself before her. She bellowed, "You sacrilegious beast! You've violated an innocent girl. For you, there is no mercy. This form I graciously gave you after your last offense was not punishment enough! You are too loathsome to merely destroy, although I would enjoy the moment. You must suffer. Death is too quick and too kind. You shall forever live, a worm in the night soil pit consuming waste, turning it into useable soil for the farmer's crops."

> With that, the demon convulsed and all but disappeared. A fiery hand extended from the goddess, plucked the worm from its curled position, and flung it beyond the village wall to the common pit. She lifted the girl's limp form and cradled her in a yellow glow, "You, my child, are young, so I admonish you only. Beware of what you long for. Things are rarely what they seem. You now must plant this flowering bush in every village and warn the young girls lest they make the same mistake as you. The flowers will forever open at the moon's full to symbolize your ordeal, and they will be known as Lady of the Night, *Raat-Ki-Rani*."

Askara sighed. "I feel a bit like that woman in the story; I met a demon tonight," Askara said.

Darian squeezed Askara closer and replied, "Well, I didn't realize the girl in the story was a peasant until I grew up. I thought she was a queen since we called the jasmine flower *Raat ki Rani*. It smells wonderful but makes you sick if you ingest it."

"Who would do that?"

"A silly boy thinking it would taste the way it smells," Darian said and laughed.

Askara laughed as well and felt the tension leaving her.

Chapter Two

Nairobi

When they walked to the bungalow, Askara squeezed Darian's hand like he was a kite high in the sky that she did not want to lose. His statement, shortly after they entered, shocked her.

"I should like to sleep out on the porch to hear the waves tonight, Askara."

She tried to formulate a reply when she saw him start to pull the cot out from the sitting room. "But the breeze dies in the middle of the night. You'll be miserable. The mosquitoes. My room is air-conditioned."

Darian spotted the table fan and said, "Right, this will keep them away," and put the fan on the small table inside the screened porch. Askara thought, he seems more concerned about mosquitoes than me.

"Wouldn't you be more comfortable with me?"

"I'm sorry, Askara, but not tonight. You need to sleep well and forget this horrible night. I can feel how exhausted you are. Rest."

Askara didn't know how to reply. Was this concern, or rejection? She couldn't tell. She didn't have the energy to argue about it. "Okay, if that's what you want. You take the bathroom first because when I get in there, I'm going to shower and wash Nagali away. I'll come to tell you goodnight."

When Askara stood in the doorway to tell Darian goodnight and hand him a glass of water, she knew the bathroom light shone through her cotton nightdress. She watched Darian's eyes follow the shadow of her legs up to her hips and the curve of her breasts, partially obscured by her unbraided hair. She felt the quiver. She knew he did too. He walked over, gathered her to his chest, pressing her close. His hands traced a rhythmical pattern in the small of her back. Leaning in, he smelled the flower scent in her hair. He kissed her forehead. His lips lingered on her face making soft, slow kisses. She wrapped her arms around his neck and kissed his lips. Darian melted. She felt his warmth radiate through her. His breaths became long inhalations pulling her into him like she was his breath, and he was hers.

Abruptly, he stepped back. "Askara, I want you; I desire you, more than anything, but this isn't right for tonight."

"What?" she replied, feeling ice freeze in her veins. She felt confused. She couldn't process rejection, especially tonight. She took two steps back, turned, and walked into her bedroom, closing the door behind her. Climbing into bed alone, she wondered had she read too much into their attraction. Maybe this is how a holiday romance ends? She cried into her pillow, falling asleep to the loud drone of the air conditioner.

The next morning, she found a note Darian left in her sitting room to meet him at the Whispering Palms café when she got up. Askara fought with herself. Should I? Should I not? What's the point, she wondered. She decided she wanted closure, a clean split.

Sipping coffee, she said casually like an old friend inquiring about a summer vacation, "What are your plans, Darian?"

"I think it best I return to Nairobi this morning. I have an appointment with Mr. Moi later in the day to discuss importing Dalal Malaysian rubber for the Nairobi Firestone plant. The project's up for bid again. The Michelin contract fell through. Moi supports the Firestone factory; in fact, he owns a majority share…evidently in another name, or so people say. We supply Firestone in Indonesia, so there's an excellent chance we can supply our Malaysian rubber to Firestone in Kenya."

Askara looked away, thinking of how she hated Darian's all-business demeanor. "Good for you."

Darian reached over and placed his hand on hers. "Will you come to Nairobi with me?"

"No," she said, withdrawing her hand abruptly. "I can't. Sorry. Mr. Reh called earlier. He'd talked to Ramsey, told him how the Nagali thing went down. Ramsey felt horrible for me, so he asked Mr. Reh to set up another contact. Both of them apologized for the Nagali fiasco." Askara lifted a folded piece of paper from her sundress pocket. "Here's Mr. Reh's number. I'm staying with him while the details get worked out. Call if you get the chance."

"Askara, Mr. Reh? Do you trust him?"

"Don't patronize me, Darian."

"No, I never intended…."

"What did you intend?"

"Askara, I'm trying to say I care. It seems we're at cross purposes."

"Maybe you should speak more clearly then."

Darian caught the edge in Askara's words. "I wish you well, but I do not agree with what you're doing. Something is not right about Reh. I will be at the Hilton Hotel until Wednesday. I would be pleased if you would join me there."

Askara picked up her sunglasses from the table and stood. "I'll come and see you off."

"I have a better idea, Askara, come and leave with me."

"Are you kidding, Darian? I'm not on holiday. I came here, all this way because Mr. Ramsey sent me to buy Ethiopian jewelry. If I go back with none, not only do I not get a commission, or a promotion, I'll probably be fired. I'm not in your enviable position of owning a company."

"Family enterprise, Askara. If I didn't have obligations…."

Askara studied Darian's face. The pain in his eyes cemented her worst fear: Maybe he's in a relationship, maybe even married—an obligation for him, a death knell for us.

"I have to go, Reh's driver, he's waiting. If the timing works out, I'll send a message, and we'll see each other at the Nairobi Hilton before you go to the airport. And where do you go this time, Darian? Singapore? Kuala Lumpur? Bombay?"

"Mauritius, then home to Bombay," Darian replied without a smile. He stood to hug Askara goodbye, dropping his white linen napkin. He glanced down at it, crumpled on the red carpet.

"Safe travels," Askara said and gave him a peck on the cheek. She walked away quickly, not looking back.

"Askara," Mr. Reh called out. "Where are you?"

"Here, on the veranda, having toast and coffee. I love this garden," she said as Mr. Reh approached.

An English style wall of yellow-ochre stones encircled the grass lawn and garden. Thick- stemmed bougainvillea plants grew up the rocks, fanning out horizontally with bright red-orange leaves that draped down the rocks to the rose beds below. A lone monkey tree towered high above the garden, its thick needle boughs leaning down to touch their shadows on the verdant grass.

"Good morning. Excellent news." Mr. Reh said and pulled up a chair, motioning for the servant to bring him breakfast. "I have made a suitable contact for you in Addis Ababa. A friend of my cousin Haroon, whom he affectionately called *Limey Jimmy*, served in the British Navy some years back. Jimmy is friends with Sir Alexander Desta, Emperor Haile Selassie's nephew. Through Jimmy, I obtained an invitation for you to meet Sir Alexander in Ethiopia," he said, handing her a piece of paper. "Here are the particulars. You go to the front gate of the palace and present this letter. Evidently, the family has fallen on hard times, what with the Eritrean conflict and all, and the drought. They have some jewels and artifacts they would like to sell but only to very discreet buyers. You know, the Emperor's a proud man. On my honor, I have assured them of your utmost discretion."

"How wonderful. Do I need a set appointment? Or do I just show the letter at the palace? I'll telegram Mr. Ramsey. He'll be super excited."

"Just show the letter. I took the liberty to clear it with Mr. Ramsey before Jimmy contacted Sir Alexander."

"Thank you," Askara said, feeling pre-empted.

"Right. I shall have my driver take you to Nairobi so that you can book the next scheduled flight to Addis Ababa," Mr. Reh added. "I would escort you myself, but I have sisal buyers coming from Israel to inspect the crop shortly. But I will meet you there soon. My sister invited us to stay with her family."

Askara found leaving simple. Mr. Reh, busy with his visitors, hardly told her goodbye. He shouted as the car pulled away, see you at my sister's house in Nairobi.

Askara felt glad to leave. Something about Mr. Reh irritated her. His pseudo-British manners? His condescension? She couldn't decide, but the drive to Nairobi, rising 5,450 feet higher than the white sandy beaches of Mombasa, made her forget all about it. The dramatic change to gray clouds and cooler air suited her.

Askara enjoyed the city bustle, especially roundabouts. Sensible traffic flow management, she thought, much better than intersection lights, plus each formed circular gardens with grass lawns, colorful bougainvillea, and roses. She assumed roses were a product of colonialism. Mr. Reh's driver informed her his boss had tried several years for best of show in the annual rose exhibit but without luck.

Askara savored the idea of a valuable Ethiopian jewelry purchase until her mind returned to Darian. The excitement of new scenery faded. She teared up. She would see Darian soon, she assumed for the last time. She wanted to say so much to him. But what? She wasn't sure. He had said in Greece that he was falling for her, but on their last night in Mombasa, he said nothing. He seemed to her inaccessible at times, formal and distant as if he lived in another time and place. Maybe he does, she thought, with a wife and kids. No ring doesn't necessarily mean no wife. I learned that the hard way. But what if he is how he presents himself? He leaves things unsaid. That could be personality, or it could be cultural, she figured. Askara's thoughts tangled in a Celtic knot someplace between her head and heart, leaving her wary. She decided to go straight to the Hilton to see Darian, asking the driver to drop her there and saying she would call later for him to take her to Mr. Reh's sister's house.

When the driver swung into the Hilton entrance, a doorman stepped forward to let her out, and she handed him her bag. Askara felt her hands go cold and clammy with anticipation. She had agreed to meet him but had never specified when. She phoned his room to ask him to meet her in the café. When he entered the café and spotted her at a table overlooking the bustle of downtown Nairobi, her breath grew shallow. She gave him a timid smile.

Darian took her hand and said, "You look lovely, Askara. I'm so glad you've come."

His calm manner relaxed her. She thought him genuinely happy to see her. They talked, between interruptions by zealous waiters in starched black-and-white uniforms, about her upcoming stay at Mr. Reh's sister's and Darian's business success with Mr. Moi. Askara gazed at his golden-brown skin, strands of gray peeking out from his close-cut black hair, and thought, what a good-looking man. She took a sip of strong Kenyan coffee.

"Darian, what are your plans now that you landed that deal?"

He smiled faintly. "That's what I want to know. What are your plans?"

"I'm going to Ethiopia to buy jewelry."

"From someone reputable, I hope."

"From the Emperor's family. How about that? Mr. Reh arranged it."

Darian grimaced, "Mr. Reh, who also made your other arrangement. Right. When do you leave?"

"Soon. I need to book my flight," she said. Askara summoned her courage. "Would you like to go with me?"

"No, I can't, not at the moment. I'm due in Mauritius…."

Before Darian could add more, Askara changed the subject to the traffic on the street below. She pointed at a stalled car blocking a transport lorry by the roundabout exit. The sound of car horns, muffled by the thick window glass, sounded like buzzing insects.

"I thought roundabouts worked better than intersections," Askara said, fidgeting with her coffee cup handle.

"They do. But people are the same, so what can you expect?" Askara felt Darian's amber eyes bore into her when he asked, "Who will you go with to Ethiopia, Askara?"

"Um, if you don't go?"

"I cannot, no matter how much I would like to. I promised to visit friends in Mauritius, my parents' best friends. They are family to me." Askara looked down at her dessert plate to avoid his gaze. "Why don't you come with me to Mauritius? Delay the Ethiopia trip by a few days. We need more time together. Since I first saw you, Askara, I have had a powerful feeling about you, something hard to explain."

"Try."

"I feel responsible for you somehow."

"You make me sound incapable, Darian. I'm responsible for myself. I've…."

Darian interrupted. "Not incapable. Don't misconstrue my words. You are very capable, unique, extremely accomplished, and independent. But possibly the prospect of traveling with me appears mundane to you?"

"No, Darian, it's not that. Look, my basic salary is small. I depend on sales commissions to keep up my San Francisco lifestyle. Plus, if everything goes well, I should get a promotion out of this one. I can't go with you—I can't afford to."

"All right. I had to ask. You know I would like to spend more time with you, but I will wait."

Askara's face burned. "Your familial obligations allow that?"

"Askara, I work for my uncles. They don't own me."

"Does anyone?"

"No," Darian said with a dismissive shake of his head, missing the implication.

Askara felt relieved. She said in a gentler tone, "I would like to spend more time with you, too. Could you come to California for a visit?"

"Yes, I should like that very much, Askara."

FIGHTING BACK HER TEARS, ASKARA SAW DARIAN OFF AT the airport later that afternoon. In the airport lounge, he kissed her, a passionate kiss that caused more than one person to stare. Askara smiled and said, "This is hardly the time or the place...."

Darian cut her off mid-sentence. "You are here with me now, so this is the time, and this is the place. I shall miss you. Call me, telegram me, write in care of my parents' address, but let me hear from you soon. I'm worried about you on your own in Ethiopia.

Askara could feel her heart beating against his chest, and his heart answering. Askara gathered her courage and replied, "Darian, you don't have a girlfriend, or a wife, do you?"

"Of course not! What kind of man would I be? I thought I had told you. I had been married, Askara. Didn't I say at dinner in Athens? My wife died tragically." Askara's eyes widened. "Evidently, I did not. I'm so sorry. It is hard for me to talk about, even now."

Askara jumped with the loudspeaker announcement: *Last call for Mauritius. Air India Flight 503, boarding at Gate 7.*

"Darian. I'm so sorry for your loss. I wish you didn't have to go."

"I must go. Time and place cannot separate us. We found one another."

Askara decided to book a room at the Hilton. She couldn't face staying at Mr. Reh's sister's, visiting with strangers, when all she wanted was to swim and get a grip on her feelings. She left a message at the front desk for the driver to give to Mr. Reh, checked into her room, and changed into her swimsuit. The gray sky had turned to warm sun that danced on the blue tiles of the pool, sending diamonds of light rippling along the wall. Foreigners lounged, baking themselves like sugar cookies. A buxom French woman in a topless bikini gesticulated and bragged in a loud voice about her latest safari while her male admirers drank cocktails decorated with pink paper parasols.

Askara slid into the cool water and began laps, building speed until her muscles stung. Rhythmic breathing and exertion brought her peace. After twenty-five laps, she paused by the pool's edge to defog her goggles.

"Good on ya."

Askara turned toward the speaker. "Pardon. Are you talking to me?"

"Good on ya, kid, strong laps," the woman replied, whisking wet curls back from her face. "A fair stride, considering you breathe every other stroke."

"Oh, thanks. Are you the swim instructor?"

"No, a farmer," the woman said in a broad Australian accent. She thrust her right hand out, "Sara. Sara Sanford." Askara's hand shrunk in the vice-grip.

"Askara Timlen. What do you farm?"

"Peas right now. I'm an agricultural expert, working for the U.N. in Lesotho. I teach crop management to a women's collective. Know where Lesotho is?"

"I've heard the name. Southern Africa?" Askara said, wiping the stinging chlorinated water from her brow.

"Fair dinkum, I'll say, smack inside South Africa, surrounded by it, but Lesotho's an independent Black African country, north of Jo'berg, up in the mountains."

"What are you doing here in Kenya?"

"Holiday. Month's leave. Thought I'd tour a bit, a walkabout, you know, see the place before my contract's up."

"Where's home?"

"Outside Melbourne," Sara said with a Cheshire Cat grin. "How 'bout you? Where's your home?"

"California."

"Immigrant?"

"No, my dad came over from India, my mom's American. I was born there."

"Bloody hell, so you're an American Indian," Sara said with a laugh. "I want to go to America someday, buy Indian jewelry—you know the Red Indian type—silver and turquoise. And I want leather chaps like cowboys wear."

Askara smiled and quipped, "Fair dinkum."

They talked between laps. Afterward, they ordered drinks and sat poolside. Sara described growing up on a racehorse ranch outside of Melbourne. "Never felt at home on horses," she said. "My brother Jimmy, he's the rider in the family. Now he runs the business. I like two feet on the ground, a born farmer." She cracked Betty Windsor jokes, imitating the queen from her Corgi's viewpoints until Askara's sides hurt from laughing. She described Lesotho like a magical kingdom high in the mountains where locals ride sturdy, sure-footed ponies that swim gushing rivers and trek all day without resting.

"The people are very gentle, don't know much about growing crops in their thin soil, so for years, most supplies have come from South Africa. With apartheid, we never know if the borders might close and cut off the food supply, so experts like me," she said with a smile, "are teaching the people to plant simple crops for survival. They have no farm machines to speak of. Everything's done by manual labor, mostly by women, often with children strapped to their backs while they scratch and plant the fragile soil. I love working with them. In Australia, I never mixed with non-whites, not that I didn't want to, but with the color bar, no opportunity ever came up."

Sara told Askara she was the first Australian woman to go to university in New Zealand for a crop science degree, a male-dominated discipline.

"How was that?" Askara asked.

"Hard. Not the work, the attitude. Since I don't care for society's conventions, I blew it off, the prejudice. Working in Africa suits me. Lots of variety. I passed through Malawi on my way up. Beautiful country, a long lake with some land and people around it. I plan to go back."

"How do you get around?"

"Land Rover—only way to go. Hell, those things cross gushing rivers. The Brits did something right," Sara said, smiling, her pale blue eyes, the color of the Hilton pool, narrowing to crescents.

"You travel by yourself? That's brave."

"Sometimes. A Danish couple started out with me from Lesotho but headed to Tanzania. They're hitchhiking through Africa. They'd been in South Africa for three months. I gave a lift to another Aussie and his girlfriend. They came all the way to Nairobi with me."

"Are you staying here at the Hilton with them?"

"No, just came here after touring Tsavo Park, practically the end of the *Big Trip*, thought it would be my last. Know what I mean?" Sara said, laughing and slapped her knee.

Askara smiled at Sara's obvious enjoyment. "I don't get it."

"I met this crazy Yank. She said, why don't we tour the park. I agreed. She was decent company, a bit nuts, an artist. Anyway, we're out in the bush, and another Land Rover comes up. The bloke tells us there's a kill about two miles ahead, on the left, so stay on the road. We get up there and can't see anything. Then we spot a zebra, you know, with its guts ripped out, but nothing else around. I wanted to drive in closer, but the Yank said, let's leave the Land Rover on the road and walk over for pictures. She'd rented a camera in Nairobi with a huge telephoto lens but couldn't figure how to use it. I waited in the Land Rover, told her to stay close to the car and take some shots from there. She was fumbling with that bloody camera. I felt sorry for her, so I walked over to help. From our left, we heard a huge roar. I froze. I spotted a female lion crouched in the bushes, blood dripping from her mouth. I bolted to the Rover, jumped into the driver's seat, started the engine when the male charged from the right. I laid on the horn. He veered off. The Yank leaped into the back seat. I floored that damn Rover and drove out as fast as it would go. That bloody Yank was laughing so hard; she couldn't stop. Crazy. I'm here for some R&R, you know, to get over that safari."

Askara wiled away the afternoon listening to Sara's stories, forgetting her loneliness and feeling grateful she wasn't making boring conversation with Mr. Reh and his sister.

"Wanna go clubbing tonight?" Sara said. "See some Nairobi nightlife?"

"Sure, sounds good."

SARA AND ASKARA ATE DINNER AT AN INDIAN RESTAURANT, the Bamboo Shoot, where a line of cars queued up for takeout *chicken tikka*. They sat inside at a dimly lit table under a mural of the Taj Mahal. The waiter told them an American had painted it. Sara smiled. "Yep, the very person I took on safari. That's her signature. She should sign *Crazy Yank*."

They washed down the hot, spicy food with a generous amount of chilled Tusker lager, laughed and talked, and later ambled to the nightclub several blocks down from the restaurant. The nightclub vibrated with European pop music, flashing colored lights, and hordes of people gyrating and bumping into one another on the dance floor. From their table, Askara watched the dancers while she sipped another Tusker. Two African women in tight dresses, rhinestone jewelry, and spiked high heels circulated and reported back to an African man in a European suit, their pimp, Askara assumed. Trendy Asian women and their dates danced in a small group, stopping to laugh and point at one another's antics. At a large table, a hot political debate flared up. The mixed group of African, Asian, and whites appeared to be university students.

Sara and Askara danced but gave up when stray men skulking in the club's shadows moved in like hyenas. A man shouted from the stage front. People yelled back at him. The music died abruptly, someone had tripped the cord, and the man's shouting became intelligible.

"Power to the People, brothers." He raised a clenched fist. "Power to Black Brothers in America struggling for freedom."

A man yelled back at him, "Struggle? You don't know the struggle; you're a rich American."

"Hey, brother, I'm one of you. I came here to be with you. We're Africans."

The indignant Kenyan yelled, "I'm not *your* brother! I do not know you. You are American from America. I am African from Kenya. What do you know of *our* struggle? Look at my brothers in South Africa. We need freedom. Down with apartheid," he yelled and raised a clenched fist.

Dancers made way for the Kenyan to approach the American, who was having difficulty keeping his balance near the stage. The Kenyan shoved him backward with a rough movement and jeered, "You can be my brother when your country stops financing apartheid in South Africa. Until then, we may both be black, but we are not brothers. You're still American."

The disc jockey plugged in the cord; music flooded the club again, louder than ever. Initially, people appeared stunned and listless but picked up the pace and began gyrating away.

"Let's get out of here," Sara said. "You can bunk at my place. It's close, a hostel."

"Thanks. I've got a room at the Hilton. Has two beds. Want to stay there? Your choice. I probably burned a bridge today. I couldn't hang out with proper tea-sippers, but your company would be fun."

"What's your plan now, Askara?" Sara asked as she lounged on the bed in the hotel room.

Eating papaya, admiring its orange-red pulp and black pearl seeds, Askara paused to reply, "Going to Ethiopia to buy some jewelry, maybe artifacts, for my boss Mr. Ramsey."

"How will you go, fly?"

"Yeah, I asked the concierge today about flights. The next one goes in a few days to Addis."

"You'll miss the scenery. What a lousy way to travel in Africa," Sara said. "You in a hurry?"

"Yeah. I need to get there soon. I have to return to America for my job."

"I could show you the Africa you'd never see otherwise. People pay a fortune to go overland. I'm offering you a trip for free." Sara grinned, her sky-blue eyes sparkling. "I've got some time off. I want to see some more of Africa. Come along."

"Overland? Isn't that dangerous?"

"The first hassle I've seen was tonight, and I've traveled thousands of miles in Namibia, Botswana, South Africa, Rhodesia, Malawi, and Tanzania, to Kenya. I mean, I've had hassles—couldn't find petrol, flat tire, wrong directions, swollen rivers, lion attack—but nothing crazy threatening if you leave out the blokes who wanted to marry me."

Askara thought, wow, what an opportunity. I can't pass this up. I may never come back to Africa, and it'll only add on a few days. Ramsey will understand after I land this sale. Reh may be ticked off because I'm not following his plan. Who cares? Darian has his trip lined up. I'll see him in California, later. "Okay, I'm game."

Sara grinned, "A play on words? *Game* in Africa could be dangerous."

Chapter Three

Signs

Askara and Sara left two days later after outfitting the Land Rover with containers of water, non-perishable food, extra petrol cans, a new tire, blankets, camping supplies, and a young African guide.

Askara's farewell at Mr. Reh's sister's house was chilly, even though Mr. Reh, who had a *soft spot* for her, as he declared, wished her well. After trying in vain to convince her to fly, he promised to notify Mr. Ramsey of her departure and asked her to keep in touch. Askara realized the family was horrified by her traveling companion, a strong, squarely-built woman, with an odd way of talking, with a hunting knife barely concealed in her trouser leg and a smaller one dangling from her leather belt. Askara smiled.

Sara waited outside while Askara said farewells but tossed a crumpled, outdated edition of the *East African Standard* newspaper at Askara with a boisterous laugh when she climbed into the Rover. "Look at page five, under *Not a Good Week for President Nixon*."

The committee wants the President to appear in person and cites the precedents of Presidents Abra-

ham Lincoln and Woodrow Wilson. The President, sitting in isolation in his San Clemente, California retreat, is certainly waiting for the Congress vacation in August and hoping that he can sit out the crisis as the American public tires of the televised hearings.

Askara's face reddened. "Bastard. He should be in jail. Everyone knows he's guilty."

"Yeah, but he's smart. He figured you Yanks are too indifferent, that he can ride this thing out."

"How? John Dean testified before the Senate Watergate Committee that Nixon is a liar, that he knew about the Watergate cover-up on television."

Sara smirked. "People have short memories. Nixon resigned what, last month? Bet that new guy, his VP, pardons him. That's the game guys like that play. Who knows, you Yanks may even one day consider him one of your best presidents. Strange things happen."

"Disgusting thought," Askara said and looked over at Mr. Reh's sister and waved goodbye. "Let's go. I can't stand the way that woman looks at me."

Askara scanned the small gathering—Mr. Reh, his sister, her eleven-year-old son and eight-year-old daughter, skinny things with hollow eyes, and his two female cousins, shawls pulled up on their heads, peering out like cats from a gutter—all huddled in a small space on the veranda.

"Check out the sour look on his sister's face," Sara said and laughed. She waved with exaggerated animation and yelled, "G'DAY" to the crowd, crammed the Land Rover into first, and stomped on the gas pedal, raising a dust storm. The vehicle surged forward and sped down the driveway.

Askara turned to see Mr. Reh's sister grimace and pull her scarf over her mouth. Sara glanced over at Askara when she attempted to reprimand her, but they both exploded with laughter.

"Burned that bridge. Napalmed it," Askara said after she caught her breath. "Good on ya."

Askara started to toss the newspaper into the backseat when her eyes caught a familiar name: *Haroon Reh*. She scanned the article. Wow, Haroon was educated in England, she thought. She checked the paper's date, months old. Recently deceased at age fifty-two? Strange, Mr. Reh made it seem years ago that his cousin died, but it was less than a year.

> *Haroon Reh made his childhood home, Kampala, his residence again after London education. He left behind a wife and four children in Kampala, his mother, and a sister. Cause of death: Accidental drowning in Lake Victoria. He'd been partners in a Mercedes car import business with his cousin Mr. Nadir Reh of Nairobi and a local Ugandan government official, Mr. Nagali, previously of Zambia. The president's domestic crime unit is conducting an investigation.*

ASKARA AND SARA HEADED NORTH FROM NAIROBI, COOLED by a thunderhead sky that promised rain. Their young Samburu guide, Malhadele, a kitchen servant from the Hilton, sat perched on the Rover's back seat with the gear. He had pleaded with Askara at the Hilton, saying his father was sick, his mother needed help, and he speaks Swahili, Masai, and Samburu. "Memsahib, you give me ride home. I help you." When Askara talked to the kitchen manager, the boy's cousin, he consented.

When they stopped along the way, people stared at the two foreign women with the skinny African boy in an oversized short-sleeve shirt and baggy slacks that rippled as he walked. Askara nicknamed the boy *Dele*, a name he appeared to enjoy.

They reached Nyeri early afternoon, stopping for lunch at a small lodge in the style of a Kikuyu village with grass huts, wooden tables and chairs, and carved gourds for lampshades. From Nyeri, they drove to Nanyuki, turned left at the road to Thompson's Falls, and located Dele's uncle's where Dele was to stay while Askara and Sara visited two nearby game parks. The uncle's house, a small mud-wattle grass roof hut surrounded by a garden, was obscured from the road by banana trees. Dele stretched out under the shade of the banana trees near the goat pen to wait for his uncle while Askara and Sara drove to the Sportsman's Arms Hotel to board the tourist bus to Secret Valley Lodge, famous for leopard viewing.

The thirty-minute drive to the lodge through a dense bamboo jungle choked by vines that twisted the sunlight into interlocking patterns of light and shadow made Askara feel she was caught in a trap. When she spotted the lodge—a rustic wood, two-story structure built on stilts, partially hidden by dense vegetation—it increased her feeling of dread. She pushed the sensation down, tried to ignore it.

They ordered shanties, Kenyan beer with ginger ale, and sat on the veranda watching elephants hover around the water hole. A baby hid under his mother, nursing, while she scooped water and snatches of grass with her trunk. Later, two leopards arrived. The owner notified his guests to watch the mother and son rip up the raw meat secured to the platform before the leopards disappeared back into the jungle.

When the women left the viewing deck to escape the mosquitoes and eat dinner, Askara mentioned her appetite had lessened after seeing the show. Sara laughed, saying the show had whetted hers. They found the dining room almost empty, except for the lodge manager and his tedious, drunk South African friend who boasted about hunting expeditions. The manager, a British man, built like a barrel, with a ruddy face, thick-fingers, and balding yellow hair, zigzagged over to their table.

"Good evening, ladies. Enjoying your stay?"

"Yes, thank you," Askara said and looked down at the menu.

"American accent?" the South African shouted from across the room.

"Yes."

"Where from? I *turrred* America once."

"Northern California."

"Ah, Frisco, '68. A lot of bloody long hair hippies." He paused and groped for something impressive to say. "Nice city. But some of your American states are sixty-five percent non-reflectives. Wouldn't visit them."

"Non-reflectives?" Askara asked as Sara rolled her eyes.

"Eh, what? Negroes, Blackies, like here in Africa."

Askara wrenched the cloth napkin in her lap, twisting it into knots, her face boiling like hot water. "You...."

Sara cut in. "You do what here?"

"Me?" the South African man asked, refilling his Meerschaum pipe with an unsteady hand. "Professional big game hunter. Take foreigners on expeditions in Kenya and Tanzania."

Askara saw Sara was ready to scorch the man and interrupted. "What do you do here at the lodge? You don't hunt these animals. Or is it bait and shoot?"

"Bloody hell! No sport in that," he said in slurred, pretentious Queen's English. "I live here between safaris, an imperialist dream."

The two men broke out into gales of laughter. The women's silent glare shut them up. They retreated to the bar for a refill of Macallan scotch, which the hunter purposely ordered in a loud voice. The women motioned for the waiter, ordered sandwiches brought up to their room, and walked out to book their return bus ticket for the early morning shuttle.

The next day, after collecting the Rover, they toured Mt. Kenya. The mountain's snow-covered peaks stretched up to skewer flat-bottom white clouds. Sara pointed to the three peaks. "Second only to Mt. Kilimanjaro and smack dab on the equator. Next trip, I'm climbing Kili."

"I'll join you. Just say when. This scenery is so amazing. Thanks, Sara, for convincing me to see Africa by car. I was feeling low in Nairobi. Overland is just what the doctor ordered."

They drove to Mountain Lodge, a wooden lodge hiked up on stilts, at the southwest edge of the Kenya National Game Park. The building emerged like a specter from the dense rainforest. Their balcony had a view of the watering hole below. The aroma of wet, fertile earth hung heavy in the evening mist laced with wild animal scent. Mysterious night noises—monkey screeching, elephant trumpeting, baboon screaming—set off a chain reaction that made Askara think of women shrieking in horror. For her, the night grew sinister. She felt threadbare, nerves on edge. The distractions of new sights and sounds could not overcome the anguish she felt inside. Her mind drifted to the panic she felt from Nagali. But he was in the past, far away. Why couldn't she shake his creepy stare? She saw his probing eyes superimposed on innocent men, like their waiter. Then they would evaporate. She questioned everyone and everything because nothing seemed as it should, even Darian. She had trouble gaging him also. Partly it was cultural, she knew. But not mentioning his deceased wife? Askara hoped her death would merit an early footnote someday. She had never experienced death at close range but wondered what it did to a person. Maybe it makes one forget for one's own survival, she thought. But it is possible to forget too much.

Darian said he and Askara had something powerful. Really? The more she thought of him, the more melancholic she felt. The feeling of him, the scent of him, the warmth of his body, she desired. But she swore to herself, after her last failed relationship, that she would never fall for a man again based on physical allurement. She found Darian attractive, but beneath the attraction, something bothered her. He seemed so sure of them, but she wondered why. A vague impression would dissipate, only to form again, like he had stepped out of a shadow at the Oracle and flooded her eyes with Aegean sun until she could not see anything clearly…not even him.

Askara jumped and reeled back to the present when a bush pig grunted and pawed at the salt lick below. She told Sara she needed to lie down for a bit, so Sara walked down to visit the other guests in the lounge. Alone in the room, Askara's thoughts quickly returned to Darian. She could see him in her mind's eye—that night in Mombasa. She could feel his strong, capable hands holding hers, his kind eyes full of desire searching hers, their bodies pressed close in the heat, and then nothing. She had thought he desired her; she needed him to want her so that she could lose herself in him after the horror of Nagali. But Darian refused, saying this isn't right tonight.

She blocked the scene from her mind. She closed her eyes, reclined on the bed, and drifted, not fully awake, not fully asleep. A chill came over her. Her eyes opened. She thought for a second that she saw Darian standing at the foot of the bed in a white tunic and pants. He smiled. The thin gap between his front teeth showed beneath his black mustache. She heard, or thought she heard, words woven into the jungle night sounds: *Askara, I love you.*

The door swung open abruptly. Askara bolted upright in bed.

"You look like you've seen a ghost, Askara. Just me. You all right?"

"Yeah, just exhausted."

"Yeah, me too, but two shandies put that right. Gonna wash up, got a chess game down there with an English bloke." Sara raised her eyebrows and smiled. "Game's on. Grub's good. Come down."

"Sure. I'll shower and be down in a few minutes."

When Askara stepped onto the viewing deck, a mongoose scurried up the stilts near the viewing blind and disappeared into overhanging branches. The waiter, approaching with drinks for the group, said, "This mongoose, he sleeps on the ledge above the fire extinguisher all day long and plays all night. Ladies watch your purses. He is very naughty. While you watch animals, he steals from you."

The guests formed a congenial group, chatting over drinks. A British man Alex, on business from London by himself, made sure he sat next to Sara. A woman named Harriet Laurel from Alabama cornered Askara. She talked non-stop, recounting a story from her earlier visit to Kenya when she had traveled with her sister and met a man, a Mr. Reh, in Nairobi who ran a safari business and an import-export company. He invited them to join him and his female cousin from Pakistan on a safari.

Harriet Laurel said, "He had little in common with his cousin—she didn't drink—so Mr. Reh welcomed our Southern laughter, conversation, and deep appreciation of whiskey."

"Mr. Reh?" Askara said, stunned and wondering, does he hit on foreigners? A rush of acid hit her stomach and quickened her breath. "Did you meet Mr. Reh's friend, Mr. Nagali?"

"No. You know Reh? Nice man. Arranges great safaris. Cheered me up after a tough time."

"Yeah," Askara said, hardly getting the word out before the woman started up again.

"My husband, Robert Edward Lighthaus," she said his name with disdain, "*Bob-Ed Shit House,* and I had recently gotten a divorce."

Askara offered a meek, "Sorry."

"You see," she said, tossing her curly brown hair back, gesturing like she was wrestling with her hair clip, "one day in December, a birth announcement came in the mail. My dear friend had a baby girl. She named her Amanda. I got really upset, I mean about the name, for no reason. Well, later that same morning—it was a month after Bob Ed had left me for that blonde bimbo hairdresser—anyway, you see, I got a phone call. A woman's voice asked to speak to Amanda. That was his slut's name, Amanda. She was calling, asking for herself, to harass me!"

Harriet Laurel paused and inhaled a large gulp of whiskey. "Anyway, a few days later, you know, when I was in the public library, a book fell off the shelf, right there in front of me, and opened up to a biography of Amanda Jones, an eighteenth-century woman in England. I read the first few lines. That Amanda had seduced her estranged brother, not knowing who he was, and turned up pregnant with his child. When the locals found out, they said she was a witch and burned her. But a curse fell on everyone who damned her. They all died from smallpox. Well, you can understand my fear. I panicked and ran right out of the library to the nearest church, a Catholic one. I'm not Catholic, but I figured the priest would still help me."

"What happened?" Sara asked smirking.

"I found the priest. Sir, I said, I've got to talk to you. I explained about the Amanda thing. He asked if anything was bothering my conscience, anything I needed to confess. I said, 'Hell no, sir. I'm not the slut. You do something.' He shook his head and told me to go home and get out of the heat. I thought, Good Lord, he's crazy! I ran out of that Catholic church as fast as I could. Two days later, Bob Ed came over to discuss our divorce, you know, the nasty stuff about who gets what. Well, we were sitting in the living room, and I started telling him the Amanda story. Suddenly and for no good reason, a huge tapestry above my head came crashing down. Knocked me clear to the floor. I could of been killed."

Alex broke in, "Harriet Laurel, did you see anything, an apparition, hear voices?"

“Why, no. I’m not nuts! You’re as bad as that priest. Nothing else happened, nothing but Bob Ed Shit-House marrying that beauty parlor slut Amanda. What do you think of that?” She took a swig of her drink and slammed the glass down. Her companion reached over and gave her a consoling pat on the hand.

Sara laughed out loud, a gut-shaker that made Harriet Laurel sit up, ramrod straight. “That’s the story?” she asked. “Fair dinkum, you’re a lucky woman. You weren’t hurt.”

Alex replied in an overly earnest voice. “Harriet Laurel, sometimes we get messages, warnings, *before* something bad happens, a chance to shift a destiny pattern, you know, change what’s coming. Your finding that book about a woman named Amanda was a sign. Did you ever consider the tapestry falling a wake-up call? Like something was coming down around you, and you needed to be aware, to wake up.”

“No, sir. How strange. A wake-up call?” She looked around at the group. “Any of you ever had something like that happen? I doubt it. Sir, you must be one of those people who sees signs in everything. I stick with reality,” she said, tapping her glass for a refill. “Thank you very much.”

Chapter Four

The Way North

The following morning Askara and Sara left the game park. Strong Kenyan coffee revived Sara from her hangover, but Askara still insisted on driving. They retrieved Dele from his uncle's and headed north toward Isiolo. The descent into the plains north of Mt. Kenya brought a wave of heat that rippled images and danced off the tree-dotted horizon.

When the Land Rover spooked a young Grévy's zebra foal, his brown stripes melded with the parched land. Gazelles, impalas, and tiny Dik-Dik deer fled the noisy intruder, running to hide among the wildebeest, buffalo, and giraffe. A herd of warthogs bolted, their black tails straight up in the air.

At Isiolo, tarmac road gave way to a dirt track through the bush. Life slowed accordingly. Askara pulled a red bandanna across her face and tucked her long braid into a canvas hat. Yellow ochre dust covered them. Sara shifted with a moan without opening her eyes. Dele slumped across their gear in the backseat as the hours crept on.

When they camped for the night, Dele unpacked, set up the tent, made a fire, and cooked rice with canned meat, adding two squash his uncle had given him. After dinner, Dele picked bits of meat out of the dirt and tossed them into the flames, saying, "Safer, hyenas no smell." The three nestled close to the fire and gazed up at the canopy of glittering stars that arched over their heads and stretched to the distant horizon.

"Hey, Sara, thanks again for convincing me to travel overland. You're right. What an amazing place, a once-in-a-lifetime adventure! I'm sure I can explain the delay to my boss since he's traveled all over the world. He'll get it; he's a good guy."

Sara mumbled, "Must be."

They slept smothered by stars. But when the heat escalated at sunrise, they rose quickly, gathered their things, gagged down mud-thick Kenyan coffee—Dele's first attempt at making it—and ate fried bread and eggs before breaking camp. Bush country, long expanses of cracked, dried earth dotted by thorny acacia trees and shrubs, unfolded in front of them. They traveled identical scenery for hours with Sara at the wheel.

"Only an African could make sense of this terrain...or an Aborigine," Sara commented, looking at Dele in the back. "A genuine wonder the kid can sleep in that position." Sara pulled under the sparse shade of a dusty acacia tree. Ahead, a gigantic sun danced blood-orange on the horizon.

"Where are we, Sara?"

"Hell, if I know. Where's the damn map? Dele wake up. Where are we?"

Dele sat up and rubbed his eyes in surprise. Askara moaned, looking at him. "Sara, he looks scared. Oh, shit, I think we're lost."

Sara wheeled around to the boy and shouted, "Bloody hell! We're lost in the bush—with our guide. Where do we go, Dele?"

"I sleep, memsahib, see no thing."

"We'll make camp here—no use going in bloody circles in the bush this late. We can't afford the petrol. Dele make a fire. Askara, help me set up the tent."

"Will we be okay here, Sara?"

"It's not much different from other spots I've camped—I hope. We can't afford much backtracking," Sara said, grinding her boot tip into the cracked earth. Sara glanced at Dele's thin, gangly silhouette gathering sticks in front of the scarlet globe. She mumbled to Askara, "Why did we think a child could guide us in rough country?"

An agonizing scream erupted and shattered the early night rhythms while they ate dinner. Dele whispered, "Baboons." They heard animals running, panicked in the dark just beyond the camp. The women jumped. Dele handed them burning sticks. "Hold close," he said, his eyes wide. After several minutes, the hysteria died down. Dele remained frozen in strained silence, listening. The women watched him. Suddenly he jumped up, brandishing a handful of burning sticks. Orange sparks left motion memories against the black night. He pointed, "See, he comes."

Askara spotted a pair of yellow reflective eyes circling the camp. Sara loosened the knife from her leg holster, grabbed a burning stick, and waved it. Askara brandished two sticks.

Dele raised his hand. "Leopard watches. Hates fire. Stay close to fire." The women squeezed together as close as possible without burning each other. The cat stalked them, studying their movements for an hour, and then disappeared. "He's hungry. Hunts baboons or grazers." The night erupted in screams. "A kill. Fast hunter. Must be young. Now he eats," Dele said, stoking the campfire. "Good."

The exhausted women drifted off to sleep next to the fire, leaving Dele to watch the darkness and stir the coals. The sounds of hyena yipping drew closer. The women jumped up and grabbed smoldering sticks. Dele said in a grave tone, "Hyenas take babies, eat them." He tossed a glowing piece of wood in the direction of the yipping. "Samburu hate them! No good hunters, mean, ugly. Eat dead meat left by leopards."

When morning arrived, they broke camp, loaded the Rover, and began backtracking so Dele could get his bearings. When he spotted a slight cloud of dust in the distance, he motioned Askara to follow it. In a few minutes, the dust makers, three Masai warriors, ran into view. They approached the Land Rover with long, thin, metal spears in hand, wearing red-ochre loin wraps decorated with jingling cowry shells. Their braids, coated with red mud, touched the large concentric halos of beads that extended down their chests. Their ear lobes, stretched into flesh loops, supported hoops of beads.

Dele spoke to them in Masai then turned to the women. "These Moran say they scout lion. He kill their calf. They kill him. These warriors, they drink blood from cow's neck with milk, warrior food. Lion fears Masai Moran. They tell way we go." Dele got directions for the track north. He displayed respect like a submissive pup. The Masai turned, and in long, even strides kicked red dust into the blue sky as they grew smaller in the distance. Dele said to Askara and Sara. "Samburu women more beautiful than Masai. Many, many necklaces."

They backtracked and spotted a lorry piled high with car tires. They followed the truck over the rutted dry earth, weaving through acacia thorns. When the lorry stopped at a small watering hole, Dele yelled for Askara to stop. He walked over to speak to the men. When he returned, he informed the memsahibs that he had arranged for them to caravan with the lorry to Addis, saying, "Safe. Men good from Nairobi. I know cousin. They stop at my village for night. You follow next day."

Late that day, the lorry and the Land Rover pulled into a small enclave of earth-red cow dung huts with conical grass roofs. Skinny chickens pecked in the dust. Children played a hopping game with small rocks. Everyone rushed over to see the strangers with Dele.

A woman with squiggles of silver in her close-cropped black hair ran up to embrace Dele. Her beaded loops of elephant hair formed a mantel around her neck and shoulders.

"Dele's mother? She must be important," Askara whispered to Sara.

Dele pointed, saying, "Mother." The woman studied them with a distrustful look until Dele spoke the word *shillings*. She softened to a smile.

They stayed the night in the village, sleeping on grass mats Dele's mother pulled out into the clearing in front of the family dwelling. The lorry men camped within sight of the huts but kept to themselves. Dele's mother brought them spongy flatbread, slightly bitter cooked pieces of goat meat, and a clay pot of water. Dele told them, "Special food for memsahibs."

Arising early to move out with the lorry, they whispered goodbye to Dele when he came to bring them more water. Askara and Sara pressed wads of bills into his hand. His smile stretched from ear to ear. In the early gray dawn, they drove off, following the lorry.

"I'm gonna miss that little bloke," Sara said, wiping road dust from the windshield.

"Me, too. I felt safer with Dele along, even though he's just a boy."

They dropped back from the lorry so that they would inhale less dust, and gradually slipped further behind. When Askara saw a broader track, with a sign for Moyale, barely discernible through the yellow haze, she figured it led to the border. They didn't need the lorry anymore, even if they could find it.

Approaching the border at Moyale, they saw men in military uniforms searching vehicles at the gate. An officer hailed the Land Rover with his pistol in the air.

"Good afternoon," he said. He leaned into the driver's window and glanced around at the contents. "Madam, passports. Step out of the vehicle." He motioned to two men. The guards trotted over and began emptying the Land Rover, throwing the gear on the rutted, dusty ground.

Askara asked, "Why do you have to go through everything?"

Without looking up, a guard continued to investigate the gear saying, "Routine for firearms. Only guns registered with the Kenyan government, okay. No illegal guns for Eritreans."

"Who?" Sara said.

"Ethiopian rebels fighting civil war. Illegal arms come across border points." The guard started reloading their gear, throwing everything in like sacks of grain. He motioned an *all-clear* to the border officer processing their paperwork.

"Are we in any danger traveling?"

"No, madam, not in the south. Problems in the north."

The women hopped back into the Land Rover, shoving things out of their way. The officer returned their stamped passports, the border gate lifted, and they drove into Ethiopia.

Pulled over to the side, behind a small building, they spotted the lorry full of tires. They saw military guards with automatic rifles aimed at six men lined up along the truck with their faces pressed into the wooden rail and hands raised above their heads. Border guards, like busy ants, crisscrossed back and forth, tossing tires onto the ground, and pulling rifles out.

"Bloody hell! There must be sixty rifles there."

With a nervous laugh, Askara said, "Thank God we were slow. Dele couldn't have known about those guys, could he?"

"No," Sara said with a metallic ring to her words, making the sign of the cross with a nervous laugh. "Didn't know there was a full-on civil war going on, no news about it. Check our visas. How long do we have?"

Askara pulled her passport from its leather pouch. "Three weeks."

"More than enough."

"But is it smart to continue?"

"Sure. We'll be south of the conflict."

Sara veered toward the petrol station. A fleet of Land Rovers and buses queued up at the lone pump. "This'll take thirty minutes, at least. Let's exchange money at that bank. Don't know when we'll see another. When they returned, and after a long wait in line, Sara filled the Land Rover and the holding tanks. "Good to go. I'm driving this stretch."

ON THE THIRD DAY FROM THE BORDER, THEY REACHED DILA after overnights in Yableo and Agere Maryam. In Dila, friendly villagers came out, shook the women's hands, vigorously and often, and tried to talk to them, apparently pleased to have guests in their quiet village. Dila appeared the nearest thing to paradise that Askara had seen in this part of Africa. A stream laced through the settlement nourishing dense banana trees, pineapple plants in fertile loam soil, and abundant fields of onions, peppers, and grains.

Askara walked down a winding path, through dense foliage and past banana trees heavy with green bunches, to the stream where a man sat at the water's edge. Careful not to disturb him, she continued walking to where the stream rushed over rocks, breaking and tumbling before it flattened and followed grassy banks.

"Memsahib," the man shouted. "Use care."

"Thank you. I'm staying away from the rocks."

"Memsahib, shadow follows you. Watch out."

"What?"

"Someone watches. Shadow follows your feet."

Askara jumped and looked down, wondering what he meant. She leaned forward involuntarily. She shook her head. The image of Nagali's amulet shimmered in a calm inlet of the stream. Her eyes fluttered uncontrollably. She focused on the opposite bank where women washed their clothes, beating them on the rocks, and spread them out to dry. She felt dizzy. She saw the women fluttering up close and then far away like a camera lens shifting. Askara sat on the grass and shut her eyes. She felt nauseous, but the sensation passed. When she looked up, the man was no longer there. She had hoped to speak to him.

Askara returned to the village center where she saw Sara playing a game with children. "What's that?" she asked.

"Not sure. I think we're playing *Mancala*. I'm winning, at least I think I am. They make it seem that way. I have the most pebbles. That must be a good sign." The children giggled and sat close to Sara, as close as they could without being on top of her. They presented her with a smooth, yellow rock striated with quartz veins. "I think I won the prize," she said, looking up at Askara.

When Sara stood, the children stood. When she and Askara walked, they walked. The children escorted them to the village market, a grassy area with covered vendor stalls. Under the woven grass canopies, neat piles of vegetables and fruits fanned out on the ground. An older woman displayed conical hills of spices—yellow, green, red, and brown—neatly arranged on woven grass mats. The villagers greeted the foreigners with broad smiles and chatter. Sara and Askara bought several pineapples and several bunches of bananas, sliced them with Sara's knife, and hosted a picnic in the market for their entourage of curious children.

"Hey, Sara," Askara said, "a man by the stream said something strange to me. *Someone watches. Shadow follows your feet.* What do you think he meant?"

"I'm surprised anyone here speaks English. Those lines are a lead-in. I read your fortune for money comes next."

"But he left. That was all. He seemed nice, but it freaked me out, reminded me of the crazy soothsayer in Nairobi, Nagali, the guy I told you about."

"Get over it, Askara. You're hypersensitive. Look at this beautiful place. The people are warm and kind. Relax. Enjoy Africa."

"You think it's in *my* head? Like that crazy-ass woman Harriet Laurel? Thanks a lot."

"I didn't say that. I know that Nagali bloke scared you. He sounded creepy, but we are here; he is not. Let's have a good time."

EARLY THE FOLLOWING MORNING, SORRY TO LEAVE IDYLLIC Dila, they pushed on toward Addis Ababa, the capital. The rough terrain transitioned to lush vegetation and orderly groves of trees. European-style wooden houses replaced the conical huts. Children darted in and out of scallop-edged cactus plants as high as banana trees. The only wildlife they saw were baboons sitting in the grass on their bare, red butts picking nits off one another.

Askara roused from passenger stupor to study the map. She saw a stop listed for Lake Ziway, between Adami Tullu and Meki, where hippos lived at the north end. The caption, *submerged in cool water, not to be missed,* piqued her interest.

"Askara, does it say that although the government tries to protect them since they attract tourists, the farmers in the area hate them because they can devour a year's crop in one night of grazing, so poaching's an ongoing problem?"

Askara rolled her eyes. "I want to see them. Okay?"

"You're the one on a business trip, not me. If you've got the time, I've got the time."

Chapter Five

Addis Ababa

Askara wiped from her glasses a dusty memory of the arid lowland terrain. Ascending to the Ethiopian capital of Addis Ababa through lush vegetation, grassland, and forests, they reached the city—Addis, for short—home to 600,000 people. Askara had expected a city like Nairobi but found this nation's capital awash with poverty for most…and extreme wealth for a few.

Beggars abounded. From the time the women drove into the Hilton parking lot, adolescent beggar boys watched them, sometimes jeering, or making passes, but hanging back to follow. The women felt glad when the valet scared them away. After putting their things in the room, they decided to walk to a nearby Bank of Ethiopia to exchange money since the bank's rate would be better than the hotel's.

As Askara watched the beggar boys lining the hotel perimeter, she came up with a plan. "Okay, I've got it. We enter the front entrance of the bank where they have guards, but we leave from the rear door, no beggars on that side for some reason. Sara, you know what I just figured out? That man by the stream, the one in Dila who said—someone watches, a shadow follows your feet—referred to these beggar boys. I see them shadowing the guests."

"Wish he'd said what to do about it," Sara said. "Okay, follow me. I have the route mapped out in my head."

They rushed into the front door of the bank, exchanged travelers' checks for Ethiopian birr, hid their money and passports in pouches tucked into their jeans, and exited through the back door, despite the *No Exit* sign. Checking outside for the boys, they saw a guard beyond the bank's manicured lawn, who prevented the beggar boys from loitering. Askara and Sara slipped away unnoticed.

"Askara, let's go to the palace, see your friend, and split. This city's too big. Too crowded."

"Friend?" Askara laughed. "I don't even know him."

"Your *contact*. Come on. Cities aren't my thing."

They walked past butcher shops, fly-invested shacks with bloody animal carcasses dangling from ropes. The stench of blood and entrails in the heat made Askara gag. They skirted the open-air market, but when Sara spotted crafts, cloth banners, woven baskets, leather goods, and musical instruments, she yanked Askara into the labyrinth of stalls.

Sara picked up a diamond-shaped wooden instrument and plucked the one string. The merchant held up another with six lines for her to try. "Look at this thing," she said to Askara.

"Looks like a lyre."

"This is more like it," Sara said, "lifting a large instrument with twelve strings. She strummed.

"Sounds like a whining dog, Sara. You're not the string type." Askara pointed to the drums. "That's you."

Sara picked up a wooden drum, wiped the dust from the stretched cowhide, and beat an aggressive rhythm.

"Yeah, I'm buying this." After haggling with the man for half-an-hour, she whittled him down to one-fourth the original price and bought the drum. When she left the stall, a runner slammed into her. Sara listed to the side and grabbed her neck. "Damn bastard got my St. Christopher. I hate that."

"Are you okay? Is that all he got?"Askara said, steadying her.

"Yeah."

"Let's get out of here. You'll never catch the guy, Sara."

They took the main boulevard back to the hotel since it afforded an expansive view, avoiding passersby, mostly Europeans. For the remainder of the afternoon lounging at the hotel, Askara withdrew into a tourist magazine in the foyer. Sara walked over to talk to the desk clerk about sites to visit. Thirsty for beer, she motioned for Askara to join her. When they entered the dark bar to Bob Dylan's *Knockin' on Heaven's Door*, Sara grinned. A woman and two men immersed in conversation saw Sara and Askara walk in and waved them over.

"Sit with us," the woman said in English with a lilting Italian accent. "I'm outnumbered." She introduced herself and the men as Italian engineers working on a dam project in Ethiopia for the government. She added, "You will keep us from arguing."

After greeting Askara and Sara, a fortyish, attractive man said, "You must understand Ethiopia. In some ways, the potential is great, in other areas…tragic. The key is the Emperor. He controls everything. We must have him sign-off on our design, first."

The woman straightened her olive-green tailored pants suit and added, looking at Askara and Sara, "He's a divine ruler, a direct descendant of the Queen of Sheba and King

Solomon. Selassie is the first and last word here." Sara snickered. The woman glared at her. "Be careful. What did you say your name is?"

"Sara."

"Be careful, Sara. Justice in Ethiopia is a fragile thing. The country has many problems, rebels in Eritrea fighting for independence, starvation, drought, social unrest. Take care with your opinions—for your safety."

The other man broke into the chilly atmosphere. "What do you do, Miss Sara?"

"I work for the UN in an agricultural program, teaching sustainable farm methods to a women's collective in Lesotho."

"That's quite a wonderful cause," he continued. "You must be exceptional to be working for the U.N. at such a young age." Sara beamed, hearing his comment. "Would you and your friend—Miss Askara, was it?—like to join us for dinner tonight? We are to meet two Ethiopian government engineers here at 8:00. It would be enjoyable to have more company."

Askara guessed he meant the woman engineer bored him, and new female company would liven things up, although she wondered how she would. She felt like a wet rag. But she knew Sara would rise to the occasion…happily.

Later, back in their room, Sara cajoled Askara. "Look, it might perk you up. Come on. You need a change. You're down. Best way to beat it? Go out and socialize, take your mind off that bloke you like, or that soothsayer, whatever's bothering you."

"True, but I don't think dinner will do it."

"I bet a swim before dinner will do the trick. I checked the pool. It's big and empty."

"Okay. I'll go down for dinner with you, but only because I don't feel like being alone."

Askara's mood improved immensely after swimming a hundred laps like someone was chasing her. She had not shared with Sara what made her crazy. She felt someone watching her since that Nagali night. Paranoia, frayed nerves, and fatigue made her believe people were staring. Earlier, on the boulevard, she thought she caught, out of the corner of her eye, someone pointing at her. She looked away. She kept her thoughts to herself, not wanting to alarm Sara or to turn her off. She needed Sara's companionship, her good humor. As Askara applied her makeup and dressed for dinner, she decided to try her best to be upbeat.

Two Ethiopian men approached the dinner table, where the group sat. The taller of the two, Mr. Enda Gaggeret, introduced himself and said, "And this my friend Mr. Tessenei Humera. We both work for the government as engineers."

Mr. Humera, the smaller and darker-complexioned man, spoke English with a strong Scottish accent. "Please, call me Tess." He made a slight bow and extended his hand to the women. When he reached Sara, he blurted out, "I didn't realize Italians had such eyes."

Sara smiled. "I'm Aussie, from Melbourne. Not an engineer, an agricultural agent for the U.N."

Tess smiled. "Ah, one of the wild ones. I have Australian friends, fine people."

"My friend Askara's from America."

He studied Askara for a second. "I would not have guessed. Welcome. Glad you could join us."

Enda lapsed into Italian with the engineers, but Tess, who had studied in Scotland for six years, spoke to Sara and Askara in his Scottish burr. "Ladies, how do you find Ethiopia?"

"Fascinating, great diversity...in the people and terrain," Sara replied. "Hope you don't mind me asking, but why did you go to Scotland for higher education? It's so cold there."

"I could have gone to Italy, but I chose Scotland. I got used to the weather, and you are correct. It is cold. You see, after becoming independent, many African countries received internationally funded opportunities for study abroad higher education, you know, to become experts in one's field and return home to shape our new countries. There were national exams in several disciplines. If you scored well, then you might get a scholarship. That's how it worked for Enda and me."

"Oh, yes, we are many tribes. Seventy unique languages. Different religions, Coptic Christian, of which I am, and followers of Islam, and other faiths. Ethiopians have been Christians from the earliest time. Did you know that? As early as the fourth century, Ethiopia protected Christians fleeing persecution in neighboring lands. To fully enjoy our past, you must see Lalibela, the city of monolithic churches hewn from rock, built in the 12th century by Emperor Lalibela. Fascinating."

"Where's that?" Sara said.

"Wollo province, north-central Ethiopia."

Enda left the discussion in Italian with the engineers to add, "Oh, yes, and Axum, the ancient home of the Queen of Sheba. Magnificent steles. The largest is twenty-one meters tall. They are on the road to Gondar in a field. According to legend, the Queen of Sheba's tomb is there."

"According to legend?"

"Yes, Miss Askara, according to what we Ethiopians believe. Gondar, in northeastern Ethiopia, our ancient capital, was home to royalty. One church—Debre Berhan Selassie—has famous murals, excellent examples of our religious art."

The Italian woman, fueled by shots of whiskey, said, "I've been to Gondar. Well worth a visit. Ruins of castles and churches fire the imagination—not Florence—but a must-see, anyway."

Servers brought out bowls for hand washing followed by large circular platters of injera, spongy flatbread, with side dishes of goat meat in gravy, spicy vegetables—squash and green beans—and red chili lentils.

Enda smiled. "The proper Ethiopian way to eat." He pulled off a piece of injera, cradling the goat meat in it, and placed the bite in his mouth without spilling a drop of gravy.

Tess laughed, "Foreigners must master eating with their hands. Quite an art, as you can see. Only the washed fingertips touch the *injera*—no shoving the food up a down-turned fork like the Scots. We use the direct method. Please, ladies, help yourselves. We all share. I'll tell you a story about my first formal meal in Scotland, my welcoming dinner at university if you're interested."

Sara stuffed a piece of food in her mouth, gulped, and said, "Please do."

"When I sat at the table and saw so many silver forks, spoons, and knives, I thought someone had made a mistake. There were not enough chairs for so many people. I moved my chair close to the woman next to me, my dean's wife, to leave room for the others. She gave me a very odd look. I assumed she was also confused as to how so many could squeeze in at the table. To simplify matters, I collected all the silverware at my setting, excepting one fork and one knife, placed them carefully on the extra smaller plate, and pushed it toward the center of the table, so others could easily reach it. The dean's wife, my hostess, watched without expression. Then she quietly gathered her extra silverware and did the same. The others followed her cue. As the dinner went on, I was surprised no other guests arrived. I considered that poor manners on their part. We, seven guests, spent an enjoyable dinner together. A week later, I questioned a fellow student who had attended that dinner, asking why others had not shown up. He replied, everyone had. But what of the extra silverware? I asked. He laughed and explained that it was the British way of setting the table. Each person's setting includes multiple plates and silverware. At first, I felt humiliated. He slapped me on the back and said, old chap, that night, you became the dean's favorite. She realized you didn't understand English dining etiquette. She taught us all a good lesson in manners."

Sara grinned. "Betty Windsor would have loved that."

When the Italian engineers initiated a conversation about harnessing the power of the Blue Nile Falls for electricity, Sara listened, but Askara drifted.

Enda interrupted, "At all costs, we must keep the falls pristine. I disagree with your analysis." An uncomfortable silence ensued.

Jumping into the void, Sara said, "I'd like to see the Blue Nile Falls. I think it's a nine-hour drive from here. But what's Asmara like? I plan to drop off the Land Rover there before I fly back to Lesotho."

Enda replied, "Asmara was an Italian stronghold during World War II; therefore, aspects of Italian culture remain.

Several Italian restaurants are excellent. Asmara's a lovely European-type city with broad, tree-lined streets and outdoor cafes. The shopping is cosmopolitan and expensive."

Askara asked, "Is it in Eritrea?"

"Yes," Tess replied, "that's the province."

"Is that where there's a civil war?"

The Ethiopians looked stunned by the question. Askara shrunk, hoping Sara would jump in to save her when Enda spoke up. "There is conflict, dating back to 1962, not a major concern. Eritreans want to have their own country. A silly idea, actually."

Tess added, "They promise Ethiopia free access to the Red Sea port of Assab, a lifeline for us down here *if* we give them independence. How ridiculous. They can't manage themselves, much less a port."

Askara changed the subject quickly. "Do you know Sir Alexander Desta, the emperor's nephew?"

"Yes, I have met him on occasion, a very polished gentleman," Enda said. "He's a member of the British Royal Navy…or was. Why do you ask?"

"I have a letter of introduction to him."

"You don't say." Enda's eyebrows raised in surprise. "How did you get that?"

"Through a friend."

Enda asked, "Why? Will you write an article about him?"

Askara, not wanting to discuss business since the jewelry sale would indicate the royal family needed money—and she was sworn to secrecy, or thought she was—responded slowly. "My friend told me they have a wonderful art collection, not open to the public, but shown by appointment upon special request. My friend asked Sir Alexander, with whom he had served in the navy, to show it to me. I have a professional interest in art. I work for an art and artifacts dealer in San Francisco."

"You are lucky. I have seen some of that lovely collection, as good as any I saw in Italy during my studies. Good for you."

The Italian woman fumbled with her napkin, and interrupted, "How is it, Enda, that you went to Italy for your education? If I am not mistaken, very few Ethiopians are literate, possibly five percent, yet you and Tess received professional degrees."

Askara cringed at the woman's lack of tact, but Enda replied graciously. "I am a lucky person. You see, I received education from Catholic missionaries in Asmara. They arranged with your government to grant me a scholarship to study engineering in Rome. I lived there for several years."

"And you, Tess, why Scotland of all places?"

"I, too, won a scholarship. I had good fortune. As a young boy, I was chosen from my village to come to Addis to study with the Church of England missionaries, who had started a school, with the help of our Emperor. Our Emperor is a great believer in education. He opened Ethiopia's first university in 1961. Initially, I studied agriculture, but when awarded a scholarship to Scotland, I shifted to agricultural engineering."

Sara asked, "What about women? Are they educated? Do they get scholarships?"

"Some," Tess said. "The women who go to university mostly study to be social workers and pharmacists. We still have a long way to go in education. First, we need to teach the masses to read and then build from there, a slow process. But we have 4,000 students at Haile Selassie I University."

"Did your wives go to university?" Askara said. "We would have enjoyed meeting them too."

"Tess and I have young children, so our wives are very busy."

"Well, I hope we meet again. I'd love to visit with your families," Askara said. "Please excuse me now. I'm tired. Nice to meet all of you and thank you for the invitation."

THE NEXT MORNING ASKARA ASKED THE CONCIERGE TO book her a taxi to Jubilee Palace. When she and Sara arrived at the palace, the guard at the gate, standing at rigid attention in his military uniform with a pistol in his belt holster, stared at the women. They attempted to explain why they had come. He did not understand English. After what seemed an exceedingly long time, he took the letter, called another guard to stand in his place, and retreated into the lavish tree-shaded garden. A half-hour passed. The women stood outside the gate, finding marginal relief from the heat under large-leaf branches that draped the palace's stone wall. They attempted to question a guard, but he remained in unblinking stillness.

"What's going on, Askara?"

"Don't know. Maybe someone needs to find Sir Alexander so that he can come to the gate or something."

"At this rate, they're digging him up," Sara said and wiped the perspiration from her brow. "Do you think they understood? I mean the letter's in English. Maybe no one here can read it."

With her excitement over the potential jewelry purchase fading, Askara turned to Sara, who was tossing pebbles on the stone steps. "Wanna leave?"

"Wanna stay? Nothing's going to happen. That bloke disappeared."

Just as Askara started to reply, she spotted an officer striding toward them in a crisp military manner. He spoke to the guard in Amharic before speaking to the women in English.

"I am sorry for the delay, madam. I am the only one on duty who reads the English language. Unfortunately, Sir Alexander is presently out-of-station and will not return for four days. Please be advised that you may return on Friday, in the afternoon, to meet him as your letter requires."

Askara said, "Do we come back to this same gate?"

"No, madam, please come to the front entrance. A guard will take you to Sir Alexander, no problem."

"Thank you." Askara walked away in the heat, deflated, wondering if she should have asked for the letter back. "Any ideas, Sara?"

"I'd like to go to the post office to mail my postcards. The women's collective in Lesotho will be excited to get mail."

"Excellent idea," Askara said, hoping a letter from Darian would be there c/o *Poste Restante*, thinking hardly likely. She fantasized about Darian meeting her in California after she landed the sale and had time off. She intended to take him on a tour of California, from Big Sur to Mt. Shasta, even down to San Diego, whatever he wanted. The thought of him lifted her spirits. At this moment, she felt hopeful.

They navigated the city with the help of a small map the Hilton concierge had given them. The massive post office, a modern concrete building with rectangular windows, looked like a cross between a prison and a palace. The long, paved walkway leading up to the multi-story building meandered through manicured grass lawns, orderly flower beds, and gigantic shade trees that softened the prison aspect.

At the counter, Askara conversed with the clerk in rudimentary English to discover she had received no mail. Sara bought stamps and dropped her postcards into the mail slot. They walked a short distance to Africa Hall, another vast, modern building, home of the U.N. Economic Commission for Africa. Entering the foyer, Askara admired a two-story stained-glass window—slumping precariously at the top—that depicted Ethiopia's history while casting colorful shapes on the white marble floor.

Askara read the plaque on the wall under Emperor Haile Selassie I's portrait, commemorating his many achievements. The Economic Commission and the Organization of African Unity set up headquarters in Addis Ababa; he'd opened the country's first university, named after himself, and it listed honorary degrees from all over the world, the most recent being from the University of California at Los Angeles. Askara smiled irreverently at the litany of his accomplishments. Below, a small plaque acknowledged Ethiopia's leading artist, Afewerk Tekle, the creator of the immense window. Ain't that the way, she thought. Artists never get their due.

Sara walked over. "The bloke's amazing. I read the emperor's speech pleading for protection for Ethiopia, and other smaller nations, against fascism."

"Where's that?"

"A plaque down the hall. The one near the photo of him."

"They're all near photos of him."

THE WOMEN WALKED OUT TO THE TREE-LINED BOULEVARD where Citroens and Mercedes sped by. Sara rolled her eyes. "No dearth of money for some people." She spotted a grand church and motioned for Askara to follow her. The entrance plaque read: The Emperor built Trinity Church in 1941 as a burial place for members of the Imperial Family. "This plaque doesn't have his photo, yet," Sara said to Askara, raising her eyebrows, her eyes smiling.

Inside, paintings depicted the Emperor's divine lineage, as a ruler descended from King Solomon and the Queen of Sheba. Askara craned her neck to look up at the cupola decoration, Titian-like fat cherubs floated in the heavens to herald the birth of the Emperor. "This is getting old, Sara. What do we do now? We have days."

"How about the Blue Nile Falls? Get out of the city until Friday? We'll come back for your meeting at the palace; then, you can ride with me to Asmara to return the Land Rover to my U.N. contact. From there, I'll fly to Lesotho. You fly to California, jewelry purchase in hand, or to India to see your bloke."

"I'll fly to San Francisco from Addis, that's quicker, more direct. Okay? Are you fine driving to Asmara alone?"

"Well, if you don't go to Asmara, I won't either. I'll arrange to leave the Rover here in Addis for him. Ethiopia is one country I would not travel alone. I'd like to see the north though, supposed to be beautiful. The highest peak, Ras Dashan is 4,619 meters, less than Mt. Kilimanjaro, but supposed to be amazing. Next trip. Okay, Blue Nile Falls, it is. Then outta here!"

Chapter Six

Blue Nile Falls

The two-day trek from Addis Ababa to Dangla, a small town south of Lake Tana, passed more easily than negotiating the beggars in Addis, Askara thought. The vast lake, Ethiopia's largest, was accessed by only two roads, one from the north from Gondar and the southern route from Addis. Askara and Sara pulled into a village in late afternoon. They quickly secured a room for the night at a small bungalow-style hotel, ten rooms separated by flimsy partitions under a shared thatched roof. The room was barely large enough for two single beds. When they strolled the town in search of a restaurant, the usual groups of wide-eyed children followed them, although no one tugged on them or begged.

Sara said, "I'm starving. Let's get some grub. Seems our motel's the only one in town, and that's the only restaurant over there. Guess it's the best choice, eh?" The modest restaurant, the size of a walk-in closet, had two tables outside shaded by a grass mat roof. Both were empty. "Guess we have our pick. Dinner crowd's not huge."

The owner handed them a crumpled, discolored piece of paper with squiggly lines on it. Askara rolled her eyes and walked to the narrow counter, pointed to four eggs, a bit of onion, and crusted bread. She nodded, *yes*. She pantomimed cracking and scrambling the eggs in the heavy black skillet that rested on the charcoal fire. The man laughed and nodded in agreement. She pointed to a pot of cooked white beans and a blackened teapot. He smiled and started dinner.

Women with water urns balanced on their heads walked past their table. Men strolled together, seemingly with no work to do. Children laughed and kicked sticks in the dusty road, stopping to check if the foreigners were watching them. An elderly beggar across the way, propped up against a wall, chanted a monotonous refrain with his hand extended, eyes glazed white from the Bilharzia water snail disease. Askara winced. Villagers greeted him and gave the old man bits of food as they passed. A young woman came out to retrieve him in the pale evening, leading him inside the shack.

"That's the way it should be," Askara said as they ate. "People helping people."

"Yeah, village life's far better, even if meager. Beats starving to death in a crowded city like Addis. Even the kids here are different," Sara said, whisking a fly from her plate. "Sun's down. Better finish and get back to our room."

At the motel, they washed at the outdoor shower, a water tap encircled by a grass mat. Reclining on rickety cots, Askara read in the yellow light of the kerosene lamp until the jabbering guests quieted. Sara had gotten sick to her stomach after dinner. Exhausted, she fell asleep quickly. Hours later, they woke to shouts. From the door crack where the flimsy wooden panel did not meet the jamb, Askara peeked out at the silhouette of a man illuminated by car lights. He stumbled toward their door and knocked hard, causing the wood to quake from the impact, and Sara to shift in her sleeping bag.

The man shouted in English, "Get out of my room. You are in my room." He slammed his fist harder, cracking the wood a little.

Askara shouted, "You're wrong. This is our room. Check with management."

"Look, bitch, my room. Open the door. I want my room."

Excited chatter erupted down the line. Another slam and the door nearly split. Askara pulled on her jeans and motioned for Sara to do the same. "What do we do?" she whispered.

"Ignore him. He's drunk. He'll leave," Sara said, sitting on the bed's edge, trying to pull her jeans on.

The man slugged the door again. "Sara, on the count of three, scream as loud as you can. One, two, three...." They screamed; the guest chatter hushed. No one came.

"Goddamned-bitches get out. I have a gun. I'll shoot the door open."

Askara turned to look at Sara, imagining blood splattered all over their tiny room. She surged with rage. She leaped back from the door, almost tripping over her bed. "No place to hide," she moaned. "Leave us alone, bastard. This is not your room!"

She motioned for Sara to flip her bed over toward the wall and get under it. Askara yanked back the latch and stepped out. The man stumbled backward, caught his balance, and lunged at her. Askara dodged him. He tossed a lit cigarette into her hair. She smelled her hair sizzle. While she pulled the smoldering tip out, he charged. She thrust out her hand, fingers stiff, and slammed him in the well of his throat.

He gasped and squeaked, "Bitch!" He doubled over. When he came up, he had his hand on a pistol aimed her direction. Askara jumped sideways. Two men leaped from the darkness into the car light, tackled the drunk man from the side, and wrestled the gun from his grip. They shoved him onto his stomach, forcing his head down, yanked his hands to the small of his back, and roped his wrists.

Askara rushed at him and kicked him in the butt, yelling, "Stupid bastard, you tried to shoot me!" He turned to look at her. She spat on his face before the men pushed her aside. The driver jumped out, grabbed his drunk friend, and pushed him into the waiting car. The car sped away with its lights turned off. The loud, clanking engine grew fainter in the blackness until Askara heard it no more. She stumbled back into their room, locked the cracked door, and heard excited gossip explode down the length of the building. She collapsed on her cot.

Sara crawled out from under her cot and righted it. "My God, Askara, I didn't take that stupid bloke seriously. The bastard had a gun? He could've killed us. Wow! You got so pissed off. Didn't know you had it in ya."

"Being threatened makes me crazy. I hate shit like that."

"I'll say." Sara inhaled with a nervous laugh. "I'm the one with a knife. Not much help, was I? I still feel lousy. Must be food poisoning."

"I saw you dead in your bag, Sara, blood everywhere. Made me go ballistic," Askara said, dry heaving. "Hey, do you have anything for sleep, valium, or anything? I figure no one's coming tonight. I need to sleep. We'll leave at first light."

"Okay. Yep, I carry some in case I can't sleep. Want one? Want them all?"

"One's enough. Thanks."

IN THE MORNING, WHEN THEY LEFT THEIR ROOM, A SMALL crowd of mumblers milled around the motel. They stared but did not come close. Askara and Sara threw their backpacks into the Rover and took off before sunrise. They drove toward *Tis Isat Falls*, Blue Nile Falls, stopping at Dangla to hire a day guide since their map didn't show the way.

Askara had not spoken more than two words on the drive, so Sara made light conversation. "Two Niles, you know. The Blue Nile starts up here from Lake Tana, flows toward Khartoum, Sudan. The White Nile starts in central Africa, flows to Lake Victoria in Uganda, then goes north from there. Both Niles converge in Khartoum. They flow north together to the Mediterranean. Pretty incredible, don't you think, Askara?" Sara got no reply, only a grunt. "The headwaters drop 1,980 ft. from these highlands. The falls should be amazing." Still, Askara didn't reply. "Hey, look, want to talk about last night? I know you're traumatized."

"You're quite the expert, Sara. No."

"Expert on what? The river? I read that in a mag in the Hilton."

"On mental states. Hell, yes, I'm traumatized, but more than that, I'm super pissed. I wanted to tear that guy apart. I need to run, hike, whatever, to get this out of my system."

"Good idea. Seeing the falls is just the ticket. We'll hike until you're exhausted."

Pulling into Dangla, they spotted the sign, *Guides for Hire* scrawled in large, red letters on a piece of wood tacked to a shack. They stepped out of the Rover. Men swarmed them. Askara got agitated and yelled at them to back off.

Every one of them waved a paper offering his guide service. She saw a young, skinny boy hanging back and pointed at him. "You, we will pay for you, a one day guide."

The boy stepped forward. The others glared at him and nodded. "Pay in office."

After a quick transaction, they were on their way. Sara drove through what looked like wildland until their boy guide pointed out a set of overgrown tracks. "No bus could drive these paths," Sara said. "Are you sure he knows the way?"

The boy spoke up, "Short. No buses. Better way."

"Just like the Aussie outback. Okay, we'll follow the guide's signals. Bush blokes are amazing."

They heard the thunder of water before they saw the falls. Turbulent, frothing water hurled off the rocky ledge with mesmerizing power and split into arteries that splintered into smaller veins. Silver beads sprayed onto brilliant green moss-covered rocks. The air vibrated. The falling water appeared to halt midair for a second before crashing down to the blue-green pool below where it exploded into a fine mist. Rainbows painted the banana trees and palm cactus. Along the rocky cliff, fugitive water from a series of tributary falls escaped the dense overhanging vegetation, flowing like iridescent sheets. Beyond the valley, the turbulent stream became a green ribbon snaking through the jungle.

Askara stood and listened, eyes shut, losing herself in the thunder, drifting weightlessly with the mist. When she opened her eyes to stop swaying, she spotted Sara seated on a rock above. The sound takes your mind away and your anger, she thought.

After climbing to every vantage point possible, they left to drop off their boy guide. Passing breaks in the vegetation, they could see white egrets standing on islands of vegetation in the stream. The boy asked them to leave him at his home in Bahir Dar. His eyes lit up when they paid him a handsome tip and gave him a writing pen. By the time they returned to Dangla in the late afternoon, a celebration seemed to be forming. People loitering on the only road waved and shouted when they saw the Land Rover. They followed the vehicle, making high-pitched cries, waving their arms.

"A festival?" Sara said. "Cool."

Askara turned around to watch the villagers seep into the Land Rover's wake like muddy water. "Don't know. Looks like they're following us." A sense of dread came over her. "You don't suppose this is about the trouble last night, do you?"

"No. Hope not. But no telling what gossips said since we don't understand the language. Let's go to another village for tonight. We have enough petrol."

"Good idea. I don't like the looks of this." Ahead three policemen blocked the road, standing rifles-in-hand. The women groaned in unison, "Oh, shit!"

The police hailed them. One came to Askara's door and said in English, "Madam, hello. Get out. Come with us." Another opened the driver's door and pulled Sara from behind the steering wheel before she could grab the keys.

"Why?" Askara said.

"Police station," the officer replied.

On the walk to a mud-wattle bungalow, the village police station, Sara whispered to Askara, "Don't say much. Don't agree to anything. They have to let us contact our embassies." Askara nodded in silent agreement.

"Please sit," the policeman said and shoved two simple wooden chairs up to a scarred, dark wood table. He sat across from them, busily writing on legal size forms, not speaking or looking at them. They sat in silence for ten minutes before the door burst open. Another man—tall, dark, and neatly dressed in a khaki uniform—marched in. He had a prominent jagged scar at the right corner of his mouth. He sat opposite the women.

Oh, God, this doesn't look good, Askara thought, inhaling audibly when two guards bolted the door and stood at attention.

The police officer spoke to the tall official, "Commissioner, these are the foreign women."

"Yes. At ease." The officers backed off to stand behind the Commissioner and face the women like a human wall. "Grave situation. I am District Commissioner of Police. A wire reached my office this morning about the incident last night at the motel. Explain what happened. But first, hand over your passports." Askara and Sara produced their passports, shoving them across the table towards him. He inspected their photos compared to their faces, noted information on a writing pad, turned to the visa stamps, jotted more notes, and pushed them back across the scarred table. "Begin," he said, nodding to Askara.

She recounted the events of the night as the Commissioner, with an impassive face, rapidly took notes in Amharic. When she finished her story, he looked directly at her and asked, "Do you have weapons?"

"No, sir."

"Why did you open the door?"

"I thought he would shoot us."

"Unarmed, you opened the door to a man who said he had a gun?"

"Yes."

He turned to Sara, "What were you doing?"

"I was in my bed, sick. I didn't believe the guy. He was drunk."

"How did you know?"

"From the way he slurred his words."

"Did you think you could have taken his room by mistake?" the Commissioner asked.

"No. I figured he said that to get us to open the door," Sara replied.

"For what purpose?"

Sara faltered, "To rape, or rob us, or both."

"So," he said, looking again at Askara and then back to Sara, "you opened the door to a man you thought intended to rape and rob you?" the Commissioner asked, exasperated, jotting more notes. He kicked backward from the table, making his chair screech across the floor. He paced up and down in front of the women, glaring at them, his face rigid.

Askara spoke up. "Commissioner, sir, I opened the door because I thought we had a better chance if we fought. We screamed. No one came, although every room was occupied that night. We had heard the chatter earlier. When we screamed, they all went dead quiet. No one came to help us. What were we to do?" Askara's voice cracked with emotion. She blinked back tears.

"This is a very grave matter," he said, drawing lines to connect clusters of notes on the pad in front of him.

Sara interrupted, "Sir, we'd like to contact our embassies. We have that right."

The Commissioner, dismayed, looked at her and said, "Yes, madam, you have that right. We abide by laws here in Ethiopia. If we did not, I would not be here. But what service do you want from your embassy?"

"We want to tell our story to the Australian and American embassies."

"Please, please, ladies. This matter, we settle here with me."

"You refuse?" Sara asked, growing angry, her voice like a sharp blade.

"Not at all, but Addis is far away. You are in my district."

Sara shot a look at Askara and said, "Don't say anything more."

The Commissioner, offended, said, "Madam, I am here to help you. You do not know our system. We have a long history of tribal justice, strict codes of behavior. Crimes against women and children carry maximum penalties. This man, an Ethiopian Merchant Marine, we must punish. The villagers informed me he had followed you around the village, watching you. He knew where you ate, where you booked a room. He had no booking at the motel. The man drank home-made beer with friends down the road. He told them that at his last posting in Mombasa, a powerful man hired him to follow the brown American. They didn't believe him. He then boasted he was such a good tracker that when the woman started traveling overland, he was still able to follow her through remote villages without her knowing."

The women looked at one another. Askara blurted out, "His gun was loaded, right?"

"Yes, madam. He could have killed you. The motel owner and his brother jumped him from behind. When his friend dragged him away, the manager contacted us. I have their reports. The entire village knows about it now. I have waited for your return all day."

Sara smiled. "Well, can we go then? You have our story, and you caught your man."

"You must sign papers first." He pushed identical-looking papers across the table at them.

Amharic? Askara thought, recognizing the odd Arabic-like squiggles. "Is this the police report?"

"Yes, madam. Just sign on this line here," he said and pointed to a blank line at the bottom.

"But what does it say?"

The Commissioner answered confidently. "It is the accurate description of the case and acknowledgment of the punishment decreed. I need your signatures for the document."

"What's the punishment, sir?" Askara said.

"Death by hanging. Tomorrow."

Askara's eyes widened. "Death?"

Sara mumbled, "Oh, God."

"Yes, madam. He attempted to kill you. Lucky for you, the brave motel owner and his brother saved you."

"But help came. We weren't hurt," Askara said, her mouth dry, her fingers cold.

"Our tribal justice is good. We respect our women and children, foreigners also," the Commissioner said with a puffed-up chest.

Askara wanted to shout, *right, and you respect the women as much as the cattle and goats because they do all the work.* "I will not sign the man's death warrant!" She threw the papers across the desk.

Sara shoved her papers at the Commissioner. He grabbed the documents and bellowed, "You realize he tried to kill you?"

"He didn't though," Askara retaliated, "and I will not go through my life knowing I caused a man, even that bastard, to be hanged."

The Commissioner looked ferocious. "This is our system of justice, madam."

"Well, not mine. Are we free to leave?"

"Yes. But...please reconsider. How will this look for me? What will the Inspector General say? How will you face the crowd outside?"

"I don't care about the Inspector General. That's your problem," Askara said and grabbed their passports from the table. "We're signing nothing, and we're leaving *now*."

The guards moved aside. Askara and Sara stormed out to see villagers spread across the road—smiling, waving, and whooping high-pitched reverberating war cries that got the crowd jumping. That sound, a war cry, made a chill go up Askara's back. She looked straight ahead, avoiding eye contact with the locals.

Someone in the crowd yelled to the policemen who escorted them to the Land Rover. When he replied, an uproar broke out. The villagers shouted with contorted faces and waved angry fists.

"What the bloody hell is wrong with them?"

"I don't know, Sara, but they're pissed off! Let's get out of here fast."

Coming up behind them, the Commissioner said, "They want a hanging. They want justice." He positioned himself to shield Sara while she climbed into the driver's seat. "Leave now, before they stone you."

The Land Rover edged forward, pushing through the furious crowd. Something pinged against the rear bumper. Then another rock hit the Rover. Sara edged past the last group and floored the pedal. Askara turned to see the angry mob, fists held high, hurling stones that dropped short in the dust.

Sara drove in silence for several miles while Askara chewed her nails. "You know, in all my travels here in Africa, in Russia crossing the Siberian Desert, in New Guinea, I haven't encountered a hassle like this. Makes me want to return to Lesotho, fast, get back to my women's collective."

Askara looked at Sara. "Before this, I'd never seen a real gun, much less been threatened at gunpoint. I've been in countries from the Middle East to Asia, conducted business deals—with all men—no problem. Good God, what a nightmare. There's no way that guy followed us, right? Half the time, we were lost, and no one was behind us. Am I right, Sara?"

"Yeah, the bloke was lying, drunk, making himself seem important. We would have spotted him at some point because we backtracked a few times when we were lost in the bush. Don't worry, Askara. Somehow, he thought making that up might save him. I'd say anything if I thought I was going to be hanged. The guy lied. End of story."

Askara mulled over the incident, trying to make sense of it. She had felt frazzled since meeting Nagali. Her nerves were shot, plus she was exhausted from the heat and dust. But something stuck in her mind: the man in Dila said a shadow follows you. Could the merchant marine be the shadow? Was the man by the stream somehow seeing her future, seeing this attack? Creepy. She thought back to Harriet Laurel and that absurd story about Amanda, her husband's mistress. The British guy at their table had asked Harriet Laurel if she had considered she was given signs, like a heads-up, to help her prepare. Harriet Laurel scoffed at the idea, really shut the man down. Askara thought, what if I am missing signs? What if the merchant marine wasn't just a drunk boaster? What if someone had hired him to track us, to attack us? The idea overwhelmed her. She moved away from it as fast as she could and fell into a deep sleep.

The women drove into the night, only stopping for petrol once until they reached Debre Markos, where they found a decent motel for the night and left at dawn to return to Addis Ababa.

Chapter Seven

Jubilee Palace

On Friday, Askara and Sara drove to Jubilee Palace, parked nearby, and again inquired at the front gate for Sir Alexander Desta. A guard escorted them to a station where he motioned for Askara to take off her small backpack for inspection. Spreading everything on the table, the inspector guard carefully sifted through the contents: hairbrush, paper, pens, map of Addis, Chapstick, crumpled receipts, a small, wooden elephant key ring, faded pictures of jewelry from a magazine, and a water bottle. He shoved everything along the table for her to re-pack. He grabbed the backpack, pressed a numbered sticker on it, and placed Askara's bag in a wooden safe he locked with a key while she watched. He motioned for Sara's, but she had no pack.

"Passports," he said with a stiff face devoid of any semblance of life.

Askara loosened her belt to slide out the leather pouch tucked into her skirt waistband. She felt embarrassed, handing him the passport that was warm and pliable from her body heat. He flipped through the pages a few times before pausing on the page of her Ethiopian visa stamp. After carefully studying the visa, he noted in a ledger her name, passport number, and visa number before handing it back. He motioned for Sara's passport and conducted a similar check.

"Which hotel you stay in Addis?" he said and jotted their replies beneath their names in the ledger. "Get pack from guardpost at front gate when leave," he said and pointed to a small kiosk further down the compound wall. Askara nodded in agreement. "Sit, wait," he ordered, escorting them to a bench in the shade.

"That bloke's a born diplomat," Sara said after he left. "Every embassy should have one just like him."

Askara burst out laughing. "Yeah, a prize. Almost as good as that police commissioner."

"Whew! That bloke was furious. He wanted a hanging, bad. Maybe he'll get a demerit for losing the chance."

"Well, we don't...." Askara quit talking when a guard approached.

He greeted them with a smile. "Good afternoon, madam. Sir Alexander will receive you. Follow me." Sara remained seated. "You, too, madam."

He escorted them down a flagstone path through the tree-shaded garden. The scent of jasmine and damp earth propelled Askara's attention back to Kenya, now so far away. Her time with Darian was becoming a dream—hazy and diminished by exhaustion.

They arrived at a heavy wooden door and entered the palace. The polished white marble floor cooled the air and made their footfalls echo along empty corridors that radiated out like spokes of a wheel from the central foyer. Murals in the vaulted ceilings and tapestries on the walls brightened the otherwise muted halls. The guard led them to ornately carved wooden chairs with a decorative gold leaf scroll along the upper back, pointing for them to sit on the padded red leather seats.

The guard peeked into a door and said, "Sir, your visitors."

When he led them in, Sir Alexander rose to greet them like they were old friends. "Hello, ladies, welcome." He shook their hands and offered them seats in chairs adorned with the gold leaf crown of Judah symbol, two upright lions supporting the crown with their paws.

"Who is Miss Askara?"

"Me, sir. I submitted the letter of introduction regarding the potential purchase of Ethiopian heirloom jewelry for my employer Mr. Seth Ramsey in the United States, a dealer of jewelry and artifacts." She looked at Sara. "Sara Sanford is my assistant on this trip. We understand the confidential nature…."

"Yes, yes. The royal family has a vast number of heirlooms, which, naturally, are not for sale, but we purchase, from time to time, from lesser families, jewelry and artifacts we deem of merit. I facilitate the sale of such articles on behalf of the family."

"But not *museum quality*," Askara said, playing the game.

"Quite so," Sir Alexander said with a smile. His eyes sparkled beneath his expansive brows that stopped briefly at the bridge of his nose. Askara recognized Sir Alexander knew what he was doing and would be a smooth negotiator. Ramsey had okayed a large budget for the purchase, but if she came in under and procured top quality items, her commission would increase.

He turned to Sara. "Miss Sanford, are you a buyer-in-training?"

"No, sir, I'm an agricultural adviser. I work for the U.N. in Lesotho, but I am assisting Askara on this trip."

Sir Alexander's eyes widened. "I, too, am an agricultural adviser here in Ethiopia. We are developing a new strain of wheat for the highlands, a heartier one. We grow corn, barley, and sorghum, but wheat could become a major export soon. As it is now, we haven't enough to feed our people. But we hope if this variety proves successful in our climate, to achieve that goal."

"That's wonderful," Sara said, lighting up. "In Lesotho people depend on imported food to survive, but if South Africa cuts us off, the people will starve. I'm teaching modern techniques to increase pea production without harmful chemicals."

"I understand. Farmers in Ethiopia have used the same methods for 2,000 years, but the world is changing, and we must modernize along with it. Look at North India, the Punjab. They now produce enough wheat for the entire country, proving crop science and proper management practices make all the difference."

"True," Sara replied. "But it takes government support to fund projects."

Sir Alexander tapped a quick rap on the shiny teak table, "Quite so. You Australians are a perfect example. You took a wildland and made it into a prosperous country in two hundred years. You export to most of Asia. Why? Because Australians have what it takes: drive and determination. Humans are reticent to embrace change, but I believe one must leave old ways when they no longer serve. Progress demands change."

Sara beamed. "Yes. I'm sure your wheat project will succeed. I'd heard of it in my university studies in New Zealand."

"Wonderful!" the prince replied, elated. "Well, ladies, I have a bit of business to attend to, another appointment at 2:30. Shall I show you the collection?"

THEY WALKED DOWN THE MARBLE CORRIDOR TO AN IMPRESSIVE carved door—birds, crocodiles, and flowers framed in a hexagonal border, all crowned by the lion of Judah emblem. The prince tapped on the door. "Fine example of Yoruba artistry, a gift from Nigeria to the Emperor."

The guard saluted as they walked in. Sir Alexander ushered the women into an antechamber that reminded Askara of a room in the British Museum with glass and teak display cases, peach-colored walls, and a gray-and-white diamond marble floor. The aroma of age—confined air and ancient paper—permeated the hushed silence. Filtered sunlight eased through the wooden slat blinds and lit the room in horizontal bands. Five display cases absorbed the floor area. Each contained neatly labeled jewelry and artifacts on an indigo velvet liner.

Askara wanted to spend the entire afternoon looking. Sir Alexander hurriedly walked them past the cases of antique jewelry sets—rubies, pearls, sapphires, and diamonds in straw-colored 24-carat gold settings—to jewelry made with beads, semi-precious stones, shells, and gold and silver filigree.

"Here, Miss Timlen." He unlocked the case, inviting her to study the pieces. She lifted a heavy necklace, a tribal design with a large, central amber bead, flanked by filigree silver that alternated with amber beads that became progressively smaller toward the clasp. Islamic design, she figured. She studied each bead carefully to find flaws in the translucent amber. "Would you say Islamic?"

"Yes, from Yemen, the late 1800s, I believe. But the amber is Ethiopian. A noble family had it assembled."

"Price?"

"$3,500 U.S.," Sir Alexander said, looking at the scribbled notes in his hand.

Askara picked up another necklace of yellowed oval beads with hairline black cracks running across the surface. She shrugged.

Sir Alexander noted her displeasure. "You dislike this piece?"

"Ivory. The market's not good in America." She lifted a strand of donut-shaped amber beads, burnt-orange with darker veins of brownish-red. "Where are these from?"

"Burma," he said, referring to his notes. The late 1700s to early 1800s. "Unusual color for amber, don't you think?"

"Yes." She ran the long loop of beads through her hands, studying the variations.

"They are $2,500 U.S."

In another case, she pointed to a thumb-size amber bead with a small square of turquoise inlay. Gold caps at either end secured it to a woven gold braid.

"Himalayas. The 1830s to 1850s, I believe. Not for sale. Lord Mountbatten gave it as a gift to his Majesty. It should be in another case."

"Lovely," Askara replied, disappointed she could not bid on it. She spotted a large solitary blue bead cradled in three places by a gold braid. "Lapis?"

"No, blue chalcedony, 24-carat gold braid. Fine specimen. The Achaemenid Empire of Iran, 550-330 B.C. A gift from the Shah to his Majesty."

"Not for sale?"

Sir Alexander chuckled, "Obviously. In fact, I'm surprised to find these out of order. Allow me to point out the items for sale, or we may be here quite a long while. I do see your interest is keen. Unfortunately, I haven't enough time today. I would like to invite you and Miss Sara here for lunch with me tomorrow. I shall arrange for you to have the entire afternoon to look. I believe you have not yet viewed the set your employer showed interested in, a wonderful necklace with matching earrings. It must be out for cleaning. I don't see it here. So tomorrow, then?"

"Thank you so much. We'd love to."

Sara had been inspecting artifacts in the case in the room's center. She kept returning to a small, dark metal cup with a simple raised design, worn thin in places. The metal glowed in the oblique rays of sunlight coming through the blinds.

Sir Alexander approached Sara. "Miss Sara. Nothing here is for sale."

"I was just looking. What is that?" she said, pointing. Askara walked closer to look.

"That small cup—such an unpretentious thing—is His Majesty's greatest love. It has been in our family for years. As the legend goes, that small bronze cup predates Jesus the Christ by several hundred years."

"Come on. You're teasing," Sara said with a smile. "That thing is over 2,000 years old?"

"Yes, Miss Sara, I am in earnest. Let me explain. There is a grand legend that goes with that small, unassuming cup. Have you heard of the prophet Zarathustra who lived in ancient Iran?"

"No."

"He was born in 630 B.C., scholars assume. Ironically, Aristotle considered his teacher Plato to be the embodiment of Zarathustra, although Zarathustra had lived centuries earlier. Curious. The religion that grew from his teachings is called Zoroastrianism. Islam, Christianity, and Judaism all have tracings to that monotheistic religion."

Askara broke in, "I've heard of it."

"Yes? It is one of the little-known ancient world religions still practiced today. The majority, called Parsi, reside in India, around Bombay. They fled from persecution in Persia."

Askara said, "I have a friend who's Parsi from Bombay."

Sir Alexander nodded at Askara and continued, "The prophet Zarathustra declared there is only one God, eternal and uncreated. That one God ruled over lesser ones. In the ancient text, the name *Ahura Mazda* denoted the one God. *Asha*, a lesser deity, represented fire. Zoroastrians consider fire holy. As legend has it, this cup held the eternal prayer flame of Zarathustra. That's why my uncle considers it the most precious artifact in his collection."

Sir Alexander unlocked the case, pulled out the small cup, and placed it in Sara's hand. She held it, running her fingers over the low relief design. She smiled. "Legend's bigger than the object."

Sir Alexander said, "Quite. I doubt the story myself, but my uncle is a fervent believer. In his presence, I could never disagree. In fact, it would upset him to know I have shown you his prize. Normally, this cup stays in its own locked case in a guarded room. Probably the guards are cleaning that wing of the palace. The Emperor believes the legend. I cannot fault him. An old man needs a bit of magic in his life."

Sara handed the cup to Askara. A warm sensation began to run up Askara's arms. She felt removed from Sara and Sir Alexander, although standing beside them. The prince's words seemed to waft through a long tunnel. His voice changed. She wondered if he was speaking English.

"During the Empire of Medes, 614-550 B.C., the cup was handed down from Zoroastrian priest to priest who are called Magi. In 330 B.C. Alexander the Great conquered the known world looking for the cup, supposedly. By that time, strange powers were attributed to it. How do you prove legends? You believe, or you do not. The Emperor believes every word. No one contradicts him."

Sir Alexander's words pulled a montage of images across Askara's vision. She saw a priest in ceremonial robes carry the cup up temple steps and pause to dip his thumb into the cup's oil wick flame to anoint his followers.

Sir Alexander's words came in more clearly than before. "...over two centuries passed before the legendary cup reappeared, this time in Tibet, and then again in India."

His words faded again. Askara drifted to snowcapped mountains where a rock-hewn monastery carved from the bowels of a sheer cliff appeared to float in the sky. She saw an elderly man in a faded saffron robe raise the cup in front of monks, repeating the same words over and over. The metal cup glowed fiery red. The man spoke in a foreign tongue, yet Askara understood his words: The new emissary is soon to come. Blessings upon him.

The image faded. Askara felt fatigued and disoriented. Sir Alexander gently took the cup from her hand and held it in the sunlight for Sara to see the slight embossment on the surface.

"When the Wise Men from the East, the Magi mentioned in the Christian Bible, saw the Star of David, they traveled with the cup to the holy child's birthplace, presenting it as a gift to honor the child's birth. Miss Sara, see how the light plays on the surface? Imagine it filled with an oil wick flame; this is how it gained its name, the cup of the shining sun. It is a thing of simple beauty. As you said, such a grand legend for such a small thing, but we humans like stories, keeps life interesting."

Askara blurted out, "How did the Emperor come to own it, sir?"

"Well," Sir Alexander said, "the early Christians—possibly a disciple—brought the cup to Ethiopia after the crucifixion, or so my uncle thinks, to the holy city of Axum. Some surmised it held the healing ointment the Magdalene used when dressing Christ's wounds. In 1929 the cup was found at Axum when a peasant boy unearthed it while searching for his errant goat. The animal had fallen into a crevice. When the boy lowered himself into the small opening to pull out his goat, he discovered a chamber. There the cup lay, half-buried in the soil. The herder sold it at the local market to a vendor who again sold it, and from there, it changed hands several times before a representative of the archeological museum in Asmara heard about it. He contacted the Emperor and purchased it on his behalf."

Askara said, "Could that story be accurate?"

"Well, Miss Askara, personally, I do not think so, but I say that in strictest confidence. The Emperor does. I have shown it to you out of academic interest only." Sir Alexander carefully replaced the cup and locked the case. "This should go back to the safe. Well, ladies, I must go to my appointment. I shall order my assistant to serve tea in the garden for you. We will meet again tomorrow for lunch, shall we? I would enjoy an agricultural discussion with you, Miss Sara. Good day."

After saluting Sir Alexander as he exited, the door guard escorted the women into the hallway, where he motioned for a second guard to accompany them back to the garden. While Askara and Sara sat under the shade of a large tree waiting for tea, they glimpsed the Emperor greeting a man in military uniform at the far end of the garden. The Emperor, a thin, elegant, small-boned man stood with his shoulders squared and back straight in his crisp uniform. His military cap bore the insignia of the Lion of Judah. Decorative ribbons—red, blue, yellow, and green bands—supported medals of gold that covered his entire left chest and looked as if they would weigh him down. His carriage defined him, Askara thought. Proud, stiff, royal.

His visitor remained rigidly subservient in front of the monarch, hands clasped in front, chin tucked slightly, head angled down. The visitor saluted, made a slight bow, and departed quickly. The Emperor glanced at the women, said something to his guard, and stepped back into the palace.

"That's something special, seeing him. *Ras Tafari Makonnen*. I read that on a plaque at Trinity Church, his real name," Sara said.

"Yeah, really something. He's so regal. The reggae musician, Bob Marley, thinks Selassie's god, or something. Rastas believe Emperor Haile Selassie is their savior and will liberate them, stop war, and bring peace to the world. Rastas—short for *Rastafari*—are named after him, Ras Tafari Makonnen."

"Nothing like hope, eh? We can say we saw him," Sara smiled.

Askara stopped talking when a guard approached with tea. He served them from a silver set, placing a tray of dainty frosted cakes, cookies, and small cucumber sandwiches on the table. With a slight bow, he disappeared.

"Yum, my favorite, napoleons," Sara said, licking the pastel-colored icing from her fingertips. "Tomorrow should be fun if they have more of these goodies."

When they finished, a guard reappeared with Askara's backpack, placed it at her feet, removed the tea tray, and pointed to the exit gate.

Chapter Eight

The Coup

At the Hilton restaurant for an early dinner, Askara reached down to retrieve a notebook from her pack when her fingers struck something hard. She fumbled to grasp the object, her eyes widening. With a violent shiver, the blood drained from her face. Her hand jerked back like a viper had struck her.

"What's wrong? Are you sick?"

Askara straightened up, lifted the pack into her lap, looked in, and re-traced the object's contours with her hands. "Oh, God." Sara walked over and placed a consoling hand on Askara's shoulder. Askara pulled open her backpack to reveal the object, saying, "Shh."

Sara stood in stone-cold silence, looking as if the air had been pummeled out of her. She slinked to her chair, slumped down, and groaned. "We're in deep shit."

Askara said, "How do you think...?"

"Don't know. Let's go."

They paid in cash, leaving their food untouched. Running back to the room, they used the back stairs near the pool. A boisterous party on the ground floor blasted pop music, providing a good distraction. Askara unlocked their door, flipped on the light, and gasped. Everything—chairs, cushions, pillows, mattresses, bedding, and their clothes—lay strewn across the tile floor.

"Oh, God. What do we do, Sara? The Emperor must think we stole the cup."

"Emperor nothing. He would have sent out soldiers to bring us in. Someone came through the window to do this."

"Who?"

"Don't know. Let's get the hell out of here. Now!" Sara grabbed her clothes, stuffed them into her pack. "Yuck, I hate the feeling of some bloke fingering my underwear."

"We have to take this back to Sir Alexander. Give me your bota bag." Sara threw the leather bag to Askara. She emptied the water into the sink and slit along the bag's seam with her razor, crammed the cup inside, and stitched the leather closed with a needle from the hotel's complimentary sewing kit. She gathered her things. "Now what?"

"Our embassies. We'll hide until they open. Yours first. Yanks have more clout."

"No, Sara, let's go now. Military guys guard it. We can beg them to let us in."

"Yeah, with Ethiopian guards on the outside. We can't trust anyone. You saw Ethiopian justice at the Blue Nile. Somehow, I don't think it favors us." Sara looked outside, gave an all-clear, and they slipped down the backstairs to reach the Rover, unnoticed. She jumped into the driver's seat. "We'll check into a cheap hotel on the far side of the market, pay in cash. They won't ask to see our passports."

"Maybe we should call Sir Alexander now, tonight? He'd help us," Askara said as they pulled out of the lot with their lights off.

"Have his number? No, that's not a good idea. Ever thought he might be behind this? He showed the cup to us. Magically it was in a case in the room with the jewelry you were to view when it wasn't supposed to be. He acted like he didn't believe the legend. Maybe he just wanted us to think he didn't believe it. No, we'll lay low until dawn. Then we'll go to the American Embassy. See what they can do for us first."

"Sara, it's highly unlikely Sir Alexander had anything to do with the theft. I'm surprised you would suspect him. Maybe you didn't pick up on it, but he was attracted to you."

"I felt that. Wouldn't that be a perfect cover for using us as patsies? You're too trusting, Askara. I liked the guy, but this is serious stuff. We can't trust anyone."

In the middle of the night, they awoke in their motel room to the sound of gunfire, people running down nearby alleys, distant screams, and muffled blasts. A male voice shouted in Amharic from a truck loudspeaker. Askara recognized the words, *Haile Selassie,* when the people in the alley wailed.

"Good God, Sara, is it a coup?"

Sara yanked on her jeans and t-shirt and laced her boots, careful to stick her large knife into her leg band. Askara crammed on her tennis shoes, trying to zip her jeans at the same time, and fell onto the bed. The frenzy outside grew louder. Motel guests ran up and down the hallway, gossiping hysterically. Someone shouted, "Mon Dieu, un coup d' état!"

Askara and Sara raced for the Rover, escaping through alley shadows. In the distance, Jubilee Palace glowed with floodlights. Gunfire cracked the thin purple-gray dawn. Barrels of trash burned orange and yellow in the streets. Without turning on the vehicle's lights, Sara pulled out into a narrow street. They crossed the city on back roads and alleys, sometimes getting caught in a slum labyrinth, backtracked, and found another way.

The dawn light illuminated the road sign north to Asmara. Sara drove as fast as she could but not so quickly as to attract attention. Life appeared normal the further they went from the city center, vendors pushed their carts to market, goat herders kept their animals on the paths.

Maybe, Askara thought, the news hasn't escaped Addis, or perhaps the Emperor suppressed the coup, or there wasn't a coup. But someone put the cup in my pack. Someone wanted it smuggled out. Why plant it on me? Askara thought herself into knots but drew some conciliation from the fact that Addis shrank and disappeared in the rear-view mirror, and bright morning sun peeked over the hills. She relaxed a little. They crossed a stone bridge over a deep gorge, slowing to watch turbulent water writhe like a brown snake five hundred feet below the road.

When Askara took her turn at the wheel, they almost skidded off the road. A herd of goats and cattle leaped onto the road in front of the Land Rover. She stomped the brakes. The Rover slid sideways before it stopped. A gigantic baboon ran up from behind the spooked animals, a silver-hair, angry-faced male with fangs bared in his open red mouth. The animals careened off the road as quickly as they had come on and disappeared into the tall grass. Askara watched the frantic herd boy running after them.

"Maybe I should drive again, Askara. Your nerves are shot. You almost ran us off the ledge."

"Sorry. How can you be so calm, Sara? We're in deep shit here. How do you think we'll be able to leave the country? You think our embassies will help if we're suspects in a coup?"

"Look, we've done nothing wrong."

"Ha, Sara, *you* may be. I happen to have the emperor's prized possession. Think about that! You may get off. I certainly won't."

"Try to calm down. The last thing we need is to draw attention to ourselves. Communication here is slow. We'll leave the cup in Asmara with your consulate, make it across the border before anyone even knows about what happened in Addis if they even find out. I can guarantee you Haile Selassie won't broadcast there was a rebellion against him, much less that someone stole his prized object. I'm driving now. Pull over."

Askara snapped, "Yeah, drive. You're better at it anyway," and swerved to a stop.

Sara took the wheel without another word. Askara dozed off, rocking side-to-side on the uneven tarmac. When Sara's sudden braking jolted Askara awake, she opened her eyes to see a crowd of people milling on the road. "Oh, God, what's this?" she said, rubbing her eyes.

"Peasants. Calm down; it's not a roadblock."

They slowed, stopped, and got out. People glanced at them briefly but continued to stare down the ravine. Below a sharp switchback, tangled in thick vegetation, an overturned truck had crashed into a rock. Dull light from the crushed cabin flickered. Men who had edged down to the site pulled two bodies from the wreckage. People on the road chattered and pointed. Sara and Askara loaded up and drove on in silence.

They stopped at Dese for food. Askara felt like vomiting. Aware people watched them, she took deep breaths through her mouth to quell the churning in her stomach. On the edge of a breakdown, sick, scared, and vulnerable, Askara longed for Darian's kind smile and reassuring calmness. She was convinced Nagali had cursed her with his amulet. She was sure of it. Darian had warned her not to proceed with the Ethiopian deal, but she hadn't listened. She and Sara were going to die. All this for a stupid heirloom jewelry purchase for Ramsey. Darian would help them if he knew. She decided to contact him, knowing Asmara would have a Telex office. She'd send word for Darian to come. He would clear this up if she could reach him.

Sara blurted out, "I can hardly eat with these bloody beggars watching. Why in God's name can't something be done about them? Look at this land. So damn fertile. Plenty of water. Poverty is a government crime."

"There's more wrong here than what we see, Sara. Huge buildings in Addis, yet no one uses them. Stone lions of Judah edifices everywhere when people can't find food. And for who? The Emperor. Yeah, there's something way wrong, Ethiopia is a humanitarian nightmare."

They pushed on all day and into the night, stopping at Kobo to sleep. Sara lamented, "From here, we could have gone to Lalibela to see the rock-hewn churches. Not this trip. Not for us. Look, Askara, the bloke I know at the Italian Consulate who works with the U.N., he'll help us. He'll sort out the cup theft. We'll explain our story, leave that cup with him, and even if it was—or is—a coup, we will not take the rap for the theft. Our ambassadors will support us. Hell, we're too dumb to have thought of a heist like that. An ag agent and an artifacts buyer? Hmm, well, you might be a suspect, I guess."

"Gee, thanks, Sara. Wish we could find out what happened, better not to ask, though. From the look of the people in Dese and Kobo, nobody's bothered. Your contact may save us. Even if they throw us into prison, he'll contact our embassies. We'll get out."

After a restless night in a cramped motel room, they began driving at dawn. The drive north toward Mekele laced through beautiful mountains and opened out into broad, fertile valleys. Askara watched the scenery flow past them. "It's like Shangri La in hell."

"Okay, Askara," Sara said, "we're approaching the Eritrean province. I've seen some of the poorest people yet walking this mountain road, those women in tattered, dirty cotton shifts, frayed skirts, bug-eaten shawls draped over the babies cinched to their backs. No wonder there's a civil war going on. People are starving. We'll hit Asmara soon." Sara stuck her head out and inhaled. "Hey, smell that? Eucalyptus. Love the smell. Makes me feel everything's gonna be all right."

"That's good. Glad one of us feels that way."

Sara said with a tight laugh, "All I need is a *roo*. God, I love that, the smell of home. This mess will be over by tomorrow. I can feel it. We'll explain what happened, and I'll fly back to Lesotho. You?"

"California. Ramsey, my boss, will flip. He has a bad temper, doesn't like failed deals, especially when he fronted so much money to get me over here. I can kiss off any commissions, probably for the next three years."

"Yeah, this hasn't been easy by any..." Sara's words trailed off. She hit the brakes hard. "Shit! A roadblock." She grabbed Askara's arm. "Don't offer any information. Stuff your pack under the seat."

Ahead, they saw a stopped bus. Passengers stood frozen, lined up on the outside, faces to the bus, while Ethiopian soldiers searched their bags, boxes, and chicken coops. An officer approached the Rover, saying something incomprehensible to the women, and motioned for them to get out. They watched army officers toss their camping gear on the ground, mangle their clothes, and disassemble the vehicle seats to check underneath. The bota bag lay on the road in a dirty heap with their tent and sleeping bags.

Sara spotted an elderly white couple near the bus and walked toward them. A soldier blocked her way. "I want to speak to them," she yelled in English. "What is this about?"

The soldier shouted at her, grabbed her by the arm, and yanked her to a standstill. Sara jerked her sleeve from his grasp. He raised his hand to slap her when the couple rushed over, shouting in Amharic. The short British man raked his palm through his white bristle hair, pushing back from his forehead. He spoke. To Sara's amazement, the soldier backed off.

"Hello. Do not be alarmed—a routine check for guns. I am Mr. Smith, headmaster of the Mission English School in Asmara. My wife, Helen." Sara shook their hands and introduced herself and Askara, who had rushed up to join them.

"Guns?" Askara said.

"For the Eritrean rebels. There has been a civil war going on here for years. Such a nuisance. They check everyone for smuggled guns, even us, and we run a mission for their children." The sound of the bus revving up interrupted his words. The passengers gathered their things and began climbing back in, but the army officers made a motion for Sara and Askara not to move. "Now, now, I will handle this," Mr. Smith said and walked over to talk to one of the officers.

Mrs. Smith watched. The officer gesticulated wildly and spoke harshly to her husband, who politely tried to reason with the man's anger. Her face contorted in concern. She pursed her lips. Turning to the women, she said, "Oh, dear, this isn't going well. They want you girls to report to the police station in Asmara."

"Why?" Askara asked.

"I don't know. They aren't telling him. You're not in trouble, are you?"

Askara and Sara replied in unison: "No."

Mr. Smith returned, red blotches growing on his shocked face. "I am sorry, girls. They want to take you to the police station. They don't believe this could be your Land Rover. Is it?"

"No," Sara replied. "It's not. I have it on loan. I'm returning it to a colleague in Asmara. I work for the U.N. in Lesotho."

"Ah, that's the difficulty, is it. Well, perhaps the Mrs. and I should accompany you to the police station in Asmara and clear this up. You're at a severe disadvantage, not speaking the language. Let me go propose the idea."

"Thank you! We really appreciate your help. Not speaking Amharic is a huge problem," Askara said.

"Yes, thanks a lot. Some silly mix-up, no doubt. Good to clear it up."

Mr. Smith, after several minutes of animated conversation, showing his documentation and the passports of the women, told his wife they would allow them to ride with Askara and Sara to the police station in Asmara to clear up the matter, with two officers driving behind them. Mr. Smith gathered their bags from the waiting bus. He and Mrs. Smith climbed into the Land Rover and crammed their belongings wherever they could.

"This is easier. I would hate to think of you two in jail," Mr. Smith said, settling in the jumbled gear.

Mrs. Smith looked out the window at the military guard following their vehicle, "Yes, we've lived here thirty years. This misunderstanding will soon be cleared up. We know most everyone at the station, educated their children, and grandchildren."

Sara asked Mr. Smith, "What about this war? I hadn't heard of it until recently."

"Well, it's been going on a long time, but the Emperor suppresses news about it. He rules with an iron hand, you know."

"Does he?"

"Yes, quite."

Sara said, "I mean, currently? Um, I know he's old."

"Oh, yes. One might say Selassie's more a dictator than a monarch, but I don't say that out loud."

"Hush! You just did. Don't talk like that, Philip," Mrs. Smith said from her backseat perch. "It's too dangerous."

"Quite. But these girls are foreigners. They won't repeat it."

Askara saw that Mrs. Smith had picked up the bota bag and held it in her lap. "Are you thirsty?" she asked.

"Oh, no, dear," she answered and chuckled. "Oh, I don't know why I picked this up. It seemed so warm and comforting, like having my cat in my lap. How funny. Are you thirsty?"

"No. That water's not good. So, you moved here to work at a school?" Askara said to change the subject.

"Actually, we came out after the war to start a school. At first, it was only a day school, but after three years, we added a dormitory, and we kept expanding. We house a hundred children now in two large dorms, even those of foreign diplomats."

Mr. Smith added, "I came out before I met Helen. I was stationed here during World War II when our military chaps ousted Mussolini. Italians had ruled this northern part, Eritrea, since 1889. When we took it from them, we chopped it up. The highlands and the coast, mostly Christian, went to Ethiopia. The northern and western lowlands, mostly Mohammedans, got lumped with Sudan, which we also ruled at that time. Caused problems, still does."

"Why did you come back, Mr. Smith?" Askara asked.

"Sense of duty. You know Ethiopia was one of the first Christian countries. Be a shame to let Communists take over. The best way to strengthen the faith here, I figure, is through education. After the war, I put in for a missionary posting, practically brought Helen out here on our honeymoon, dear girl." Askara caught Mr. Smith's affectionate glance at his wife.

"Do you like the Emperor, Mr. Smith?"

"Well, yes, I have met him on occasion. A very polished gentleman, quite intelligent. He has done grand things for the people, gave them their first written constitution, supported education. He spoke before the League of Nations against fascism. That was in 1935, as I recall. He was exiled from '36 to '41, during the Italian occupation. When he returned, he made many changes for the better, brought Ethiopia out into the world, you might say. Best of all, he kept Ethiopia officially Christian. But power changes people."

Mrs. Smith broke in. "He's much more popular in Addis and in the south than up here in the north. And he's even more popular abroad, seems to me, than here in Ethiopia. Back home, in England, they see him as a pivotal upholder of Christianity in this area of the world."

Mr. Smith interjected with an edge to his voice. "Eritreans hate him. They persuade the peasants to oppose him. He deployed half his army to contain the struggle up here, but the Eritrean rebels resisted, so he declared martial law. But the Eritrean People's Liberation Front defeated his forces at Asmara. That shocked everyone, not to mention the Emperor. Yes, it is awkward for us now. Many of our friends and many of the grown children we have educated have joined this leftist Christian group that opposes Selassie's rule. Because of that, we are out of favor. They watch our school; they interrogate our teachers. And we came here to do God's work—not get involved with politics."

Sara laughed. "I thought God's work was politics. I mean, look at all the wars fought in his name."

Mrs. Smith's face tightened. She stared out the window. Mr. Smith replied, "Yes, you can see in history upholding the truth requires a great price, but one cannot be daunted by hardship, or by opposition, can one?"

Askara jumped in to soothe the tension. "It's so kind of you to help us out."

"Not at all, dear," Mrs. Smith said. "After we clear this up at the police station, would you girls like to see our school? A lovely red brick wall encircles the buildings and gardens. I planted most of the flowers myself. One can grow almost anything in Asmara. Here poinsettias are tall trees, not potted plants."

"Here, turn here, Sara," Mr. Smith interrupted. "The station is down that way."

Asmara looked like a gentle city, even though the Smiths informed them fighting had been heavy for six years, and martial law ruled. The orderly European architecture, wide tree-lined boulevards, and rose gardens spoke of a different era. Palm trees towered over Queen Elizabeth Street and Haile Selassie Avenue. Women in white dresses with bright-colored hems that matched their shawls walked the boulevard, greeting one another in passing. Askara watched, hoping she could enjoy the city after clearing up their debacle.

When they pulled into the parking lot at the station, Mrs. Smith smiled and said, "By the way, girls, do you know what year it is?"

Sara said, "I hope so!" They laughed.

"No, I mean here in Ethiopia. Seriously, we are eight years behind the European world. It is 1966. The Ethiopian calendar has twelve months of thirty days with a thirteenth month of five days, so don't let this confuse you when this comes up at the police station if you have to sign forms."

Askara said, "We'll be doing good if that's the only confusing thing."

THE POLICE COLLECTED THEIR PASSPORTS AND ESCORTED the two women, along with the Smiths, to a large room with a rectangular table with chairs. A policeman motioned for them to sit and told the Smiths in *Tigrinya*, Eritrea's dominant language, that the Commissioner would come soon to discuss the case.

Fifteen minutes later, the police commissioner greeted them cordially in English. "Someone has informed us of a stolen"—at this Askara's mind went blank, and she heard *artifact*—Land Rover."

Sara shifted in her chair. Askara heard Sara's reply as if Sara sat in some distant place and shouted across a body of water: "Sir, the Land Rover is not mine. I borrowed it through a co-worker on a U.N. project in Lesotho, where I currently live. I am to return it to Mr. Antonioni, who works with the Italian consulate here in Asmara."

"Is it his?"

"No, sir, it is a U.N. vehicle, part of the agricultural unit in Africa."

"Why did you not declare it at Moyale when you entered the country?"

"I didn't know I had to. No one told me."

"Sir," interrupted Mr. Smith, "this seems highly irregular. Are you accusing the girls of stealing the vehicle? I am sure a call to Mr. Antonioni will clear this up."

"We received a wire from Addis. A vehicle of this description was stolen yesterday in a skirmish near the palace. It was seen driving northward from the city. We received orders to stop the vehicle and hold the occupants for questioning."

"There must be a mistake. Please let me give Mr. Antonioni a phone call," Sara pleaded.

"What skirmish?" Mr. Smith interjected before the Commissioner could speak.

"An attempted coup, have you not heard, Mr. Smith?"

"Why no, we've been in a rural village working all week while the children are on holiday."

The Commissioner continued, "I have too much work to devote time to this issue. Everything is unstable. We have martial law and a strict curfew to enforce."

"What about the Emperor? Is he...?" Mrs. Smith faltered.

"Alive. Emperor Selassie may be a prisoner. We are not sure. He may have escaped. There are conflicting reports. All of Addis is in turmoil. All of Asmara is in turmoil. The Imperial forces are fighting with Eritrean rebels all over our city. We, Eritreans, may yet have our own country, but I did not want it this way. Fighting has broken out between rival Eritrean groups. The Imperial army, stationed here, patrols the streets. You are not safe. Get to your school and stay there."

"And the girls, surely you wouldn't want to chance a foreign incident?" Mr. Smith said, raising a bushy, white eyebrow in their direction.

"True. I will put the foreigners in your custody until we clarify the matter. At this time, no one is to be trusted. Some even say the Emperor himself initiated the crisis so that he could attack rebel forces in retaliation for the February demonstrations. I do not know the truth, but I know we are set on a course, a deadly one. We certainly cannot risk the addition of foreign intervention at any level. Take the women; they will be safe with you. I will send a messenger to your school tomorrow. Go straight there. Park the Land Rover in a locked shed, and you, sir, keep the key and their passports. The women are not to go anywhere without you."

"Quite right," Mr. Smith said as he rose and shook the Commissioner's hand before hurriedly exiting with Mrs. Smith, Askara, and Sara.

Mr. Smith insisted on driving. He took back roads to the school, avoiding military trucks plying the major roadways. He assured the girls that the mission school grounds with its high brick wall afforded privacy and protection. Mr. Smith ordered the school workers, the gardeners, and the maintenance man, to stand guard in shifts at the entrance gate.

Sara and Askara felt relieved to be in a safe, comfortable place, one with hot water, home-cooked food, and English conversation. After dinner, they turned in early, saying they were exhausted. Askara quickly hid the bota bag under her bed for safekeeping.

“What should we do with it, Sara? There’s no hope of clearing this up with Sir Alexander. He must be in a precarious situation.”

“Yeah, sad. Such a nice man. I think we should tell the Smiths about it, let them handle it. They have contacts here. You need to get rid of *it*.”

“I don’t get the feeling the Imperial army issued an order to detain us, or else, I figure, they would have arrested us on the road. If the police had gotten a government order from the Emperor, they wouldn’t have released us to the Smiths. Plus, the order would have specified we stole something from the palace, but not a Land Rover,” Askara said and rolled over in her bed to face Sara, who was thumbing through some books in the bookcase.

“Askara, the only trouble with all this—aside from the monumental trouble of having this bloody thing planted on us—is with the government in turmoil, who can we trust? Someone wanted that cup. God knows why, I don’t. A silly crude thing with a fancy story. I figure someone wants to use us as pawns, probably related to you, Askara.”

“What do you mean by that?”

Sara put down a book. “Well, if two foreign women, one American and one Australian, are killed in an uprising in Ethiopia, it’ll get attention for the revolutionaries, won’t it? Maybe that’s what the Eritreans want, international recognition. They’ve been fighting for what, thirteen years. Here’s a big chance for them.”

“What good would that do?”

“Our deaths would cause an uproar back home, especially yours…in America. Nixon could use this to direct attention away from his troubles with Watergate. The Eritreans could finally expose Selassie as a dictator—not an enlightened monarch—and draw attention to their cause. That would be news in Australia, I can tell you."

"Hmm, in America, I might be a one-sentence item in the evening news. We have too much going on with Watergate."

"Yeah, but Nixon's strength was always foreign policy. He could use it. Oh, well, don't worry. The Melbourne paper will mention a Yank was with me when I drew my final breath, when I uttered, 'I love Australia. Take me home now,' before I drop lifeless to the ground with the sun setting on the mountains of northern Ethiopia."

"You have a weird sense of humor."

"Better weird than nonexistent. Hey, don't worry, be happy, no problems, eh, mate? We'll sort all this out tomorrow. Let's catch some zeds for now. G'night."

During the night, the sound of heavy trucks, sporadic gunfire, and an explosion roused everyone in the house, but the compound remained secure. At breakfast, Mr. Smith read the newspaper headline: *Asmara Police Station Attacked in the Night. Two Dead.*

"Looks like you two won't be going to make a statement to the police today. Thank God, you were not there. Someone bombed the station last night," Mr. Smith said to the girls over tea.

"I heard the explosion," Askara said.

Mrs. Smith added, "It woke us up, too. All Asmara heard it. We tried to call a friend about it, but all the lines were down. They still are. You girls will stay here today. I'll send the gardener to Mr. Antonioni's office with the message to contact us about the Land Rover."

"Seems the airport's shut down, too. No flights in or out for several days," Mr. Smith said, reading. "I hope this settles fast. The children are due back from vacation next week."

"I'm due back at work in Lesotho. It's planting time for peas."

"I need to return to California, or else I won't have a job."

"I think you girls should fly home at the first opportunity," Mrs. Smith said. "This is no place for you now. I am sure this vehicle business can be cleared up easily, maybe forgotten, a small matter in light of the situation. We can drop the vehicle off to Mr. Antonioni for you later when this gets cleared up. The paper says there are food shortages in various areas because the military won't allow trucks on the road for fear of carrying arms, you know."

"Whose carrying arms?" Askara said.

Mr. Smith nibbled at his toast slathered with marmalade, "Well, that's just it. According to the BBC, the Imperial forces are losing ground. The Marxist revolutionaries want to set up a military government and make Mengistu Haile Mariam head of state, but the Eritreans probably will not back him either. Oh, this is a proper mess. We have weathered many changes here for over thirty years. I hope we can make it through this one."

Mrs. Smith walked over and gave her husband a reassuring pat on the shoulder. A knock at the door made everyone jump.

"I'll get it," Mr. Smith said and rushed to the rear door of the kitchen. "Heregu, how did you get here? I thought no one could be on the streets."

"Good morning, sir. I came the back way to check on you."

"Come in. So nice of you. As you can see, we have guests." Askara looked up to see an attractive Ethiopian woman about her age.

"I know. I heard. That is why I came."

Mr. Smith introduced Sara and Askara to Heregu, a former student, now married and a mother of two, working toward her law degree. "A prize student and a dear friend," he said.

Mrs. Smith hugged Heregu. "What do you mean, dear? You heard we have guests? From whom?"

"I was at a gathering, a political meeting. Someone said two foreigners were here. I thought maybe your son and his wife had come from London for a visit."

"Lands, no. As you can see, we have other guests."

Heregu gazed intently at the women and said, "For your safety, you should leave the country now. There is much strife and turmoil. You will not be safe here, and you endanger the Smiths."

"We intend to leave as soon as possible," Askara said, wondering if Heregu had another reason on her mind.

"You could come to my house for a visit. I live close, just down the alley over there. We are preparing for a wedding, my brother's. You might enjoy that, take your mind off things."

"Is it safe?" Sara said to Mr. Smith. "Should we go?"

"Yes, no one will see you. Might as well try to enjoy yourselves a bit. A shame really, Asmara is such a lovely city, but you cannot go about. What a nuisance this outbreak is."

Mr. Smith wrinkled his brow and pushed his specs up on the bridge of his nose. "Yes, go for a little while. Learn about the culture. Heregu will enjoy speaking English. She always does."

Heregu led them along the narrow path to her house. They entered through the back door after Heregu tapped an all-safe signal to notify her family—her parents and two younger sisters living upstairs and her husband and their two children downstairs. She led her guests to the sitting room but left them while she made tea. Askara inspected beautiful circles of lace, crocheted like a spider web while Sara sat slumped on a brown calf hair stool and stared at the closed curtains.

Heregu's husband walked in to greet the visitors. He extended his hand, shook theirs, and motioned for them to sit again. Askara realized he most likely did not speak English, or at least not well enough to have the confidence to address them. Two little two girls followed him in but hid behind him until he pulled them to the front to greet the visitors. They giggled. Soon they danced around the furniture to attract the guests' attention. From upstairs, a woman's voice called. The girls evaporated, followed by their father, who exited with a respectful bow.

When Heregu returned with a tea tray, she said, "My brother's wedding is tomorrow. You must come. There will be traditional food and dance. The women made honey beer! You will see a happy celebration in Eritrea. Did my husband disappear? He speaks no English. Did the girls come down?"

"Yes, we met them, adorable," Askara said. "Sara and I would love to come to the wedding if we're still here."

"Where else could you go with martial law?" Heregu said, pouring the tea.

They passed the afternoon at Heregu's, helping prep food for the next day. Her father came to greet the guests, asking Heregu to translate. He explained the traditional dance while he and his granddaughter demonstrated the steps.

Askara asked Heregu if the political trouble bothered her, would it affect the wedding celebration, but Heregu said, "Eritreans know conflict. Life goes on. Soon everything will be quiet again." A hard rap at the back door made Sara and Askara jump. Heregu motioned for them to stay still. She rushed to the door and stepped out to exchange words with someone. She returned quickly. “You must go now. Mr. Smith needs you. His gardener came to escort you. I will call for you tomorrow morning.”

Chapter Nine

Nuns On The Run

Askara and Sara entered the Smiths' house to find Mrs. Smith weeping. Everything was in disarray—books, cushions, papers, and furniture. Shattered china bowls, like blue and white puzzle pieces, covered the tile floor, making it difficult to walk. Shards crunched underfoot. Mrs. Smith sat on the burgundy stuffed chair, whimpering.

"What happened?" Sara said, kicking things aside to rush over to her.

"What happened, indeed," Mrs. Smith said, beginning to sob into her monogrammed handkerchief. "Two men broke in while you and Mr. Smith were out. They wanted the foreigners; they said you stole something from them. They wrecked the house. Go, look at your room."

Askara blurted out, "We stole nothing!"

They rushed upstairs ahead of Mrs. Smith, who climbed slowly, gripping the banister. The entire room was upside down—mattresses, pillows, the bookcase, their clothes—heaped on top of one another like an earthquake had jolted the house. Askara started toward her bed but halted, spotting the bota bag in the far corner.

Sara tried to remain cool since poor Mrs. Smith was falling apart. Working to control her anger, she said in a measured voice, "Did they say what they thought we took and from where? Was it the Rover?"

"No, no, not the car, you took something in Addis. They will find it, at any cost. What is it?" she said, bursting into large, rolling tears. "What have you girls done?"

"Nothing," Askara said, scared now, too scared to tell the truth to anyone but a U.S. Embassy official. "It's a mistake!"

Sara added, "Someone is trying to stick us with something for political reasons, I think, to get international coverage for the uprising."

"But why were you accused first of stealing the Land Rover and now something else?"

"The Land Rover thing is crazy. If I could call Lesotho, you could talk to my boss. He'd clear this up. I'll contact Mr. Antonioni. He'll vouch for me. I'll go see him now, to hell with the curfew!"

"No! I cannot let you. You could be killed. We could be, too, for harboring you. Nothing is safe now. I will send my gardener to fetch Mr. Antonioni. Stay with him for more protection. Those people will come back here for you. They will not give up. You should leave Ethiopia. Let your governments sort this out. I must say I like you girls. I don't think the Good Lord wants me to condemn you, but things do not look good. What did you do to bring this on?"

Askara shouted, "All we did was visit Jubilee Palace. I had a letter of introduction to Sir Alexander Desta, Selassie's nephew. We met him and had tea. After that, everything went wrong. Someone attacked the palace, so we fled Addis. Mrs. Smith, we have nothing to do with the coup."

"That's right," Sara added. "This is some political thing. That night we heard frantic voices on loudspeakers. People ran. We jumped into the Land Rover, escaped the city on back roads. That's the truth," Sara said, patting Mrs. Smith on the shoulder.

Mrs. Smith looked at the foreigners. "Girls, I don't remember your telling me you had been at the palace."

"It didn't seem important. I mean, we didn't meet the Emperor or anything," Sara said in a fake, nonchalant tone.

"Oh dear, oh dear me, that must be the reason. You were seen there—two foreigners—and then the trouble happened. Maybe someone thinks you are foreign agents or something. This is terrible. You are not safe, and neither is anyone you contact. We had better leave Mr. Antonioni out. The Eritreans aren't fond of him anyhow."

Mr. Smith rushed in, wide-eyed with terror. "What happened here? Helen, are you all right?" Mrs. Smith gushed tears, halting to blow her nose, and recounted the break-in. Studying Sara and Askara, he said, "I contacted Mr. Antonioni this afternoon. He confirmed your story about the Land Rover, spoke very highly of you, Sara, but this is difficult to clear up. I went to the police station with my information. No one could help me; they have either fled to the rural areas or joined the Eritrean forces. The place is in utter disarray. No one knows if the Emperor is alive or dead. You must get out of Ethiopia—now. You are in grave danger. And it seems you put us in grave danger as well."

"But how? The airport's closed," Askara said, choking on her words.

"Overland to Sudan? Can we cross the border?" Sara said. "I have a dear friend in the Ministry of Agriculture in Khartoum. He'll help us. I'm sure of it."

"That is an awfully long way, not to mention dangerous. Eritreans patrol that border," Mrs. Smith added, dabbing the handkerchief at the corners of her eyes.

"But Sara is right. Although not quick, that is the only way. I shall contact Mr. Antonioni again. He can arrange a letter for your exit at Teseney, although it is not a regular border post, stating you must cross there because of the conflict. With official papers, you will be all right, I hope. You could go the other way, toward the Red Sea, but you would get stuck there, and the rebel strongholds may prevent your passing in their land. Let me have your passports. I'll have them, well, um, I'll have them *adjusted* a bit."

"Dear, whatever do you mean *adjusted*?"

"Don't worry, Helen, I won't jeopardize us." He turned toward Sara and Askara. "You must do what I say. I know this country better than you. You will leave the Land Rover here, go by bus. They are still running for now. But you'll need disguises."

"Disguises? You can't make them into Africans," Mrs. Smith said, astonished.

"No, but I can make them into nuns. They could wear habits. I shall go to the bishop and plead their case. Surely, he will help. Get ready. I'll be back directly." Mrs. Smith followed him downstairs.

Askara sat on the bed for a moment, holding the bota bag in both hands. She looked at Sara. "Should we leave it here? Bury it, toss it from the bus. What?"

"We're stuck with that thing for now. It could cost the Smiths their lives. We'll take it to Sudan, give it to Mr. Dahab, my friend. He's high in the government. He can return it, melt it, or do whatever. I don't care."

"Okay, but Sara, why don't you go back to Lesotho. Let me do this on my own."

"I'm in it now, both feet. I'll see it through." Sara said with a wry grin, "Besides, my dad wanted me to be a nun. He'll laugh from his grave when he sees me in a habit."

Askara grew quiet. A warm glow flowed into her hands from the bota bag. She saw Sara turn into mist, and she felt herself become weightless. She saw a sun-drenched vista, a mountain meadow, that filled the space between her and the faint outline that was Sara. Shepherds with their bleating goats ambled along a dirt track. On the horizon, a whirling tunnel of dust and debris rose to the sky. Someone yelled: Run, run for cover. Hide the children.

Askara watched screaming women in loose, woven robes dart near and far gathering children into their arms. A young girl ran toward a stone temple on the hill, her black hair tangled in the leather bag hanging from her shoulder. A temple priest met her at the entrance and thrust something into the bag. "Run, child, run," he shouted and waved her toward the hills. A horseman struck down the priest. Another rider swooped in, grabbed the girl, threw her across his pony's back, cut the animal sharply to the right, and fled in a whirl of choking dust. The girl, still clutching her leather bag, slipped from the horse's back. Her screams ripped the air.

Sara waved her hand in Askara's face. "What's with you? Are you deaf?"

"What?"

"Mrs. Smith wants us. She's calling. Come on!"

"Sorry, Sara. I was somewhere else."

"Yeah, well, we need to be somewhere else, or we'll end up dead. Let's go."

Askara retracted her grip from the bag. Moist fingerprint impressions faded from the leather. I think I'm going mad, she muttered under her breath. She stuffed her clothes and the bota bag into her pack and followed Sara downstairs.

Mrs. Smith said a prayer, Sara stared at the clock, and Askara hung her head. After they ate in strained silence, Mr. Smith appeared with their passports, bus tickets, and nuns' habits. They listened to his commands while Askara fought off vomiting.

"I'll drive you to the first village bus stop outside the city, only a few kilometers, in case anyone is watching the Asmara station. He handed them the habits. The bishop requests that you mail them back from Khartoum, if possible. You're in his prayers."

Mrs. Smith directed them to the cellar door. "Go down these stairs. Follow the tunnel to the storage shed at the far end of the complex. Take this lantern. Mr. Smith will pick you up there in the bishop's car. Don't let anyone see you. God bless and keep you safe."

Askara and Sara hugged Mrs. Smith, now shaking visibly in her cotton dress. They thanked her for her hospitality and promised to visit again in better times.

Reaching the end of the tunnel, they heard the motor cough and sputter. Opening the storage shed door, they crawled low to the ground, into the backseat of the car. "On the floor," Mr. Smith said and covered them with a burlap drape. "Not a word. If I am stopped, remain motionless, no sounds."

They rode, shrouded and silent, over bumpy roads. The car slowed but never stopped. Mr. Smith spoke in a cheery voice as he slowed. A reply would come. Then he would speed up again. He pulled over in an isolated area and told the women to put on the habits quickly. They hopped out and threw the habits over their clothes. At the village bus stop, Mr. Smith escorted the nuns to a waiting bus and tipped the driver. He waved farewell, climbed into his car, and sped off in the opposite direction.

Their bus started with a noxious cloud of blue smoke and pulled out of the village. The driver careened around blind curves, drove in the middle of the road, and swerved to avoid camels and on-coming trucks as he talked over the motor's loud drone to the man seated near him. Dust entered through the permanently jammed windows, while heat from the dented metal floorboard reduced the passengers to coma-like lethargy. He crammed on the brakes. The bus skidded, dislodging overhead bags and caged chickens, before wheezing to a stop.

Passengers grumbled and retrieved their belongings strewn along the floor when uniformed men stepped on board and ordered everyone off, except the nuns. Soldiers searched the interior, studied the nuns' transit papers, and disembarked. Passengers loaded back on, and the bus pulled away. Askara and Sara said nothing. The vehicle lumbered into the night, rocking the passengers to sleep.

After several hours, the driver stopped at a small group of huts. Passengers disembarked and disappeared into the night like ants escaping a disturbed anthill. Askara and Sara remained on the bus. They stretched out on vacant seats and slept until dawn when the passengers miraculously reappeared. The bus pulled away into a fresh morning of rising heat.

"I'm so hot in this veil thing, can't stand it," Sara said, struggling to loosen the confining material.

"Leave it. We're almost there, from what I could make out from a road sign. We're about 15 km from the border. Did you notice two Land Rovers passed us?"

"No, I was asleep. Why?"

"They circled back, came alongside the bus, and the men looked in. Did it on both sides. I bent my head forward and peeked. All they could see was black cloth. You had slumped over anyway."

"Military?"

"No, regular clothes, like the 1950s in America, same as the way men dress in Asmara."

"How many?"

"Three, maybe four, in each Rover. It was hard to see."

"We're in deep shit."

"Yeah. What do we do?"

"Wait and see what they do, I guess."

Askara lifted the bota bag from her pack, placed it on her lap, and immediately warmth rushed up her arms again. She wondered what if there was something to the legend. Maybe the images she'd seen weren't her imagination. If the cup had power, she needed that power now. She was desperate. She concentrated on the thought: *Help me see where those men in Land Rovers are.* An image floated up like a leaf on buoyant water, breaking through the surface, expanding across her visual horizon. The men stood, guns in hand, at the border gate. One of the men pointed back the direction of the bus. Askara cringed. She begged, *help us escape.*

A reply came in a voice she thought she had heard before: *Get off the bus. Now!*

Her eyes shot open. She bolted upright, climbed over Sara, and accosted the driver, shouting, "Stop! Stop! I need to get off. Now!"

The driver jumped sideways. She yelled again, this time in his ear, over the loud drone of the motor. He swatted her away. Passengers sat up to watch. Askara slapped the driver hard on his shoulder, shook him, yelled at him, swore at him. She popped him on the head with the back of her hand and yanked at the ignition key. Sara watched, stunned, as the driver crammed on the brakes. The bus lurched to a bucking halt. The engine died. He yelled at the nun and shoved her away, trying to start the engine. It would not turn over.

Askara yelled, "Sara, grab our bags; we're jumping off." Their robes flapped like raven wings when they fled into nearby scrub brush and hid behind a massive tree of tangled branches. They crouched low.

The disgruntled passengers climbed down but did not try to approach the crazy nuns. They walked into the woods to relieve themselves while the driver and his friend lifted the hood.

Sara looked at Askara. "What the…."

"Shh…."

A Land Rover sped up and braked fast, raising yellow dust that made it difficult to see the three men who jumped out brandishing automatic weapons, shouting orders. The passengers dutifully lined up, faces pressed into the scarred metal bus, hands overhead. A man shouted and held them at gunpoint. One passenger pointed in the nuns' direction.

Sara whispered, "Do we run?"

"No. Stay still." From a nearby rock outcropping, monkeys screeched and ran.

The passengers turned to look at a military truck barreling down the road at them. Gunshots thundered in the warm air. Passengers scrambled under the bus. The Land Rover men returned fire. One man fell twenty feet from where Askara and Sara crouched. After a brief exchange, the remaining Land Rover men surrendered at gunpoint.

Soldiers jumped from the truck, collected their weapons, tied their hands, and shoved them in. They drove away, leaving the dead man contorted in the dust.

Sara and Askara stumbled back onto the bus with the other scared passengers. No one seemed to care about the nuns. Everyone appeared dazed. The bus engine choked and sputtered on acceleration but settled into a metallic hum. The driver sat rigid, gripping the wheel, glancing in the rearview mirror at the nuns.

"How the hell did you figure that?"

"The Lord works in mysterious ways, sister. I'll explain later."

"Fair dinkum. Praise the Lord."

THEY REACHED TESENEY, A LIVELY MARKET TOWN SEVERAL kilometers shy of the Sudanese border. Askara took heart when she heard James Brown's *I feel good* blasting from a ramshackle brothel, a small bungalow where women lounged seductively at the door.

Low mountains loomed beyond mud-wattle grass huts clustered in the small valley. Monkeys and baboons raced around large boulders and darted between trees and shrubs. Askara spotted a bombed-out bridge in the distance, no doubt a rebel skirmish, she assumed.

The bus driver swerved to follow a rutted road along a shallow riverbed. The bus choked, gasped, and coughed like it had bronchitis. A few hundred yards farther down, a gutted bus identical to their *Quick Bus* lay overturned. Easy to guess what happened to those passengers, Askara thought, glad she and Sara had made it this far, but she knew they weren't safe yet.

Crossing the border into Sudan proved easy. Askara felt heartened by the respect paid to nuns. When they disembarked at Kassala, the other passengers, except for an elderly couple, loaded onto a waiting bus and departed, going east. Kassala buzzed with the excitement of a festival. Sara and Askara walked to the far end of town, toward the low hills, and quickly changed behind the rocks into their jeans and t-shirts, glad to shed the heat-absorbing black habits. They rolled them up, stuffed them into a crevice between boulders, and walked back into the town center.

They walked to the first event they saw and settled down in a makeshift tent to watch the entertainment, a Hadendoa troupe. The dancers jumped high into the air on one leg, came down on the toes of the opposite foot, and quickly rose again, swinging long swords in figure-eight patterns. The musicians pounded a repetitive, hypnotic drum beat,

"Amazing those blokes can do all that at one time. If you didn't land a foot right, you'd stab yourself."

They drifted to where a circle of women played cowhide drums. Men clapped the beat and sang. A group of women danced in colorful dresses. Arching their backs, with arms extended backward, they jackknifed forward in a whipping motion. The synchronized circle of dancers stomped the rhythm with the shell anklets on their feet.

"Sara, look at those bands on their foreheads. Those huge crescent earrings and nose studs are pure silver. They're wealthy."

"You would be hung up on jewelry. How quickly you forget our situation, Askara."

"Hey, we did it. We're home free now, well, almost. I'm ecstatic."

They drifted over to the police dog demonstration in front of the station. The dogs resembled black-and-tan German Shepherds. One had erect ears. The rest had one standup ear and one floppy. The dogs performed simple tricks like rolling over and sitting. One dog did nothing, no matter how much the policeman pleaded. When he asked for volunteers from the audience, six men stepped forward. He took the watch of one, shielding it from the dogs' sight, walked toward the biggest dog, and put it near his nose. At the policeman's command, the dog that should have picked the watch's owner from the group trotted to the wrong man. On the second try, the dog nipped a man. The crowd exploded with laughter. The policeman hushed the crowd with a raised hand and tried again. This time the dog found the correct man but bit his arm. That man yelled and jumped back in terror. Remaining volunteers bolted. The audience laughed so hard they couldn't rise until the dog chased them away.

"Best show I've seen. Those poor blokes should do everyone a favor and feed that dog to the hyenas."

"That's awful, Sara! The dog was confused."

"Permanently," Sara said with a smile. "I'm so hungry I could eat the hind leg of that camel over there. Let's get some grub. How long do you figure before our bus arrives?"

"Mr. Smith said if we made it across the border, there'd be a bus to Khartoum once a day. I've been watching the road; no bus has come since we got here. We're out of Ethiopia, safe. I'm okay with waiting."

They found a restaurant and ordered curds, flatbread, and goat meat. They sat at the table closest to the road to watch the festival and keep an eye out for the bus. A man in his twenties approached them. Askara froze.

"Are you enjoying our festival, ladies?"

"Yes," Askara said, relieved, "very entertaining."

"May I join your table? What brings you here?"

"Holidaying, a walkabout in Africa," Sara replied tersely. "And you?" she said, pointing to a rickety chair.

"This village is my home. I go to university in Cairo for engineering. I returned to see my family and the festival. I am Atmed. May I buy you colas?" he said.

Sara introduced herself, saying, "Colas would be great. This is Askara."

"Have you seen the display of prayer rugs at the marketplace, my brother's shop? My family owns an ancient one. It is displayed every year for the festival. It has gone to Mecca with my family for seven generations."

"I'd like to buy one."

"So, you could look at it on the wall?"

"Yeah."

"Prayer rugs are for praying."

"I'd use it in a different way."

"You people do not understand. Jesus said a prophet greater than himself would come. That was Muhammad, 570 A.D., the best and greatest prophet."

Askara regretted their invitation. She tried to divert the conversation. "Atmed, how many brothers and sisters do you have?"

"My brothers and sisters are the faithful of Islam, upholders of the faith. Many. All others are doomed. At Judgment, people's eyes will relate what they saw, ears heard, hands done, mouths said. People will walk a thread; those who fall are sinners and will go to hell. Only the righteous go to Paradise." Atmed's eyes widened; his nostrils flared. He cocked his head to hear the loudspeaker announcement, the mullah's call to prayer. "Enjoy your colas. I must go. Nice talking to you," Atmed said and joined the other men walking to a rocky outcropping above the road to face east to Mecca.

Askara and Sara watched them unfurl their prayer rugs. "Whew, eat up," Sara said. "Hey, that bloke stiffed us for the colas. Wrap up the food. I don't want to be here when he gets back, or in the same town."

"Yeah, let's get out of here."

CHAPTER TEN

Intrusion

Near the bus stand, Askara and Sara met a weathered man who spoke English and drove a bush taxi. He offered to take them to Wad Madani, and for an additional fee, they could be the only passengers. The women jumped at the opportunity.

They rode for hours in silence, dozing off and on, while the car bumped along a rough track through the dry scrub brush. When the vehicle braked abruptly, Askara and Sara sat upright, excited. But the town Gedarief was not Wad Madani, the home of Mr. Dahab, Sara's friend she had met at a U.N. agricultural conference.

"We stop here for tonight. The motel has tasty food. Push off at dawn."

Over a plate of bean gruel and bread, liberally washed down with beer, Mr. Neal sat with the women at their request. They figured he could be an asset by keeping other men away.

He recounted British rule in Sudan as if he had lived it. "We are brilliant, you see. We British in Sudan. My father was a British soldier, my mother, Sudanese. Back in 1885, the Mohammedans killed Governor-General Gordon, right at his palace in Khartoum, and for the next fourteen years, they controlled Sudan. But General Kitchener defeated them at the Battle of Omdurman...."

Askara tuned out the conversation, bored by colonial pride, and wondered if the British would align with him as he did with them? She didn't think so.

Sara, listening with interest interjected: "Brits have a way of ruling I find cruel. The divide-and-conquer thing like in India, and China...if you consider opium. Pit people against one another. Let them fight it out, or get drugged out."

"Right, successful approach."

"Disgusting," Sara said, leaning forward on her elbow to look straight at Mr. Neal. "I read here in Sudan the Brits pitted the lighter-skinned Muslims of the north against the darker-skinned Christians of the south to encourage civil war."

"Keeps 'em busy. Politics, pure and simple, the old divide and conquer at its best."

"But even now they're still divided, aren't they?" Sara said. "Northern Muslims figure the black southern tribes, mostly Christian, are inferior. They use them for house servants."

"What makes you an authority? They'd all still be in the bush if not for us British."

"Maybe they'd get along better that way."

"Don't fool yourself," Mr. Neal said, knocking his chair over as he stood. "Meet me here at 6:00 a.m. I plan to reach Wad Madani early." He grabbed his crumpled canvas hat from the table, tossed some bills near his plate, and marched out.

Sara counted the money. "At least he didn't stiff us, bloody bastard."

"Sara, why can't you just let things be? The guy's a mess, but we need the ride."

"I can't stand blokes like that. If you asked him about Australians, he'd say we're all bloody criminals. Same narrow mind."

"Look, the farther we are from Ethiopia, the safer we are, and the closer to getting home. Let's not blow it."

"Right. You still haven't explained what went on. How'd you know what to do, jumping off the bus and all?"

"The cup told me. I held it in my hands, and I got a message. Don't ask me how. Like a mental imprint or something, not like a schizo hearing voices. It's weird, but it worked."

"Wow, maybe that thing's powerful, or maybe it's your imagination. Sure you want to give it back?"

"No, I'm not sure. I know this sounds nuts, but I don't think the cup wants to go back. In Khartoum, I'll cable Darian to see if he can verify Sir Alexander's legend. I think in the wrong hands, it could be disastrous."

"You believe that bullshit? Askara, you know the cup's valuable, belongs to the Ethiopian royal family, came to us in a coup, and someone wants their hands on it. That's the bottom line. You can't keep it."

"I know that. I don't want it for *me*—not at all—but I don't want it for *them* either, whoever *they* are, the jerks who are after us. I could give it to a museum, but there are provenance issues."

"Yeah, good idea, the British Museum is full of old things like that."

"Anyway, don't talk to Mr. Dahab about it until I contact Darian."

Sara raked her lips over her teeth. "You're really hung up on that bloke, aren't you?"

"It's like, um, he seems too good to be true, but I want to get to know him better."

"You know what they say if something's too good to be true...."

"Sara, I like him a lot. But I haven't had enough time to figure him out. Life got so crazy. I mean, look at us, accused of a royal theft that probably spawned a coup, and we're on the run for our lives. Good God, this is nuts."

MR. NEAL DROPPED THEM OFF MID-MORNING IN WAD Madani with a curt "Goodbye," after he counted his payment and tip. Sara asked shopkeepers on the main street for a phone number for Mr. Mohammed Dahab with the Ministry of Works. After several tries, she got one. When Sara called, he was not at his office. The clerk suggested she walk down the street and ask for Dr. Ali Dahab, a veterinarian, Mr. Mohammed Dahab's cousin.

The vet greeted them cordially when Sara introduced herself and Askara. While they drank tea, he inquired about their journey and made small talk, checking his watch often.

"Yes, yes, Mohammed spoke highly of you, Miss Sara. He hoped you would one day visit, as you promised. I have sent my servant to notify him. You met Mohammed at a U.N. conference. I believe you are an agricultural expert, yes?"

"Yes."

"I am sure Mohammed will take you to see our famous agricultural project, the Gezira Scheme. We produce fine cotton here in Sudan. The scheme lies between the Blue and White Niles. Many of our cotton factories are right here in Wad Madani."

"Yes. I'm aware. Mr. Dahab told me all about it when we met at the conference. I'd like to tour the scheme, if possible."

"Certainly, Miss Sara, our pleasure. We are enormously proud of our scheme's productivity and quality of fiber. The project is a unique blend of private enterprise and state ownership, the largest farm in the world under one management. It comprises 12% of the total cultivated area in Sudan." His servant walked in quietly like a shadow and stood until the doctor acknowledged him. They exchanged words. He dismissed the boy with a nod.

"It seems Mohammed went to Khartoum for the day. He will return this evening. Meanwhile, ladies, shall I arrange a tour for you? My driver is free. Unfortunately, I have work, or I should accompany you, but the information officer at the scheme is my personal friend. He will enjoy escorting you. He's fluent in English, foreign-educated."

"Thank you. That would be great!" Sara said. Askara smiled in agreement and nodded with little enthusiasm.

They spent the afternoon driving along the fields, all ninety acres of the Gezira Scheme, with Mr. Aziz Elrayah. They passed sections of fodder, garden vegetables, wheat, lubia, groundnuts, and the prize crop, Extra Long Staple Cotton. Mr. Elrayah bragged, "This cotton is the best in the world, Sudan's lead export."

Women in colorful dresses with their hair wrapped in bright scarves pulled the white fiber cotton balls from tall, dry brown stalks and tossed them into their shoulder bags. Askara was surprised at the field laborers' elegance. They could have been fashion models in another time and place. When Mr. Elrayah pointed out the *Hindi* wheat, tall and golden-yellow, swaying in the breeze, the word *Hindi* pulled Askara's thoughts back to Darian. She wondered if he was already home in Bombay. She hoped so. She felt desperate to talk to him, to hear his calming voice.

Sara fired questions about the cotton at Mr. Aziz, the name he requested the ladies call him. Askara tuned out, content to watch and daydream. She didn't care about the *Sakel* cotton with extra-long fibers, or that experts from all over the world came to bid on it, or that for the last sixty years British manufacturers have dominated the market. She perked up a little when he said, "Sakel cotton can be found in Europe's high fashion creations, from skirts to coats, gloves to accessories, especially Prada."

In the late afternoon, Mr. Aziz showed them Wad Madani, a sprawling city of 74,518 people, before he dropped them at Mr. Mohammed Dahab's home, an enormous house by local standards, enclosed by a tall manicured hedge. It was a former British headquarters house. Mr. Dahab walked out as soon as the car came up the drive. He stood in his flowing white galabieh to greet them, two boys cavorting around his knees.

"Miss Sara," he said, opening the car door for her, "this is a grand pleasure. Thank you for coming to meet us."

Sara shook his hand. "Wonderful to see you again, Mohammed. This is my friend Askara."

"Pleasure to meet you." Mohammad called to his wife Fatima to come out of the house. Fatima, noticeably younger, a pleasant-looking woman with high cheekbones and protruding front teeth that gave her a permanent grin, greeted them. "Salida," she said in a soft voice.

"She speaks no English, but she'll soon teach you Arabic," Mohammad said. One boy darted behind his mother's sari. "That's Daanish, a naughty boy." The boy leaned around his mother's leg at the mention of his name and flashed a smile. The other son Danni, a lanky ten-year-old, held onto his father's tunic and stared at the women with a sullen expression.

Mr. Dahab showed Sara and Askara to their sizeable room with three beds and an attached bathroom. They washed up and rejoined the family in the sitting room where the rest of the children—two more boys, ages fourteen and twelve, and an infant sister—sat mesmerized in front of a TV, watching the story of a young boy's journey to market for his elderly grandmother.

Later, at the dinner table, Mr. Dahab smiled at his guests seated with his family. "Miss Sara, it gives me great joy to see young people like you go out into the world and meet others of different cultures and religions. You are the hope of the future, a one-world where we are all brothers and sisters. I expect glorious things from you and the youth of your countries. May Allah bless you."

Sara and Askara, with the help of Mr. Dahab, conversed with Fatima and learned that she, the youngest of fourteen, was born in a village on the Rahad River. Mohammad explained that Nubians in the Islamic religion, marry within their own family, usually to a first cousin, Fatima being his. Men establish their careers, and only then can they marry. Wives are generally ten to fifteen years younger than their husbands, fifteen in their case. The women, typically uneducated, stay at home and have as many babies as Allah wills.

When they finished eating, a girl appeared and gathered the children for bed. She balanced a baby on her hip, led the Dahab's youngest by the hand, and the others followed like sheep.

Sara said, "Another daughter, Mohammad?"

"No. This peasant girl, still a child herself, lives with us. She married at age twelve, became a mother at fourteen, and just three days ago, at age fifteen, her husband divorced her. Her father, my gardener, took her back. They live in my compound. She helps Fatima."

"That's sad," Sara said.

"Yes, life can be difficult. Allah blessed me with a good education and the means to support my family with honor. We help where we can. Peasant marriages are based on cattle. To marry, a man must have several cows equal to the beauty of his wife-to-be. Cows cost fifty pounds sterling. One hundred is an adequate number. Often a man pays the girl's family in installments of cattle after the marriage, which can go on for a long while, an entire lifetime. In this girl's case, the husband divorced her before paying what he owed. The father now supports his daughter and her baby. Often divorced women are left to die if no man supports them."

"But if the men are so much older, there must be a lot of young widows," Askara said.

"Not as many as you'd think. The life span for a woman here is only about forty years."

At 8 p.m., the TV broadcast ceased for the night with a picture of the Sudanese flag—a simple green triangle overlapping three broad stripes, red, white, and black—that waved in a breeze while the national anthem played. Mohammad and Fatima, with their two elder sons, stood at attention until the song ended. Sara and Askara followed suit.

Mr. Dahab explained afterward that in the Sudanese flag, red stands for struggles in the Arab lands and martyrs. White stands for Islam, peace, optimism, light, and love, and black for the Sudan and the Mahdiya Revolution. Green represents prosperity, goodness, and agriculture.

"We, Sudanese, are proud of our flag. It took many struggles for us to be free of British rule. They planted the seeds of seventeen years of cruel civil war here. They divided us, making the southern Sudanese, who are Christians, go naked and think of themselves as separate from the Muslims in the north. It will take long for the wounds to heal." Seeing that his guests looked tired, Mohammad told them to make themselves at home, and in the morning, he would take them to meet the commissioner of the largest province in Sudan, the Blue Nile province. "And tomorrow evening, Fatima has invited friends over to meet our foreign guests."

The next evening proved to be Askara's worst idea of a party, the women relegated to one room while the men enjoyed the living room and garden. The women couldn't converse, but they did communicate in pantomime, which at least she enjoyed. The husbands talked loudly about politics in Arabic and English. Fatima had sent the children to spend the night at the watchman's quarters at the far end of the garden. Sara and Askara were relieved when the guests left, and they could retreat to their room.

Sara lightly snored while Askara lay awake thinking of Darian, wondering if it made more sense for her to fly to the U.S. directly, or to ask Darian to meet her in Khartoum, or should she fly to India? What about the cup? Would it even pass customs? Should she hide the cup here on the grounds and be done with it? She couldn't decide. She hoped Selassie was okay and the uprising was over, for everyone's sake. She had no intention of keeping his possession, but she had no idea of how to return it.

Askara was still awake in the middle of the moonless night when she heard the heavy iron gate creak. She figured the night watchman was at his post or making his rounds. A man's shout woke the household. Screams and running followed. Askara looked out and saw two men fighting at the gate. One fell. Mr. Dahab charged out in his pajama suit, baton in hand. He slammed a man down to the ground and struck at another who rushed in from the shadows. The nightwatchman staggered to his feet, lunged at his attacker, and threw him to the ground. Mr. Dahab yelled. Lights flooded the compound. Neighbors woke and turned their lights on. Soon the night was as bright as day.

A man jumped Mr. Dahab and shoved his face into the pavement. Three neighbors broke through a side gate, grabbed the man from behind, and dragged him into the bushes where they beat him until he became motionless. Sara grabbed her knife. Askara grabbed a metal statuette. They rushed down the stairs and found Fatima in the kitchen, gripping a large kitchen knife.

Mr. Dahab shouted in English, "Don't come out!"

With the help of the neighbors, Mr. Dahab and his night watchman tied up the attackers and dragged them out of sight. The nightwatchman locked the gates, ran to speak to Fatima, and stood, rod-in-hand, at the entrance. Another man paced the driveway holding a long, curved dagger. Fatima, having no way to explain in English, shook and cried, but Askara and Sara needed no explanation. She motioned for them to go to their room.

Not long after, police cars screeched to a halt at the front gate. Doors opened, men jumped out and shoved handcuffs on the tied men, pushed them inside two of the vehicles, slammed the doors, and they sped away. Agitated officers remained, arguing at the gate. Mr. Dahab limped back into his house.

Sara looked at Askara. "Doesn't look good. Too much of a coincidence."

"What do we do now? I never wanted to bring harm to these people, Sara."

"We'll go to Khartoum, fly out. Those bastards came for that damn cup. I'm sure of it. They're killers. When I asked the commissioner tonight at the party if he had heard news of a coup in Ethiopia, he said he'd heard conflicting stories. In one, the Emperor was taken prisoner, most likely by the same rebel leaders who organized the mutiny last January, but he doubted it. In another, the coup was a false alarm; a factory near the palace had caught fire. Chemicals blew up. People panicked, thinking it was the palace. He said: 'Not to worry. Our Sudanese borders are strong. A coup in Ethiopia stays in Ethiopia. It will not affect us here. Sudan is a strong country.'"

"Should I bury this thing here, Sara? Leave it in Sudan and be done with it?"

"That's not going to stop *them*, whoever they are. I'd give it to them if it were me, Askara, but they'd kill you in the process. By the time they'd get close enough for us to know who they are, it would be too late. We've got to get out of here. We're endangering innocent people. Hell, we're innocent, but you know what I'm saying. Try to get some shut-eye. We'll work out a plan in the morning, depending on what Mr. Dahab says."

In the morning, officials from the Sudanese police, army, and central government converged at the Dahabs' to hear accounts of the night before and survey the grounds. They repeatedly asked Sara and Askara if they had any idea why the house had been attacked.

No, they lied.

"A national intelligence agent from Khartoum, who reports directly to President Nimeiry, identified them as Eritrean rebels from Ethiopia," the police commander said. "They're in jail. You girls entered from Ethiopia at Teseney.

Did you see anything unusual at the border? Did you have any difficulty crossing?

No, they lied.

The Commissioner ordered the women to stay in Khartoum for two days—at the government's request and as guests of Sudan—for their safety. "Please, ladies, do not consider this house arrest," he said. "This is for your protection only while we question the assailants. Mr. Mohammad Dahab has arranged a room at the Sahara Hotel in Khartoum, where his cousin Brigadier General Dahab will look after you."

Mr. Dahab said he was very sorry to see them go, especially under such circumstances, but he had his orders. His cousin would watch out for them until they got cleared to fly out. Mohammad said he would pray for their safety and a quick return to visit his family.

THE WOMEN ARRIVED IN KHARTOUM, THE CAPITAL OF Sudan, the largest African nation, in an official government car. The driver, an intelligence agent, described the city like a tour guide would. He pointed out the bridges over the Nile that connected Khartoum to its sister cities, Khartoum North and Omdurman—the city just south of the confluence of the Blue and White Niles.

"The Blue Nile reaches Khartoum after a long journey from the Ethiopian highlands," he said. Askara recalled the image of Sara watching the powerful water thunder over rocky cliffs. "The White Nile snakes north from Uganda's Lake Victoria, the second largest lake in the world, and descends into the Plain of Sudan. They meet here in Khartoum. The two Niles flow 1,900 river miles north to the Mediterranean Sea."

Sara, wanting to pick a fight, spoke up. "I don't get it. They aren't white and blue. So why call them that? Looks to me like one's browner, and one's slightly blue, that's all."

"Visitors say that. The Blue Nile, torrential and variable, looks clearer, especially at the headwaters in Ethiopia. The White Nile does not change much. It's a steady brown season to season. My family and I come down on hot nights to walk the tree-lined promenade along the Nile. My children play on the grass. There's always a cool evening breeze, even on the hottest day."

"So, how does this hotel thing work out? Are we locked in our rooms?" Askara asked.

"No, madam, you are not prisoners. You can move around. Some of my men will move with you. Don't worry. You will not be aware of them. They are professionals. This is for your protection only, until we figure out that break-in, most likely an attempted robbery, but Eritreans? Why would they risk crossing the border? We have no record of their visas. Your safety is Sudan's responsibility."

THE WOMEN SETTLED INTO THEIR ROOM AT THE SAHARA Hotel and enjoyed lunch in the elegant hotel restaurant. Sara ordered soup, rolls, Lebanese salad with dill-lemon dressing, and spicy chicken, plus a chilled beer, glad the Islamic code did not apply to foreigners. She and Askara drank two each, hoping to relax.

"Hey, Sara, after lunch, let's go to the museum. Okay? An afternoon of art would be fun, a good diversion." She leaned in closer to whisper, "And we can find out about flights, and I can send a cable."

"Great idea, going to a museum," Sara said in a loud voice, glancing around to see the wait staff at their stations. She held her damask table napkin over her mouth, pretending to whisk crumbs aside, and whispered. "Askara, either these guys are really good at blending in, or it's all bullshit. I think we're under house arrest. And, yes, I need to book my flight to Lesotho."

After eating, they walked out the front entrance of the hotel and caught a taxi to the Sudan National Museum. No one seemed to follow them. "Cool, Sara said, "more bullshit."

They followed the museum docent around the mock Nile River that skirted Nubian temple remains, which they learned were *salvaged*—not stolen—from their original site, according to the docent. A row of stone lions lined the promenade as well as a series of conspicuous security personnel. Sara nodded their direction. Askara grinned.

"What's with the stone lion thing," Askara said, "and those men? Are all rulers lions? Are all men spies?"

"Maybe on the first. Yes, on the second. Hey, look at that." Sara trotted over to a case labeled Skull of Paleolithic Man, circa 12,000-8,000 B.C. from Gebel Al Sahaba. "Even the teeth are intact. Pretty amazing. Wonder how Christians date the Adam and Eve thing to 4,000 B.C.?"

"Yeah, and what about our ape connection?"

"Fair dinkum, what about the apes following us?"

Askara spoke in a loud voice, "I particularly like these blue-glazed quartz beads from the Middle period, 2000-1750 B.C. and Queen Yusata's golden toe cases. Who would have thought? Toe cases. Makes it hard to run. Or maybe they'd help?"

"Wonder who *she* ran from?" Sara snickered.

Askara whispered, "See anybody behind us now, Sara?"

"Nope, they fell back, probably outside for a cigarette under a shade tree. What's our plan?"

"Ditch 'em and get the hell out of Sudan."

Chapter Eleven

The River Nile

Askara and Sara enjoyed their air-conditioned hotel room until a hard knock startled them. Askara jumped up and wrapped the bota bag in a towel, and tossed it to the far end of the closet. Sara motioned for her to sit down, and with a finger to her lips, she whispered, "Shh."

"Brigadier General Dahab here," an aggressive male voice shouted from the hallway. Sara opened the door. The Brigadier and a man who introduced himself as the veterinarian, Dr. Dahab, Mohammed's cousin, greeted the women but did not enter the room.

"Hello ladies, I trust you are comfortable. Mohammad sends his regards and has asked Dr. Dahab to show you the racehorses today. I cannot accompany you, but I will meet you again."

Askara tried to beg off, but the men would not hear of it, especially since Sara showed an interest. The vet Dr. Dahab insisted the races were unparalleled in all of Africa, and since he owned the best horses, he knew the foreigners would enjoy the outing. He left no room for disagreement. Askara shut up, realizing it would be futile, especially after Sara told them her father bred racehorses.

After a twenty-minute drive, they arrived at the stables. Walking the corridor of the nine-stall barn with its white-washed plaster walls, sand floors, and thatched roof, Askara felt pleasantly surprised. She had expected worse, much worse.

Sara asked Dr. Dahab, "Where did you study veterinary medicine, sir?"

"Scotland," he said. "Five years, didn't make it home for the birth of my third child, examination time."

"Your wife didn't accompany you for all those years?" Askara asked.

"Tut, tut, no. I had to study, no time for translating shopping lists."

"Sir, my father owns a stable in Australia. I grew up around racehorses. I don't understand this. These animals look sick and hurt. One has a deformed hoof. You don't race these animals, do you? What about those four Arabians over there? Are they yours? They look too young."

"This filly," he said, pointing to a bay Arabian with flared, drippy nostrils and bulging eye whites, "will win tomorrow. You must come to the races as my guests. My animals are of great stock. Many winners. After the races, we will dine on a Nile houseboat to celebrate."

Askara rolled her eyes, trying to get Sara's attention. "Sure," Sara said, watching grooms shuffle past, leading horses in for treatments. "I'd like to see the races. My brother Timmy breeds thoroughbreds on his farm outside of Melbourne," she added, watching Dr. Dahab give a shot to one, a glucose drip to another, and searing a lump on the third horse's leg with a heated rod. The stable smelled of sizzling flesh. Askara turned away. "I guess these horses are out of the race tomorrow?" Sara said.

"No, they'll be fine, fit as ever," the vet said and shouted orders at the grooms. Sara curled her lip in a snarl and started to say something, but Askara grabbed her arm and shot her a shut-up look.

They rode back to the hotel in silence until Dr. Dahab said, "Tonight, we will dine with my dear friend Charles. The Brigadier is busy. I will fetch you at your hotel at 7:00."

Askara faltered, trying to think of a way to decline. Sara jumped in. "That would be nice. We'd love to meet your wife, doctor. Please bring her."

"No! She doesn't speak a word of English. The children need her at home," he said and remained quiet for the duration of the drive. He got out of the passenger's seat when the driver pulled into the hotel's valet parking lane and quickly opened their door. "I will give my wife your regards. Thank you. The men, over there, are at your disposal, anything you need."

Askara glanced at the thugs he had pointed to. After the car drove off, Askara growled, "He repulses me. Hard to believe he's Mohammed's cousin."

"Hell, they're all bloody cousins, the whole damned country. Can't expect to find many men like Mohammed here—or, for that matter, anywhere in the world. He's truly kind. That's why I accepted the offer. I don't want to offend Mohammad. He can't help it if his cousins are fools."

They quit whispering when the thugs drew closer to follow them into the hotel foyer.

"Fools, that's only half of it," Askara said at the elevator, fumbling in her pack for her address book. "As soon as we lose these goons, I'll send a telegram to Darian and tell him to meet me here ASAP. I saw Western Union's down that way about three blocks and a travel agency. Let's go up to our room and leave by the back exit near the ice machine.

These guys only watch the foyer."

"Good idea. How fast can your bloke get here? I need to get back to Lesotho."

"Don't know. Not sure where Darain is. If I don't hear back fast, I'll book a flight to California."

They walked to a business center, sneaking through three hotels along the strip, always exiting from the back. No one followed. Sara booked the next available flight on Air Sudan for Johannesburg. Askara sent telegrams to the two addresses Darian had given her, his business in Bombay, and his parents' home. *I need you. Meet me ASAP. Sahara Hotel. Khartoum. Urgent. Askara.* They sneaked back to their hotel and walked into the bar for a cold beer, making sure the front desk staff saw them.

ASKARA AND SARA DRANK MORE THAN THEY INTENDED, figuring they should have some fun before the dreadful dinner with the vet Dahab and his friend Charles.

When the car came to collect them, only the driver was there. He said the others were already at the restaurant. Sara, feeling good after several beers, entertained Askara during the drive over with crazy stories about her brother Timmy, a likable bloke but wild, she said. Once, he wrestled a python to pull a wallaby right out of the python's throat. Askara couldn't decide if Sara was joking or not, but the story made her want to hurl.

They composed themselves before they walked into the restaurant, but one look told Askara this dinner would be a nightmare. Sara grinned and whispered something rude that made Askara blush. She tried to recover her composure before introductions.

Charles, an agricultural scientist, tried his best to impress Sara. Waiting for food, he cleared his throat to get their attention—especially Dr. Dahab's—and in a high-pitched voice informed them, "I am the major importer/exporter of seeds and agricultural feeds to Cairo. I have many contacts in Egypt. I was born there."

"Is that right?" Sara said, taking a healthy gulp of beer. "Quite an accomplishment."

"Yes, but the research I do, on plant sex hormones, is not my major interest."

Askara stifled a laugh. She could guess from the looks of him—long, knobby fingers, concave chest, and a pitted, sallow complexion—that hormones of any type would not be his primary interest. "What is your major interest, Charles?"

"Theology. I am a Christian. I studied theology at university. I won a scholarship to the United States to get a Doctor of Divinity degree."

Askara choked on a piece of injera. "Excuse me," she said, "please go on."

"I didn't go. The war between Egypt and Israel broke out, and the scholarship got canceled. It was the worst day of my life."

"I'm sorry," Sara chimed in, looking at Dr. Dahab slumped with boredom in his chair.

"No matter," he said. "I came to understand God's reason."

Sara, now intrigued, said, "What *was* God's reason, Charles?"

"To save me from idiocy. You see, I had written to 289 institutions for their applications. When they wrote back to me, I studied their stationery, especially their logos. Each carried symbology in their letterheads and brochures. Intrigued, I set out to write back to each one asking for an explanation of the particular holy symbols so that I might make the wisest choice."

Sara and Askara looked at one another and smirked. Charles stopped, shook his head in confusion, and began again. Dr. Dahab chomped a piece of meat like he had to kill it.

"Do you know, not one of them could explain their sacred symbolism. What is worse, some institutions did not even realize they had it. One university replied: Sir, if this is some joke, we do not find it amusing. Our logo, the first letters of our institution's name, is merely that. The designer created a pleasing composition within a triangle, nothing more. Please do not contact us again." Charles rubbed his forehead. "Their reply stunned me; the reference to the Trinity was obvious. Well, I figured I could not get an excellent education from such ignorant people. One by one, they all failed the test. Those institutions knew nothing of God's message for me."

Sara dropped her napkin on the floor and slowly leaned over to retrieve it, trying to choke back a laugh. Askara saw her and sat rigid, pursing her lips, wishing herself somewhere far, far from the absurdity of the moment. Immediately after dinner, Askara said she had a migraine and needed to return to the hotel room, causing Sara to pat her back and nod emphatically.

Dr. Dahab, who had not spoken all night, growled, "I'll call for you at 1:00 p.m. tomorrow. My driver will take you back to the hotel now. Stay in your room. The Brigadier's men are posted outside. Goodnight."

THE NEXT DAY, DR. DAHAB, A MEMBER OF THE QUALIFYING panel, watched and evaluated the horses as they entered the racetrack. He disqualified one for lameness, which made the owner furious. The man stormed off, pulling the limping animal behind him.

Sara leaned over to whisper to Askara, "Most of these aren't racehorses. They're built like bloody prehistoric ancestors of a horse, the Przewalski, or some other Mongolian version. Look at those thick necks and stubby legs. Thought they would be Arabians. These horses should pull plows."

During the race, the all-male crowd did not talk, shout, or do anything but watch. Then they rushed to the pay-off booths waving tickets in their hands, yelling and jostling to be first in line. Before Dr. Dahab's horse raced, he asked Sara and Askara to walk with him to the stables. They saw him give his young mare an injection in the shoulder.

"What's the shot for?" Sara asked.

"A little fluid, so she won't get dehydrated in the race."

When his horse bolted out of the gate in the lead, Sarah leaned over to Askara and whispered, "Potent shot." But after two rounds on the dirt track, the filly fell behind and finished last. The vet said nothing more that afternoon to the women, or anyone else. His driver dropped them back at the hotel and handed Sara a note: Dinner with Brigadier Dahab, pick up at 7:00.

THAT EVENING DR. DAHAB, ASKARA, AND SARA JOINED Brigadier General Dahab and one of his army officers, accompanied by his Egyptian wife, for dinner on the Nile. They parked in a grassy lot, walked down a short pier, stepped onto a houseboat, and entered another world. The river flowed silently, reflecting the last orange light of day, and came alive with strings of houseboat lights like fireflies dancing in the evening breeze.

The Brigadier General Dahab asked, "How did your horse fare today, cousin?"

"Useless mare ran a miserable race. She's too old!"

"Old? Two years?" the Brigadier General said, reaching for a chilled beer.

"Two years too old." The vet ordered the servant to bring him a beer. Bottle in hand, he stood up, trudged to the forward deck, and sat alone, downing that beer and calling for more until seven bottles flanked his feet. He stretched out on the wooden bench.

Sara and Askara sat back to enjoy the River Nile. Chilled beer, beautiful view, yep, this is enough to, Askara paused her thought, make the night worthwhile. She looked out at the broad expanse of muddy water flowing sedately north. The huge orange sun melted on the horizon. Molten bands of red-orange danced on gentle waves and, like ancient whispers, faded. A breeze came up to chase mosquitoes away. This is a dream worth having, Askara thought.

Sara excused herself and called to Askara to tour the small houseboat with her. One tiny bedroom, a sitting room with couches and chairs, a dining area, and a small toilet comprised the first level. They climbed metal stairs to the upper deck. City lights emerged in the purple dusk. The kitchen servant rushed to light Chinese lamps hung along the deck for the guests, the amber glow dancing on the ripples as the boat parted the black water. The voices of children playing among the trees along the promenade drifted by.

Sara tipped her head, directing Askara's gaze. "That's pleasant."

"Yeah, they're having a splendid time, rattling off in Arabic. Don't even miss us."

"You think she's really that bloke's wife? No one else has brought a wife."

"Hadn't thought of that. Her husband's drunk. Brigadier's high. Pompous doctor's comatose. And she looks bored. I'd say let's focus on a beautiful night on the Nile. Way cool," Askara replied.

"Yep."

The Brigadier bellowed, looking up at them. "You know, ladies, this river gets so hot in the summer that the vegetation on the bottom rises to the surface and ignites, catches fire right in the water. Burning clumps of grass float down the river."

Askara shouted, "How could that be?"

The Brigadier shouted back, "You don't believe me? You think I'm a liar?"

"No, not at all, sir, that's not what I meant. I didn't know that could happen."

"There are many things you foreigners don't know about our part of the world."

The officer rallied to mollify the situation, "Brigadier, sir, how can we expect a young American to know anything about our world? It's enough that she's here to learn."

The officer's wife stood up abruptly and walked upstairs to join the women, her spiked heels clicking on the deck boards. She looped arms with Askara and Sara and led them to the far end of the boat, where the vet snored on the level below. He roused, looked up, straightened his crumpled shirt, and stumbled to the other end where the men stood enjoying shots of whiskey.

The women leaned on the rail and listened to the soft waves lapping against the boat. The officer's wife, slightly older than Askara, spoke in Arabic and patted Askara's hand affectionately. Dressed in a crimson sari with gold embroidery, her long black hair tied up in a tight bun, eyes lined with kohl, red lipstick catching the glimmer of Chinese lanterns, the woman looked both dramatic and awkward, like a child who had gotten into her mother's makeup. Askara couldn't decide if she were a dolled-up wife or an escort for the night, but she liked her.

In brittle English, the officer's wife said, tapping her chest, "Egyptian, born Cairo. No Muslim."

Askara pointed to herself. "American. Father Indian. Mother American."

The woman smiled and tapped near Askara's dark eyes and did the same near Sara's blue eyes. She twirled her hand in a questioning gesture, asking, "Sister?"

Sara smiled. "No. Friend. I am Australian. My name is Sara. Hers is Askara."

"Samia," the woman said, pointing to herself.

They learned, or thought they did, that Samia had a three-year-old boy. She patted her swollen stomach to convey she was pregnant.

Their conversation ended abruptly when a speeding car skidded sideways toward the river with tires screeching. The car braked suddenly at the grass bank. A couple stumbled out. Illuminated by the car lights, they waved to the boat. The man in a white galabieh and turban yanked the woman toward the dock. The woman's tight sequin dress sparkled in the lights. Samia clucked disapproval. Sara whispered *whore*? Samia nodded, *yes*. They watched the couple climb into a shaky rowboat, the man almost dropping the oar into the river, and paddle out to the houseboat, waving, shouting, and laughing. The riverboat guide slowed the houseboat to let them pull aside.

When they climbed on board, the woman threw her arms around her man and kissed him, causing Brigadier General Dahab to utter sharp words in Arabic. Their back-and-forth exchange grew aggressive. The Brigadier shoved the man. His officer stepped in and calmed the situation. The vet rallied from the shouting and walked over but said nothing. Sara and Askara looked at Samia for an explanation. She avoided their gaze.

The servant appeared and muttered something to the Brigadier, who motioned to Askara, Sara, and Samia to follow the servant into the dinette. Before Askara could get out of range, the man swaggered forward and grabbed her shoulder.

"I am Malik Dahab, cousin to Mohammad, living in Ethiopia, home on holiday. Pleased to meet you, madam."

Askara said, "Hello," watching his date rub up and down his leg seductively with her spiked heel, while she stared down Askara. Sara yanked Askara away. Askara said, "I want out of here. How do we do it?"

"Bloody hell, I want out of here, too, but I don't know how when we're floating down the river."

"The promenade follows the river, and there are hotels all along it. If we can get to one of them, we can catch a taxi back to our hotel."

"Great. What do we say?"

Askara thought for a few seconds, "I'll get sick."

"They'll tell you to sit down and rest."

"Not if I'm vomiting. Follow my cues."

Samia watched Askara gobble mouthful after mouthful of food, hardly stopping to breathe, or chew. Samia pantomimed, patting Askara's belly. Askara laughed and shook her head, *no*.

When Askara left the table to talk to Dr. Dahab, standing alone at the rail, watching the Nile slip by, Samia walked over to her absurdly drunk husband. He pulled her onto his lap and kissed her neck. Angry, she pushed him away. Malik Dahab and his woman were all over each other, leaving the Brigadier to pace up and down on the deck, grumbling in Arabic.

Askara lunged forward, hitting her stomach hard on the boat's rail.

"What is it?" the vet said, grabbing her by the arm.

Askara slumped, then straightened up. "Nothing, pain in my stomach."

"Have a beer," he replied.

Askara thought how absurdly brilliant. "Thanks." She gulped down the beer. She felt her stomach rumble. Gripping the rail, she glanced down at the vet Dahab's ring. "That looks like an Egyptian scarab ring." The design was unmistakable, a large beetle with its body divided into halves by a central groove. She lifted his finger and held it up to the dim Chinese lantern to see the color. "Lapis?" The thick gold band and stone beetle covered the entire lower segment of his fourth finger. "Great imitation." She burped. "Looks authentic."

Dr. Dahab stepped back from her. He fingered the ring. "A museum piece from the tomb of King Tutankhamen. Naturally, it's authentic!"

"Not possible," Askara blurted out and sucked in a deep breath. "Those treasures belong to the Egyptian government. You were duped."

"Watch your words! I purchased it several years back from a friend, head of the archeology department at the University of Cairo."

"That's a state treasure that should be in a museum, not on your finger."

"Well, it was on one person's finger before, wasn't it? I take excellent care of it. It brings me luck."

Sara overheard the conversation. "Didn't bring you much good luck today at the track, did it, doc?"

Dr. Dahab looked like a wild animal with the lantern glow in his eyes. He growled, "How dare a woman, especially a foreign woman, speak to me like this!" He slammed his hand down on the boat railing.

Askara lunged forward and groaned, gripping her stomach. "Oh, God." Leaning over the boat rail with her hair falling like a curtain around her, she plunged her index finger down her throat and retched. The smelly mess splattered on the boat deck. Everyone jumped away. Only Sara approached to drag Askara by her hand to the small ledge below where the dinghy was tied.

The woman, exclaiming in Arabic, fell off Malik's lap when he jumped up. She wiped the hem of her slip dress in disgust. The men backed away to the other end of the boat, ordering the servant to clean up the mess. Samia rushed down to help Askara onto the dinghy. Then she climbed in. Sara rowed them to the pier, jumped out, tied the dinghy, and gave Askara and Samia a helping hand. Samia led them down the tree-lined promenade to a public drinking fountain in a small garden where Askara splashed her face and rinsed her mouth several times.

Sara whispered to Askara, "What now?"

"Okay?" Samia said, rubbing Askara's back.

They heard screeching car wheels follow the curve of the road above. The car raced to the dock and skidded to a halt. A man jumped out and shouted in Arabic to the houseboat.

He fired a barrage of bullets. Everybody on the boat dove for cover. The Brigadier shouted something in Arabic, stood, and fired back. Bullets sprayed the car, zinging on metal. Someone inside screamed. The man on the pier collapsed, moaning. Two men jumped out and dragged him into the car. They opened fire on the boat again. Askara, Sara, and Samia ran toward a hotel. They heard a woman scream, "Allah...." Gunfire drowned her words.

Samia choked, pleading for the hotel guards' help. They yanked the women in, closed the massive doors, and bolted them. The reception clerk pulled guns from a drawer to hand to the guards. The men rushed out a side door towards the river while the clerk stood guard with his rifle leveled at the front door. Askara and Sara tried to calm Samia's wailing.

"Look at her, Sarah, poor woman's hysterical."

Their conversation halted abruptly. An officer ran in and spoke to the clerk. For a few minutes, no one made a noise. When a policeman shouted, the clerk unbolted the door allowing him in. The officer rushed to speak to Samia in Arabic. The clerk translated for Askara and Sara, telling them that Samia's husband had been shot in the arm and taken to the hospital, and the officer would drive her there now. Another officer would come to take them to meet the Brigadier.

NEAR MIDNIGHT SARA AND ASKARA ARRIVED BACK AT THE Sahara Hotel under police guard. By the next morning, every police official had read the crime report—written in triplicate—before passing it to the Brigadier and President Nimeiry. The women were quickly cleared of any implications, being the Brigadier General's guests. The verdict, dispute over money, was the explanation given to Askara and Sara.

Askara wondered, why no mention of our border crossing, the coup in Ethiopia, or even Mohammad's break-in? What could that mean? She felt momentarily relieved but increasingly anxious. Nothing added up.

When Mohammed Dahab arrived at the Sahara Hotel mid-morning, he found Askara and Sara eating breakfast, in clear sight of a table of police officers enjoying their breakfasts. He sat down, ordered coffee, and looked directly at Sara. "Miss Sara, is there anything you can tell me? I am worried. Praise Allah, you were not harmed, but I cannot believe this is *not* related to the break-in at my house. Who could have such ill luck?"

Sara sighed. "Who were those men? Who were the men at your house?"

"The police aren't saying, not even to me. I called on the Brigadier early this morning. He told me every policeman is searching. They found the abandoned car near the train station, bloodstains on the seat. The Brigadier told me one man captured at my house that night is Ethiopian by birth. He had just begun working a temporary contract at the Gezira Scheme, the very day of the break-in. He's in jail pending further investigation."

"Is last night's attack in the paper today?" Askara asked.

"No. That would shame our family. The Brigadier's father-in-law, a pious and powerful man…this would not look good for him. Malik, the stupid boy, has a wife from an influential family, and two children. That family would cast him out. In fact, my cousin, the Brigadier, said he could not speak of certain details with me. But he suggested that you must leave Sudan as soon as possible. His men will guard you until then. I do not know what this concerns. I fear someone has involved you in difficulty beyond our knowledge. Leave. Yes, that is best. We have troubles in Sudan—what country doesn't?—but we are good to foreigners. Your governments should understand that. I will be sorry to see you go, especially under these circumstances. Fatima and the children already miss you. On your next trip, I shall show you the beauty of Sudan. I must go now to inspect a project at Al Ubayyid. My cousin, also named Mohammed, will check in with you. Expect him later today."

"Don't worry about us. We will get to the airport on our own," Sara said without hesitation.

"The hope of the world lies with people like you. A one-world-family is our only answer to peace," Mohammed said, rising from the table. He shook Sara's hand, and then Askara's. "We will meet again. Inshallah."

Askara's mood brightened after going to the telex office when Sara and Askara eluded their guards. Darian's message made her giddy: he would meet her the following afternoon in Khartoum. When they entered the hotel, they settled their dining bill with the front desk and ran up the stairs to their room. Packing quickly, Askara grabbed the bota bag and felt for the cup, wrapped her jeans around it, and stuffed the bundle into her backpack. From their upstairs window, they saw the guards had drifted away, only one remained, smoking a cigarette under a tree near the entrance.

"They're getting lax, Sara. They didn't bat an eye when we walked in. I wonder if they want us to escape. That would be easier for them. Or maybe they'll let us run, so they can shoot us and say it was an accident?"

"Interesting. I'll check the back lot right now." When Sara returned, she quickly closed the door behind her. "No guards in the rear. Yep, they want to appear to guard us but not really. Askara, they want us to get lost. Perfect. We're their worst nightmare now; the Brigadier knows it. He can blame his own guy, fire him, whatever, for our escape, but the truth is then we'd be out of the Brigadier's hair. A taxi driver's sleeping in the shade back there in the lot. Let's go."

When they rushed up to the driver, they startled the man by requesting he drive them around the city for hours, give them a tour since they were flying out later. He grinned. He agreed after telling them it would be expensive. After two hours of stopping at points of minimal interest, like the local camel corral, the taxi driver dropped them at the youth hostel near the airport, as they requested. They sat out front for several minutes, pretending to deliberate on his tip while checking if anyone had followed them. Seeing no one suspicious, they gave the man a wad of bills and jumped out of the taxi.

They would share a large dormitory room with three German girls, who spoke no English, the desk clerk informed them upon registration. Luckily, when they got to the dorm room, the Germans were out. After locking their gear in cabinets, they took a taxi to the Nile business complex near the parkway to pick up Sara's airplane ticket and walked along the river to relax.

"Ugly bastards, aren't they?" Sara said, looking at a crocodile gliding by the shore. "Did you see the one near the houseboat dock?"

"No."

"Yeah, he was upstream, had his mouth open, a tick bird standing in it."

"Why didn't you point it out to me?"

"Would have, but the vet Dahab was talking to you."

"Did the croc eat the bird?"

"No. They have a relationship. The bird goes into the croc's mouth and eats the leeches stuck all over the inside, does the croc a service. In exchange, the croc doesn't eat the bird. Strange, like I watch your mouth, you watch my back."

"Ugh, weird." Askara looked at the sunlight skittering on the water. "You know, Hindus consider the Nile River holy. They spread some of Mahatma Gandhi's ashes on it near Lake Victoria, the White Nile part."

"Yeah, why?"

"Don't know. To honor him, I guess. Hey, Sara, you leave early morning. Do you realize this nightmare's almost over? We lived through it, thank God. Darian arrives later in the afternoon. I wish you could meet. You'd get on great. We'll fly out early the following morning for Cairo."

"What about that damn cup?"

"Darian will take care of that. He said, *not to worry* in his telex. He'll come up with a plan."

"Boy, you are trusting, aren't you? You haven't had the time to get to know him very well. That bloke must love you to come so far to pick you up."

"Yeah, I know. I've thought about that. I'm surprised. I mean, we're still getting to know each other. But there's such energy—a force I can't explain—that pulls us together. I couldn't face going to the airport alone. I'm so glad Darian will be with me."

"Askara, I'll miss you. I thought traveling with that other Yank was intense, but this? Wow! You've been a great friend, can't imagine getting into more trouble, or being with a better person during that trouble. I most definitely plan to come to the States and take you on a road trip to Arizona to buy Navajo jewelry and leather cowboy chaps, maybe after a year, when my stint in Lesotho ends. But seriously, I worry about leaving you here. Are you sure you can't come with me to Lesotho? Have Darian meet you there?"

"Too late. He booked a flight already. Bombay, Cairo, Khartoum."

"Askara, promise me you'll hang out at the hostel after I leave. Don't go anywhere. It's not safe here."

"Sure. I promise. The canteen food looks pretty good. I don't plan on leaving the room, except to eat and shower. I may sleep until Darain arrives. I'm exhausted."

"Me too. If I were you, I'd toss that damn thing in the garbage can and be done with it. Selassie's not going to miss it, poor guy."

"Yeah, I wouldn't want to be in his shoes. I'll see what Darian thinks. We may leave it here in Sudan, maybe with a note, so eventually, a museum could house it in an antiquities department."

"Good idea, right next to the queen's toe cases," Sara laughed.

Chapter Twelve

Vision

Sara tried to dissuade Askara from riding to the airport with her. But Askara wouldn't stay behind. Standing in the airport foyer, Askara gave Sara a big hug goodbye. "Who would've known when we were swimming laps how life would go? Fair dinkum," Askara said with a grin.

"I hope to hear from you soon. It's difficult, the phone thing at my barracks, but keep trying. I won't sleep well until I know you're safe in California. I'll see you when my assignment is up, just about a year from now. Please, Askara be safe. This is no joke. And ditch that damn cup. It's nothing but trouble. It's a life wrecker, not a life maker."

Askara waited in the departure lobby and watched Sara cross the pavement and climb the stairway into the plane. Sara turned with a raised fist and a big grin. Askara answered with broad arm sweeps until Sara disappeared.

Immediately a feeling of grief and foreboding flooded over Askara. She turned away from the dirty glass to face the waiting room, feeling all eyes were on her, slipped out the main door, hailed a taxi, and stared at the city sprawl on the ride back to the hostel. When she returned to the room, no one was there. The German girls must have gone out sightseeing, she thought. She relaxed on the bed to read her book *No Room in the Ark.*

Askara awoke hours later in the sultry heat, the ceiling fan's creaking the only noise she heard. Her thoughts rushed to Darian and their last night in Mombasa—ages ago, it seemed to her, another world. She saw him standing under the fan in Mombasa, admiring her in her thin nightdress. She felt his closeness, his warm hand on her back, the scent of his aftershave. We wasted precious time together, she thought. Askara yanked back from the memory telling herself: no use going backward, we'll make up for this when he arrives. I'll show him how I feel. Askara reached for the bota bag she had wedged into the wireframe of her bed. She removed the cup and cradled it on her stomach. The sensation of drifting on water overtook her. Waves gently rocked her. She relaxed. The tight cord in her back fell slack. The fan's robust whir slowed. Her heavy eyelids closed.

SHE HEARD THE MELODIOUS SOUND OF WOMEN CHANTING. Askara drifted with the music. Darkness transformed into color; a pale sky blue deepened to indigo. A pulsating light in the distance lured her toward a luminous sphere. A gentle hand pulled her, whose she didn't know. She dove into sunlight diamonds on water and emerged where flat rocks surrounded a well.

Looking down at her clothes—a rough-weave cotton robe that touched her sandaled feet—she shook the water from her tangled hair, grasped a rope, and pulled up the heavy, creaking bucket to fill her earthen jug. Walking uphill to a stone temple flanked by cedar trees, she balanced the jug on her head and greeted a group of men and boys with a smile as she passed. A little boy touched the hem of her robe and mumbled a prayer.

Her adoptive father emerged from the inner sanctuary and took the jug from her, saying, "Thank you, Asha."

They joined hands, chanting a blessing. May our supreme god, Ahura Mazda, bless our bounty. We give thanks to the creator. The elderly priest looked out at the landscape and said blessings for the guardians of the separate creations: cattle, plants, earth, water, stone, and fire. Dipping his hands into the blessed water, he passed them over a small bronze cup whose lighted wick floated in oil. He touched Asha's forehead, saying, "Daughter, these blessings I give to you: good thought represented by cattle; immortality by plants; piety and devotion by earth; wholeness and health by water; the Kingdom of the Lord by stone; and Truth by Fire. May Ahura Mazda bless you in this life and in those to come."

The girl kissed her fingertips and pressed them to his sandaled feet, "Respected One. I will always defend the purity of Fire."

"Asha, keep in your heart—good thought, good word, good action—and you will be an *ashavan*. Care for this world with reverence for all things. This cup of fire, he said, holding the small bronze cup aloft, is it not a beauty to behold? The flame of divine life cannot be polluted…nor sullied. It burns forever pure and acts as a scourge to eliminate evil."

"Yes, Respected One, but how does evil come into the world?"

The Respected One answered, "First as a spirit that takes form in destructive acts, thoughts, and deeds. The world is a battleground. Some beings grow strong in evil and allow the dark spirit to rule. We, Asha, are Defenders of the Light."

"Respected One, surely you can destroy the Evil Spirit. You have that power."

"We all have our assigned work. I am not a destroyer. There are those of us who have been here, and more will come, to carry the torch of righteousness and use fire to cleanse. The legacy of goodness eclipses with time, and new leaders step into the ebb and flow of creation, like waves of the river they flow. Occasionally the river floods and wipes away life, so revitalized life may appear. Honor the divine cycles but, Asha, always work for the Light of Ahura Mazda."

"Respected One, villagers worship the stars, moon, and sun—not Ahura Mazda. Are they evil?"

"No, child. They worship what they see. Do not disparage them. They cause no harm. In time, many lifetimes from now, they will see beyond and understand. One can only worship from where one stands in creation. Some, on the distant mountains, for example, see the wide valley expand to the horizon and grasp the essence of sky and earth. Others, in the meadow, see only the grass and insects at their feet. Some see nothing; their eyes are closed. Like living in a cave deep within the earth, you believe it night when it is day. The cave is dark, yet sunlight shines above."

"Can the Just be deceived?"

"Those pure of heart see and understand. But remember this, Asha, victory over evil comes in many forms: as a bold wind, the mightiest in strength; as a powerful golden-horned bull who no one will challenge; as a fiery camel able to see far into the darkness of night; as a sharp-tusked boar, a formidable enemy; as a hawk, the swiftest of birds who listens to the cries of all; and as a powerful ram with backward curving horns able to climb high crags. Many forms. Ultimately, victory comes to the righteous; despair comes to the evildoers.

Fire and sun symbolize the battle of purification, in the physical world and in the world of spirit. Without them, The Deceiver would destroy all that is good. Fire cleanses."

"Father, what about the night when no sun shines?"

"The night with a moon, even a crescent, protects us. The night with no moon scares the weak of faith. Ahura Mazda ordained the waxing and waning to rouse the spirit. The Lord created twins, rival spirits, who come in many forms to teach, one holy, one wicked. Enough. We must work now. Take my prayer cup into the temple."

"Yes, Respected One," the girl replied. "But can you tell me, um, my destiny, why you adopted me?"

"Asha, this will become clear. You have a duty. Your way will not be easy. I will be near you in spirit, but you will have difficulty seeing me. You become blinded by the world. But the inner flame will help you remember. You will realize who you are, yet the way is not obvious."

THE TEMPLE, CATTLE, AND THE RESPECTED ONE DISAPpeared in indigo light. A swoosh of wind brushed Askara's face. Her body, propelled forward, jolted to a stop. Her heart thumped wildly with irregular wallops and wheezes. She gasped for air. She grabbed her travel clock. 4:30? Ten minutes. Wow, what an intense dream, she said to the empty room. The white-hot cup left marks in her damp palms. She shoved the cup away and crammed it under the bed, throwing her pack over it.

Shrieks outside the window startled her. She pulled back the thin curtain to see two mangy cats fighting over a locust. She heard footsteps approach. The German girls burst through the door, chatting away.

Hallo! They said, seeing Askara, and grabbed their meal tickets. They pantomimed for Askara to join them for dinner in the canteen. She nodded *yes*, happy to have company, even if they couldn't converse. When they returned, the German girls put on fancy dresses, styled their hair, and left Askara to her solitude.

She lifted the cup again and ran her finger over the simple embossed pattern of raised curvilinear mounds outlined by greenish-black patina stains in the crevices. As a visual object, she found it undistinguished in design and color. But to hold it was to feel the warmth of the sun after a cold, dreary winter. Penetrating, sustaining, enlivening. She traced the subtle pattern over and over with her finger, following the same channels each time. Her eyes closed. She floated.

A never-ending circle of cattle trudged along the cup's surface, horns and bodies interlocked, leaving afterimages in their wake. A fiery sun rose to its zenith, set, and rose again. In the delicate interweaving of hollows, a procession of draped individuals marched to a temple flanked by trees.

Askara opened her eyes. She saw the crudely designed, time-worn, unevenly colored metal cup, the same cup she had seen at the Emperor's palace. She detected a faint glow. Askara realized the light did not follow the physical laws of this world. It came from the cup. She trembled. Someone wanted this cup badly, had tried to kill for it, and would try again she told herself. Askara felt duty-bound to find a safe place for the precious cup, but where and how? She now understood her dreams were recollections. How was that possible?

Askara stretched out on the cot, pulled the crisp, white cotton sheet up to her neck and rested the cup on her stomach. Warmth radiated into her. She slipped away. She saw herself, a youthful woman dressed in a tunic, standing to the left of a stone temple. She poured water into a cattle trough and breathed sweet earth where hooves had churned up the grass. A dark-haired man approached. He waved and shouted and ran up to her.

"Asha, come. See what I've found."

Asha stopped her work and walked toward him. "What?"

He reached into his bag and withdrew something. "A gift for you," he said and placed a folded piece of leather in her hand. "Open it."

She pulled back the leather to see a rock with a deep blue center. The blue, like the last color of the evening sky, shimmered.

"Lapis lazuli. I found it in the hills," he said. "I will make a pendant for you. Lapis is a powerful stone, an enhancer of spirit."

"Thank you, Dastur. Does this have any other meaning?"

"Like the elder women whisper?"

"Well, does it?"

"Would you want it to?" the young man said with a broad smile.

"If a meaning, like what the elders say, is intended, I would like that."

"Asha, I shall shape this stone of perfect core, and with it, my love adore. Is that what they whisper? Asha, I have ten cattle. Will you accept my offer and marry me?"

"With promise pledged, I accept. Have you asked The Respected One?"

"Yes, long ago, when we played pebbles on the temple steps as children. He advised me then to let you win the game so that you would marry me someday. He advised me three years back to work hard, earn cattle, and ask for you. Last summer, I told him I had nine. He said, earn ten. I have ten now."

The priest approached. They bowed and touched his feet. "My children, I see the time has come for your union. You have a mutual fate. Fill it with blessings." He clasped their joined hands to his. Let us go in."

Inside the temple, The Respected One chanted a blessing and passed their intertwined hands three times over the flame that rose from his small bronze cup. "Blessings. May you always be guided by Truth, and may the Light of Ahura Mazda forever illuminate your way. Be now one, husband and wife."

The image faded. The sound of a plucked string reverberated in Askara's ears. Brilliant light pricked her eyes. Thousands of pulsating stars raced by. A gleaming silver moon crested in a gray dawn. Askara plummeted like a rock, hitting the cot with such force that it knocked the breath out of her. Her eyes flew open. She saw glimmers of both worlds. Then neither.

Chapter Thirteen

The Legend

Darian wondered if Askara would meet him at the airport, or the Sahara Hotel. She had not replied after he sent the telegram with his arrival information. Strange, he thought. The fasten seatbelt light came on. The airplane landed with a jolt on the runway that resembled a zipper holding together the yellow desert on one side and the green irrigated fields on the other. Darian realized he was nervous—not about the landing—but about seeing Askara.

Her telegram, an urgent request to come to her, plagued his mind. Had she contacted him out of necessity, or longing? Hoping for the latter, he assumed the former. He had decided on the flight down from Cairo that he would let Askara make the initial move. Would she approach him as a trusted friend or lover? The plane's engines roared to a halt. His heart accelerated.

Getting through customs and immigration seemed endless. Darian climbed the stairs behind a group of large Sudanese men in white galabiehs. Askara rushed past them. She threw her arms around Darian's neck and kissed him several times. Two men turned to watch and winced disapproval.

"Askara," Darian said and looked down at her face flushed and wildness. "I've missed you."

Askara grabbed his hand in hers, held it close, and said, "I am *so* happy to see you."

Darian wanted to wrap her in his arms and kiss her a thousand times, but he didn't. They trudged toward baggage claim, pushed forward by the crowd. He whispered, "You seem different."

"I am. A lot has happened. I have so much to tell you."

After retrieving his bag, Darian hailed a taxi. But when he said the Sahara Hotel, please, Askara broke in saying the Nile Hotel.

"I'm glad you met me at the airport; otherwise, we'd be in two different places."

"I haven't stayed at the Nile. Someone recommended it. Look, do me a favor," she said as they walked up to the front desk to check-in.

"Anything."

"Book us into a room together, but don't give my name, say I'm your wife."

Darian smiled, but Askara's urgency unnerved him. He feared her affection might be an empty victory. The porter opened the door and set their bags down in a spacious room with one king bed drowned by colorful pillows. The porter pulled back sheer curtains to a small balcony with a view of the city sprawl. With palm extended, he smiled a toothy grin. Askara quickly tipped him a Sudanese pound and motioned for him to leave.

"I'll go down to request a room change, Askara."

"Why? This is clean."

"The set-up."

"You mean only one bed? We signed in as husband and wife. Don't you think we can share a bed, at least for pretense."

Darian, taken aback, said, "If that suits you, it suits me."

"You share my heart, you share my bed," Askara replied.

Darian pulled Askara close. "Askara, I want you to share my bed and my life. You have been in my heart longer than you can imagine." He leaned down to kiss her. Askara met his passion. They became a world apart from the busy city.

Later, nestled in Darian's arms, Askara asked, "Am I the only one in your heart, Darian?"

"You have been since we met at the Oracle, but I want you to understand my life. Askara, I was married in India to a wonderful woman, my cousin Minoo. I have wanted to tell you about her so many times, but things got in the way. I came to love her very much. Ours was an arranged marriage. We were promised by our parents, who were best friends, from the time we were children. They were convinced we were a good match. We grew to be."

Askara raked her front teeth over her bottom lip, nestled into Darian's warm chest, stroked the side of his face, and said, "Okay. Tell me. I want to know about your life."

Darian began to tell the story he kept hidden, locked away, the one he could no longer contain. He said to Askara as a boy he had played with Minoo at celebrations, weddings, and when her parents came to visit. He found Minoo, several years his junior, fun. She liked kickball, flying kites, and riding bicycles; most girls did not. She was a plump girl with long black hair pulled back from her face in thick braids that Darian yanked until she gave him candy, *lollies*.

When she grew tall and thin, she reminded him of a young willow tree. That's when he stopped speaking to her. He could think of nothing to say. She would not look at him, much less smile. Darian grew to dislike her, but he watched her—when her friends were not watching him—and wondered what had happened. Her rounded face had disappeared. He wasn't sure what he saw in its place, something different and alarming, something he couldn't pinpoint. He avoided her for a couple of years. After all, he was a *mature* teenager, and she, a kid.

In time Minoo became hard to overlook. With high cheekbones, a huge smile, and almond-shaped black eyes, she became a younger version of her mother, Darian's favorite auntie. Minoo was a fourth cousin, not a first, he explained to Askara, and in Indian society, all adults are called aunties and uncles. Askara replied she knew that; after all, her dad had relatives who visited. But Minoo's mother was his favorite auntie and always had been. Minoo sparked with electricity, he recalled, just like her mother. Her eyes seemed to generate their own light, like her mother's. Still, Minoo ignored him, so to lessen the snub, he told himself she was gangly, awkward, and stupid.

When Minoo turned fifteen, she disappeared. Her father, a civil engineer, took a post near Darjeeling and sent Minoo off to convent boarding school in Dehradun. She wrote to him occasionally, not spontaneous letters, but dutiful ones, a cousin-sister's effort prompted by her mother. Over time, her correspondence changed to friendly, chatty letters about her school: how bad the food was; how in winter they had to take cold showers when the hot water geyser broke, which was as bad as getting shocked by one; and how she loved English literature, especially the Romantic Period poets. She began to sign the letters, *your loving cousin-sister Minoo*. Darian felt that phrase made the gray cold of England bearable.

Askara squirmed in Darian's arms. Pulling Askara closer, Darian explained his feelings. Askara was the first person since Minoo he genuinely cared for. He had realized what he had said about needing to protect Askara was because of what had happened to Minoo. Askara told him she was not squirming because she was jealous; at least she didn't think so, but by comparison, her love life had been shallow, plagued by poor judgment and failed relationships. Hearing his story made her feel superficial. Askara focused on Darian's words again and relaxed in his arms to imagine what his and Minoo's life had been.

To celebrate Minoo's twentieth birthday, the extended families gathered in Hyderabad for a grand reunion. Minoo had completed her undergraduate degree in English, Darian, his doctorate at Oxford. Darian was busy sending out job applications in London because the professor's pay was much higher than in India, and he had come to love the city. Just two days before the family reunion, his father told Darian he intended to announce his son's engagement to Minoo at the gathering. Darian was stunned; he had no idea the four parents had been planning this while he was studying—and dating—in London. He had decided he wanted a love marriage. He liked the Western idea of falling in love with someone and not accepting a woman—even his childhood friend—because his parents had chosen her. He told his father he had thought about an arranged marriage and decided he didn't want to marry that way.

His father's reaction floored him. He had never seen his father move so fast. He stood up, slammed the teak chair into the study wall, and in two quick strides, stared into Darian's face. Darian could feel the heat coming off him. He wondered if his father intended to slap him. His father was so furious and yelled two inches from his face: You will marry Minoo. We made this promise to our friends. Your mother and I have waited for you two to complete your educations. Your marriage is not current news, son. You have known this all your life, so has Minoo. You do not have to marry today, but we will announce it at the family gathering. Life is busy. Time flies. The wedding can be in December, or in March, your choice.

Darian had never contradicted his father. He saw the shock on his face when he did. He explained with all due respect that he did not want an arranged marriage. He had been abroad and thought differently now. He wanted a love marriage. Love marriage, ha, his father snorted, a stupid Western concept. Look how many of them fail! You are not a Westerner, son. But we are a chaste Parsi family, a good family, and we have expectations. If Parsis do not secure bonds with one another through marriage, we as a people will perish. We will exist no more. Fulfill your duty, son. Marriage is not, as Westerners think, a thing that can be taken lightly and dispensed with easily when it becomes inconvenient. Marriage is a sacrifice of one soul to another, a commitment, a discipline not to be taken on emotions alone. That is why we chose a girl we knew so well, one we could see would be well-suited to you, spiritually and mentally. Love will come to your union, he assured Darian.

Darian realized from the pain and disappointment in his father's eyes that the battle wasn't worth fighting. Darian could not and would not jeopardize his relationship with his parents, so he consented. He shrugged and told his father: You win.

At the reunion, Darian made an excuse to go to the car to get something. He considered driving off but knew that would be the coward's way. Walking back in, Darian glanced around the large veranda full of women in fancy saris but saw no one who resembled Minoo. For a minute, he wondered if she had felt like he did and bolted. Then he heard his father's deep voice.

His parents approached with a young woman sandwiched between them. She towered over his mother and came chin high to his father. Darian did not recognize her. The woman had short hair tipped in purple that fell in soft curls around her face, large gold hoop earrings, and purple nail polish. She smiled. Her face lit up. Minoo? Darian asked. She extended her hand and said, Darian, has it been so long? You look more British than Indian. Darian's father, not missing a beat, replied he could change that when Darian settles in India. His mother shot her husband a disapproving look and grabbed Minoo's hand, saying, come, *Beta*, let's show you to the aunties.

Darian watched his mother and Minoo disappear into the crowd of women at the far end of the veranda. When his father asked, son, what do you think, Darian replied he was dumbfounded. He saw in Minoo a modern woman who also embodied the grace of her culture. She glowed. He asked if Minoo knew about the announcement. Of course, his father replied. Darian continued watching Minoo exchange pleasantries with the women. She positioned herself for a full view of the veranda where Darian mingled with the men. After that meeting, Darian and Minoo spent days together, going to restaurants, meeting relatives, and falling in love.

His father described their March wedding ceremony as *the show of a lifetime, the only show worth the effort.* Shortly after, Darian got a letter of acceptance for a teaching job from the University of London. When they left India, Darian looked at his father and saw the sadness even his brigadier uniform could not shore up, his crisp trousers slumped at the hem, his arms dangled like useless ropes. His father had always believed Darian would join the family business, but now his only son and his new daughter-in-law Minoo were to live in London. His father complained he wouldn't get to know the pleasure of children playing at his feet.

He enjoyed teaching at the university, and Minoo landed a journalist job with the *Daily Times*. Minoo quickly rose in the ranks, from food reviews to politics. Times were good. They lived in a small flat in northwest London, not far from Hampstead Heath. They were happy. On long summer evenings, they would stroll on Parliament Hill. They returned to India every year to visit family who would greet them with: When will you have children? You're not growing any younger.

Children were a touchy subject that Minoo and Darian argued about. Minoo wanted to wait. Darian did not. She preferred to establish her reputation as a serious journalist before having babies. He would have been pleased to come home to someone calling him Papa.

But five years into their marriage, on a beautiful warm midsummer evening, Darian was home alone, waiting for Minoo so that they could walk Parliament Hill. She was in the Theatre District having tea at a street café after work when a car bomb exploded. Bricks, glass, and mortar catapulted in all directions. Rescue workers found Minoo's body under the debris.

Darian's parents and Minoo's flew to London the following morning. They escorted Minoo home to India for a Parsi burial in a Tower of Silence. Darian was a widower at thirty-one. Minoo was only twenty-seven."

"I didn't return to England after the funeral. I stayed in India and wallowed in grief for many months. I didn't go out. I didn't see anyone other than my and Minoo's parents. I am sure my father pressured his brothers to hire me to get me out of the house. I would have never guessed a political science professor would do well at business, but I did. Work saved me. No dearth of women tried to comfort me, but rather than being attracted to them, I resented them for their sympathy. No woman has meant anything to me... until you, Askara. From the moment I saw you resting on the stones at the Oracle of Delphi, I knew."

"What?"

"I would do anything to protect you, to love you."

"Darian, I'm so sorry. I'm not the best in intimate relationships. I blow up, get offended, and scared, but I want this to work. I want it very much. Thank you for coming to Sudan to help me. Thank you for telling me about your life. I understand now that I misread you. Tonight, my heart feels heavy yet light, like a buoy in water. I want you close to me. I need you."

Much later, Askara called for room service to bring tea and sandwiches. Sipping tea, she said, "I have a story to tell you and something to show you. Be open-minded, okay? I need to fill in the background."

Askara recounted her journey with Sara through northern Kenya to Ethiopia, the coup at Jubilee Palace, and the events that made her and Sara flee to Asmara and then to Sudan. Darian listened thoughtfully, making her repeat parts of the story as if he were visualizing the sequence in detail, every person and place.

"Where's that cup now?

"In my pack," she said, pointing across the room.

"You carried it everywhere with you?"

"What else could I do?"

"I thought you would have stored it somewhere, an airport locker, a hotel safe, anything. God, it's worth a fortune, at least to Selassie."

"It's ancient but not a looker. The bronze is worn in places." Askara faltered and picked her words carefully, "The value is, well, beyond the object," she said and withdrew the unpretentious cup from her pack. A warm glow radiated in the dim room.

Darian exclaimed, "What's going on?"

"I have to explain before you hold it. Unusual things happen." She put the cup down on the bedcover. "I've had odd sensations, like, well, visions when I've held it. You may, too. The glow thing, that's new."

Darian sat in numbed silence, exhaling slowly. Darian touched the cup but pulled his fingers back. After several moments of silence, he spoke. "What do you know about Zoroastrianism, Askara?"

"I know it's your religion, and Sir Alexander mentioned it."

"This cup…well, there are coincidences, Askara. Our prophet Zarathustra, Zoroaster to the Western world, lived in ancient Iran. Fire is holy to us. Askara, this is alarming because I heard stories told by my mother's mother, the grandmother I mentioned, the one I was so fond of, about a sacred cup. One summer night, we were looking at the stars. In India, you pull your *charpoy*, your bed, out onto the roof on hot nights. I was restless and irritable, so my grandmother told me a story about a small boy and a cup to get me to fall asleep. I can see her pulling her white *dupatta* scarf up over her head. She pointed up at the stars. I remember there were millions of tiny points of light splattered across the black sky. I'll tell her story as well as I can remember it."

Once there was a poor peasant boy with a noble heart. He worked all day in the fields to help his mother. His father had died in a flood, leaving the young mother alone to care for the boy. As soon as he was able, the boy began working at any tasks the villagers gave him, tending goats, threshing wheat, gathering herbs, anything. His mother also worked extremely hard in the wheat fields, sowing, carrying heavy bundles, harvesting, and threshing.

One day when he was walking into the village with a sack of wheat to grind into flour, he saw an old man lying on the dirt path, weak from starvation. The boy poured water into his mouth and helped him to a shade tree. The man asked, what is your name and what do you do? The boy replied I care for my mother doing many kinds of work. We are poor.

The boy led the old man back to their hut, a simple structure of sticks and woven grasses, and laid him on a cloth on the grass-mat floor, telling him to rest. The boy returned to the village, exchanged his sack of wheat berries for ground flour, and returned to the hut.

The man lived with the boy and his mother for three months. The boy and his mother worked extra hard to feed him, but they never complained. One day the old man said he had to leave to continue his pilgrimage to a holy temple far to the north. He promised to return and repay them for their kindness.

Months passed into years. The old man did not return, and the boy grew up honest and strong. He worked long days, and in the evenings, he went to listen to the village priest teach the ancient wisdoms. One particularly hot summer evening, after the harvest was in, the old man returned to visit the young man and his mother. He presented them with a small bronze cup saying, son, your kindness to me was a test. God found you worthy of an important task. To the west, there comes a Teacher of Truth. The brightest star on the horizon points to where he will be born. To herald his arrival, you must go by camel and deliver this blessed present, this small cup. His mother will understand the significance. He pointed up to the starry sky and told the young man to follow the star to his destination, many sunsets away, and along the path, two others would join him. Upon delivering the cup, he would receive a great blessing for him and his mother.

Without questioning, the young man set out to deliver the cup. He followed the bright star. Two men joined him with their camels, and the three rode to the child's birthplace to offer their gifts. He returned home to his mother, and from that day forward, he and his mother wanted for nothing. People sought his wise counsel and gave him gifts of wheat, fruit, and goat milk. Whenever he or his mother needed something, the thing would come to them. People from near and far revered him for his spiritual knowledge. They called him *Magi*, priest.

"ASKARA, WHAT DO YOU MAKE OF THAT STORY GRANDMOTHER told me?"

"I'm not sure."

"The gift—that cup—was taken by Zoroastrian priests, Magi, to the Christ child. Could this be *the same* cup? Is that why Selassie prized it so much? If so, this would be the most valued cup in the history of the world...if the story's true and the cup's real. It seems unlikely the emperor of Ethiopia would own it, though."

"Darian, come on. That's too far out even for me. There's no mention of a cup in the Bible, myrrh, yes, frankincense, yes, but a cup, no."

"Agreed, but it's an interesting premise. I think, in India, we look at holy men in a different way, even Jesus. Some people in India say Jesus traveled around India and received the blessings of many great rishis in his day. He studied ancient wisdoms. In Tibet, they say he wore saffron robes like a monk. I do see parallels between Zarathustra's teachings and Jesus' teachings, but maybe all great spiritual teachers share the same teachings. Why not? Different times, different places but the same message. The Magi, the wise men who came to Jesus's birthplace, were Zoroastrian priests."

"Wait a minute," Askara said, placing her hand on Darian's forearm. "You actually think your grandmother's story could be real?"

"I haven't thought of that story since my childhood. I considered it a bedtime story. Why did I recall it? What if this small, bronze cup did belong to Zarathustra, just as Selassie thought? The cup could have resurfaced in history for Jesus's birth. Many people could have possessed it along the way. If they could have, then even the current descendant of the King of Solomon and the Queen of Sheba, Emperor Haile Selassie of Ethiopia, could have possessed it."

"You are not the pragmatic man I met in Greece. You seem willing to believe that things of great value could become lost and resurface periodically."

"Yes, I imagine as a buyer of jewelry and artifacts, you could give me an example of valuable ancient things you have seen. But can you establish provenance for every item?"

"No. Many times valuable jewelry goes missing only to be found again in a different era with a new owner. Black market, politics, an excavation, floods, earthquakes, many factors come into play. Look at all the art the Jews owned in Europe that the Nazis seized. Many of those pieces resurfaced later in private collections."

"So? Zarathustra composed the *Gathas*, holy poems. They survived. We Parsis read them like you read the bible. Why not an object? If words can survive thousands of years, metal objects can also, in fact, more easily if they are not melted down for warfare."

Askara felt relieved that Darian believed her. She hesitated but handed the cup to him carefully and watched him trace the curves and hollows in the delicate rise and fall of the form. "Close your eyes and see if the cup shows you anything," she said.

Darian closed his eyes. Night rushed past him. He felt his body pressed wafer-thin into folds of darkness. He flowed like water, rushing, filling every space, collapsing, and expanding in darkness. From the roar of nothing came the music. Each note of the plucked strings pulsated indigo to bluish-white.

Darian ran. His body ached with exertion; his breath flew just beyond reach. He bolted toward a temple. Spooked cattle scattered. Dust turned the blue sky brown as Darian rushed up weathered stone steps. An elderly man ran across cracked, dry earth, tufts of yellowed grass collapsing beneath his feet, pulling a girl with him. Darian chased after them shouting, "Wait! It is I, Dastur." The holy man glanced behind and slowed to a stop. The girl bent over her knees, choking on the dust. "Respected One, what is it? Where are you taking Asha?"

"Ruffians attacked the temple. I feared for our lives. I thought you one of them, Dastur."

"I saw a cloud of dust, cattle stampeding. They stole some of them. But you and Asha are safe. That is all that matters."

The holy man replied, "God Vohu Manah will protect the cattle. Judgment shall come to the wicked, and the Just shall shelter in the pasture of Truth and Good Purpose. Those demons of bad purpose by their hateful acts condemn themselves. So be it." He looked at Asha, wide-eyed and trembling. "Daughter, be not afraid. My worry was for you, not the cattle."

The thin sixteen-year-old looked up at the elderly man. "Respected One, I fear nothing in your presence." She moved closer, her delicate hand taking his. He brushed the hair back from her face. She smiled at the Respected One.

"Dastur," he said, holding him with a fixed gaze, "You have a duty to perform."

"Anything you wish."

"Hear me well. Remember my words long after I am gone from this world of matter. Across time these words shall find you. When they do, obey."

"Yes, Respected One."

"This girl, Asha, given to me as a daughter, is very dear to my heart. She has many trials and joys to experience before she can sit with me in the pasture of Ahura Mazda. Your destiny, Dastur, is to protect her. Her destiny, she will learn in time as a protector of the cup. You share great love. There will be long periods of separation, yet your purpose remains. The work of Ahura Mazda prevails even in the darkest times. Hear my words."

The elderly holy man pulled a small bronze cup from the lining of his robe. The cup glowed as if the sun rose in its center. "Of the best things in existence, created with truth by Ahura Mazda, our God of Good Purpose, was his daughter, Devotion of Good Action. She reminds us of the power of virtuous thought and deed. To the Evil One, I say be gone, deceive not my daughter, nor impede her on her journey. For she speaks for the goodness in us all. Instruct her through Truth. Bless Dastur, so he may aid her when the Evil One comes to challenge them." The holy man looked down into Asha's eyes. "The cup's power and enduring strength to uphold Truth must be protected. As a foe of the Deceiver and a supporter of the Just, this cup symbolizes the struggle of Light and Dark inherent in every human soul. It attracts and repels, saves, and destroys. It amplifies the tendencies of its owner. Let the power of the cup guide us in devotion to Good Action, now and forever. I will be ever near you."

Asha bowed her head. "Yes, Respected One. How will I know you are near? Will we see each other like we do now?"

"No, at times, your eyes will be cloudy. You will have to see with your heart. You will have to remember me and call on me. I am always near, but you will fail to see. Daughter, there will be hardship in your life, as well as times of joy, such is the nature of human life, but yours will differ from others. Once the cup chose you, your life stepped out of the normal cycle. Your life is no longer your own. You must be committed to right action, now and forever. The cup follows laws of nature too challenging to explain to you, but every action has an equal reaction. You will learn what the cup requires of you. You have been the protector of the cup earlier, and you will be again, Asha. For your welfare, devote yourself to Good Action.

"And you, Dastur, guard with mighty power and abiding strength this mission of Truth. Defeat the Defiler, and I shall meet you at the appointed time on the Chinvat Bridge to escort you across to the Creator of Life. Your enemies shall forever reside in the House of the Lie."

DARIAN FELT HIS BODY STRETCH AND CONTORT. HE SPED down tunnels littered with vision fragments caught in crystalline prisms. His head slammed into a wall. His eyes flew open. He saw cattle run across the wall, and like city lights fading at dawn, they disappeared.

Darian struggled to speak. "Askara, did you see that?"

"No. I felt relaxed, but I saw nothing."

"I had a vision," Darian said and shoved the glowing cup away from him, "of you as a teenager with a holy man, our teacher. I do not know what you are destined to do with this cup, but I know this cup is powerful. I am sworn from that time to protect you...and you the cup. If these visions weren't so clear, I'd say we're both crazy, but we're not."

Askara slipped her hand into Darian's. "Thank you for coming. Now you know how I feel. I understand the rightness of protecting this cup. But I am scared. What's the cup trying to do, and why? Did your vision tell you? People I have never seen hunt me. Selassie sits locked in prison, or worse. The world's become a sinister place. We need to find a refuge for the cup, a place for it to exist in neutrality, away from the world. I think the cup wanted to leave Emperor Selassie, but I don't think it wants to stay with me, or with you."

"I'm duty-bound from ages past to help you," Darian said, stroking Askara's hair. "We'll figure this out. We need to focus on being normal, like husband and wife tourists. Turn the lights on. Let's dress, go out, and act normal." He lifted a small box and a big package from his suitcase and placed them on her lap. Askara smiled and unwrapped an emerald-green cotton salwar kameez suit stitched with golden embroidery.

"Beautiful. The cotton's so soft! Thank you."

"You can go incognito…my North Indian wife with a wheatish complexion."

"Should I cut my hair?"

Darian stroked her hair. "That would be a crime but wrap it in a bun. You will be my *pucca* Indian wife, who doesn't talk much. They are looking for an American in jeans."

"Right. Traveling with an Australian woman with sky blue eyes."

He handed Askara a small velveteen-lined jewelry box. She lifted the pendant cabochon of deep blue lapis lazuli circled by irregular white pearls on a gold link chain.

"Wow! I love it. Extraordinary work. The links are embossed with a mango swirl design."

"I got lucky. I told a jeweler friend in Bombay to notify me if any family jewelry from a maharajah's house, or a noble family, came through his shop for sale. With times as they are, many royals sell off items to pay the taxes on their estates. They would rather retain land than jewelry. Anyway, this piece came from Rajasthan. Supposedly a great-grandfather had won the stone in a polo match from someone who had worked on excavations in Egypt. He had the stone set for his wife. When the granddaughter inherited it, she found it old-fashioned. She asked the jeweler to sell it for her. It seems she feared a curse followed it like the King Tut jewelry."

"You mean this could have been a temple stone?"

"Possibly. My jeweler friend said lapis lazuli is reputed to be a very spiritual stone and, if correctly used, brings blessings to its wearer. After I bought it, I took the necklace to have it blessed by a temple priest. Now my Askara is blessed and protected." Darian clasped the pendant around Askara's neck. "The jeweler said to wear it all the time, except when you shower. Pearls grow more lustrous when worn next to the skin, he said, but they don't like soap. It dulls them."

"It's so wonderful," Askara said, admiring it in the mirror. She gave Darian a robust hug and a lingering kiss. "Darian, I feel safe with you here. Thank you for coming, for helping me, and for not thinking I'm nuts."

"Askara, we're in this together. And I'm hungry. Starving. Shall we go down for dinner? The kitchen closes in a few minutes."

"Sure. At dinner, I want to tell you about the Gezira Scheme. They produce fine quality cotton. Normal conversation...that's what we need."

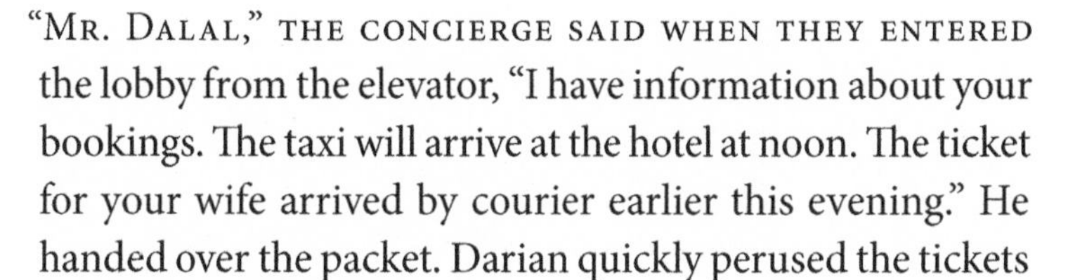

"Mr. Dalal," the concierge said when they entered the lobby from the elevator, "I have information about your bookings. The taxi will arrive at the hotel at noon. The ticket for your wife arrived by courier earlier this evening." He handed over the packet. Darian quickly perused the tickets and thanked him with a tip.

“Darian, I should contact Mr. Ramsey and let him know the jewelry purchase fell through. He’ll be pissed off. I don’t want to be fired, so I’ll say I made another contact for estate jewelry in India—not exactly lying—and I’ll return soon, two weeks max.”

“If that’s what you want. We will telex in the morning. Although I’m not sure what *not exactly lying* means.”

“It means saving my skin but doing no harm.”

“I do have contacts in India for jewelry. At least that is true. There’s one thing I’d like to do before we leave. I want to see the confluence of the Niles. I will never be back to Khartoum, and I would regret not having done it.”

“Don’t sound so fatalistic,” Askara said. “Sudan’s interesting. We’ll come back for a pleasure trip.”

CHAPTER FOURTEEN

Departing Khartoum

The Khartoum International airport, teeming with people, made Askara's skin crawl. She hoped Darian's unusual plan would work. He stowed the cup in his carry-on bag rather than risk the less than reliable baggage department. It fit nicely into his toiletries with his brush and shaving soap. Askara realized her anxiety stemmed from her attachment to the cup. She wanted to feel the connection it conveyed to something grander than her normal life. She pushed to the back of her mind the legendary importance of the cup, but now at the airport, the seriousness of her situation again hit her like a train. Terror seeped into her heart.

She trusted Darian and herself, but no one else. The immensity of the responsibility frightened her. What she once considered a conveyor of perception, like a Ouija Board parlor game, had become a deadly trial. She looked over her shoulder, repeatedly, watching everyone around her: menacing adults, scary children. The more she watched, the more they stared at her. She could hardly stand still in the check-in line. She hopped on one foot then the other, tiny steps like she was warming for a sprint. One hour before departure, too long, she thought. Anything could happen.

They approached the ticket agent. He looked over their passports, inspected their visas, and crosschecked them with their tickets. He looked across the counter, tipped his head down to peer over his half-frame glasses, and said in staccato English, "Ticket for madam, one name. Passport, visa, another name."

Darian spoke up, "Yes. Correct. We were just married. She will change her passport name when we're home in India."

"Change name later?" the clerk repeated with a puzzled look.

"Yes. My wife will take an Indian passport, like mine, in our married name: Dalal." He pointed to his worn passport.

"American?"

"Yes. My wife is an American. May we go now?"

"No, go." The clerk motioned for another man to walk over to his station. He spoke in Arabic to him and turned back to the couple. "How long been Sudan?"

Darian pointed to his visa. "Two days." Darian said nothing more. Askara turned to check the agitated line of passengers behind them.

"You," the immigration clerk said, pointing at Askara, "from Ethiopia, come?"

That was the last bit of information Askara wanted to be proclaimed in public. She edged up to his counter, leaned forward, and hissed, "Yes."

"Come how Sudan?"

"Teseney," she said exasperated.

The clerk shifted his footing and motioned with an aggressive wave of his hand for an additional agent. With harsh Arabic words, he silenced the grumbling line. Askara glanced back to see tense faces boring a hole through her. She thought she recognized one man's angular face, his thick features, and eyes hidden by his sloped forehead. But where had she seen that face before? She turned back to the clerk. When his manager reached them, he rattled away in an agitated manner.

The manager gathered their passports and said, "Follow me. Bring bags."

Askara saw the sloped-forehead man leap forward in the line. The crowd shoved him back. The ticket agent rebuffed him loudly in Arabic. Whatever he said hushed the others in the queue. The man darted toward the manager, who was leading the couple away. Security guards grabbed him by the shirt. In a heated shouting match, they dragged him to the back of the line.

The manager escorted Darian and Askara into a room flanked by two guards with guns. Seated behind a small desk, an official in a white galabieh and turban stood up to greet them. The manager explained something in Arabic before the official motioned for Darian and Askara to sit. The manager handed over their passports and tickets and stepped aside, retreating to a corner.

Darian blurted out, "Sir, what's the problem here? We have a flight to Cairo shortly."

The man replied calmly in English, "I am sorry, sir, madam, for this inconvenience. It is very confusing, two names for one lady. Your wife?"

"Yes."

"She has not your name in her passport?" he asked as he fumbled through pages of Askara's worn, dull green passport, full of visa stamps from various countries.

"No. We recently married. My wife is an American. In the United States, women go by their family name, or by their married name. She goes by both. The passport has her family name. We were not married when she got that passport. See, it is eight years old."

"Ticket in married name?"

"Yes."

"Why not passport name to match?"

"I forgot to tell the hotel concierge when I asked him to purchase the tickets. He went by how we signed in at the hotel."

Askara spoke up. "The next passport will be in my married name, Dalal, not my name, Timlen."

The man looked at her, expressionless. "American."

Darian snapped, "Look. You cannot detain us. We have valid papers and tickets!"

"We detain you if we want," the official countered. Darian noted the title on his badge: Chief Inspection Officer.

"Sir, Chief Inspection Officer, with all due respect, we've done nothing wrong," Darian replied and stood up so fast his chair fell back and hit the wall.

The man jumped up to face him, purposely showing the gun strapped to his waist. "Sir, there was an attempted coup d'état in Ethiopia. Sudan is on high alert."

"What does that have to do with us?"

"Two foreign nuns crossed border at Teseney, where your wife entered Sudan. There was a gun battle. Border guard said nuns caused it. In confusion, the nuns entered Sudan."

"So? That is no reason to hold my wife and me. Surely you have the nuns' names in your records. My wife is no nun. She's married to me."

The man looked perplexed. He didn't answer.

"I want to contact the American and the Indian Embassies," Darian hissed. "Get them on the phone. You have no legal right to detain us."

Askara, taken aback by Darian's aggression, added. "Yes, I want to talk to my American Embassy immediately!"

"Please. We settle this here."

"Very well then," Darian growled. "Settle it! Come out with it, man. What do you want? Baksheesh?"

"No, sir!" the official replied indignantly. "We, Sudanese, do not take bribes."

"What?" Darian said. Askara saw he was disgusted, biting his lower lip.

"I must examine your bags. A precious item went missing in the coup. The government of Ethiopia wants it back."

Darian continued, "Check our bags then. Quickly. I demand our telephone calls. You are holding innocent foreigners illegally. Our governments will deal with you on this! I am from the Gandhi family. This is an insult!"

The man's eyes widened. "Madam, why you entered Teseney?"

"I covered a festival…for National Geographic. I'm, um, a photojournalist."

"Tribal Dance Celebration? Myself, I have attended. Very good. I was born in the area. I attend many times. My sister danced last year." The officer searched Askara's backpack, blushing when his hand caught in her lace panties at the bottom of the pack and slid the bag along the dusty tabletop for her to repack.

"Here, let me help you," Darian said and dumped the contents of his carry-on bag onto the table. The items hit the table and spread out—a clean undershirt and underwear, alarm clock, socks, hairbrush, shaving cream in an old container, razor, and packs of cigarettes. "There you have it. Do you smoke? Here, take these," he said and tossed the cigarette packs toward the officer. They were for the hotel desk clerk, a tip for excellent service, but I couldn't find him," The officer smiled and stuffed the packs into pockets of his galabieh. Darian checked his watch: "We have ten minutes before our plane departs."

"No gold?" he asked and slit the lining of the suitcase.

"Just what I have on." Darian shouted, "You ruined my bag."

The officer checked his watch and sat down to light a cigarette, tapping the table with four fingers. Darian withdrew his wallet, slipped four Sudanese hundred-pound notes to the man, and began replacing his belongings in his carry-on bag. The Chief Inspection Officer quickly stamped their papers, called to the guards in Arabic, and waved them and the manager out of his office.

Security guards escorted them to the door leading down the stairway to the runway. Darian and Askara could see the metal stairs at the front of the plane were still in place.

"Thank God," Askara whispered, "We're almost out of here."

Two men ripped through the flow of passengers behind them. The crowd split. Askara turned to see the sloped-forehead man sail through the air at her. He wrenched the pack off her shoulder. She stumbled, but Darian caught her. The men bolted down the stairs, charged out the door past the airport agent, and headed toward the field where a private plane was taxing. Security guards shoved people out of the way, carving a path through them, and chased the men, guns raised. The ground crew waved directional flags and motioned for the passengers to hurry aboard. Everyone trotted up the metal stairs. The ground crew pushed the stairway ramp to the side, and the doors closed.

Darian clamped down on Askara's hand, shoved their tickets toward the steward, who pointed the direction to walk, and they pushed down the narrow aisle. When they found their seats and collapsed, out of breath, the plane began moving. A stewardess instructed the passengers to quickly stow their bags and secure their belts for immediate takeoff. The plane taxied into position. In the field on the right side of the runway, four airport guards stood over a face-down body while the other man kneeled with a gun pointed at his head.

Askara dug her nails into Darian's hand. He turned to her and said in a pseudo-calming voice, "You look lovely in your lapis necklace, wife. Glad you're wearing it. Sticky fingers may have lifted it, had it been in the bag. Relax now."

Askara fought back tears. Her heart fluttered like a hummingbird's wings as flight regulations in Arabic, French, Italian, and English drowned the nervous chatter of passengers. She leaned forward and grabbed the airsickness bag to breathe into it. After several minutes, she leaned back in her seat.

"He didn't recognize it, Darian. He didn't know what he saw."

"Had no idea, just an old shaving cup."

Resting on Darian's shoulder, Askara slept and dreamed of birds flying high on favorable winds in a cloudless sky, cutting large pieces of blue that fell like flower petals to the ground. They spiraled ever higher until they faded from sight.

CHAPTER FIFTEEN

Bombay Revelation

Bombay was overwhelming, Askara thought. The weight of people and buildings seemed too much for the reclaimed land to support. Traffic noise—crowded streets, screeching brakes, grinding diesel engines, shouting street vendors, and constant jackhammering—created a discordant symphony, the sounds of progress and demise. Askara knew she was no match for this city. Bombay made her feel more fragile, not less.

The cement absorbed the fierce Indian sun and radiated heat at night, slightly modified by the Arabian Sea breeze. In Darian's area, Juhu Beach, trees and vegetation softened the effect, but Askara longed for the cooling San Francisco Bay fog. She missed home. Even here, with Darian, a feeling of doom shadowed her. She wanted to rest and forget, but she could not.

Askara's imagination spun out, attributing ill-intent to every person who looked her way. She watched hands for guns, knives, bombs. She understood that the shaky feeling haunting her, the queasiness in her stomach, and the fear of strangers had started that night in Mombasa when she met Nagali. The person looking back at her in the mirror no longer had radiant brown eyes. Her eyes, dulled by distrust, told the story that no one, not even Askara, could listen to. She wondered if Darian sensed her desperation? She knew she was no longer the person he had met at the Oracle of Delphi, who was strong, young, and overconfident. He must perceive that. She understood from experience that weakness in a partner becomes a burden. Darian's goodness could carry him for a long while. But what then? Everyone burns out sooner or later, she knew.

From Darian's apartment, Askara saw an eclipsed view of the sea through interlaced trees and asked Darian to take her on a stroll. They walked past blocks of flats—multi-story citadels with small balconies, manicured yards, and wrought iron compound walls—that opened directly onto the beach. Juhu Beach, unlike the Indian Ocean beach at Mombasa with white-flour sand and swaying palm trees, belonged to a large, crowded city. The strip of dingy yellow sand held back the Indian Ocean on one side, with the help of a row of trees, and looming high-rises on the other. Children cavorted at the water's edge. Hindu women with damp saris clinging to their calves braved the gentle waves just far enough to say their prayers and release marigold garlands. Down the beach, near a five-star hotel, a small carnival offered pony rides on thin, scruffy animals, games, and amusement rides.

Usually, Askara enjoyed what a place offered, but Bombay, she decided, must grow on a person. The charm must come with familiarity, she assumed. To her, Bombay felt ominous. She slipped her hand into Darian's as they walked the beach, aware that Indian couples rarely showed public affection, but she needed him close.

"You will learn to love Bombay. Everyone does; it's the commercial hub of India, very cosmopolitan. If you can get it, or do it, in India, Bombay's the place. Plus, there's Bollywood, our Hollywood. In India, stars are modern-day gods and goddesses to their adoring public."

"Bombay has a different feel from other cities," Askara said with care, knowing how much Darian loved Bombay. "How long have you lived here?"

"Six years. In Juhu, two. It took time to book my flat. Here you buy a flat before the building construction starts. It seems the building process goes on forever. Inevitably there are hassles about adulterated cement, unavailable materials, delays in water connections, and on-and-on. A lot of money greases hands, even to get utilities connected. The irony is all the while the value of the apartment escalates. Space is limited. An apartment doubles in value before the owner even takes possession. Where else does real estate do that? Look. Over there, as far as you can see, is landfill. Bombay is reclaimed from the sea as the demand for housing grows. Sometimes I think the city will sink under the weight of it."

"How funny, I had thought the same thing. Is it unusual to have a flat to yourself, to live alone?"

"Yes, in my building-society, everyone has a family. It's unusual for a man like me not to have a wife, two or three children, maybe in-laws, all living under one roof."

"In a one-bedroom flat?"

"Yes…small families. A mother, father, two children. The living room can convert at night into a bedroom. Look at us in Bombay, in India, for that matter. We are conditioned to living in proximity. We feel connected, protected, valued. An extended family might have ten people living together in a space Americans would consider cramped for three. But if you're rich, you live like royalty here; your house is a palace. India's a different world that takes getting used to, but there is no place like it. India becomes part of your soul. India is the lover that enchants you and pulls you to the center of her universe. When she whispers her name in your heart, you run, forgetting all else."

Askara looked at Darian. "And if I whisper my name in your heart?"

"I dropped everything to meet you in Khartoum, didn't I? You have whispered your name in my heart." Darian hugged Askara. "And how long have I known you?"

"When do we begin counting?"

They walked back to Darian's flat and greeted the guard sitting dutifully at the entrance. He pulled back the metal gate and saluted. Askara glanced at the cement compound wall topped by shards of jagged green glass. "Does everyone live like this?"

"If they can afford to." Darian pressed the elevator button for the third floor. "Shall we have lunch? I told Professor Doctor we would come around four o'clock for tea. He's my friend, the one I mentioned, the expert on the Gathas and Avestan texts of Zoroastrianism."

"Is that his real name, Professor Doctor?"

"Yes. Zoroastrians originally took their names from their professions, so he's a professor with the last name of Doctor."

"Do we take *it* with us?"

"Yes. The professor is my trusted friend. The company driver will pick us up."

"You don't have a car of your own?"

"No, I have the use of a company car and driver when I'm in Bombay. I hate driving in the city. No one drives himself if he can help it. You will see what I mean. I far prefer to pay a chap to battle the streets for me," Darian said with a laugh. "Driving is *not* a part of Bombay I love."

AFTER A HARROWING RIDE THROUGH CONGESTED STREETS and clogged roundabouts, the din of car horns still echoing in Askara's ears, they arrived at the tip of the peninsula, Nariman Point. Professor Doctor's house, an old, sprawling monster with wrap-around verandas and high ceilings, provided a calm oasis in Bombay's urban chaos. Huge broadleaf trees, alive with the chatter of birds, shielded the house from the blistering sun. A slight afternoon breeze blew in from the water, not enough to alleviate the heat, but a humming air conditioner in the main room helped.

Professor Doctor, an elderly scholar, greeted them. His gracious manner made Askara feel immediately welcome. Over afternoon tea, they talked like old friends. He explained he had retired from university life at seventy and now, ten years later, remained active in his study of ancient texts of Zoroastrianism, as well as that of other religions.

"How is it, Miss Askara, being half-Indian in such a grand country as the United States of America?" he said and took a sip of hot, sweet Darjeeling tea.

"I've never thought about it. I am what I am."

"Quite so, but how do others treat you? Do you experience discrimination?"

"Not that I am aware of. From my coloring, it's hard to place me. People think I'm Italian, or Greek, usually. In California, people of Mexican ancestry are my color, but I don't speak Spanish, so that's a giveaway."

"You are unmistakably Indian to me, in your features, only lighter...like a Kashmiri. Those are undoubtedly Indian eyes," the old man said and winked.

"Darian interrupted. "Sir, are you flirting?"

"Indeed, exactly. You can allow an old man to enjoy a pretty face and a kindly manner."

Darian said with mock severity, "Only if I'm present in the room."

The professor turned to him. "Son, would you go to the kitchen and order more tea from the servant? My cup appears empty." Darian stood to go. The professor laughed. "Dear boy, you must sharpen your skills. How do you expect to win this lovely creature, much less keep her?"

"By not bringing her to visit you, Professor. Obviously, a dangerous thing to do."

"I'm afraid that I am the least of your worries." The professor's face constricted. He looked at Askara. "My dear girl, you have stumbled into a hornet's nest, I believe. Darian informed me Sir Alexander Desta told you the cup is the emperor's prized possession."

"Yes."

"Did you happen to bring it along?"

Darian pulled the cup, still wrapped in a length of cotton, from his leather bag and handed it over. The professor slowly unwound the cloth and held the ancient bronze vessel in his hands, gazing at the surface design, rubbing the contours. His eyes closed. He remained silent for a few moments. Then he spoke slowly. "My dear, you certainly have gotten yourself into something. I'm afraid more than you can handle."

"What do you mean, sir?"

"This cup is beyond valuable...it's absolutely priceless. The people who want it, who know about its power, will not give up. They will pursue you to the ends of the earth and take it back by any means."

"Why do you say that?" Darian asked.

"Dear boy, I recognize this vessel from various accounts. Never would I have dreamed I would one day hold this cup. Have you held it?"

"Yes, sir."

"And did it talk to you? Did it show you things?"

Darian replied, "Yes, in a way, like seeing a dream."

"Exactly. That is how it works. This cup has a life of its own, a role to play, and the people who hold it are pawns in the game."

"Pawns for what?" Askara said, briefly distracted by sounds from the kitchen, metal pots clanging on tiles, pinging, and wobbling like spinning tops.

"The game of life. Pawns for the history of humankind. Pawns for the Divine." The professor watched the aged bronze glow bright like fire kissed by a breeze. "There are, and have been, from time immemorial, objects, physical objects, which embody spiritual truth. They are gifts from the gods to us poor humans; since we are so blinded, we no longer see the moving hand behind the motion, the essence in the object, the truth beyond illusion. Certain objects are teachers, precipitators of action, givers of reward, and agents of retribution. They provide experiences that ultimately shape our world, but not always peacefully, I'm afraid. They give us what we need to play out the grander scheme."

"What do you mean, sir?" Askara said, perched motionless on the edge of the large cushioned chair, leaning closer to the cup.

"The grander scheme? What is Real…what lies beyond this level of existence, this veil of illusion."

"Sorry, sir, I don't get it."

"My dear, we all have a mission here, no matter how small, from the street sweeper to the greatest ruler. We play parts that fit like a jigsaw puzzle. Each part depends on the other, no matter how awkward the perimeter may appear. We are honed and shaped to fit exactly into place in this puzzle of life, both giving and receiving to realize our ultimate nature, our Divine Nature."

Darian put down his teacup and looked at his friend. "What do you know *specifically* about this cup, Professor?"

Professor Doctor relaxed into his overstuffed chair, saying, "Certain things from my studies."

He laid the cup to the side, rubbing his hands, and started to explain. Ancient writings and modern texts maintain the cup was Zarathustra's prayer cup, but the written information many compiled came later, as there was no written record from the time, only oral history handed down from person to person in the form of legends. Zarathustra meditated upon it, thus imbuing the cup with tremendous power. According to Zarathustra's teachings, life was a battle between the Upholders of Truth and the Upholders of the Lie, the *Just One* in the first case, and the *Deceiver* in the second.

Professor Doctor picked up the Zoroastrian bible and read Yasna 34: "*...then we wish Thy fire, Lord, strong through Truth, very swift, mighty, to be of manifest help to Thy supporter, but of visible harm, O Mazda*—his name for the One God, the professor interjected—*with the forces in his hands, to Thy enemy... Truly, both wholeness and immortality are for Thy sustenance. Through the dominion of Good Purpose, Devotion together with Truth will make grow these two enduring powers.*"

Askara, perplexed, asked, "Can you explain that simply, sir?"

"Yes. This cup wields great power, to be used for good or evil, depending on who controls it at the time. It cares not which. It brings lessons with either, but the lessons differ."

"Good and Evil are rival twins, according to the teachings," he continued. "They set the stage. We, humans, play the game of life over and over and eventually hone our perimeters into perfect pieces of the divine puzzle. The twins represent the two sides of the same divine struggle and the two sides of each of us. Both allow opportunities for growth until, ultimately, we leave the struggle behind and realize The Divine. The cup that held holy fire has been referred to as the Cup of the Shining Sun in various texts. The fire element destroys and renews. It cannot be polluted as can earth, air, and water. Only fire purifies. But to what end?"

Darian repeated the name. "When I held the Cup of the Shining Sun, I saw a light glow like the rising sun."

"This cup has come into your lives by absolute purpose," the professor said. "There are no accidents."

"In my vision, I was shown that I had been the protector of the cup. But why?" Askara said, pushing tendrils of hair back from her damp forehead.

"You will find out. The cup will lead you, as it has done, to where it wants you to go."

"Why did Selassie have it?" Askara said.

The professor sighed and told them that accurate history is difficult to pinpoint at the best of times. But, from his research, Zarathustra lived around 630 B.C., according to ancient texts, and King Solomon possessed the cup earlier, about 900 B.C. Zarathustra inherited it after King Solomon's rule. The professor knew Selassie had obtained the cup just before his coronation in 1930 and found it no coincidence that Selassie descended from the royal lineage of King Solomon and the Queen of Sheba.

The professor concluded, "The cup chooses where its power manifests, and with whom."

"That's fascinating," Askara said. "After someone smuggled the cup into my pack, only hours later, a coup broke out, and the militant group took the emperor prisoner. Maybe the loss of the cup toppled his rule? If true, someone who knew about the cup's power used me to carry it out of the palace. Why me?"

"Someone wanted to change the tide of political history in that part of the world," the professor replied. "I have no idea why they targeted you, but possibly being a foreigner with a letter of introduction provided a suitable instance to carry out the theft. You, Miss Askara, appear to be an unwitting agent in the heist, a pawn. Allow me to sum up the cup's history. Possibly we can uncover a pattern that addresses your question."

Professor Doctor went on to say that he had found one account that placed the cup with Plato, who lived 428 to 347 B.C. And that Aristotle, Plato's prize student, believed Plato was Zarathustra reincarnated. Aristotle became tutor to the young Alexander the Great. And it was Aristotle himself who supposedly encouraged Alexander the Great to search for the legendary cup.

"Alexander must have been successful," he concluded. "After all, he conquered most of the known world by age thirty-one—India included—and died a year later in 323 B.C. Could he have conquered the known world with the power of the cup? Yes. Could he have died when someone stole it? Yes."

From the professor's research, the cup disappeared at that point, until it resurfaced at a pivotal time in history: the birth of Jesus. The professor recounted the biblical story of the nativity, reminding Askara that in The Gospel of Matthew in the Christian bible, wise men from the East came to honor the child's birth. The Three Wise Men were Magi.

The number three also may have referred to the number of gifts—gold, frankincense, and myrrh—usual gifts for royalty at that time, as frankincense and myrrh were used as wound salves and for holy incense. Ancient Ayurveda, traditional Indian medicine, still uses them in remedies, he added. Some scholars believe the Magi presented to Mary a cup filled with powders of those valuable tree saps, plus gold. Possibly the Magi brought healing medicine to the child's birth as a symbol for what lay before him, he conjectured.

"Miss Askara, you may have heard what some in India believe, that Jesus did not die on the cross. He lived to return to India, where he had studied with holy men in his so-called *lost years*. His grave is in Kashmir, where local followers of Islam revere him as a Muslim saint. Some records contend that a disciple brought the sacred cup to Axum in Ethiopia, an early center of Christianity, to preserve it."

"I had wanted to visit Axum and Lalibela to see the ruins, but the coup broke out in Ethiopia."

"Poor Selassie. No definitive news of his fate, I hear. But the faithful cup showed up in Jerusalem again, near the ruins of the ancient tomb of King Solomon. That was before the Crusades. A scribe recorded the cup in Jerusalem around 1096 A.D. when Godfrey of Bouillon, the Duke of Lorraine, took back Jerusalem as a Christian land. Scholars believe Godfrey knew the legend of the cup. He attacked Jerusalem to confiscate it. Confusion arises whether the duke sought Zarathustra's cup, The Cup of the Shining Sun, or the Holy Grail, or if the two were one and the same. The Crusades dragged on. Godfrey did become the first European ruler of the Holy Land.

"From that time forward, there was little mention of the cup until sources pointed to Napoleon Bonaparte as possessing a valuable artifact, a chalice of some sort. In 1872, some fifty years after Bonaparte's death, Italy invaded Ethiopia, scholars believe in search of the cup. No real mention of ownership showed up, to my knowledge. Ironically, when Emperor Haile Selassie came to power in 1930, film footage of the coronation events of the day showed him accepting the scepter of governance. A small cup with a wick and flame was barely discernible on a table in the background. Investigators contend Mussolini invaded Ethiopia in 1935, looking for the sacred cup. Some reports point to Hitler as having obtained the cup, not necessarily evidenced by historical documentation, but by his meteoric rise to power. Possibly, Selassie had lost it? Others conjecture that Hitler committed suicide upon losing the cup to the American General George Patton.

"Possibly you Americans possessed the cup when you bombed Nagasaki and Hiroshima three months after Hitler died? Certainly, that implied a reckless use of power, a type associated with the cup, depending on its owner. But here we are in 1974. The Ethiopian emperor is currently a prisoner in his own palace. A young American woman shows up at an elderly professor's house in India with one of the most sought-after prizes in history, evidently stolen from Selassie in a coup, and, oh, the trouble she brings."

"I'm so sorry, Professor. I had no idea. I'm terrified. I don't know what to do."

"You, my dear, are in a precarious situation at best. But as for our involvement, all of us, we had no choice. The cup chose us, not we the cup. We must act with great care to determine the most prudent course to follow."

"What course, sir?" Darian said, his voice stretched thin like galvanized wire.

"Well, as you understand, the cup's immense power, for good or evil, depends on who controls it. We must find a peaceful sanctuary, a spiritually neutral home for the cup. A place away from the dominance of any one person. Only the strongest can resist its lure. Look at Alexander the Great's example. In thirteen years, he conquered the known world, but Alexander died with his palms turned up, symbolizing even Alexander the Great goes without possessions, empty-handed when facing death. Alexander succumbed to the lust for power, as many have. Emperor Selassie certainly did much for Ethiopia, but even he became an autocrat in time. Who knows when faced with such power how strong he, or she, is? I certainly do not trust myself," the old man sighed. "Too many greater than I have fallen." He handed the cup to Askara. "Put it away."

"Surely, there are some," Darian said. "I believe the power could be used for good. It had been at times."

"Yes, undoubtedly, but the users for good haven't made history's headlines. Acts of goodness rarely do. My suggestion? Take it to the north, to the Himalayan foothills. A spiritual society known for The Truth flourishes there. I knew their holy man long ago when he was a professor at university. After his enlightenment, I sat with him, an experience like facing God. Now he is referred to with an honorific name: Satya Baba. I believe he may help you, or at the least, know what you should do. You can trust him. Tell him I sent you. Waste no time. Pursuers know of the cup's power and will not be deterred. The cup will guide you, Miss Askara; it chose you. Be silent and listen when it speaks." Professor Doctor scribbled something on a worn piece of paper and handed it to Darian. "Son, take her to this ashram. We will meet again." With a salute, Professor Doctor said, "Namaste," and shuffled down the corridor, ordering the servant to escort his guests to the door.

The journey to Darian's apartment, dodging vehicles, and holy cows, seemed to go on forever. Askara liked the professor, but he had increased her sense of dread way beyond what she had felt before. The magnitude of the cup's importance shook her. She felt waves of nausea slosh in her stomach. When Askara glanced at Darian, who was lost in thought, looking out the window at Bombay traffic, she saw a sadness in the fine lines radiating from the corners of his eyes where previously she had seen only kindness. She knew she didn't have the strength to do this alone but felt guilty that she had pulled Darian into her trouble.

THE FOLLOWING MORNING DARIAN WENT TO HIS OFFICE to advise his uncles he would be away. "I'm taking my fiancée on holiday," he informed them.

His uncles greeted the news with dismay saying, Who? We had no idea. We must meet the girl. But Darian refused, explaining he had no time, promising they would meet Askara later. The uncles warned Darian to guard his heart, reminding him Americans are different, not like our women. They don't understand about family. Remember your Parsis duty. You haven't known her very long.

When Darian arrived home, Askara greeted him at the door. He stepped in, bolted the door, and stroking her hair, said, "It's almost over. I took leave from the office. I booked our tickets to Delhi. From Delhi, we shall take the train north, stay with my friend Lakhbir, go to the ashram, give the cup to that holy man, and be done with it. Let's pack."

CHAPTER SIXTEEN

The Punjab

Negotiating the Delhi airport arrival proved a little easier than departing Bombay, but Askara's anxiety mounted, seeing the crowd of strangers. Darian guided them to the taxi stand and waved.

"Ashok Hotel," he said and held the door for Askara. "That was crowded, but not dangerous. The Sudanese airport frightened you, Askara, but those guys are in jail now, I'm sure. Relax. No one followed us. The worst is behind us. Soon all of this will be over. We drop off the package, and we're free. Then we will fly to California."

"Really? I thought you only had a few days off. Didn't you tell your uncles you'd be back in a week?

"I will reschedule my trip to Asia, or better yet, we could fly that direction, and I can keep the meeting. Have you seen Singapore? It's beautiful, clean and lush, with parks and gardens everywhere. They have an amazing orchid garden, just out of the city, every type of orchid you could imagine."

"I'd love that. I've blown my assignment with Ramsey. I tried. Too bad your jeweler friend in Bombay had nothing to show me. Guess wedding season's coming, and everyone has purchased all the heirloom jewelry sets already. Add that to a demented contact, Nagali, and a coup. How was I to know? This buying trip was a train wreck."

Darian made no reply. He figured no one would work alone in a heist like that, especially for such a prize. The mention of Nagali set his teeth on edge. He couldn't help thinking somehow that repulsive man was linked to all this, although he realized that was irrational. He loathed him for scaring Askara. She had not been the same since that dinner party. She was no longer the upbeat, confident woman he had met in Greece. There she had made him laugh more than he had in years. Now, weighed down, burdened by apprehension, she seemed scared of her own shadow. He wondered what Satya Baba, the holy man, could—or would—do for them. But if Professor Doctor recommended him, that was all Darian needed. Once the cup was in safekeeping, he knew Askara's laughter and confidence would return.

The elegance of the Ashok Hotel, more like a maharajah's palace filled with beautiful carpets, tasteful furnishings, and remarkable artworks, provided a comfortable place to rest until their train departed that evening. Darian figured it would take Askara's mind off her worries. He was right. The company perk, a short-stay room for in-transit businesspeople, proved just the thing.

Askara showered and dressed in the pale blue salwar kameez Darian had given her. "*Pucca* Indian," he commented when they walked down to the restaurant.

"I don't feel *pucca*. Indian women are so elegant with their temple-art voluptuous figures. I'm a swimming jock." She looked around at the women in the restaurant. "I mean, Darian, look at them. Kohl-lined eyes, glistening burgundy lips, exquisite silk saris, precious jewels set in 24-carat gold. Just for a meal? In California, we'd be in workout clothes."

"Maybe that's better." Darian smiled. "Health is wealth."

"Be serious. Look at these men. More jewelry on them than an American woman would wear." She surveyed the large, chunky gold rings on the men's hands. She took Darian's hand in hers. "You only wear this pigeon-blood ruby ring with pearls and that simple coral cabochon ring. How come?"

"Maybe class and money are not the same, Askara. Yes, these rings are all I wear. They mean a lot to me. The ruby ring has been in my family seven generations. The coral, my father gave me for good luck in travel. All I need. All I want."

"Being content is powerful."

"Aren't you content, Askara?"

"Not currently. How could I be? My mind spins out like now. Here we are in a fine restaurant. I'm enjoying you, loving your company. Should be heaven, right? Not. Another part of my brain is revisiting the Bombay street dwellers. They cook, eat, birth, and die right there on the streets, and along those noisy railway lines. I never knew their lean-tos were made of billboard canvas movie star portraits, lengths of cheap sari cotton, and old newspapers. How do they sleep? How do their children play on that filthy pavement? How do they call that home with families huddled in 6' x 6' plots along the wall, their lives demarcated by metal train wheels rumbling and shaking? The disparity makes me crazy. I look around here, white damask table linens, marble floors, velvet window drapes, silver tea service, waiters in white uniforms with red handkerchiefs in their lapels to match their red tassel caps. They serve the grand jewelry-laden ladies and their gentlemen, stuffed into Western business suits, who wear ostentatious Rolex watches. And what do we do, Darian? We sit here just like them. How do I reconcile that?"

"Hunger. Everyone must eat. Better a clean restaurant than a *chaat café*. But that's not the issue, is it?" Darian watched Askara wince and gulp wine. "None of this is news to you, Askara. You've traveled, seen the world. You deal in treasures. Without them, you would have no work. Correct?"

Askara burst into tears. "I can't do this, not any of it. I wanna go home." She dropped her head. Her hair fell around her face like a curtain. Darian watched her clinch the damask napkin in her fist, twisting it around her index finger.

He waited for a moment and said, "Relax, Askara. We will be at your place before you know it. Here," he said and handed her his handkerchief. "Wipe your tears. I know this is incredibly stressful, but it is almost over. Tell me about your place in California. I want to visualize it."

Askara dabbed kohl smudges from her eyes, took a long breath, and perked up describing her home. She referred to her small home as her *houselet* and described the area in Marin County, north of San Francisco, as a peaceful setting in the hills, with lots of redwood trees. The hills, golden yellow in dry summers, turn vibrant green in spring, she said, but the live oak trees remain gray-green all year and grow thick in the ravines. The hilltops, undulating grassy curves, like a mythical serpent's back, rise and descend in the coastline fog with a life of their own. As you climb the path from redwood trees to grassy hills, she added, if the mist hasn't come in, you see the Pacific Ocean. At night the amber lights on the Golden Gate Bridge glow like jewels until the fog rolls in and hushes the landscape with a timeless feeling.

"Sounds enchanting," Darian said. He saw the light return to Askara's eyes.

"Yeah, you can sit on my front steps and watch the fog swallow hill after hill until it engulfs my house. We have bougainvillea, too. Everything grows in a Mediterranean climate, but my favorite flower is fuchsias. They look like ballet dancers in big purple skirts. I have hanging pots of them on my front porch, purple, pink, and white. From my back deck, all you see are huge redwood trees. Fog drips from them like rain onto the ferns. Another tree, madrone, with branches like entwined bodies, is very sensual. Their red bark is like paper. It peels back in curls, and you see smooth blonde skin underneath. Mule deer, local deer with big ears, come up to the house. They're almost pets."

Darian smiled at Askara and took her hand in his. "You'll be home soon."

The waiter brought out several dishes. They sat and ate slowly, talking in hushed tones.

"City life, that's much different, I mean, in San Francisco. I prefer to live outside the city, away from things. But it's only a thirty-minute drive on the freeway to the heart of San Francisco. I have all the advantages the city offers and the quietness of country living. Suits me. I grew up in the Sierra Mountains in a small town."

"How old were you when you left home?"

"Eighteen. I went off to college. After that, my parents moved, so now when I go back, I'm a tourist. Lake Tahoe's a huge lake, second cleanest in the world, next to one in Russia. Sapphire-blue, cold, and clear, in the deepest part. Blue-green like an aquamarine jewel near the shore and a little warmer but not much. In the summer, you can look up at a snowcross in the ravine on Mt. Tallac, above the yellow sand beach. You can swim in clear blue water and look at snow, all at the same time. Amazing. When I was young, I decided I'd marry on the shore of Lake Tahoe, at sunset, when the water turns to gold."

"We'll see it together...soon."

"So, Darian, tell me something about you that I don't know already."

"Like what? How charming I am? Or maybe how I was almost a priest?"

"A priest?"

"Really. My father was worried. I'm the only son. He wanted me to keep the family name going, but I considered another life in my youth. I wanted to be a priest. My father's a strong character, a doer, an out-in-the-world achiever type. My mother's a scholar, loves learning, a spiritual person. She wanted me to be a priest. She said she saw in me from a young age that sort of quietness and interest in our religion. My father objected."

"She didn't get her way?"

"No. As close as my mother had gotten was my name. She named me after a Zoroastrian high priest. My given name is Dastur. Mother named me after Dastur Dhalla, a Parsi High Priest who lived in Karachi, India, now Pakistan. Dastur means the head priest of a Parsi temple."

"But you go by Darian. Who gave you that name?"

"Kids at school."

"Your mother and father accepted a name school kids gave you?" Askara said, taking another bite of basmati rice stained orange from saffron.

"She liked the reason my schoolmates gave me the name," Darian said with a smile.

DARIAN SAVED A DOG FROM BEING BEATEN WHEN HE WAS playing in his schoolyard in Bombay. A man across from the playground, sitting at a *chaat café*, kicked a pariah dog away from his table. The poor, starving dog screamed. Darian bolted out the gardener's side gate of the school and ran over to help the animal. He yelled at the man, who, naturally, ignored him. When the man lifted his foot to kick the dog again, Darian yelled at him to stop. He didn't. Darian grabbed a cup of chai from the table and tossed the tea on the man's clothes. The man jumped up to strike him, but the café owner rushed over. The man bolted. Darian thought the owner would be mad at him, but he explained he wasn't because the man had already paid, so it was his loss. He told the boy to run back to school, so the headmaster would not know he had left. When the story of Dastur fighting an adult to save a pariah dog circulated among his friends at school, the boys nicknamed him Darian after the Persian ruler Darius the Great, whom they were currently studying in school. The name stuck. Even his parents accepted the nickname in time, although they continued to call him Dastur.

When his mother picked him up that day, Darian recounted the story for her. She walked him over to apologize to the café owner. They saw the emaciated dog lying under a piece of burlap behind the tea stall. The dog came to Darian like she wanted to thank him. That's when his mother realized the dog was pregnant and starving. She agreed they would take the dog home and care for her until she had her pups. After bathing the dog, Darian made a bed for her in his room where two days later, the dog whelped eight puppies. The servants helped care for the pups while Darian was at school. When the puppies were old enough, they found homes for all of them. Darian kept the scruffy pariah mother dog. She turned out to be a real beauty, with silky white markings in her black fur, after she recovered.

She lived for twelve years and was Darian's best friend. The first thing he would do when he came home on holiday from boarding school was run to see his dog.

Darian's mother wasn't happy that her son had thrown tea on someone. But years later, his mother told him she had been as proud as she had been mad, even though she didn't act it. She took him to their priest for a lecture. The priest told him: Dastur, the world may not meet your expectations, but a wise man looks for maximum goodness in life and experiences the joy of living. Life can glide like the moon across the heavens, but at times life can be rough. The priest said, "Remember...Zarathustra taught that man should adjust to life, to all its diversity of fortune and people, and be a bearer of joy and light, even in gloomy times. Give happiness and be happy," the priest said and admonished Darian to uphold the core Parsi values of good words, good deeds, and good thoughts. The priest agreed the man had acted cruelly, but Dastur should not. He warned Dastur, "Many tests come in life. Do not resort to anger and aggression to deal with them. You will only get hurt."

"Simple. Direct. I like it. Maybe I should be a Parsi?" Askara said.

"Too late. To be a Parsi, you must be born of Zoroastrian parents. Some, the Iranian and Kurdish Zoroastrians, believe you can convert, though."

"Your parents won't accept me, will they, Darian? They must have loved Minoo, the perfect choice for you, the choice they made."

"Not perfect. We had conflict, but there was a strong bond; genuine love did develop. Askara, my parents will love you, my choice of wife. Do not doubt that. They want me to be happy. They will love you for bringing me joy;

they will love you for you, but they will insist our children follow the Zoroastrian religion."

"Let's cross that bridge later, Darian. We're not married. We may never be if things don't go right. Much less have children."

"Don't say that. Within the next two days, all this difficulty will be a bad memory, nothing more."

Askara winced. Her lip quivered. "Darian, do you think we will ever get out of this? I mean, okay? I'm not a fighter. I'm a wimp who's scared, terrified."

Darian edged his chair closer to reach around her shoulder. He whispered into her ear, "Askara, without a doubt. Yes, we will get out of this. Believe me. Trust me. Think of what you have already faced in Kenya, Ethiopia, and Sudan. You're a strong, brave woman. It's almost over. We have a great future waiting for us." He glanced at his watch. "It's later than I thought. Did you want dessert?"

"I am so exhausted from all of this, Darian. I know I'll be better when this stress is alleviated. I'll be me again. And no, I don't want a dessert. Thanks, though."

"Time to go then." He signaled for the waiter. "Room 26, please, have our luggage brought to the lobby," he said and signed for dinner. Grabbing the bag at his feet, they hurried for the elevator.

Chapter Seventeen

Delhi Departure

The Delhi train station, a moving monster, trains arriving and departing on eighteen tracks connected by a network of walkways to sixteen platforms, stunned Askara. Hordes of people pushed and shoved. Agile men climbed on top of the cars; others clung to side grips. Suit-clad businessmen clutching their briefcases, weary from work, pushed inside with friend groups to sit at tables and play cards on the commute home. Women, laden with shopping items and noisy children, elbowed their way into the ladies-only cars.

Coolies with large suitcases balanced on their heads raced everywhere on the platform like ants foraging for food while station hawkers shouted their wares in high-pitched voices: lime peelers; hairbrushes; snacks; bottled water. Food vendors squatted on the platform, frying savory samosas and sweet *jalebis*, loops of fried dough drowned in orange-colored sugar syrup, for hungry customers.

Darian grabbed Askara's hand to pull her along. "Track ten, northbound, over there," he said and nodded the direction. "Hurry."

Askara followed single file, clutching the back of his shirt. He cut through the crowd, rushed up metal stairs to a walkway that crossed high above several lines of tracks, and descended on the far side. Their train screeched into the station seconds later and groaned to a stop briefly, ready to accelerate again. Frantic riders pushed and shoved, getting off, getting on.

Darian checked the roster, pointed to their first-class sleeper compartment, and picked up their luggage before an advancing coolie could reach them. They rushed the length of several cars. Askara hopped up the steps first. Darian shoved their luggage up on the landing, jumping on just as the train began creeping forward. He checked cabin numbers as they pushed along the tight corridor.

At their door, he turned and smiled at Askara. "Made it." The train lunged forward, throwing Askara into his back. He opened the heavy door and helped Askara in. He tossed their bags onto the upper rack before the train bucked and knocked him to a sitting position. Darian laughed. "Riding trains in India is a survival art, like hunting and gathering in ancient days. Timing's everything."

The train gained momentum. People milling around on the platform smeared against the dusty window glass. Only Sikhs stood out in their colorful turbans, pale blue, peach, and crimson. The sight made Askara think of her father. She missed him. She could always count on him. He wore his warrior heritage, even dressed in blue jeans and a t-shirt. She saw him in these men, the stance, the confidence. He always made Askara feel protected. The last time Askara had visited India with him, she was a teenager. Soon, she thought, for his daughter's wedding, he will come to India again, and he will wear a pink turban for the celebration. The image made her smile.

The Delhi sprawl followed the railroad tracks for miles. Cramped stacks of ramshackle apartments with doors and windows wide open to the acrid smell of diesel and the noise of screeching wheels became family dioramas of crying babies, children clutching their mother's legs as they cooked, and men reading newspapers.

Finally, the landscape transitioned from crowded city to fertile green Punjabi farmland. Askara settled back to daydream; the train's clatter made conversation difficult. Darian read the *Times of India*. The train soon rocked Askara to sleep. But a loud rap at the cabin door roused her when Darian opened it to see the conductor. He inspected and punched their tickets. Askara turned back to the window. In the feeble light of a dusty evening, she watched young boys bathe water buffaloes by a canal, men pedal rickety black bicycles, and an entire family on their scooter going to market—husband steering with small children braced between his legs, his wife riding sidesaddle behind him while holding an infant.

"Soon they'll bring dinner, probably after the next stop," Darian said.

"I'd like to wash up first. I feel sticky. Which way do I go?" Askara replied.

"Lavatory's down the corridor, on the right. Take your hand towel. Hold on to the rail. The train lurches."

When Askara returned from the lavatory, she said, "Not too bad. Your turn."

Askara had slumped down with a book, hiked her feet up on the opposite seat, and gotten comfortable when she heard hurried footsteps in the corridor. Three sharp raps on their door and Darian's voice shouting outside made her jump. She leaped to unlock the door. Darian fell inside, tugging at his disheveled shirt, and bolted the door behind him.

"What's the matter?"

"Someone kept pounding on the lavatory door. When I opened it, I saw a man run this way. I thought to our door."

"Darian, no one knocked on our door. You're as jumpy as me."

"I'll be glad when *it's* gone." He combed his damp hair. The train slowed. "We're approaching a station. Let's step out for a few minutes. I need fresh air. I'll carry the bag."

The train lurched to a stop in the open-air station. Several passengers from their car disembarked to join others strolling the cement platform. The smell of damp rice fields and the sound of crickets filled the air. A male American voice bellowed, "Fertile all right. Reminds me of the San Joaquin Valley, but here people shit right in the fields. Disgusting." Askara tried to spot the man, but people hovering around the food vendors blocked her view. She cringed. No wonder American tourists have such a bad reputation, she thought.

A man with wrinkled brown-leather skin sat at a roller press pushing long stalks of sugar cane through metal cylinders. The shafts cracked, fibers splayed out, and pale-yellow juice flowed. He handed her a glassful. Askara drank the sweet liquid, read the sign, and gave him three rupees. The old man deposited them in a cloth bag tied around his neck, took her used glass, submerged it twice in a bowl of cloudy water, and refilled it for the next customer.

Darian smiled at Askara. "Sorry, I wasn't paying attention. I would not have recommended that. Let's hope your stomach can handle it like an Indian's."

"Oh, God, I hope so," she said. Looking past Darian, she saw a man standing with two other men staring their direction. She glanced behind her. Seeing no one, she turned to face them, but the men had moved away. She pointed their direction, telling Darian, but he couldn't see them. They melded into the crowd at the far end of the platform and disappeared.

"Darian, let's go in. I don't think that was anything, but…." Askara jumped onto the metal steps just as the conductor shouted. The train lurched forward. Darian jumped on and held the rail.

When they reached their cabin, Darian accosted a uniformed railway ticket collector and spoke to him in Punjabi, pressing a roll of rupee notes into his palm.

"What was that about?" Askara asked when they settled in their compartment.

"I told the guard some *thuggees* had watched us and for him to patrol our corridor until we get off."

"Robbers? Will he?"

"Of course, that's his job, plus I made it worthwhile." When a knock sounded at their door, Darian stood, demanding in Punjabi, "Who's there?" Hearing a meek reply, Darian turned to Askara, "Dinner's here."

The server brought in a covered tray, put it on the table, smiled, and retreated without a word. The smell of curried chanas and poori, puffed fried bread, filled the cabin with the aroma of turmeric, coriander, and cumin. Darian inspected a small bowl of *raita,* yogurt and cucumber salad, saying, "Best you avoid raw food." He sipped the hot chai, pointing to carrot halva triangles topped by pistachio bits. "That's good for me…but not for you. You don't want to get sick, especially now."

"Ha, caught you. I know it's been cooked. Darian, you just want it all!" Askara said and nibbled at a corner of the halva. "I'll take just a taste. I can't resist."

"My friend, Lakhbir Phoolka, will meet us at the Tanda station. We'll stay overnight with him. His driver will take us to Satya Baba's ashram the next day. We'll leave *it* with the holy man, return to Lakhbir's by nightfall and spend a couple of days relaxing. See, it's almost over."

"I hope so. How well do you know Lakhbir?" Askara said, investigating smudges on the teacup rim. "He's an old friend, more a brother. We went to Sanawar School together, a boarding school, the best in India. I trust him implicitly, and we need his help. He knows of that ashram; his cousin lives near there."

"Okay. I'm nervous, indulge me. Do you think those three men were looking at something on the platform, or at me?"

"You. Most likely. Many people look at you. The curse of beauty, I suppose. Can you recall their faces?"

"One. He stood in front of the others. Dark complexion, a bit taller than me, thin, and he wore a plaid short-sleeve shirt, a Western shirt."

"Indian?"

"Couldn't tell."

"That fits millions. Forget it, your imagination's turning simple gestures into threats. I understand. I'm jumpy, too," Darian said and checked his watch. "I'll set up the bunks. Let's get a bit of shut-eye. Don't worry." He hugged Askara. "You're safe with me. You know I would do anything for you, Askara. Anything."

WHEN THE TRAIN JOLTED TO A HALT IN THE TANDA STATION at dawn, Darian was ready. He checked the corridor, nodded all-clear to Askara, and they disembarked. Askara scanned the crowd for the man who had stared at her, but she saw only men greeting their families. When Darian spotted Lakhbir in the distance, he waved him over.

"*Sat-Shri-Akal*," Lakhbir said in a boisterous voice, saluting Darian with his hands clasped in respect.

Darian returned the greeting and said, "Lakhbir, so good to see you! This is Askara."

"Pleased to meet you, Miss Askara. Thank you for bringing my brother to me." He pointed toward a waiting Mercedes. "Shall we go."

Lakhbir's friendly demeanor, his immense size, three inches taller than Darian's six feet, and his manner of unabashed confidence, as if the world existed to serve him, made Askara feel comfortable. She saw the Sikh in him.

They bumped over roads that laced through acres of planted fields. Lakhbir flourished his meaty hand and said, "Mine. Wheat and basmati. Miss Askara, my rice is the best in the Punjab, the best in the world, with such sweet aroma."

"How will the wheat harvest be this year, Lakhbir?" Darian asked.

"Excellent. Yield should be the highest in five years. Rain at the correct time, that's what makes it. Miss Askara the Punjab is the most fertile area in the world. Dark, rich earth. Nothing better. Give me land. Forget gold, forget diamonds. Give me soil and the opportunity to sow!" When Lakhbir grinned, his upturned mustache touched the sun lines descending from the corners of his eyes. "Miss Askara, how do you like our Punjab?"

"A relief from congested city life, that's for sure. I haven't seen that much of it. I look forward to seeing more."

"Darian, I told you Bombay's too crowded. You must move here. Buy some land, raise some crops, start a family."

"I know little about crops. I'm a businessman, not a gentleman farmer like you, Lakhbir."

"I could teach you. There. Look there." A massive cement house four stories high with a wrap-around veranda loomed into view. "That's home."

Lakhbir punched a code into the electric gate opener, the gate slid back, and they drove in, stopping at the front. Lakhbir jumped out of his Mercedes and opened Askara's door, offering her his engulfing hand. A diminutive woman at the door waved and started down the steps.

Askara rushed ahead and met her mid-way. "Pleased to meet you, Amrit, I'm Askara. Thank you for having us."

"Our pleasure," Amrit said and nodded to her servants to unload the luggage, tipping her head to direct them upstairs.

Askara followed Amrit into the foyer. Pearly-gray marble floors, carved teak doors, cornice molding, Kashan silk carpets, a claw-foot settee with matching chairs filled the entrance room. An immense three-tier crystal chandelier threw a thousand rainbows on the shiny marble when the sun hit the prisms and made the house seem more a museum than a family home. Askara wanted to wander around the immense house and investigate the paintings, vases, and sculptures. Still, she sat next to Darian on the settee in the living room to listen to the men exchange updates about their mutual friends over tea.

After the servants removed the trays, Amrit said, "Can I show you the garden, Askara? It's lovely in the morning light." They walked through two elaborate living rooms to exit an etched glass French door to the garden. "Roses, my mother-in-law's love," Amrit said, walking down the stone steps. Roses of many colors—white, pink, peach, red, and dark blue—arranged in geometric patterns created a wave of color that transitioned from light to dark. "Smell them," Amrit said. "Peace is my favorite. The scent reminds me of a childhood candy we called *lollies*. Askara, do you have a garden in the United States of America?"

"No. I work for a man in San Francisco, an international dealer of artifacts and jewelry. I travel with my job, so I have no time to manage a garden."

"You are lucky! I would love to travel."

"Where?"

"Venice, Italy, to ride in a gon-do-la, that is correct pronunciation, yes?"

"Absolutely. I've been there. Venice is a fascinating city."

"I will never go, though."

"Why?"

"Lakhbir loves his Punjabi dirt too much. He cannot leave, not even for a holiday. Plus, he would not leave his elderly parents. They live here with us. He worries about them." Askara observed Amrit's youthfulness and innocence, figuring Lakhbir must be fifteen years her senior, a good man but far from innocent. "In one year plus, we will start our family," Amrit said with anticipation. "We've been married two years now."

"You don't sound as if you want to wait."

Amrit flushed, "Well, no, it's not my choice. Lakhbir wants to wait to see how suited we are."

"Arranged marriage?"

Amrit smiled. "Of course. But Lakhbir's second marriage," she said in a soft voice. "His first was a love marriage. She left him for another, ran away to Australia. That hurt him. Things are good with us. I want to have several children. I love them. I come from a large family, three brothers and three sisters. I'm the eldest."

"Do they live near here?"

"Jalandhar, not too far. Lakhbir has one sister only. She lives in Malaysia with her husband and three children. His parents live in that part of the house," she said and pointed to the left. "Very kind people. You will meet them at lunch. Lakhbir runs the family farm. His father moved here after Partition when the government created Pakistan for Muslims. Sikhs from that side moved to this side, the Punjab in India."

The words *family farm* seemed a misnomer; Askara thought it more like the Gezira Scheme. "Well, it's a lovely place to live and raise children. As lovely as Venice in its way, but someday you may see Venice. Don't give up. Take the children for a gondola ride."

When they rejoined Lakhbir and Darian in the sitting room, the men were locked in a serious conversation. Askara could tell by the tone and the look on Darian's face, his brow like a furrowed field, that their topic was politics. The men broke off quickly.

"Well, Askara, how do you like our garden?" Lakhbir said.

"Beautiful, the roses are amazing. The fountain in the center's very elegant."

"Yes? We ordered it from Agra, a Mughal design, took a year to make it. I find it gives such pleasure to sit on the back veranda on a hot night and listen to splashing water, like music. And the smell of *Raat-ki-Rani* sweetens the entire garden."

"Yes. I've smelled that flower in Kenya, Lady of the Night."

"Interesting your life has brought you here now, Askara."

"Yes," she replied, not knowing to what Lakhbir referred. Askara assumed Darian would not mention anything about their mission. She hoped not.

"I am pleased Darian has found you. Such a tragedy, what happened to his wife Minoo, a lovely girl. I feared I would never see him happy again, but here he is, extremely happy...because of you. We thank you."

After lunching with Lakhbir's parents, Askara and Darian retired to their upstairs bedroom to rest. The swamp cooler dripped water on woven *Ruhkhus* grass mats, filling the room with a scent as sweet as peppermint candy. Makes sleep come easily, Askara thought, as she drifted away. A sharp spasm shot through her entire body. She shook. She ripped off the sheet as if it was smothering her. Darian grabbed her by the arm.

"Askara! Wake up. You're safe." He pulled her trembling body to his chest.

"Oh, God. What a dream. I was running. Men chased me along canals in Venice. I tried to hail a gondola taxi. I couldn't get the boatman's attention. One paddled to me. He was Death. Men in long black cloaks rose from dripping underground caverns. They tried to grab me. I ran under a stone archway and hid in the shadows. Water dripped into my hair from a crack in the overhead stones. The water sliced into my scalp with each drop. I couldn't breathe. I heard footsteps echoing along the stone corridors. Louder. Louder. A guy yelled: There she is. I tried to run. I couldn't move. My feet were glued to the cobblestones by bright green moss. I tried to kick it off. That woke me. What a nightmare. It reminded me of a scene from the weird thriller movie *Don't Look Now*. Ugh. Darian, I'm so glad in a few hours this will be over. I want to move on, enjoy each other, have fun. The dinner party tonight will be a welcome relief. I look forward to socializing at a mixed dinner where women and men converse. It'll be more like a family gathering. I remember when I was here as a teenager with my dad, the dinner parties were fun. After dessert, the young people played in the courtyard. Those are fond memories."

"Good company is good medicine, something we both need. You get ready first."

Chapter Eighteen

Uninvited Guests

Askara made small talk with the guests, several of whom commented that her Indian heritage and grace were recognizable although she looked more Kashmiri than Punjabi because of her lighter skin. She enjoyed Lakhbir and Amrit's friends, but she was mentally and emotionally exhausted. Her mind kept drifting back to her goal, to leave the cup at the ashram and resume a regular life. After dinner, she feigned a headache, attributed to travel fatigue, and excused herself.

On her way upstairs, she stopped on the landing to investigate the vase collection of Lakhbir's mother, Mrs. Phoolka. Askara made a quick appraisal of the items: Chinese porcelain, seventeenth century, mountainscape with cranes, valuable; Dutch, Delft blue, hand-painted, average quality; Greek, red ochre figures on black, Attica imitation, poor knockoff, no value. One enormous silver vase piqued her interest. Amrit had told her this vase was from a maharajah's collection. Made from ancient silver rupees, it once carried holy water from the Ganges to the maharaja's summer palace in the foothills of the Himalayas. Good story, Askara conceded, possibly too good, but quality craft.

Askara trembled, feeling suddenly alone and chilly, on the second floor of Lakhbir's sprawling house. A house like this should serve a large, extended family, she thought, not for four, more like twenty-four. Even the stairway landing suffered from the vastness. Lakhbir's dynamic personality couldn't animate this much space; no one's could.

She climbed into bed and listened to the party carry on downstairs, relieved that tomorrow her stress would be over, and she could resume a normal life. She knew she would miss the cup. It had given her a glimpse of herself, an expanded version, a better version that made routine duties, daily events, and worries trivial. The cup validated her in a way she perceived but could not understand. She had looked through a window and seen more to her life. She hoped to sustain the new awareness, realizing as much as she wanted to get rid of the cup that much she wanted to keep it.

Askara fantasized scenarios. She would keep the cup and not let its power change her. She would do only good deeds, feed the poor, help the ill, support charities. Her rational mind reminded her how many people far more disciplined than she had failed. What if, she countered, a person like me, someone little interested in being a public figure, used it for the good of the world? I could do this, Askara convinced herself. But a creeping feeling deep down said she could not. She was no match for the cup's power. An image of her father floated across her vision. She heard him say, as he often did: power corrupts; absolute power corrupts absolutely. She shook her head. His image disintegrated, but he and her mother lingered in her thoughts. Askara missed them. She wanted to be with them, to hear them reassure her, to feel their love. In the darkened room, alone in a land far from home, Askara lifted the cup one last time. She unraveled the length of cotton and admired the subdued beauty of the legendary prayer cup. She held the prized possession in her hands one last time.

THE ROOM SHIFTED. WALLS OPENED OUTWARD AND FLATtened into grassy pastures. Askara slid down a tunnel of pulsating lights. A chill ran down her back; goosebumps popped up on her arms. Deep silence descended, followed by an explosion. Stars hurled across the night like silver bullets, ripping the dark fabric open. From the gaping wound, Askara saw a small fire expand into a gigantic blaze that danced in front of her. She collapsed at the edge of the light, the breath knocked out of her. The crystalline form of her ancient teacher, The Respected One, appeared in amber flames. He stepped through the fiery veil and sat beside her.

Daughter, I commanded you here. The Deceiver will strike at you again. Be clear of mind. Things will not appear as they seem. Hold fast to your instincts, trust in Ultimate Truth to guide you. Do not despair. The Deceiver feeds on despair, thus rendering you weak and the Deceiver powerful. Your faith in Absolute Good must be your guide. I will be ever close to you, as close as your beating heart. But you must listen. Be still and listen. I am always with you. Heed when I speak.

"How will I know if it's you and not the Deceiver?"

Call out: Magi, Magi, Magi. If my image does not warp or disappear, then you know it is I who speaks. If you hear a voice giving you instruction, and see me not, demand I appear. Call me. If I do not appear, do not heed the words, for it will be The Deceiver speaking. You are in grave danger in this house. You must leave. Go immediately.

"What about Darian?"

He will not leave yet. He has work to do. You must leave alone.

"*Magi, Magi, Magi.*" The image didn't falter. "I leave without him?"

Yes. The enemy approaches. RUN, Asha. RUN!

Flames consumed The Respected One. Askara plummeted through darkness, slamming onto the bed, the air knocked out of her. For a second, she lay motionless. Her foot spasmed, then a molten rod shot up her leg. She leaped upright.

She heard the party downstairs, especially Lakhbir's boisterous laugh. All seemed normal. Askara threw on her jeans and t-shirt, wrenched her hair into a ponytail, strapped on her sandals, wrapped the cup, and crammed it in her small backpack with her traveler's checks, rupee notes, a crumpled salwar kameez, and her passport. She paused, asking out loud, "What do I do now? The gate is guarded. Three Alsatians patrol the grounds. I can't leave without Darian."

The guard dogs howled, growled, and yelped. Their screeches erupted but fell silent, dead silent. Dinner guests paused then chattered on. Askara peered through the curtains. A guard lay slumped near the gate. Sleeping? Amrit's shrill scream slit the air like a raptor claw. Running feet scattered. Loud male voices shouted. Askara panicked. The only way down was the stairs up from the sitting room. She couldn't climb out the window. She was on the second floor. She strapped on her backpack and stepped out to the landing. Crouching, pressed against the wall between two vases, she heard a thwack. Someone hit the floor with a groan. The wooden banister shook.

Darian bounded up three stairs at a time, yelling: "Run, Askara, run!"

Someone yanked Darian from behind. He turned and jumped the man, knocking them down the stairs. A pistol fired. Askara leaped from the shadows to see Darian's limp body sprawled across the lower stair when a dark figure lunged at her. She grabbed Mrs. Phoolka's silver rupee vase and slammed it into the man's face. She heard a bone crack. He stumbled. She swung again, hitting him on the side of his head. He fell backward down the stairs. Askara rushed to Darian, leaning down to try to lift him. Blood from his shoulder pooled on the marble.

A voice yelled: Run from the Deceiver. Leave Darian to me.

"Magi, Magi, Magi," Askara cried out. The image of The Respected One appeared, hovering above Darian's body, pulsing soft and bright three times. A flame wrapped Darian's body in a shroud. The voice commanded: Go!

Askara rushed out the garden door, past the motionless guard slumped at his gate station, shoved the gate open, and careened into the black night, leaving the pandemonium behind her, women screaming, men shouting, people running.

She repeatedly fell, hitting unseen rocks and scrubs, scraping her hands, scuffing her knees. She remembered the driveway pavement straightened and turned left where the road began skirting the fields. She smelled the musky scent of upturned earth. She ran into the field until she doubled over, grasping her gut, retching repeatedly until only the bitter taste of bile remained. She edged her way along a raised mound between two fields and collapsed in a shallow irrigation ditch. Car lights sped away. One vehicle, then another. She wanted to run back for Darian, but incoming car lights speeding toward the house confused her. Reinforcements? Askara realized there was no turning back.

She moved slowly in the dark, keeping the barely discernible scar of the road to her left. In pale silver dawn, she trotted toward village lights. The gash in her ankle from tripping over a post made every step agony. She limped along dim, narrow alleys toward the village center, looking for the bus station. She smelled a diesel engine warming up. She crept closer. A driver stepped off the only bus with its motor running and disappeared. Askara sneaked on and climbed into a seat where she slouched, partially hidden among baskets of chickens and sleepy peasants. The station master appeared, approached her, and demanded her ticket. She nodded and slipped him enough rupees to take a bus to Delhi and back again. He stuffed the bills into his pocket, punched a ticket, handed it to her, and waved for the driver. The bus pulled away and swaying gently on the flat road lulled Askara to sleep. She woke in full daylight to stifling heat when the bus lurched to a stop.

Askara climbed down with the others and asked for a chai stall. A man pointed, rattling off in Punjabi, wobbling his head side to side. At the chaat café, she collapsed on a rickety wooden stool to drink steaming hot chai and gobble fresh chapatis with curds. She tried to relax in the morning heat. Soon every face and every movement spooked her. She saw that people stared at her rumpled Western clothes and her bloody foot. She limped back to the bus station.

The next, and only bus of the day, the clerk said, would come at 2:00 that afternoon, a seven-hour wait. "Madam take room at guesthouse over there," he said and pointed down the main road to a small building. "You are being tired. Your foot, she bleeds."

The guesthouse consisted of a few rooms on a central courtyard, crowded with large shade trees, home to hundreds of darting, chirping parrots. There was one room left. Askara took it. She washed her bloody foot at an outside spigot and limped to her room, where a cotton mattress slumped like a decrepit animal on the saggy rope charpoy frame. After using the odiferous communal toilet, she returned and fell asleep.

Askara woke when the manager knocked. Opening the door, she saw he pointed to his watch. She splashed water on her face from the bucket he offered her, gathered her pack, and limped back to the bus station. People milled around, waiting in the dust and heat for the bus, but no one spoke English. She couldn't recall the holy man's name, not a surname but a string of respectful epithets. They hadn't stuck in her mind, nor the name of his ashram, not even the town. She had assumed Darian would be with her; he would know. No one here seemed to know the guru or his ashram when she tried to ask.

In the distance, she spotted a young hippie guy buying a Coca-Cola. She approached him. "Hi! How are you?" she said, hoping he spoke English.

"Cool."

"Great, you speak English."

"Yep. I'm American. You are too, right?"

"Yes. Can you help me? I need to find someone, a spiritual teacher who lives near here in the mountains somewhere. I don't know his name."

"Wow. Far out. Been looking for the holy guys. Gone all over India, to all the temples down south. Far freakin' out.

I'm ready for GC. Got blessed all over, I mean, wow, every temple, the works, marigold necklace, red paint on my third eye, ashes. Such a blast."

"GC?"

"God Consciousness. Don't know your guy. In the Himalayas, holy men live in caves, don't eat, live on air, breatharians they're called, don't wear clothes even when the snow's falling. Outta sight. I plan to head up north, too, visit some rishis."

"North, where?" Askara asked, exasperated. "Which ashram?"

"Dunno. Up in the mountains. I'll ask around. I speak a bit of Hindi."

"Do you know of a spiritual colony where the master was a professor before he became enlightened?"

"Nope. They're born enlightened, right? I mean, why would a guy be a teacher and then turn holy? Sure you heard that right?"

"I'm sure."

"Let me check my book. *The Super Spiritual Wayfarer's Guide to India* has all the addresses of ashrams and spiritual gigs foreigners can visit."

"Where did you get that?"

"Bookstore on Telegraph, in Berkeley. It's great, tells which ones give you food and lodging for free, which ones you pay for, which ones you work for room and board."

"Sounds like a hostel list."

"Yeah, a spiritual motel guide for trippers. Got me around all over. Umm, here's something. Let me check the map, yeah. North a couple of hours from here, there's an ashram. A work-for-lodging type colony. Cool. Satya Baba lives there. That the one you're looking for?"

"Great, that's his name. Thanks."

"Can I go with you?"

Askara thought *no* but realized this long-haired guy in tie-dye pajamas would be a good ruse. Trackers wouldn't suspect an American hippie couple. Anonymity, at least as far as the colony gate, would be useful. Plus, he could speak some Hindi, enough to get them around.

"Yeah, sure, good idea."

The hippie inquired about which bus went to the village near the ashram and where to transfer. They bought their tickets but had a forty-minute wait until their bus would come, so they walked around the village and talked. Askara couldn't believe this twenty-three-year-old-matted-hair hippie guy had gone to UC Berkeley, but it made sense when he told her he had dropped out. Probably after competitive frisbee, she thought.

"I dropped acid…dropped out…started on the road to enlightenment. The only real education anyway. Been traveling for a year on my student loan money. Hey, ten years to repay. Far out, right?"

"Right."

"Wanna smoke a j?"

"No, thanks."

He fumbled a hand-rolled joint from the pocket of his Indian pajamas. "Look at this doobie, got it in Madras, African weed, super strong. Crazy, it grows here all over, but nobody smokes it. Nothing compares to this ganja, well, maybe Acapulco Gold. Okay, I'll be back in a minute, off for a quick hit. See you here for the bus." Askara watched him walk down the dirt path and disappear behind vendor carts.

She sat by the tea stall, sipping chai, and people watching. A man rode past in a wooden cart pulled by an emaciated donkey with haunches that erupted from abraded, hairless skin. The cart, piled high with red bricks, creaked under the weight. The donkey faltered and stumbled to his knees. The man jumped to the ground, took the leather reins in hand, and whipped the animal across its back. The donkey groaned. The man beat him again, harder. The animal struggled to stand, lost his balance and went down on one knee, the cart of bricks listing to the side. The man gathered the reins to strike the poor animal again. Askara limped over, wrenched the reins away from his hand, and threatened to beat the man with her hand raised, cursing in his face. He shouted back and tried to grab the leathers from her, swatted her away, and slapped the animal's neck with his bare hand. Onlookers gawked. Askara dropped the reins. The man yanked the poor animal forward by the bridle. Realizing the locals had surrounded her, Askara cussed at him and stepped away from the donkey to hobble back to her seat.

The vendor frying balls of dough in a heavy black iron skillet resumed his work. The cobbler fixing a leather sandal strap began hammering again; the broom hawker continued shouting his wares. The afternoon sun beat down on Askara's uncovered head. She felt sick from heat, anger, and fatigue. She shuffled over to sit on wooden crates in the shade of a corrugated tin roof to wait for the hippie.

He didn't come. Twenty minutes passed, the hippie still didn't show. She checked her watch. She limped back to the bus station and queued up at the gate where the hippie had said their bus would leave. The bus filled. Askara, extremely glad she had insisted on keeping her bus ticket, climbed on.

When the bus pulled out of town, Askara thought she glimpsed the hippie's matted yellow hair, leaning up against a wall in an alleyway, but she couldn't be sure. Maybe baskets?

Chapter Nineteen

River Rescue

The packed bus careened along narrow roads, barely missing people and animals, dodged oncoming buses and lorries, and finally stopped in a small village. Immediately, hawkers boarded, screeching their wares. No passengers got off, so Askara remained in her seat. A woman next to her holding a caged chicken made getting out impossible anyway. The driver boarded after tossing his lit cigarette butt, started the engine, and crammed the gear shifter into first. The rusted, ancient, red-and-white bus coughed and lunged forward like an unwilling racehorse out of the start gate. They drove a few kilometers to the next village where several people got off.

Askara, unsure of what to do, accosted the driver and presented her ticket. He replied in Punjabi and pointed to a blue-and-white bus parked in front of the depot shack. She walked over and boarded the empty bus. When no one came after fifteen minutes, she approached the ticket counter, a cracked wooden door propped up on barrels, to speak to the clerk. He pointed to his wristwatch, then to the silent bus. He tapped the number three. She slumped down on a rickety wooden chair next to the ticket kiosk to wait.

When the driver finally showed up, wiping sweat from the edge of his turban, she and others boarded the bus, now a metallic oven in the afternoon heat. The blue-and-white bus bumped along a narrow road between maturing wheat fields. The heat, noise, and fumes overcame Askara. Fields criss-crossed in her vision; her head dropped; her eyelids closed.

Askara saw Darian lying prone on the stairs, a dark stain wicking into the fibers of his shirt. Was he okay? She whimpered: Please, let me see him again to tell him I love him. Keep him safe. A bump in the road jarred her awake. She dozed again, despite the din of grinding gears. She saw Darian wavering in front of her. She heard his words: Askara, fulfill your duty and return to me.

Askara woke when an overhead package fell into her lap. The woman across the aisle jumped to retrieve it with an embarrassed grin. Askara, dazed, felt Darian was close. She believed him safe. But how? She shoved the image of him on the stairs from her mind. It made her sick. She could not dwell on tragedy, she told herself. She knew she must get the cup to a neutral haven at the ashram and return to Darian as quickly as possible.

A large orange sun, like ripe fruit, dropped below the distant mountain and stained its jagged edge red-orange. The stifling air cooled. Askara looked down into the ravine where a broad river flowed and women gathered lengths of colorful saris drying on the grass while their children splashed in shallow pools. Herd boys sat atop buffaloes, washing their tough hides to keep flies away.

When the bus pulled into the next village, the driver motioned for Askara to disembark. "Pathankot?" she asked. Yes, he nodded. She stepped off the bus with three other people who walked away quickly. She didn't know what to do or where she was in relation to the ashram. Tired and dirty, she considered finding a room for the night, but she thought, if I leave the cup at the ashram tonight, I can return to Darian by morning. Only one last step. This nightmare will be over soon.

A thin, gray-haired rickshaw wala approached. He stopped pedaling in front of her, lowered the support bars for the rickshaw, and spoke in Hindi.

"English," Askara said.

His eyes gleamed. "I am speaking English. Wanting ride ashram?"

"Yes."

"One hundred rupees only," he said, shiny white teeth glistening against his dark buffalo-hide skin. "Come."

Askara didn't haggle over the fare. She knew robbery when she saw it. She didn't care, not now. He helped her into his rickshaw, raised the support poles to his waist, trotted down a dirt path, crossed railroad tracks, and huffed up a series of hairpin curves. Askara realized his price was not high compared to his labor, didn't even compensate for it. She intended to double the amount when they reached the ashram. Robbery nothing, she mused, the old guy's an Olympian. She saw the village below them grow dim in the evening light—ramshackle shops, clusters of modest dwellings, glowing cook fires, and pariah dogs, goats, and chickens foraging for food scraps.

The rickshaw wala, his thin body hunched forward to grip the handlebars, every sinew taut, pedaled at a slow, even pace. They climbed the uneven path toward the ashram gate. Askara begged to get out to lessen his strain, but he made no reply, nor did he stop. At the corroded metal gate, he lowered the balance poles and stood upright with an audible gasp.

He extended his leathery hand. "Ashram, you are finding," he said. Askara handed him two hundred-rupee notes. He looked down at the money, and a broad smile peeled his face like a theater curtain, revealing pristine white teeth. "Thanking you. Namaste," he said and positioned his rickshaw to take a worn path that skirted the grassy hill. Askara watched him bike away.

She stood alone in the purple evening and knocked on the ashram gate. She called *Hello* in her loudest voice. After several minutes, a man approached.

"May I see the holy man? I know his friend, Professor Doctor, from Bombay. I have a message for him."

The guard made no reply but allowed her in. He escorted her to the veranda of the first building. Pointing to a chair, he said, "Sit," and disappeared.

She sat watching moths hover around a nearby lantern. The scent of pine trees traveled on the evening breeze. She slumped in the chair and dozed but sat up abruptly when she heard footsteps.

"Master says eat, sleep. Tomorrow afternoon, come. Follow me." He walked her to the third building up the hill. He knocked on the door and spoke in Hindi. A young woman in a sari opened the door to greet them.

"Hello, sister. Welcome. You will stay here," the woman said and pointed to a bed with crisp white sheets. "What is your name?" she asked, handing her a glass of water.

"Askara."

"I'm Jyoti. Devotee, or seeker?"

"Umm, seeker, I guess."

"How do you know of the Master?" She sang the last word like the opening of a hymn.

"His friend in Bombay. They were professors together a long time ago. I have a message for him."

"Professor? I have served for ten years now. I didn't know. Sit."

They sat on wicker chairs in a small annex to the dorm-style bedroom where Jyoti studied Askara from head to foot. Askara did the same. She marveled at Jyoti's milky English complexion, untouched by fierce Indian sun, realizing Jyoti wasn't much older than herself, which meant she would have come to the ashram as a teenager. Jyoti explained she had come on holiday and had the great good fortune to hear Master give a satsang in Delhi. She moved to the ashram to serve him three months later, despite her parents' objections. She took a training course and now served as the resident nurse and the manager of the kitchen, emphasizing that all the residents have service assignments. When Askara asked if hers was a paid position, Jyoti looked startled. When the softness returned to her eyes and voice, she replied that the service performed for the Master isn't about money. She asked if Askara had family in India. Askara said, "No. Do you?

"I have no need for husband nor family," Jyoti snapped. She stood and handed Askara a towel, saying, "The washroom is across the courtyard. I will return in thirty minutes. I have work to do. Lights out by 9:00."

When Jyoti left, she mumbled a blessing in Hindi, Askara assumed, or possibly a curse. She could tell she had offended Jyoti. Askara quickly hid the cup in her clean set of clothes and carried it to the washroom. She squeezed into a small, tiled shower stall, filled the orange plastic bucket with water, flipped the electric switch for the heating coil, and placed it in the bucket. She fell asleep on the stool, waiting for the water to heat. When she jerked awake because her head hit the wall, she pulled the heating coil out. The unit, no better than the ones she had used for a cup of tea, had hardly worked. Scooping up the lukewarm water with a plastic scooper, she poured it over her and washed her hair. The thin towel became drenched quickly. The salvar kameez clung to her damp body. Exhausted, she didn't care. She quickly French braided her hair, wrapped the cup in her dirty clothes, and returned to the room. As soon as she lay down, she fell fast asleep.

Jyoti woke Askara in the dark when a loud bell clanged for 3:00 a.m. meditation. While sitting on the floor and chanting with eyes closed, Askara fell asleep. The person next to her nudged her to sit up. After prayers, everyone walked to the dining room for breakfast. Two boys scurried from person to person, dishing out ladles of rice, dahl, and curds onto metal plates. A third boy served hot chapatis. Askara sat with the others—who only said an initial hello.

Jyoti walked over. "Sister, your seva is garden weeding this morning and then kitchen work. Report to the garden after putting your plate away."

"When can I see the master?"

Jyoti looked indignant. "Only he makes that decision. You will see him at the afternoon blessing, but to see him personally, well, that is the dream of many. I can't say when, or if, that will happen."

"But I must see him. I have something to tell him."

"I will pass on your request," Jyoti said curtly. "He alone decides."

Anger scalded Askara's face. She had not come all this way not to see him, or to deal with his underlings. She had not understood, much less enjoyed, the chanting. Sitting on the floor had hurt her back. She wanted to leave the cup with the master and get back to Darian. Yet she wondered at

Professor Doctor's glowing recommendation. She worried she had made a mistake, or that he had. What if the master won't see me? What then? she thought. She tried to hide her fear, confusion, and anger from Jyoti's probing eyes, not an easy thing to do. When everyone walked in silence, as instructed, Askara attempted to avoid Jyoti.

Jyoti's dry voice cracked when she came alongside Askara. "Weed until lunch. Don't stop until you hear the bell." Again, Askara tried to ask when she could see the master, but Jyoti turned and walked away without a word.

Askara weeded the vast vegetable garden for hours in the hot sun, stopping only to drink water from the communal water bucket. Her body ached from crouching. She had made it through the chili pepper plants with their dangling green and red chilies, past the capsicum peppers, past the green pea pods on long vines, and had begun weeding around the cauliflower plants when the lunch bell rang out. She could hardly rise to walk. She washed her hands and hobbled to the dining room.

Following lunch, Askara revived after drinking two refills of chai. She quickly realized kitchen duty was not food prep but food clean-up. She struggled to clean the plates and pans with cold water before an elderly Indian woman crouching at the outdoor tap showed her how to collect the scraps for the dogs and rub the metal dishes with sand before scrubbing with them with a soapy rag. Askara found pleasure in feeding the scrawny pariah dog that hovered near the water tap. She could feel the dog's joy with every morsel, yet there were few to feed him.

At the afternoon session, Askara finally got word she could have an audience with the master. She joined the devotees in their meditation session, waiting, although irritated and ready to bolt. He entered. They prostrated themselves before him, with foreheads pressed to the ground. Askara, too stiff from gardening and too antagonistic, raised clasped hands to her forehead and remained sitting cross-legged. The master noticed. She thought he shot her a disdaining look, but it could have been her imagination, she concluded, since he was seated on a red cushion dais far away.

Later, a kitchen boy found her to say the master would see her. Jyoti dropped by their room to check that Askara had dressed appropriately for the audience. She had re-braided her hair, rinsed the grime from her face, and tried, unsuccessfully, to smooth the creases in her cotton salwar kameez suit. Jyoti approved the decency of her look, although grimacing at the wrinkled cotton. She told her not to take too much of his time and to bow when she entered and exited. The young boy led her to a courtyard where she waited for thirty tense minutes before another servant led her to an inner room where the master sat in a wicker chair.

"Thank you for seeing me, sir," she said, surprised at his youthful appearance.

"My duty. Why have you requested audience with me?"

"Well, sir, I became friends with your friend Professor Doctor in Bombay. He suggested I come to you." The master made no reply, so Askara continued, "Well, sir, he says wonderful things about you. I need your help."

"You see, sister, the man you seek, my uncle, is no longer master. It was he who knew your friend in Bombay. I inherited his mantle some years ago."

"Oh, I didn't know. I'm sorry."

"Why, sorry?"

"That your uncle died, sir. I didn't know."

"He is alive and well…living in retirement."

"Spiritual masters retire?"

"If one can no longer perform, one must step down and allow another to continue the work. The need for spiritual guidance is great, especially among you, Westerners."

"I understand. But can I see him? I have a personal message from Professor Doctor for him."

"He sees no one. He sits in meditation only. He neither speaks nor receives visitors. He observes silence. How may I be of service? I see you are troubled. Let me shoulder your burden."

Askara's heart raced. Was it anger or disappointment? Maybe both. The master fixed his gaze upon her without saying a word. The breath caught in her throat. She felt bees were stinging her. She yawned, looked away, and calm down by picturing the redwood trees at her home.

"Sir, it's…well, it's silly. You see, I'm lonely. I miss my fiancé in Bombay. I thought the ashram life was for me. Professor Doctor said I must decide before marrying. He suggested I ask his dear friend, the holy man here at this ashram. His personal message was a request his friend help me. But in coming here, I realize I am not suitable for a life of devotion. I do want to marry. I appreciate your seeing me. I know now, I should return and marry my fiancé. I have no more doubts."

"Sister, you mean you came so far just to turn around? You have a valuable opportunity for service. I can assist you in your spiritual journey."

Askara felt him probing her and sought to deflect it. "Well, sir, I do have something that confuses me."

"What?"

"Free will and karma. How do you know what's what? Like how do I know for sure that my fiancé is my destiny? Or am I willing him to be? Where do you think free will ends and karma begins?" she sputtered.

"Allow me to tell you. From your viewpoint, they seem separate. But, in reality, free will and destiny are one-and-the-same coin, only different sides. Your actions from previous times, exercised by your free will, come back to meet you as your destiny. So, everything that happens to you now is determined by the choices you made before. With each instance, you are further from free will until you have none. You live your destiny. As you move forward, you move backward. Understand?"

Askara mulled over the tangle, knowing she did not understand, but more than that, she had no interest in trying. She wanted to exit. "Thank you, sir. You have cleared up my misunderstanding. I get it. I understand. And thank you so much for your valuable time. I'm going now."

"Going to where, sister?"

"Back to Bombay, to my destiny."

"Enlightenment is not a quick process. We must work together on this," the master said, shifting his position on his cushioned chair.

"Free will leads me back to Bombay, to my fiancé, who is my destiny. I get it. On my level, I feel like staying here, so that means I should return to Bombay, even though I don't want to. Since I am choosing to do *not* what I want, but what I feel is the higher calling, I'm obligated to return and work out the karma. I understand."

"Sister, so much mental debate tangles your thoughts. We shall resume tomorrow over tea, my garden 4:00 p.m."

"Thank you, sir," Askara said and tipped her head slightly before the boy servant escorted her out.

When she got back to the canteen building, Jyoti appeared in the hallway like a vapor rising in the sun. "Have you seen Him?"

"Yes."

"How blessed you are. Askara, I have a matter to discuss, money seva, a tithe for the ashram."

"Yes, of course, I intended to pay my way. Who do I pay?"

"Me. I'm the Secretary of Finance." Askara reached into the money pouch she wore inside her tunic and handed seven hundred-rupee notes to Jyoti. "Not much by American standards," Jyoti said.

"This is India. That's a lot," Askara snapped.

"Come now, sister, most Americans tithe thousands of rupees per day. We have a lot of upkeep here."

Askara met Jyoti's glare. "Ah, sorry, I didn't understand. I'll go to the room and get more. I'll be right back."

Askara turned and hurried down the hall, relieved Jyoti had walked toward the kitchen. She rushed to their dormitory room, grabbed her gear, ran to the gate, and slipped out unseen to sprint down the path to the village. Askara saw a bus, its motor revving, and jumped on—not knowing its destination and not caring—as long as it left quickly. She slumped down in a seat and watched oblique rays of afternoon sunlight touch the hills. Disillusioned and angry, she knew she could not return to Darian until she disposed of the cup. She would not endanger him or his friends again. She needed to dispose of the cup. But how and where?

The swaying bus lulled her to sleep. When she woke, the sun had set through a dusty thick amber haze lighted by small charcoal fires that carried the scent of curry. A ticket collector towered over her, demanding payment. She shoved the money into his open hand. He punched a ticket and passed it to her. Askara had no idea which direction the bus was traveling, but it made little difference, as long as it was away from the ashram.

WHEN THE BUS PULLED INTO A TOWN FOR THE NIGHT, Askara spotted a *Quest House* sign and booked a room. After a fitful night, she woke to a dismal, heavy feeling when the cocks crowed at first light. Feeling desperate, she decided to dump the cup, to bury it somewhere. She would retrieve it later when she found a safer place for it. She rallied after eating breakfast, a chapati slathered with white buffalo cream, and several cups of strong, smoky, sweet chai. She knew her bus would leave early, but she wandered around the town, looking for a suitable burial spot. Walking to the west side of town, she followed newly sown rice paddies bordered by a wide river. To the north, Himalayan mountains increased like stairs reaching for the clouds.

Askara walked toward the river, leaving the morning vendor bustle behind. She found a grassy spot where she could be alone to toss pebbles into the river and think. She fantasized about a sanctuary for the cup, high up in the mountains, a secret place where she could bury it and be done forever, a safe place for the power object to rest, away from human eyes and human greed. Looking at the mountains, she decided to hire a pony and guide for the trek. She clutched the pack close to her chest to ask for confirmation of her plan. She whispered Magi, Magi, Magi. The Respected One's image flickered against her closed eyelids. She thought: What do I do? Where do I go?

The answer came to her like a cool breeze over the water. Follow your heart. Act with courage. The time is near.

Askara sighed, thinking my heart tells me nothing. I have no courage. I'm lost and scared. I need help. Respected One, can you give me specifics? No answer came. She opened her eyes and squinted at the sunlight, rippling on the river like tiny gold dancers. Her mind drifted to a Lake Tahoe memory, sitting on the beach, mesmerized by sunlight playing on the aquamarine water. Askara missed her parents. She wondered if she would ever see them again. She longed to speak to her father. He would know what to do. He always knew what to do. A *pucca* Sikh warrior dad always knew. She heard his words echo from her childhood: Do your best in all things, then at the end of life you can rest, knowing you made the most of your opportunities.

A scream shredded the calm morning air. Askara jumped. She spotted a frantic woman wading out into roiling muddy water, her clothes billowing up around her. She floundered in the current. Farther out, Askara saw a girl bobbing up and down, choking and sputtering.

Askara kicked off her tennis shoes and raced down the bank to where the river curved inland. She dove in. The current swept the girl toward her. Askara power kicked, her muscles straining. She reached the girl's limp body, grabbed her tunic, reeled her in, and braced her head in the crook of her arm. Askara quit kicking and let the swift current take them closer to shore. She struggled to keep the girl's head above water. When they approached the closest point of land, Askara kicked hard using a one-arm breaststroke to bring them to the reeds along the shore. She grabbed bunches and pulled them through the weeds until she found her footing in the mud. She hauled the girl's body onto the sandy bank and cleared her mouth, flipped her over, and pushed along the girl's back from waist to shoulder with force.

People gathered around quickly. The girl's mother collapsed by her child's limp body, rubbing her thin arms and feet, screaming in Punjabi. Askara worked frantically, turning the body over, pushing up from the girl's abdomen, listening for signs of breath, breathing for her, then flipping the girl to her back. Askara pulled the child's arms up toward her head and worked them back and forward in a rowing motion. She didn't react.

Askara gathered the girl like a wet doll, draped her head down over her arm, and slapped hard between her shoulder blades: one, two, three hard whacks. The girl's body expanded slightly. Askara repeated, pushing the stomach, pulling the arms, hitting between the shoulders, listening, breathing into her. She heard a gurgle. She rubbed along her spine from waist to shoulders and pulled her arms up and out. Brown water shot from the girl's mouth. The girl sputtered and whimpered. Askara draped the girl's belly over her knees, turned her head to the side, and gave her another hard slap. Water and mud gushed from her mouth, turning the sand brown. The girl gasped and grabbed her mother's hand.

Askara stretched out on the sand, panting. Onlookers shouted for a peasant passing by in his bullock cart. They lifted the child onto the wooden bed, wrapped her in a shawl, and helped the mother climb in. Two men lifted Askara and placed her next to them, covering her shivering body with burlap bags. A woman rushed up and placed Askara's backpack and tennis shoes next to her. The cart bumped along the rough path with a noisy entourage of wailers in its wake. Askara heard an erratic drumbeat in her head…and then silence.

When the driver stopped, Askara pushed herself upright far enough to see a large house. The girl's mother shouted. The gate creaked open. An elderly woman ran toward them from the house, followed by a silver-haired man in a white kurta pajama suit. The peasants carried the child and Askara into the house. They laid Askara on one bed and the frightened child on another in the same room. The girl's mother made them drink hot sweet chai while she and her maids cleaned and dressed them. The older woman gathered Askara's hair back from her face into a tight bun, hugging her repeatedly and whimpering, *Shukria*.

Askara tried to talk, but her mouth would not form words. She heard fluid sloshing in her lungs that sounded like the ocean. She coughed. She was drowning. She jackknifed forward and heaved muddy water onto the tile floor. She sputtered like an old engine but found her voice after several tries and whispered, "Is the girl all right?"

"She lives, thanks to God and you," the girl's mother said and burst into tears.

The grandfather cradled the girl in his lap, rocking her back and forth as he spoke to his daughter in Punjabi and patted her head as if she were still a child. Clearing his throat, he spoke to Askara in educated English. "Words cannot express our gratitude for what you did. This girl, the jewel of our family, the blessing of my old age, my only grandchild…to lose her would kill us all. You have spared us such suffering. Words cannot say enough. My daughter here, Narinder, cannot swim. She, too, would have died with her daughter…if not for you."

"Who do we contact for you? What's your name?" Narinder said, wiping her kohl-smeared eyes.

"No one," Askara said and struggled to recall her name. She paused and breathed. After a couple of minutes, she said, "My name's Askara."

"You must stay with us, Askara, let us care for you. Our honor is to serve you." Narinder begged, "Please, grant us this."

"Thank you. I will stay tonight. I'm exhausted."

Narinder nodded and translated for her mother, who mouthed Askara's name as if it were a confection. "Pretty name, unique," Narinder translated.

Askara and the young girl, Neetu, rested for the remainder of the day. By evening a throng of visitors had gathered to pay their respects, an endless line of well-wishers curious to see the foreigner who had saved little Neetu. The news had circulated rapidly. Even the Inspector of Police came to pay his respects. Guests brought fruit, flowers, and sweet milk delicacies. Neetu's grandfather asked his brother, a local judge, to bring the gurdwara priest to offer prayers and bless his granddaughter and the *woman of courage,* as the villagers had named Askara.

Askara received the guests with a nod and a smile as they filed past to touch her feet and thank her in Punjabi. Dressed in Narinder's clothes with her hair braided with jasmine flowers, Askara thought she looked *full* Indian. Little Neetu watched the guests from the safety of her grandfather's lap.

Neetu's grandfather stood to salute the elderly priest, raising praying hands to his forehead. "Sat-Shri-Akal, Guruji," he said. "Come meet her. This woman is the foreigner who saved my Neetu."

When the priest looked at Askara, she felt a wave of peace envelop her like a warm breeze on a chilly night. Her nagging anguish abated. For the first time in a long while, she felt calm. Everything in the room faded, except the light shining from Guruji's dark eyes. She nodded and said, "Sat-Shri-Akal, Guruji."

After minutes of shared silence, Guruji spoke. "Daughter, you acted bravely. May God bless you and keep you strong."

Hearing his words, Askara felt her body grow full of strength. Tears filled her eyes. "Thank you, Guruji, sir." She smiled, feeling as if The Respected One were in the room with her.

She watched guests file past Guruji to receive his blessing. He walked over to little Neetu, who had warmed to the company, especially to the sweets they offered.

"Neetu," he said, "young one, remember this day. You may come to understand when you grow up. But for now, enjoy the sweets." Neetu smiled at him and swallowed a sticky jalebi. He walked back to Askara, raised his clasped hands in blessing, and said a prayer in Punjabi. He whispered, "Visit me at the gurdwara tomorrow at 4 p.m. for tea. We have much to discuss." He turned, saluted the guests with "Sat-Shri-Akal," and left.

IN THE MORNING, NARINDER TOOK ASKARA SHOPPING FOR Punjabi suits. When she questioned Askara why she had almost no clothes, Askara replied, discipline. Americans have too much.

Narinder entreated Askara to stay with them as long as she liked so that they could show their gratitude. But Askara said she had to take care of some business first. After that, she would return to visit.

That afternoon, dressed in a new salwar kameez and new shoes, embroidered *chappals*, Askara left for tea with Guruji. She waited in the garden of the gurdwara, as instructed. Green parrots flitted from tree to tree, squawking jubilantly, before flying en masse to the neem tree to chatter there. Sunlight slowed like honey to a deep yellow, village bustle disappeared, and spaces between trees filled with discs of light reflected from the fountain. Water spilling over the rim sounded like tinkling bells. Askara's mind spread out into the garden; she could feel the joy of it, the birds, the water, the flowers, the bees. When Guruji approached, she attempted to stand, but the servant motioned her to remain seated.

She saluted, palms raised to her forehead. "Sat-Shri-Akal, Guruji. Thank you for inviting me, for letting me find you."

"It seems I found you, daughter. How to help?"

Askara withdrew the cup from her pack and unraveled the cloth. She handed it to the elderly guru. "This, I must put this cup someplace safe. Will you help me?"

Guruji held the cup and closed his eyes. "So, resurfaced, has it? I know of it. But how and why did this cup come to you?"

Askara explained the circumstances at length, ending with, "Guruji, please help me. Will you keep it in a safe place? Take it. Please. Set me free."

"Daughter, I am duty-bound. Yes, I shall help you. But this cup's power can only be hidden from the world if it *is not held* in the thoughts of the living. If one thinks upon it, someone else can pursue it…as you have discovered, as Emperor Selassie found out. Sooner or later, greed takes over. Few can resist its power. I had guessed you had stumbled upon something way beyond your comprehension when I saw you at Narinder's house. I did not know what. Some of us initiated into the higher mysteries know of this cup. We, to varying degrees, are immune to its lure. Yet many adepts have become overwhelmed, particularly as time goes by, even those initiates sworn to protect it. The cup will overwhelm you, Miss Askara. I am surprised it has not already. Not today, not tomorrow, but someday."

"I don't want it, Guruji. It has completely changed my life. I want to return to the safety of my previous life."

"Daughter, there is only one way that is possible. You have been touched by the cup more deeply than you know. It is not for you to keep. On this, I agree. But you cannot think of it, nor can anyone who has experienced the cup through you. That is the mandate. Do you think that possible?"

"How can that be?"

"Tell me who experienced the cup while in your keeping."

"My Australian friend Sara. We traveled together. She was with me at Emperor Selassie's palace. Darian, my fiancé, he held it. We three only, I believe. Oh, also, Darian's professor friend in Bombay, Professor Doctor. He knows. Four of us."

Guruji said, "Pursuers?"

"Wow, I don't know. Who are they? I saw the man who lunged at me in the airport in Sudan. We were chased near the Sudanese border, me and my friend Sara. I don't know who they were. There was an incident at the Ethiopian border when we first entered, but that probably wasn't related to the cup. But later, in Asmara, two men ransacked the house where we stayed. But I didn't see them either, only Mrs. Smith did. A guy at a motel room near the Blue Nile Falls tried to shoot me for our room. I have no idea what that relates to, if anything. I never knew the people who attacked us, didn't even see some of them. Oh, wait. The friend we stayed with in the Sudan, Mr. Dahab, his house was attacked. I didn't see them clearly either. It was dark. Men fired at a boat on the Nile in Khartoum where Sara and I were supposed to be, but we'd gotten off and were hiding in bushes. I have no idea if these incidents are related. But the house in the Punjab, Lakhbir's house, the one I escaped from before arriving here, I know that was related to the cup, for sure. Again, I didn't see the attackers. I ran with the cup. I had tried to leave it at an ashram for safekeeping, but I didn't trust the person there. That's how I ended up by the river and saw Neetu drowning. I think the cup brought me to you, Guruji, so you can help me. I have no idea who is after me. I do know someone wants this cup very badly. Maybe a lot of people do. I expect Selassie must. Maybe they work for him? But Selassie is in prison now. I feel people staring at me all the time. I'm really paranoid. Maybe some are real threats, maybe not. I don't know. I feel like I'm falling apart."

"Child, I can see how difficult this has been for you. But this is not the first time you have held the cup. I perceive you were a keeper of the cup in a distant time, in a distant place. But you are here now. The world has changed. Your task has become more complicated because you no longer have easy access to the guidance you need. We will do our best. The process will destroy your memories associated with the cup for your safety. If small fragments remain, they will not be enough to link the cup to you, only generate confusion. I feel this is our best approach, your only approach. I will create a mind link. It is painless. I will have you shut your eyes. You will travel in your mind to review those who know of the cup through you, those who have been affected, and the incidents that seemed threatening, even though you don't know the people involved. Do this in chronological order from when you first became aware of the cup in your pack. Then go to your specific friend, Sara. Visualize her. Hold her in your thoughts. I will release all knowledge of the cup. Then move to your fiancé and that professor who told you the legend. Visualize all the incidents and revisit them in as detailed a manner as possible. Close your eyes. Listen and follow what I say."

"Then what happens?"

"I create a mind link to the cup based on your perceptions. Then I erase all knowledge of the cup from that link. You see, the mind makes records of all we are exposed to, all we experience. We have vast records of knowledge we are unaware of stored in our minds. These impressions lie dormant, sometimes forever, sometimes for certain periods, until awakened. It is like making a recording of music on a cassette tape. You may never play the music again, or you may play it often, but the point is that it is recorded and remains…until the tape is destroyed. We record our experiences, conscious as well as unconscious. For everyone's safety, I must erase segments of their tapes, a painless process the person does not perceive. No harm is done. In fact, relaxation comes. Eradicating connections to the cup frees you, forever. You will have no memory of it."

"So, how would that work with the attackers at the Smiths' when I wasn't there?"

"I go from your memory to Mrs. Smith's. She holds memory threads to you and to others she witnessed, and from those threads to others, and so on. This process is difficult to do, and even more difficult to explain. It is based on the comprehension of threads that bind and define us."

"Oh, I forgot to name him, Sir Alexander Desta, the man who first showed me the cup at Jubilee Palace in Ethiopia."

"He's crucial. We will start with him, then go to Sara. He is the first, you are sure?"

"Yes. Will I feel this? I mean when you erase all those memories, will it hurt?"

"Not at all. It's like sleep. Relax. The gaps will register

to you and others as memory loss, something we humans accept as natural and normal. Think of it as a skip in the tape, but the music quickly resumes. Or on a phonograph machine, when the needle gets stuck in the groove, no music comes, but when the needle shifts to the next groove, the music resumes. We listen to the music and forget the skips because they hold nothingness."

"Okay."

"I hope your friend Darian was observant. His recollections are crucial since he directly witnessed the attack you fled. When I access Professor Doctor's memories, his academic knowledge of the cup will remain intact; all else will fade. Lastly, I will focus on you after I have cleaned the cobwebs. You are most important. All memory of the cup must leave you, every bit of it, for this to work."

"Everything?" Askara said. "Even my connection to the spiritual teacher I came to know?"

"I am sorry, yes. For your safety." Guruji sat in contemplation for a moment, eyes closed. "What did your teacher say about contacting him?"

"He said to focus on him, repeat *Magi, Magi, Magi* three times to verify it is him, not the Deceiver, and I could communicate with him."

"So be it. He gave you the method. It shall remain. He can protect that gift. He watches out for you, but you forget him. You drift away in a dream. Askara's eyes welled with tears. For an instant, she felt as if she saw the wavering image of The Respected One sitting next to the guru.

"No, I will not. I will keep him in my heart."

"I hope so, but the way is not easy, and the mind is tricky, and you can be deceived. Now let us begin. Close your eyes. Take slow, deep breaths, and follow my directions."

ASKARA HEARD GURUJI CALL HER NAME. SHE OPENED HER eyes and glanced at the peaceful garden. She smiled. She reached for her teacup and drank the last sip.

"Thank you, Guruji, for inviting me over for tea. I feel so much better. I'm so glad to have met you."

"It was a brave thing you did saving little Neetu, Miss Askara. I wanted to thank you personally. Neetu has a bright future; she is a born leader. We cannot lose her. Her destiny could help us all. The driver waits to take you back to Narinder's. Any time you desire to see me, please, visit. I am at your service. Now and always."

When Askara returned to Narinder's house, the family rushed out to greet her with their news. The Tanda District Magistrate issued an alert for an American woman last seen at Lakhbir Phoolka's house. They fear someone abducted her. Narinder blurted out, "The description fits you, Askara, even the name. Why didn't you tell us?"

"Yes, I was there with a friend. I remember that. But there is some mistake. I was not abducted. I visited an ashram and then arrived here by the river. I'll return and see my friends in Tanda and clear this up. My mind felt fuzzy after nearly drowning, guess I had oxygen deprivation or something? Now I feel great, thanks to your good care, Narinder. I'll leave first thing tomorrow."

ASKARA DEPARTED IN THE MORNING WITH NARINDER'S driver, waved goodbye to the neighbors and villagers who had walked over to see her off, and hugged Narinder's family, promising to return and introduce them to Darian.

The local Superintendent of Police pulled into the driveway and trotted over to halt the car.

"Miss Askara, I informed Tanda office by telex: No need to worry. American in question, Miss Askara Timlen, not abducted. On holiday only. Rescued drowning child. Will arrive by private car late afternoon. Formal report pending."

CHAPTER TWENTY

Reunion

Darian summoned his strength and stood, holding onto the stairway banister. Disoriented, he made his way toward two figures walking his direction. Then he collapsed.

Forms grew distinct in the darkness. One man looked familiar to Darian, another not. He pulled himself upright. Quickening his gait made the heaviness fade from his limbs. He searched for Askara. Where is she? He wondered. He didn't panic. He continued walking forward to ask the people standing motionless in shadows. Have you seen her? No one answered. Darian realized the man in a white uniform—further up the path, the one directing people—would be the correct person to ask.

The scene looked pristine. Every detail from the vibrant grass to the swiftly flowing river to the distant purple mountains were starkly crisp, clearly delineated, yet stationary, frozen, like a fine-grain photo enlargement, including the river. No wind tickled the verdant leaves, no bird sailed the sky, no shadow crept up the mountain, yet the man, a bearded gentleman, with shiny gold buttons and medals on his chest approached at a quick pace to lead Darian by the arm.

"We weren't expecting you at this time, sir," he said in a comforting voice. "Allow me to show you the way."

"Thank you," Darian replied, "I'm glad to have help; I'm unfamiliar with this part of Lakhbir's property."

"You see those stone steps up there to the right beyond the garden?"

"Yes."

"Follow them. Take the path that crosses the field. Continue. You will reach the bridge. Not many approach this way, but there's always an exception. Good journey, sir."

"Thank you," Darian said and trudged on. The day, neither warm nor cool, sparkled with tiny prisms of light against the cerulean sky. Darian's strength increased with every step. He looked back at the figures along the edge of the field, huddled in shadow, flailing aimlessly, wondering why the kind uniformed gentleman made no effort to help them. He ignored them. Darian trotted, assuming Askara had outdistanced him on the path, regretting he had not asked the gentleman about her.

The stone bridge reflected the sunlight like burnished brass. Wheat stalks stirred in a nearby field. A feeling of contentment washed away Darian's worry, confusion, and pain. He felt buoyant. He skimmed his hand over the plant's golden tassels. Shiny flecks of gold coated his fingertips. Ahead, a glow settled over the bridge while the stream became animated and rolled, tumbled, and slid over iridescent rocks before calming at the horizon. The rushing water sounded like women chanting—high notes dropped low and rose again in a crescendo—yet he noticed the water's movement ceased when he looked directly at it. Darian thought he could almost—but not quite—catch the women's words.

When he approached the bridge, vicious dogs tethered one on either side reared up and snarled, displaying gaping mouths full of spiked silver teeth and barbed tails that sliced the air. When they lunged at him, Darian froze. The dogs sprang again, clanging their heavy chains against the stonework. Darian realized the beasts couldn't reach him if he didn't advance. But the guide had told him to go to the bridge, he assumed, to cross it. He wanted to cross over into the green, fertile pasture on the far side, to relax and listen to the melodious chanting water, but how to pass these ferocious dogs? Darian stepped forward. The dogs stood on their hinds, pawed the air, and snapped their powerful jaws. Knowing they would attack if he attempted to run past them, he stood still. The singing water grew louder. Darian felt his chest pulse with the rhythm. To his surprise, the dogs slumped, dropped their heads, tucked their muzzles into their flanks, and fell asleep.

Darian walked forward unimpeded. When he stepped onto the bridge, the stones liquefied and flowed around and over his feet like gelatinous water. He began sinking. An elderly man in a shimmering robe rushed toward him and offered his hand to stabilize him. The stones solidified. Darian found his footing.

"Son, not yet. Your time is not upon you. You have work to fulfill, your sacred pledge to Asha. Do not fear; I shall escort you at the appointed time. We will meet here on the Chinvat Bridge as proof of your goodness when you come again. Go now, return to your body and heal."

"Is Asha here, sir?"

"No, son. Go back now. You will be snared in the In-Between if you delay."

The stream receded and turned to earth. The bridge disappeared. Darian's limbs grew heavy as he trudged past sleeping dogs and walked across a wheat pasture. When he looked back, he saw the vague outline of the man raising his hands in blessing. Darian's body grew slower, heavier, and more painful as he reached Lakhbir's garden steps. Each footfall sent painful jabs up his legs to a black hole near his chest. He felt like a kite flying high on an unfavorable wind—twisting, turning, diving, and descending with great speed—until it smashed onto hard ground and broke into thousands of brittle shards that liquified and seeped into the earth.

LAKHBIR SHOUTED, "TELL THE DRIVER TO FETCH DR. Bhatia. Darian's losing a lot of blood." He scooped Darian up and carried him to the bedroom. He applied pressure to his arm. "Amrit, help me. Rip that sheet into strips. Tie two lengths together. Wrap his arm here, where my hand is. Tighter. And further down. Here. Good. Fetch whiskey." When Amrit ran back in, she shoved the bottle into Lakhbir's hand. He lifted Darian's head and forced him to swallow Glenlivet. Darian took sips but mostly dribbled the whiskey down his shirt. Lakhbir monitored the tourniquet pressure. "Amrit, send for the police. Askara's missing. My God, what a tragedy, and here in our own home."

When Dr. Bhatia arrived, he staunched the bleeding, removed the bullet from Darian's right shoulder, disinfected the wound, and dressed it, telling Lakhbir that Darian had lost considerable blood and not to move him.

"He won't wake soon. I gave him morphine injections. Your friend was lucky, no bone shattered, no lung grazed. I'll return to check on him directly. Only if he worsens, bring him to Guru Nanak Hospital. Otherwise, do not disturb him. Call me if there's a change."

"Thank you, doctor. I feared the worst."

The doctor looked at Lakhbir. "Quite a swollen face. You need stitches above your left eye. Drink some whiskey. I'll do it now," he said, cleaning the wound. "What happened here?"

Lakhbir recounted the break-in at his dinner party the previous evening. He explained how two men had jumped him from behind. They fought; he threw one to the floor, the other hit him in the head with the butt of his gun. Darian rushed upstairs to his fiancée Askara. The *thuggee* chased him. A gunshot echoed in the stairwell. The guests downstairs screamed, held at gunpoint by the man who had hit Lakhbir. He pressed his pistol into Lakhbir's father's temple and forced the guests into the servants' kitchen. He ordered Lakhbir's mother to hand over the key, but she stood still, not understanding. So Lakhbir grabbed the key and opened the door. The *thuggee* ordered everyone into the pantry and locked the door. By the time Lakhbir broke down the pantry door and rushed upstairs, Darian lay unconscious, his shirt covered in blood. The gardener ran into the house, shouting that they poisoned the guard dogs, the American had run away, and the gatekeeper wasn't waking up. Then pandemonium broke out among the guests. They fled as fast as they could, except for two who had waited to speak to the police.

"Must be land, Lakhbir. A deal gone bad?" the doctor said, finishing the final stitch on Lakhbir's brow. "Keep it clean."

"I have no land for sale. No one would dare take my land by force."

"Jealous relatives?"

"No, doctor. My sister lives in Malaysia, and she has no interest in our family land. Her husband is wealthy. An attack like this, for what? The wheat crop? Bags of basmati?"

"Gambling debts, son. Enemies?"

"No, sir. But why abduct an American?"

"I don't know, but when the police arrive, if you have something to hide, do it well…for your parents' sake. As for the American, she must be here on the property somewhere, too frightened to show herself. You'll find her crouched in the bushes. Call if you need me."

When the Superintendent of Police and six policemen arrived, Lakhbir rushed out to meet them, ordering his guests to wait inside. Only Amrit followed. A policeman hunched over to study the gatekeeper's body and reported: not dead, drugged. "But your guard dogs are dead, Mr. Phoolka," the SP said. "Over there, by the compound wall, we found poisoned meat. This was a well-planned attack not carried out by average thuggees. I must interview everyone. Your servant thought the men were not Punjabis."

"No. They spoke English with a foreign accent. They wore Western clothes and shoes."

"Was the American woman with you downstairs, madam?" he asked Amrit.

"No, sir, she had gone to bed early. No one saw her after that. Servants search the fields for her even now."

The S.P. pulled Lakhbir aside to whisper, "Mr. Phoolka, do you have political enemies? Could this be a ransom situation?"

"No, sir. This attack has nothing to do with me. I am sure."

Askara was surprised to see so many police in the driveway when Narinder's driver pulled into Lakhbir's compound three days later. He eased forward toward the house. Police surrounded the car. Askara jumped from the back seat before the vehicle entirely stopped and bolted past them to where Darian sat on the veranda, propped up in a chair, his bandaged arm elevated on pillows. He attempted to rise. Amrit eased him back down on the cushions.

"Thank God, you're alive," she said and burst into tears, smothering Darian in soft kisses.

"Askara," Darian whispered, "my heart broke. I thought the worst. Police searched for you. Where did you go?"

"Darian, I'm here now, unhurt. We'll talk in private. People are staring at us. What's happening? Am I under arrest?"

Lakhbir walked up and glared at Askara. "What have you done?"

"Nothing. I've done nothing," Askara snapped back. Amrit whispered something to Lakhbir, her face tense and flushed. "I'm so sorry for all of this, Lakhbir. Thank you both for taking care of Darian. Are your parents okay?"

"Thanks to God, they're well, and Darian is healing," Lakhbir replied and studied Askara's face like a hawk studying a mouse. "The burglars fled, we assumed with you. How is it, Askara, that you appear unharmed when they drugged my guard, killed my Alsatians, shot Darian, and locked us up?"

Amrit interrupted her husband, putting a firm hand on his forearm. "With Guru's grace, you have returned safely, Askara. That is what matters, Lakhbir."

Askara shot back. "This is *your* house, Lakhbir. I was visiting. Don't blame me for this debacle. The problem is yours, not mine. I know I ran into the night; I was really scared. I had to get away. But I don't remember the details."

Lakhbir retreated a bit and hissed. "That is convenient. You don't remember? The Superintendent of Police launched an intensive search for you, *the missing American*. Then you reappear one hundred miles away, after saving a child's life? Don't you see how strange this is, Askara? You have cast a shadow on my family's honor."

"You dishonor yourself, Lakhbir, trying to blame me—your houseguest—for a robbery attempt. Shame on you! Look, the shock of almost drowning—having oxygen deprivation from saving that girl—affected my brain, gave me amnesia, so back off. I've said I don't remember what happened here, much less why it happened. I do know I ended up at a river, and I pulled a girl out. Narinder's family can verify everything from the time I jumped into that river until their driver brought me back here now. Ask them. I will not sit quiet and let you accuse me."

Lakhbir looked at Darian and steadied his voice. "I am not accusing you, Askara. I'm trying to make sense of this."

Amrit grabbed his hand and stammered. "Lakhbir doesn't like me saying this, but he's running for Member of Parliament in the upcoming elections. I think that's why nothing was stolen. The *thuggees* wanted to scare us, so Lakhbir will withdraw his name."

Lakhbir snapped at Amrit to shut up, dismissing her words as an absurd notion. "What would a young girl know about politics anyway?" he snarled. Amrit blanched at Lakhbir's tone and backed away, excusing herself to fetch tea. "My wife is afraid people will appear at our door at all hours with their land problems. There's a growing movement in the Punjab, the Khalistan movement. Sikhs want their own country and government. Sometimes they come and talk to me about it. That's all. She worries as MP I would need to keep opposing forces happy. They may try to buy me off. I'm stronger than she thinks."

Darian slowly stood, leaning on Askara. "This has gone far enough. Lakhbir, I need time alone with Askara, and I expect you to remain civil when speaking to her."

"I do apologize, Askara. My temper gets the best of me," Lakhbir said and steadied Darian. "Let me help you upstairs. The servants will bring afternoon tea and dinner to your room. Rest and be together. I inspect my fields early in the morning and will see you on my return. The police guards remain day and night. We're safe. Askara, you're safe here... and you are welcome. Excuse me."

In the privacy of their upstairs room, Darian embraced Askara, nestled his face in her hair, and explained in a cracked, dry voice that he had feared the worst. For two days, he had lain consumed by pain and confusion. The morphine didn't help; it gave him strange visions. In one, he searched for Askara in a hot, dry place and in another by a river, but he couldn't find her. An elderly man in a loose, flowing garment appeared. He talked, but Darian couldn't remember their conversations when he woke. Darian knew he was running to help Askara, to protect her, but he didn't know from what. Those dreams tortured him more than the gunshot wound, he confided. When he saw the elderly man standing at a beautiful bridge that was guarded by vicious, horrible dogs, the man greeted him and told Darian he had arrived too early and that he must return to help *Asha*. The man promised to meet him at the correct time at the bridge to eternity.

Askara stroked his face. "Morphine does that. Darian, you were wounded. You must rest. I'm here now. I'll take care of you. My crazy jumbled thoughts bounce off surfaces of words, memories, emotions, but they'll straighten out soon. I'm sorry I was rude to Lakhbir, but he deserved it. I'm talking about me, but you're the one suffering."

"Askara, this will pass. I'm so happy you're back, unharmed. Your heroes came here to help, two U.S. Marines."

"What?"

"Lakhbir notified the U.S. Embassy. Now I know what you meant about the Marines. Within hours, two Marines showed up here to interview us. Impressive, young, strong, fierce types but well-mannered, and cordial in a militaristic way. They returned to speak to Lakhbir privately. I am surprised they couldn't find you. Anyway, the S.P. called the embassy in Delhi and notified them of your return.

"Askara, you saved a child's life. I hardly think your Marines, or anyone else, could fault you on that. The shirt label one thuggee wore, *Sudan Gezira Cotton,* caused your embassy's concern since you had been in Sudan."

Days passed before the Superintendent of Police notified them that embassy officials had read the Marines' notes and the S.P.'s account of the break-in, and the police report of Askara Timlen saving a young girl from drowning. They cleared Askara to leave with no charges pending, case closed. The attack, according to the S.P., was deemed *politically motivated,* given the information he received about an earlier threat on Lakhbir's life, as recounted to him by the elder Mr. Phoolka.

Chapter Twenty-One

Transitions

When Darian and Askara exited the Bombay airport, Darian expected to see his company driver, not his uncle. His *chacha* greeted him with unfortunate news. Darian's apartment had been burgled during his absence. The building society's safety committee fired the night watchman over the incident. Someone had found the man in the early morning sprawled on the lawn, unconscious from drink. That surprised and saddened Darian. He knew the man well, a chaste Hindu who did not drink. His uncle merely replied that everyone has a weakness while emphasizing the excellent news that nothing of value had been taken, not even the jade statues. No other flats had been burgled, which made sense because Darian was the only person out-of-station.

When Darian and Askara reached his apartment, Darian sent word through the gardener to find the night watchman and bring him by. When he questioned the man, he begged for his job, staunchly declaring his innocence.

"Sahib, you know I drink no whiskey. I had only *Limca* the man handed me."

"What man?"

"Your visitor."

"What did he look like?"

"Foreigner. He spoke to his friend, and his friend spoke to me in Hindi. He gave me the cola. Nice of him. Hot night. I remember nothing until day guard kicked me in the ribs. May gods judge me, sir, I speak the truth."

AFTER VERIFYING THE BURGLARY REPORT WITH THE LOCAL police, Darian decided he and Askara should depart for California as soon as possible. He knew Askara was so nervous that they would get no rest if they stayed in Bombay. Darian could not convince her she was safe. He had a hard time convincing himself. Two break-ins at two different locations in a short time seemed impossible, yet they had happened. Darian's doctor permitted him to travel since the wound had closed, and there was no sign of infection. But he warned him to take rest and drink lime juice to cleanse his kidneys of medications.

Darian rechecked everything in his apartment. He left his valuables with his uncle, in the company safe, just in case. He gave the new watchman strict instructions to patrol hourly, which the man readily agreed to do when Darian pressed seven hundred-rupee notes into his hand. Darian notified his neighbors of his vacation dates and asked them to keep an eye on his flat. He said he expected no visitors. He hired an additional gate guard, at his own expense, for increased security, and to allay the fears of tenants who gossiped that one of Darian's business deals in Asia had gone wrong and people were after him. Darian flatly denied the story.

"I've gone over everything," he said to Askara on the drive to the airport two days later. "Anything of importance,

I put in uncle's safe. My apartment is a bachelor's place. I still don't understand why anyone would break in. And once in, why tear it apart and take nothing?"

"Like Lakhbir's," Askara said, "lots of valuables, nothing stolen. Broken, yes, stolen, no. Maybe the fight stopped the thuggees at Lakhbir's, but no one stopped the thieves in your flat. They had all the time they needed. India is changing. Thieves are everywhere ...and they're dumb, seems to me. Or, they don't know what they want to steal, or they can't find it. That's the scary part."

"Not *so* dumb. They're getting in. I do not believe for a second that these two robberies aren't connected, and with foreigners involved both times. But why?" Darian said with exasperation. "What could they be after?"

"Maybe someone in Asia, one of your business contacts, thinks you are worth more than you are? I mean, monetarily. Maybe they think you're a drug runner? I have no idea. Hey, I finally got through to Sara. When I asked how she's doing, she mentioned how foggy her head's been; she can't remember parts of our African trip. She wonders if she had a sunstroke. How odd is that, Darian? Three people with memory damage. I figure we drank bad water, maybe in Sudan, got some weird parasite thing. I remember Greece very well, in vivid color, like a movie, and my trip with Sara, the first part. Then things get cloudy."

"I recall every detail of Greece. I can see you stretched out on the stones at the Oracle of Delphi, the sun playing in your hair, and later your disappointed face that night in Mombasa."

"Okay, let's not go there again. We worked through that misunderstanding. We've come a long way, Darian. Your coming to join me in Sudan was huge...is huge. No man, outside of my dad, has ever been there for me like that."

"And we will go a long way together, Askara, a lifetime. In ten minutes, we'll be at the Bombay airport, and then California, here we come."

Askara's attention drifted to her Marin County home on a hill, to her three neighbors, and to the narrow road leading up to her place that skirts a huge redwood tree, and the dirt road that appears to dead-end at her house but continues down to Woodacre. Askara got excited about the prospect of being home, feeling safe and secluded, and breathing fresh Pacific Ocean air scented by redwood trees.

"Darian, we can take walks along the ridge and see the San Francisco Bay. At night, the Golden Gate Bridge lights make the fog glow pink-gold."

"Sounds wonderful. Oh, I read in the *Times* that Selassie is in prison in his palace, supposedly unhurt. His nephew Sir Alexander fled to England. The coup, carried out by a group called The Derg, formed a provisional government. Too bad for Selassie and the region. A Marxist government could de-stabilize the whole of East Africa."

"That's a shame, but I'm not totally surprised. Something was wrong there. So many poor people and so many hungry, yet he had huge buildings constructed in his honor. Maybe those are torn down now?"

Askara felt vindicated that international news validated why she had failed to land an Ethiopian heirloom jewelry purchase for Ramsey. Selassie's private collection, she feared, would be sold off to purchase ammunition. But Ramsey might have another shot at getting what he wants on the black market, she thought, although he says he doesn't get involved in illicit deals. Askara recalled his often repeated personal mantra: "Can't do anything to tarnish your reputation and succeed in my line of work."

AFTER A VERY LONG PLANE RIDE, THEY FINALLY ARRIVED in San Francisco. Askara and Darian, stiff and out of sync with the Pacific time zone, having left Bombay twenty-four hours earlier, rented a car and drove to her home.

Lucas Valley Road looked more beautiful than Askara remembered. Golden hills swayed in the early morning breeze. Horses, sleek and well-fed, chomped tufts of grass in their white-picket-fence pastures. Askara lowered her window and breathed in the comfort of home. Darian dozed, his head bumping against the windowpane. Leaving downtown Woodacre, she followed the road uphill that split at the massive redwood tree. The sharp turn woke Darian. He rubbed his eyes.

"From one dream to another," Darian said, looking around. "The famous tree?"

"Yep. And in two more turns, we'll be at the top." Askara pulled into the gravel driveway in front of her compact house, a sugar cube with green trim. "Home sweet home. Thank God. See that path over there, Darian? It goes up to the crest. From there, you can see the Pacific Ocean if it's not too foggy." Askara eased into her carport, cut the engine, and jumped out. "Smell those redwoods. Aaah," she said and stretched her arms to take a deep breath. She walked over to Darian and hugged him. "Welcome to my home."

"Ocean and damp trees, lovely clean air, quiet, what a pleasure."

Askara reached for the housekeys she stashed on a carport rafter, untangled them from a cobweb of netted flies, and opened the front door. The small living room, monochromatic in dim light, burst into color when she pulled back the curtains. Light fell across the floral couch. "Giverny," she said, smiling. "But wait, this is the best part." She took Darian by the hand and walked him through the small kitchen to the white French doors. They stepped out onto the balcony. "Look up."

"Stunning. I've never seen trees like these redwoods." Darian wrapped his fit arm around Askara's waist and pulled her close. "How do you make yourself go to work? I wouldn't leave home."

"Rent is a huge motivator. I work from home on some projects. San Francisco's only a thirty-minute drive from here, in good traffic. I used to live in the city, but I couldn't take it anymore, the traffic, noise, cramped apartments, huge parking fines. Then I found this place."

"No wonder, Bombay...." Darian stopped mid-sentence. A rustling noise from the bushes caught his attention. A doe and two spindly-legged fawns appeared from the foliage, looking up unconcerned, and began nibbling tender green fern shoots.

"Mule deer. My neighbors. They love ferns."

Askara opened the creaky door from the kitchen to her bedroom and motioned Darian in. He eased past the oak pineapple-poster bed to examine hand-blown glass perfume bottles on the dresser.

"Where did you get these *ittars*?" he said.

"Egypt. In front of a mosque in Alexandria. An old mullah was selling them to raise money for the mosque's renovation."

"Were you on business?"

"Kind of. Ramsey invited me to go with his family last year to introduce me to some of his colleagues for future buying trips."

"Why would he send a female to conduct business in Egypt?"

"You think females can't conduct business?"

"Of course they can, but I know how some cultures work, Egypt being one of them."

"He wanted me to meet his partners, so I could act as a courier when needed for high-end items. I wouldn't actually buy them, just transport them, complete the necessary paperwork for import, bring the item back... *white-glove treatment*."

"Do you pack them? The objects you carry?"

"I fill out the customs forms and oversee the packing."

"Risky, Askara, something illegal could be hidden inside like drugs, or diamonds, or something."

"True, happens in the movies." But Askara knew Mr. Ramsey was well-respected in professional San Francisco circles, and he did not deal in black market goods. Even if he wanted to, his social climber self wouldn't allow him to blow his upward mobility goal. She realized Darian could think that of Ramsey, given the Nagali fiasco. Wanting to avoid a confrontation, she didn't reply. There was no need to explain that Ramsey stipulated his employees must be drug-free and fingerprinted. His clients, the San Francisco elite, classy museum directors and collectors, people of taste and refinement, had no interest in shady deals. "Anyway, since going to Egypt that one time, I haven't been back. I think he invited me more as a companion for his wife, Sonya. Good, I did go. At the last minute, Ramsey couldn't, so Sonya and I had a great trip, fully paid for by her husband. Her brother met us there and took us around. Well, Darian, how do you like my little place?"

"I like it very much. I thought a buyer would have a pretentious place. Yours is tasteful, simple, very appealing. The setting's magnificent."

"And California, what do you think so far?"

"I slept through most of the drive. In India, one's impression of California is sun and surfboards, neon signs, the Marlboro Man reigning his horse while lighting a cigarette, fast cars, sexy pale-haired women in teeny bikinis, surfers, that sort of thing, very commercial. But I like this area. It's beautiful."

"That's southern California. The north's different. I love to travel, but I love to come home," Askara said, detecting a vague discomfort sail across Darian's face like a shadow. "Nature here, but big-city culture is a short ride away. Both worlds. That's pretty special."

DARIAN SAT AND WATCHED *THE HUMPBACK HILLS*, AS Askara called them, swim in veils of fog. Only the near tip of a golf course in the valley below remained visible, but it soon disappeared. Redwood boughs twitched in a sporadic breeze. Askara phoned in an order for Thai food delivery, and they sat at the front window gazing out at amber light haloes in the distance, mesmerized and too tired to talk. After eating, Darian wrapped himself in a woolen shawl and fell asleep.

The moisture swollen door to her bedroom moaned when she opened it, but the noise did not rouse Darian. Askara plopped down across her bed to call Mr. Ramsey. She wasn't expecting a warm greeting, or any greeting at all since it was late, but she did hope she would not be fired. He didn't pick up. Askara left a message on his answering machine: This is Askara. I'm back. Didn't nail that purchase. Long story. I tried in India. No luck. Let's meet tomorrow morning at 9:00 at Max's. See you there. After showering, she crawled in bed and rolled over to stare at the ceiling poster of Big Sur's rocky coastline with frothing surf and seagulls and fell asleep.

Birdsong woke Askara at dawn. She reached over and felt Darian's warm body. She pressed against him and dozed until the *varoom* of the neighbor's Harley shook her windowpanes. She blinked and groaned. Darian shifted and fell back to sleep. Askara dragged herself into the bathroom to dress. Leaving a note by the bed for Darian, she slipped out of the house.

Commuter traffic, after weeks away, reminded Askara of what she did not miss, although it was nothing compared to Bombay. She hugged the slower lane until she reached the Golden Gate Bridge. Cars queued up like ants in a food line, plying inbound lanes to the city; overhead, fog erased the looming, orange bridge towers. Askara accelerated after the tollgate, reached Van Ness, turned toward the Financial District, and, to her surprise, found parking in front of Max's Café. A good omen, she figured. She often met Mr. Ramsey at Max's for morning coffee, ostensibly because he enjoyed Tassajara baked goods with his Turkish coffee. Still, Askara knew it had more to do with a certain waitress, Mimi, the petite brunette with large green eyes and ample breasts. Ramsey never wanted to go to any other coffee shop for meetings. Askara knew this about him.

Mimi greeted Askara at the door. "Good to see you again, Miss Timlen. Your boss is waiting at table six. What can I get for you today?" Mimi said, flicking a permed hair from her breast shelf.

"Espresso, please," Askara said, smiling at the blinding sheen of Mimi's frosted maroon lipstick.

Mr. Ramsey always sat at table six, by the window overlooking Kearny Street, so he could gaze at the *cafe movie*, as he called it, the street life below. He often commented to Askara about the people jockeying for tight parking places, the employees rushing to work, the tourists fumbling with downtown walking maps, the Yellow Cabs picking up foreigners who were freezing in cold summer fog and burning up in autumn's Indian Summer heat, the delivery trucks blocking traffic lanes while off-loading goods at mom-and-pop grocery stores, the street people panhandling, and the drunks staggering with paper-bagged bottles of Ripple wine. "Life in the city," Ramsey would say and smile. "Askara, it's worth viewing, a lesson in what *not* to do."

Mr. Ramsey stood, extending his suntanned hand weighed down by a chunky gold-chain bracelet. "Nice to see you again, Askara. I've worried about you. I'm pleased you're safe. YOU'RE FIRED." Ramsey sat down, smiled, and placed his neatly folded table napkin in his lap.

"Wow, that was quick," Askara said, with her eyes stretched wide.

"Joking. Gotcha. No Ethiopian heirlooms, eh? Bad timing, Selassie foiled everything."

"More like he got foiled," Askara replied.

"No success in Kenya either, Reh called to say. I'm sorry to hear of that Nagali problem. I do not know him personally. I would have never suggested him."

"I thought you did know him."

"By phone. A Canadian friend of mine is a friend of the Aga Khan. The Aga Khan knows Nagali. Nagali helped him on some business with President Amin. I presumed Nagali a sound contact."

"If you like vipers."

"Ethiopia overland? India? You realize, Askara, I will not reimburse you for that travel. You should have communicated with me…often. No purchase, no commission. Simple. Do that again, and No Job."

"I am sorry. Let me explain. I tried to call several times from Kenya. The calls didn't go through. After I left Kenya for Ethiopia, it was hard, no phones, no time. I don't expect you to pay for the overland trip to Ethiopia, although overland was cheaper than flying, or the ticket to India."

"But Sudan to India? Come on, Askara, that's hardly a direct flight."

"Wait, Sudan? How did you know about that?"

"A call came from a government official asking me to verify that you work for me. It shocked me. I don't remember his title, but I vouched for you, of course. I told him you were on a buying trip for me. Okay, I white-lied, but don't expect me to cover for you again, not going to happen. I have my reputation to protect. He said something about your port of entry that I didn't understand."

"I'm stunned. Weird. I don't think I ever mentioned you to an official. I guess maybe I did," Askara said, trying to remember.

"Weird that I vouched for you? What did you do, Askara?"

"I had to leave Ethiopia and go overland to Sudan because of the coup. The airports had closed. I crossed at a border gate that they don't use much; that's all."

"From Sudan, you should have flown back to California, but you flew to India. Why?"

"Yes. I mentioned that in the telegram. Didn't you get my telegram?

"No."

"I met someone, Darian. He thought he could help me find heirloom jewelry, from a maharajah's estate, through a jeweler in Bombay. No luck. Worse than that, Darian was shot in the shoulder during a violent burglary at his friend's house. I escaped, but I almost drowned, pulling a girl out of a river. I had temporary amnesia or something. Darian's here with me now, recuperating."

"Sorry, Askara, sounds like a B movie plot. Seriously, drowning, burglary, and love." Askara felt her face burn red hot. Ramsey altered his tone. "Okay, I had better meet your new guy. I don't want my best employee stolen from me, especially now when my book's almost ready, except for the image layouts and the text you need to complete."

"I won't let you down, Mr. Ramsey, but let me explain."

Askara recounted the business particulars of her journey, watching Ramsey fight to focus on her words when Mimi's ample figure sashayed past. When Askara described the jewelry and artifacts she had seen at Jubilee Palace, Ramsey perked up. He questioned her repeatedly about insignificant things, the room, Sir Alexander's manners, the palace grounds, even what types of shade trees were in the garden. Askara thought Ramsey was reeling off course, trying to cover his anger with silly details to show interest when all he wanted was to set up a meeting with Mimi.

"Why didn't you put offers on the jewelry you saw right away?"

"Mr. Ramsey, many of the items weren't for sale. Sir Alexander showed Selassie's collection to me to be polite. My friend Sara and I were to meet him the following day, so I could look at pieces from noble families that were for sale. Never happened. The coup broke out. I escaped Addis with Sara in her Land Rover."

"You should have been more forceful. Royals are reserved. Selassie's in dire straits now. Poor old guy. I sent you to do the groundwork for a small purchase as a lead-in for me to pursue a large one. Our chance is lost, at least for now. The Emperor may be facing the end of his reign, maybe the end of his life. At least, he's still alive. That's something. I have always admired him."

"More forceful? You weren't there. Sir Alexander had little time. Later that day, the coup broke out. You have no idea what I went through. For the record, your Zambian contact Nagali was a sham, a nightmare. The guy's a sleazy womanizer. He was hitting on me. He tried to hypnotize me. Find yourself another monarchy contact, another soothsayer, whatever. I'm fed up. You don't seem to care at all about the stress I've been under. Have you even asked me about me? *No*. I almost drowned saving a kid in India. Since then, my mind feels like mush. I have a gap in my memory, some sort of oxygen-deprivation amnesia thing. I need time off. Better yet," Askara said and stood abruptly, "I quit. I'll submit a formal letter tomorrow. Mr. Ramsey, I RESIGN."

"Askara, whoa, forgive me. You're upset. You can't resign. I need you. You're the best. My wife tells me I'm wrapped up in myself; maybe she's right. I am concerned about you. Of course, I am. You are our family friend, Askara, and you're exhausted. I see that now. Please, take a couple of paid days off, on me. Have a good visit with your new guy. What did you say his name is? Oh, yes, Darian."

"Is that all you have to say?"

"Should I beg? I'm not firing you; that's big of me. I need your help. I need support materials for the section on the history of beads. You are the only one who has worked on this project with me. Askara, it would take too long to train someone else. My publisher wants to go to press within two months. PLEASE, do not leave me now. Look, take it easy, work at home, but please start on this next week. The remainder of this week is on me, my way of saying thanks. I'll be busy with the Asian Carpet Expo anyway. Work at home, work at your own pace, take naps, rest, order out, whatever, but *please* work on the book. Stay with me. I'll make it worth your while."

"How worth my while?" Hearing her own words, Askara wondered who was speaking. She had never been so blunt. Must be exhaustion, she thought.

"Double your salary for the next three months plus a 20% bonus if we hit the publisher's deadline. How's that?"

"Agreed." Askara wanted to jump up and down and do a happy dance. "Okay, I'll start with the remaining publisher photo requests since that takes the most time...on Monday."

"Excellent. Keep me informed. Let's meet here to discuss the project at the same time next week."

"Okay."

Askara felt swelling confidence like a flower bud opening in the warm sun, spreading its petals, soaking in the light. She'd won a victory with a boss; she had Ramsey over a barrel. He needed *her* talents. He trusted *her* artistic judgment and *her* ability to write well, a piece missing from his repertoire. She had often edited his work, but she had not until now, realized her value. She mulled over his words: You're the best. He had never said anything like that before. Typically, Ramsey arranged client contacts and received the benefit of Askara's ability to mix with a wide range of people—and to charm them—as a prelude to his business pitch. She understood that, although he had never thanked her or given her credit...until now. Askara reveled in her accomplishment. She had stood up to Ramsey and had gotten what she wanted...what she deserved, compensation and acknowledgment. Previously, she thought he considered her an airhead. Not anymore.

But beneath his praise, Askara felt an undercurrent of honey-coated anger and frustration. Ramsey could slide from charming to snarky…fast. She had seen it before. She had wondered at times if Mimi had declined his offer for a Nob Hill tryst. Or maybe his stylist mentioned his hair was thinning? Ramsey had a thing about baldness. Or maybe Sonya was having an affair? Unlikely. Whatever the reason, Askara felt if she pushed him too far, she would not walk away unscathed, so she decided to seize the day gracefully, enjoy the time with Darian, and finish Ramsey's book project.

Ramsey motioned for Mimi to bring the check. He watched her hips sway toward him. Without taking his eyes off her, he said to Askara. "Oh, and thanks for dropping off the papers at my friend's house in Athens. See, you did accomplish one thing."

Ramsey glanced at the check and left several bills on the table, tapping them with his finger as if to make them stay in place. He pressed a tip into Mimi's pale hand and whispered something that made her face turn crimson. Ramsey stood, straightened his vest over his sagging middle, told Askara goodbye, and walked toward the Kearny Street foyer where a large crystal chandelier tossed rainbow shards of light on a mirrored wall. Askara watched him check his image in the beveled mirror before he exited to become an actor in the street movie.

On the ride home, Askara felt oddly deflated, despite her Ramsey victory. Fatigue played a part, she knew, but her feelings ran deeper than that. Anxiety swayed around her like a cobra waiting to strike. Distorted echoes, visions she couldn't decipher, incomplete images, and quick-moving shadows gripped her. She couldn't catch them. They swam like spooked fish. When she thought of Darian, the impressions scattered in all directions, making her anxiety increase even more. She wondered, "What is this about?

Distracted, she nearly sideswiped a car while changing lanes on the Golden Gate Bridge. She glanced back across the white-capped bay to the city shoreline at Fisherman's Wharf. She had walked there hundreds of times, eaten cracked crab from small paper plates, argued over the so-called *art* in the wharf galleries, and listened to street musicians playing conga drums in front of Ghirardelli Square, all pristine images that produced no anxiety.

Driving into Woodacre, past the small post office, past the two horses corralled next to the blue cottage, turning right uphill, she resolved not to tell Darian about her feelings. She would sift through them herself, logically. Darian had to cope with enough, and he needed to heal. Her mental gyrations would not help.

She walked in to find him drinking a cup of coffee and reading in the front room. "How'd you sleep, Sweetie?"

"I only just woke. The neighbor's dog was barking. Where have you been?"

"I left you a note on the nightstand. I drove to San Francisco to meet Mr. Ramsey."

"I didn't see it. And?"

Askara explained how she would work from home starting next week to help Ramsey get his book project to the publisher and get a 20% bonus if they hit the publisher's deadline. "Then, I'll quit," Askara said. "But I didn't tell him that. Darian, for the first time in my life, I held my ground with an employer. I got everything I asked for, days off with you—paid days—permission to work at home, and a bonus."

"An understanding man."

"Oh, he insists on meeting you, made a point of saying it. He seemed very interested in you. Hey, let's go into town for brunch and drive to Stinson Beach. Cold Pacific Ocean air is just what we need to reset our body clocks."

Chapter Twenty-Two

Disturbing News

Darian buttoned his jacket up to the neck, walking the beach in the soft gray fog that smelled of saltwater and kelp. "Fog reminds me of London."

"It'll burn off soon, I hope. Let's walk toward those rocks," Askara said, looping their clasped hands under his jacket flap for warmth.

White foam surf spread on the coarse yellow sand before the ocean sucked out again. They passed a couple huddled under a blanket where two children dug into the wet sand with bright yellow plastic shovels. Their small dog grabbed a shovel out of the girl's hand and ran down the beach with the screaming child following.

Askara threw a blanket down, removed her shoes, and wiggled her toes in the coarse cold sand, encouraging Darian to do the same. He kept his loafers on. Seagulls circled, looking for food, but disappointed, they screeched and flew away. Sand crabs walked sideways, disappearing into holes before sandpipers could snatch them.

Darian looked at Askara. "My heartbeat synchronizes with the ocean here. That doesn't happen at home with the Indian Ocean. This water is fierce, wild, mesmerizing."

"Dangerous and cold, too. No walking out to float marigold prayers here. I feel the ocean rhythm, but I synchronize with your heartbeat, Darian." She snuggled closer. "Water fascinates me, the power of it. Giver and taker. Experts say we may get a huge tsunami someday, when the *big one*, the mother of all earthquakes, cracks the San Andreas fault. People say the whole coast of California will slough off into the ocean, maybe even the whole West Coast."

"People believe that?"

"Yes. A few years ago, psychics predicted a huge earthquake would hit San Francisco. People were really scared, so Mayor Alioto threw an earthquake party down at the Civic Center."

"No quake?"

"No quake. People partied, smoked dope, ate hot dogs, listened to bands, and walked home happy. The psychics reworked their figures, said something about variations in planetary alignments, and targeted 2023 as the corrected date."

"Let's plan to be in India, or anywhere else," Darian said with a smile.

Subdued by the thundering waves that hammered the coastal rocks, Askara and Darian sat huddled together, speechless, for a long while until Darian complained his shoulder hurt from the damp. They slowly walked back to their car. The powerful waves became distant thunder.

When they rounded the last curve up to Askara's house, her spine tensed. She saw her neighbor boys tossing the football in their front yard. Parked in her driveway, she saw a familiar black Mercedes. Askara crammed on the brakes, jumped out, and rushed to her front door. Hardly touching it, the door swung wide open. Darian trotted up behind her.

"What are you doing here?" she said in a tight voice. How did you get in?"

"Askara, beg your pardon. I called out. I thought I heard a reply. Your door was ajar, so I entered. Then you drove up. Looks bad on my part, I'm sorry," Mr. Ramsey said, appearing nonplussed. He extended his hand to Darian. "Hello, I'm Seth Ramsey, Askara's employer."

"Darian Dalal. Don't you think you should have waited outside Miss Timlen's door, finding it ajar?"

"I locked it when I left," Askara growled.

"It was open. I assumed you were on your balcony. Again, my apologies."

Askara studied Ramsey, his formal manners, all smiles and goodwill, the style he fastidiously employed when chatting up wealthy buyers at the showroom, the technique she detested.

"Never mind. What brought you out?"

"Good news. I have just come from the publisher. Here's the rough draft layout of the book. I thought that would help you. For the three hundred full-color illustrations, the printer said you must make a space allowance for the credits below the images, on the right, when you plan the text. That's all. I had hoped to hand this to you earlier, at coffee, but the printer hadn't completed the layout draft." He thrust the folder into Askara's hand and turned to Darian. "This project represents years of research for me, and quite an effort on Askara's part, too. We're on a very tight schedule; otherwise, I would have never presumed to drop in."

"I'm sure," Darian replied, looking down at Ramsey's opened collar, where a gold link necklace caught in his chest hair.

Askara stifled a smile. She could feel Darian's reaction. Ramsey's polished Italian black leather pumps, three-piece pinstripe suit, open-collared shirt, and finely tailored black trench coat screamed gangster, straight out of the *Godfather*. With precisely trimmed dyed black hair and mustache and *Maybach* gold rim glasses, he looked like a cross between a mafioso and a gigolo. But Ramsey rarely, if ever, gave compliments, unless he was describing some particularly fine garment worn by an attractive woman, and then only if the woman were within earshot and the comment proved advantageous. That Askara knew. His repeated vote of confidence in her skills surprised her, especially in front of Darian. She softened to him.

"Thanks. I would invite you to stay for tea, but…. When's the deadline for the descriptive part?"

"Two weeks. Askara, you're the best. I'm depending on you. Again, so sorry it appeared I barged in. I didn't. I thought I'd heard you call."

"I'll get the first three chapters to you on Tuesday."

"Oh, and here's the advance," he said and pressed an envelope into her hand. "Nice to meet you, Mr. Dalal. I trust you will enjoy your stay in California. Do you live in England?"

"No, India…Bombay."

"Lovely city, at least, twenty years ago it was—tree-lined boulevards, fine architecture, especially the Gateway of India, and clean. I stayed in the Malabar Hill area, very posh, more Jaguars than in London. I've longed to return, but my business has grown. Pleasure travel is a luxury now, one I rarely have. Plus, my dear wife, Sonya, does not like being left at home alone with the boys, and we're expecting another soon. When they are older, the family will travel again. I would love for them to visit India, a fascinating country."

"Look me up when you do. I would be happy to show you the city."

"How would I contact you?"

"Through my family business, Dalal International."

"Excellent. Nice to meet you. See you, Askara."

Askara waved goodbye and watched Ramsey back out, turn, and descend the gravel drive toward Woodacre, thinking his memory is good. He'd only come over once before, and most people continue driving past her house, assuming it goes downhill to town, but that way is a narrow dirt path.

"He's not so bad, Askara, at least he appreciates the work you do."

Askara ripped open the envelope. "Wow. He gave me $2,000.00 in cash. The note says it's an advance since the last trip didn't turn out well. So unlike him."

"In India, you would never see that worker again. He's buying your dedication. The project must be important to him, and my being here worries him."

Askara spotted a small glass of water on her tiled kitchen counter. Ramsey was thirsty, she thought. "That door does swell, and the lock doesn't line up at times. The door *was* open. I screwed up."

"Trust me, Ramsey will get over the implication of impropriety."

Darian nestled into the overstuffed chair by the front window. Askara placed a quilt over him and soon heard a soft sound like a kitten purring. She smiled and slipped out to walk next door to collect her mail. Clara's eldest boy, Justin, met her at the door, greeting her with a huge smile and hug. When Askara asked if they had her mail, he disappeared into the kitchen to return with a grocery bag full.

"So much?" she said, quickly looking into the bag. "Mostly ads, no wonder. Tell your mom, thanks. I'll come back later to see her."

Askara tiptoed into her room and dumped the mail on her bed. Tossing the ads into the trash can, she separated bills into one pile, letters into another. She had three personal letters: one from Sara, a fat envelope, one from her friend Kathy, and one from her mother. Askara tossed pillows against the headboard and settled down to read Sara's fat letter plastered with stamps. The envelope looked like a kid's puzzle.

The letter began with Sara hoping Askara would, and could, read the news as soon as possible. She said she would call but figured the letter might reach before Askara returned. Askara flipped the envelope over to see the stamps that were dated weeks ago from Uganda, not Lesotho. How strange, she thought.

Askara glanced a few lines down. The name NAGALI, written in block letters, shocked her. Her stomach torqued. Sweat beaded on her upper lip. She forced herself to take a deep breath and started to read the letter.

Shortly after Sara returned to work in Lesotho, the regional director asked her to represent the Women's Collective of Maseru at a U.N. information session in Uganda's capital of Kampala. She took Impho, the leader of the Women's Collective, with her to deliver part of the presentation on how a change in agricultural practices had enhanced her collective's food production without using harmful chemicals. That part was good, Sara wrote, they got more funding, but what came next was a nightmare.

Sara and Mpho went out dancing to celebrate with a group from the conference. Nightlife in Kampala was famous all over Africa, and the Kololo Club was "on the map," according to Mpho. Sara was a little worried about taking a farm girl out dancing, but she learned the farm girl was much smarter than she had anticipated when a man came up to her and demanded she dance with him. Mpho turned him down flat, saying he was *too* ugly and *too* short for her taste. Sara saw the man grab Mpho by the arm. Mpho yanked her arm back. Sara motioned to the others in their group to surround them. They confronted the man.

The man shouted at them to back away, not to touch him, or they would die. Naturally, everyone thought the bloke was drunk, maybe crazy. His eyes bugged out, Sara wrote, *like the whites would pop.* He reached for a chunky necklace and held Impho in front of him, ordering her to look at it. At first, she laughed, then she started to cry and shake. No one knew what was wrong. Her body went limp. She hit the floor.

The man warned everyone to back away. He said he was an extremely famous person, President Idi Amin's soothsayer, and to touch Impho would be to die. Impho's date reached down to pull her up from the floor. He could not lift her. It was like she weighed a ton, he said later. Then he slumped on the floor next to her. By this time, the crowd had moved away from the crazy man who called himself The Famous Nagali, the president's eyes and ears, the man who would make Idi Amin the most famous African president ever. He declared Amin would be immortal because of his—Nagali's—skills, because of his power.

What he said next, Sara recounted, *blew her away.* He bragged he had deposed Emperor Haile Selassie of Ethiopia. Nagali claimed the emperor had something that Nagali wanted, and he would get it, no matter how long it took. With it, he would become the most powerful soothsayer in the history of the world. All leaders would seek him out and bow down to his wise counsel. He would be the kingmaker of all kingmakers. He called Emperor Selassie a thief. He declared the emperor would never again rule Ethiopia.

By that time, Nagali was practically foaming at the mouth, screaming over the blaring music, and dancing around like his feet were on fire. He looked insane, Sara recounted. Three huge bouncers approached and saw poor Mpho unconscious on the ground with her motionless friend lying next to her. They grabbed Nagali, and before he could utter a word, wrenched his arms behind him, and dragged him away. Nagali shouted he would have President Amin order all of them executed before dawn.

Someone threw ice water on Mpho and her boyfriend. They came to. She had no idea what had happened. She said monsters were crawling around that man's neck. Her friend rallied, but the poor bloke didn't know where he was, much less who Mpho was. Mpho was so shaken that she and Sara straightaway took a taxi back to their hotel. She climbed into bed with her clothes on and whimpered all night. They left first thing the next morning, arriving at the airport four hours before the flight, figuring they would be safer there.

Askara, Sara continued, I'm sure he's the bloke you told me about, the guy who hypnotized you at that party in Mombasa. That bastard must make a living at it. I'm so glad you got away. You must still be with Darian, so that's a relief. Don't know what that bastard Nagali was after, but that story of yours made me like Darian even more, although I don't know him. He's a keeper! As you must have heard by now, Selassie's still in prison. Not sure how this will play out for him, but he is alive. Some Commie rebel group overthrew him.

She said she felt glad to be back in Lesotho, where the people are gentle, and hoped that Askara was safe at home in California, or would soon be. Sara swore she would not travel in Africa unless she went west. She included a cutting from her local Lesotho paper, the *Mochochonono*, the Comet, about their hassle in Kampala. Her colleagues were upset about Impho and her being threatened. They were as shocked about that as they were interested in knowing about the Kololo Club. They felt embarrassed the story had made the news in Lesotho. When her boss called Sara into his office for an explanation, which made her nervous, it turned out he was only concerned for their safety. Sara said that was a big relief. She didn't want the collective's reputation tarnished.

She apologized, "I cut the article out to send to you, but I spilled coffee on it...sorry for the mess. It's still legible, though." She concluded with a postscript saying she had forgotten one thing. She had found out that Nagali, Amin's soothsayer, had correctly predicted the overthrow of President Milton Obote of Uganda in the '60s. Sara wondered if Amin was linked to that overthrow. When she asked some people in her office, no one thought so. Amin was a nobody at that time. But Amin had been impressed because later he made Nagali his prophet, his dream interpreter. "Yuck! Glad you got away from that bastard and his nasty necklace," she scribbled in the margin. "Love ya."

Sara included a second news clip about her successful project and how the U.N. had funded it for another round to expand to more collectives in Lesotho. Sara guessed she would be there longer, which suited her, and she promised to visit Askara in California in a year.

Askara collapsed, grabbed her knees to her chest, and her breath escaped with a groan. She couldn't believe Nagali had done to Mpho what he had tried to do to her. The mention of him brought acid to her throat. Her mind raced. She knew the man was a serious psychotic. She couldn't make sense of it. When she thought back on meeting Nagali, she remembered Mr. Reh had referred to Nagali once as his cousin Haroon's friend. Reh never mentioned Haroon was a business partner in that Mercedes import company with Nagali. Why? She concluded that since Haroon had died tragically, maybe Reh couldn't face bringing him up in casual conversation, which was understandable. Reh must not have known Nagali very directly. And Ramsey told her earlier that day that he didn't know Nagali directly either.

Askara's jet lag evaporated like she had drunk three cups of expresso. Her heart raced. The rage she felt towards Nagali at Mr. Reh's party exploded. She couldn't wait for Darian to wake to tell him Sara's news. She paced around her room, reviewing bits of information and impressions she had about the sequence of events. The more she thought about it, the more confused she became, so she decided to keep this piece of news to herself. Why ruin her time with Darian? Why upset a man trying to heal? She knew she would forget Nagali and move on, but first, she needed to run along the ridge until the anger drained from her.

Askara sneaked out and returned two hours later, totally exhausted. She peeked through the front window. Darian was still sleeping in the living room. Good, she thought. She entered through the balcony door, but the creaking sound woke Darian.

"Are we going for a walk now?" he said, looking at Askara's running clothes.

"Sure. Good idea. I'll take you up the hill to see the ocean. Let's have tea first."

They hiked the dirt path through the ferns and moss-covered rotting logs, each step triggering the scent of decaying leaves and fertile soil. Overhead redwood boughs swayed with the coastal breeze. Askara's head cleared. She left the fear of Nagali behind. They climbed the steep path up to the grassy hilltops. Leaning into a stiff wind, they reached the highest point where they watched indigo clouds turn gold in the setting sun. A hawk sailed over the dark green line of live oak trees in the ravine. Three large birds circled high above them, buffeted by the wind.

"Turkey buzzards," Askara said, pointing up.

"Yes, in Bombay, we have thousands of buzzards. The sky grows dark with them at times. They pick everything clean, useful, but ugly creatures. They take care of Zoroastrian dead in the Towers of Silence." A blast of wind nearly knocked them off their feet. Askara started to reply, but Darian pressed her close and said, "I love you, Askara. I want to marry you."

"And I love you, Darian." Askara felt a dizzying shift like the ground raced beneath her feet, or maybe it was the wind. "I want to marry you, too, Darian, but something bothers me, haunts me. I need to say this. You know I've mentioned several times my memory is messed up. I have a gap in my head. But beyond that gap, I perceive images of you—you but not you—although I know it is you, but from another time and place. Sounds crazy, I know. But just then, when you said you loved me, I heard you say it in another language, yet I understood. It's like weird déjà vu stuff. It freaks me out. I'm worried if I scratch through the image of us, here and now, I'll find darkness, like something bad is lurking. But what? It makes no sense. Darian, I don't want some weird darkness to define what we have now. I know this sounds crazy. I'm sorry."

Darian braced Askara against the wind. "Not really, Askara. You've been under incredible stress, we both have. Your impressions are jumbled with your fears. We Parsis believe in multiple lifetimes, but not exactly the way Hindus do. Most people cannot remember their past lives, yet some get images at times. Remember in Greece when I told you I felt I had known you before?"

"Yes. But, Darian, loving you scares me. That sounds harsh; please, don't be offended. I feel by my loving you, something really bad might happen to you."

"Askara, your fears are talking. The last few weeks have been rough. The wonderful memory I have of you, relaxing on the stones at the Oracle of Delphi, sun warming your face, you looking blissful, is hard to see when I look at you now. Something happened to both of us. For me, Askara, I woke from a nightmare that day. Hope returned when I saw you. I remember what you were wearing: blue jeans, a beige long sleeve tee shirt with little blue flowers embroidered at the neck, and very odd sandals. I saw you clearly then, but I cannot see you clearly now. Your smile lit up the Oracle that day. Our time in Athens was passionate, a getting back into life for me, but I hurt your feelings when I didn't know how to talk to you in Mombasa. I didn't think I could be what you wanted, and I didn't know what that was. Now I do. Askara, we want the same thing: to spend our lives with a loving friend.

"Yes, I do want that. We've straightened out our misunderstandings pretty well now. I know we love each other, Darian. But it's my mind; it scares me. I feel like my thoughts are sand racing through my fingers. They slip by in fragments that don't make sense and fall like confetti on the floor, little snippets of understanding, little glimpses that don't make a whole picture."

"Maybe," Darian said, pointing to his wounded shoulder, "forgetting is an art. The past is better left in the past. We need to move forward. We need to create our new picture together."

"But what if I'm forgetting something super important? Is that an art? Or is that a train wreck waiting to happen? Something important on my timecard should not have been punched out, but it was."

"Travel fatigue, too many experiences, robbery attempts, and that damn Nagali, all in a short time, is enough to make anyone feel undone. Then there's Ramsey. That man is odd, nice enough, even pleasant, but something in his manner is amiss. The more I think about him, the vaguer he becomes. Like a wisp of smoke rising from a fire, he blends with his surroundings and fades. He irritates me. Askara, I know he fancies you. I am in his way; he resents me. He is not a man to be trusted."

"Yuck. We've never had anything like that. Ramsey's always been professional. But you picked up on him for sure. He's a womanizer; you should see him fawn over this waitress, Mimi. He's revolting in that way, and he's married to a nice woman, too."

"Don't trust him, Askara. Account for all your work-related expenses and the hours you work. Don't be in his debt in any way."

"I'd give anything to get out of this project now. I've lost interest."

"But let me see," Darian said, holding Askara's hair back from her face in a ponytail. "Ramsey has already paid you a handsome advance. Correct? The man knows exactly what he is doing. He's buying you off. Why? He is worried you won't finish the book project, and he's not smart enough to do it on his own. His reputation rests on being not just a buyer of artifacts but being intellectually equal to his clients. He's not, and he knows it. The man has drive. He will get there financially. But he will never arrive in his own estimation of himself. He wants to best his superiors, but he sees himself as inferior. There's the rub."

ASKARA KEPT HER CHECK-IN MEETING WITH RAMSEY. After her talk with Darian, she intended to tell Ramsey she would not be available to finish his project. She had decided to return to India with Darian. Ramsey didn't take the news well. He argued and cajoled Askara, asking her to stay, but in the end, he conceded. He only requested she stay long enough to finish the rough layout pages and train her replacement for three days. Ramsey would handle the rest. Reluctantly, Askara agreed since she needed the advance money for her air ticket to India.

But Ramsey became increasingly challenging to work with. Nothing was quite good enough for him. He changed the order of the chapters, which threw off Askara's timeline and image placement. She assumed there was no way they could meet the publisher's deadline, but she would have a rough for the new hire to complete. A few days later, when Ramsey informed her the new hire would arrive within a week, his lousy mood suddenly lifted. He was friendly.

But it shifted again. Askara attended a meeting to get approval for her latest layout, which she had put hours into, often leaving Darian to read or to hike up the hill by himself. Ramsey objected to the changes. He and Askara argued over the placement. Askara shouted a barrage of pent-up frustrations and rebuttals before she stormed out. When she got home, she barged in and told Darian, "He doesn't trust my judgment. I had that chapter all blocked out, references, photographic rights, text, everything in order, and he said it didn't work. Like hell! The damn thing was fine. Now, everything's a domino effect, and the whole damned book is out of order because earlier Ramsey had wanted beads to come after semi-precious stones. Now he's changing. He wants beads before stones. I can't take this any longer."

"Sounds as if he doesn't want to finish the book. He can't face the consequences of his colleagues finding it below the mark. I don't blame him in a way. Being an importer of artifacts is far different from being an expert connoisseur, especially in his world."

"This not the definitive history of beads and stones, according to the illustrious Mr. Seth Ramsey. This book builds on the work of experts in a chronological way. Well, it did. And you know what else drives me nuts? He always asks about you: How is Mr. Dalal? I hope he is feeling well. Please give Mr. Dalal my regards. Yuk. He's so solicitous; it makes me sick."

"He fancies you, Askara. I told you. He'd like to see me far from here. He only asks by way of probing to see how we're doing." Askara didn't reply, thinking, I'd like to see *him* far from here…in hell. "He will get over it, and soon you will be finished with the project. Don't worry. We have a fun time ahead of us, going home to India. I'll take you to Kashmir. It will remind you of where you grew up in the mountains."

Askara smiled, looking forward to seeing the Himalayas. She realized that soon Ramsey and the book project would fade from her mind. She couldn't wait.

Chapter Twenty-Three

Moving On

Askara rushed into the house in time to catch the phone. A female voice said: hold please for connection. A few clicks later, a man's voice shouted over the scratchy connection to ask for Mr. Darian Dalal. Askara handed the phone to Darian as he stepped in through the front door.

"Hello? Yes?" Seconds passed before Darian replied in Hindi, speaking rapidly for several minutes. Askara watched him wince, his face fading to aged parchment. Darian tugged at the corner of his mustache; his brow rippled. "Yes, goodbye," he said and slowly put down the phone.

"What's wrong, Darian?"

"My uncle in Bombay, head of the company, has suffered a serious heart attack."

"Is he...dead?"

"No. But I must return home immediately; my family needs me. Askara, call for a booking, the earliest possible, while I shower and pack. Try British Air, Air India, any airline without long layovers. Price doesn't matter. Here's my American Express card," he said, handing her his wallet."

Askara hugged Darian and felt his heart thumping like a scared rabbit's. "It will be okay, Darian. I know it will. Go shower. I'll take care of this." After fifteen minutes, when Askara found the earliest flight, a business class booking from San Francisco, she shouted from the front room. "I have one, tonight at 9:00, Air India, one short stopover in Frankfurt. Is that okay? They need your verification. The shower turned off, and Darian rushed out in a towel to give the particulars of his passport and credit card. When he hung up, Askara said, "We need to leave pretty soon."

They drove to the San Francisco airport in silence, their thoughts separated by as many miles as their countries. Words failed. When Askara saw the green airport sign, she blurted out, "I'll miss you, Darian. I'm so sorry for your family. You know I love you. This will be okay." She glanced over and saw oncoming headlights glisten in the tears welling in Darian's eyes. She squeezed his hand.

"I love you, too, Askara. I don't want to leave you like this…not at all. If things were different, you could come with me now, but the family is in upheaval. The business will be, too. It would not be the right time to introduce you to the family." He checked his watch. "Drop me at international departures."

"Okay, but there's time. I'll park and catch up with you," she said, pulling to the curb.

"Air India Flight 108," Darian said and leaned over to give Askara a poignant kiss, wrenched his bag from the backseat, got out, and trotted toward the terminal door.

Askara looped around the cement multi-level parking structure twice, found a space on the third deck, parked, and rushed to the elevator. Inside the terminal, she charged up the escalator, ran down a never-ending length of the carpeted walkway, and arrived at Gate 9, where passengers queued for departure. She didn't see Darian. Thinking she d misread the gate number, Askara panicked and started r the reader board when Darian grabbed her shoulder from behind. She jumped.

"Thought I had missed you, Askara," Darian said and hugged her. "I love you more than you know. I will miss you every minute we are apart. If there's time at the Frankfurt airport, I will call. We'll figure out our next step very soon. Give your parents my best. Sorry, it didn't work out this time. Tell them I look forward to meeting them."

"I love you, Darian…I truly love you. I miss you already. When will?"

"Soon, I promise. Take care of yourself. Don't let Ramsey come around." Darian motioned for other passengers to go around him. But when he was the last person, the agent waved him over. He pressed Askara close, stepped back to look at her, and said, "Lock your door! I'll dream of you in your chenille bedspread, the morning light kissing your sleepy eyes. Take care of yourself."

Askara smiled and started to answer when the ticket agent began pulling the chain across the walkway. Darian rushed. Askara watched in numbed silence as Darian disappeared down the corridor to the plane. Feeling vulnerable, standing alone at the empty departure gate, she hurried to the parking deck and drove home with KFRC radio turned up as loud as it would go. When *Love Will Keep Us Together* by Captain and Tennille came on, Askara broke down and sobbed for the remainder of her drive.

She entered her quiet house, immediately made popcorn, and turned on her TV for company. She found an old movie to calm her nerves: *It Happened One Night.* The film had just ended when the phone rang. Askara jumped to answer it. The male caller from Macy's department store asked for Mr. Darian Dalal. Askara said he wasn't in, but she would relay the message. The clerk told her Mr. Dalal's order had come in and would be available for pick up at the Macy's lingerie department for two days during regular store hours. Askara lied, " Mr. Dalal will pick it up in the morning." She was surprised at such a late call, 11:30 at night. When had Darian gone there? She wondered. Realizing he must have ordered by phone, purchasing something fancy for her, she figured it made sense to receive a warehouse service call, but at that hour?

Early in the morning, the phone rang again. Askara leaped from her chair, almost knocking over her cup of coffee. Hearing Darian's voice cheered her, even though difficult to hear over the background noise of the Frankfurt airport's arrival and departure announcements in multiple languages. When Askara told him about the Macy's call, he replied he had not purchased anything.

"Look, Askara, that's very odd. Someone knew your number, someone who knows I was with you. Is your number listed in the phone book?"

"Yes," she replied.

"Don't...." His voice cut out. The call dropped.

Askara looked up the Macy's nearest her and called to speak to someone in the lingerie department. The clerk assured her they had no order on record for a Mr. Darian Dalal. She asked if there was a contact number for the warehouse. No, the clerk said. Askara asked for customer service. The customer service agent said that several people had called to complain about crank calls in the last few days. Seems to be an epidemic, she said, kids must be bored, too much free time.

Askara tried to call Darian but got the message—All lines to the country you are calling are busy, please try again—several times until she finally reached him two days later. Darian told her he figured in two months everything with the company should be stabilized, and Askara should join him then. Relieved Darian's uncle was improving after heart surgery, and Darian was doing well, she threw herself into Ramsey's work, now a welcome distraction.

Late afternoon mid-week, Ramsey met with Askara at the horse riding stable not far from her house to assure her the new hire, Aiden Bosman, was to be her gopher, not her lead, for the book project. Ramsey reiterated that she was irreplaceable, but he would train Aiden to see if he had potential after Askara familiarized him with the work. Askara thought that odd: Why hire someone who cannot do the job?

"Aiden Bosman, my dear friend's son, knows business accounting, got a degree in it," Ramsey said, handing the pony's reins to his youngest boy. "I plan to ease Aiden into buying if he stays in America. His family lives in the capital of Zambia, Lusaka, in the area called the Copperbelt. Aiden wasn't getting much together there, so I arranged a work visa for him. You know, to help his parents out."

Askara watched Ramsey's eldest son clear a small jump on his pony. Ramsey said, "He's good. He's not afraid. I used to ride a lot. When you jump, you have to look straight ahead, not down, or else the pony won't clear the jump. You have to keep your goal in mind to direct the horse."

"I know, I rode too."

Ramsey smiled and tightened his youngest son's riding cap. "Your turn next. Do better than your brother. You show him." The instructor came over to lead the boy away.

"Askara, I would like to give you credit for your work on my book, have your name, Askara Timlen, appear below mine on the title page. That would boost your career, my way of saying thanks for all the work you have done. What do you say?"

Askara thought Ramsey incapable of sharing glory. She paused a moment and accepted. "Yes, thank you." She couldn't decide which bit of news surprised her more, his offer to put her name on the book, or his hiring a foreigner who needed a work permit for a job he couldn't do just to help out family friends. Both scenarios seemed hard to imagine. Askara wondered if Aiden had done something illegal and had to be spirited out of his home country of Zambia.

"Aiden is about your age, Askara, a nice guy. So, what do you say? Train him, get your book credit, and then trot off to join Mr. Dalal in India. Or will he join you here?"

"I'll go to Bombay."

"Excellent. You found a winner, Askara. Hold onto him. Nothing brings more pleasure in life than a loving, calm family scene," Ramsey said, looking at his sons trotting in the arena.

CHAPTER TWENTY-FOUR

Copperbelt Blues

Aiden Bosman was not what Askara expected from the moment she saw him ride up on a Harley in downtown San Francisco. Looking from her second-floor office, she watched him back into the parking slot on the steep hill, slam the jiffy stand down with his black leather commando boot, and stand up to stretch. Askara couldn't imagine the motorcycle would not fall over. She laughed to herself: he has a lot to learn.

She heard his boots clomp on the metal elevator exit before the sound softened on the carpeted entrance to Ramsey's office. The door swung wide open and hit the wall. Aiden said his name AIDEN BOSMAN like a cannon going off at the counter when he asked for Mr. Seth Ramsey, CEO. The secretary smiled and picked up her phone, saying, your new hire is here, sir. Ramsey rushed from his office and gave the young man a hearty handshake and an affectionate cuff on the shoulder while Askara watched from the copy room.

"You're five inches taller than when last I saw you, Aiden. All grown up."

"Yessir, my parents send their regards. I'm here, ready

to work. Customs and immigration went well, no hitches, thanks to you."

Ramsey called for his employees to come out and meet his new hire from Zambia. When his secretary asked where Zambia was, Aiden blurted out in Africa, the southern part, near the middle. Looking confused, she smiled without replying.

When Askara walked in, Ramsey introduced her as Aiden's supervisor. She saw a shadow of discomfort skip across his broad, sunburned face. But he shook her hand and said it was nice to meet her although Askara knew what he meant: Oh, shit, I have to work for a woman—a brown woman my age. She felt the heat in Aiden's handshake escalate.

Ramsey led him back to his office for a private conversation, Aiden's commando boots making deep impressions in the carpet pile. Askara decided to take an early lunch to avoid the unpleasant possibility of having lunch with Ramsey and Aiden. When she walked across the street to the deli, she saw Aiden's Harley leaning onto the curb. She wondered if Aiden could lift the six-hundred-pound bike upright. She figured he could, with ego, if nothing else. How he would handle jewelry could prove interesting. Askara smirked, wondering what Ramsey owed the Bosmans to sponsor their son on a work visa when he was not the jewelry-and-artifacts type of guy, professional game hunter maybe, but jewelry, no. She only found it humorous because soon she would leave all this behind to join Darian and start their life together.

In the next few days, Askara tried to teach Aiden the basics of metal and stone verification. He seemed to know about diamonds- -*conflict diamonds*, she guessed—

but not other precious stones. He became agitated during their training sessions and made excuses to take breaks, get a drink of water, use the bathroom, take a call, or go for coffee, ostensibly for Mr. Ramsey. That she knew was ridiculous since Ramsey would never pass up the opportunity to see Mimi at Max's Café, and he would never take Aiden since Mimi was closer to Aiden's age than Ramsey's. She hoped Aiden had the sense not to hit on Mimi. Ramsey would never stand for it. That would be like stealing his prize cufflinks. Aiden may have been a boy when Ramsey last patted him on the head, but he was anything but that now. His rough young man charm, like a dust devil from a distant land, stirred up the female office staff, but not Askara. Her vision wasn't clouded. He could cause a lot of upheavals if he didn't reign in his bravado, Askara thought.

Aiden was thick in body and mind, but Askara didn't hold that against him. She praised his quick success when speaking to Ramsey. She announced Aiden was ready to start his work in earnest after she had trained him for three days, realizing three years would not make a dent. Ramsey had some reason to support Aiden, an altruistic one, Askara hoped, keeping her thoughts to herself.

At lunch on their last day of training, Askara asked, "So, Aiden, what did you do before you left home?"

"I worked at my dad's copper mine," he said, chomping on a double-patty burger. "Dad was teaching me management skills, but I realized I didn't like it. I couldn't communicate with the Chinese workers; the Blacks were okay, but they didn't listen to me. One day there was a problem between workers. I broke the fight up. I got blamed when the owner found out about it. Dad thought I'd be a natural manager since he was. Wasn't my thing. I decided I wanted to try my hand at something else, so Dad sent me here."

"Yes, management is a special skill. I don't like it either. But I thought your dad owned the copper mine."

"Nope. Manages it. A Zambian named Nagali owns it. He lives in Uganda now, so my dad's job is super important. He does everything. Mr. Nagali comes a few times a year to check on the books."

Askara dropped her fork into her salad bowl. She fumbled to pick it out of crumbled feta cheese and looked down, trying to compose herself. Her hands got sweaty. She felt the hairs on the back of her neck stand up. Ramsey hadn't mentioned that Nagali owned the mine. She was glad when Aiden finished his fries and said that he needed to get back for a meeting with Mr. Ramsey. She gathered her courage for one last question. "Aiden, how long has your father managed the copper mine?"

"Going on six years, but he worked there about eleven as assistant manager, ever since we moved from South Africa."

THE NEXT DAY AT WORK, SHE DECIDED TO CONFRONT Ramsey. She barged into his office.

"Askara, glad to see you. You've done a great job with Aiden, thank you. I know you're probably busy...."

"Why didn't you say you know Nagali?"

"I don't. I know of him. I mentioned that."

"You never said that he owns the copper mine in Zambia that Aiden's dad manages."

"It never came up. Is it important? Yes, Nagali does, but I have never met him. Nagali, as a contact for the jewelry purchase, came through the Aga Khan's friend, as I had told you. Aiden's dad doesn't live in that world; he's not sophisticated. He's a good guy, someone I count as a dear friend. Why are you so upset? Has Aiden been rude to you?"

"No, he's fine."

"Great. I have one more favor to ask of you before you leave. Could you take Aiden around a bit, you know, show him San Francisco life for young singles. I'd treat you two to dinner at the Stinking Rose."

"I'm not a good escort. Margie has eyes for him. Ask her."

"I'm not trying to fix him up. Margie would have him in bed before dinner."

"Maybe that would suit him."

Ramsey shook his head and turned crimson. "How about showing him Golden Gate Park? That's easy enough, then have a good meal. I know he's bored. Please. We had him over, but my wife's so close to delivering, well, we weren't good company for a young man."

"Okay, I'll take him, but then I'm done. I have a lot to do before I leave."

"Thank you. Let this be your farewell dinner. I wish, if things were different, we could throw you a party, but we need to be ready to go to the hospital at a moment's notice."

WHILE WALKING AROUND GOLDEN GATE PARK, ASKARA asked Aiden, "You mentioned your dad has worked for Nagali for a few years. Have you met him?"

"No, my dad always meets him alone." Watching hippies toss frisbees, Aiden continued, "People call Nagali a witch doctor. He's real tight with Idi Amin, the president of Uganda. They say Nagali casts spells and stuff."

Askara stifled her revulsion. She played innocent to tease out what Aiden knew. "What do you mean, a witch doctor? Is he a tribal healer?"

"More like a fortune teller seems to me. I don't like the guy because he hasn't been nice to my dad, and he accused me of trying to cheat him. I didn't. But my dad says he's important and not to cross him. That's why I came here. Dad said it would be better if I took a break, got away, expanded my horizons type of thing, and worked for his old friend Seth Ramsey for a few months. I couldn't believe my luck. I've always wanted to see America."

"What? I thought you wanted to apprentice with Mr. Ramsey to learn the trade."

"Not really. I'm not sure I'm the jewelry type. I got into a bit of trouble back home, nothing huge, but some guys thought I'd done something against them. My father thought I should let things cool down at the copper mine. Nagali wasn't happy with me."

"Okay, I'm interested. What did you do? Did you kill someone in a fight?"

"Nothing like that. I recommended a guy I knew, who had earlier worked at the copper mine, a childhood friend from Jo'berg, to arrange a contact in South Africa for Nagali so that he could buy diamonds. Turns out, the diamonds and my friend's contact weren't any good. The deal fell through. Stuff like that happens a lot in Africa. Nagali thought I had tried to cheat him. Dad wanted me to leave while he straightened things out. It's like I had two strikes against me, the factory fight and then the messed up diamond deal. They weren't my fault."

Askara looked at the rugged guy walking next to her, a what-you-see is what-you-get type, big, not notably smart, not notably corrupt either, just strong and naive enough to get into a lot of trouble. She warmed to Aiden, realizing they had something in common: they both had gotten on Nagali's bad side. Suddenly the pieces fell into place. That night in Mombasa, when she rejected Nagali's stupid amulet hypnosis attempt, she created a determined enemy. He couldn't let go of the insult. She realized his pattern. Aiden foiled a diamond purchase for Nagali out of no fault of his own. Maybe Mr. Reh's cousin Haroon had met an untimely death because he had failed his business partner, Nagali, in some deal. The guy is vindictive, maybe evil enough to have hired that merchant marine to track me, evil enough to cause all those break-ins. Nagali is crazy and dangerous. He constructs his life around vendettas, she thought.

"Do you know much about Nagali, like from your father?"

"Dad doesn't talk much, but some of the guys at the mine told me stories about him from his Zambian days before he moved to Uganda. Nagali worked in the same copper mine he owns now, the one my dad manages. Nagali was nothing special, a nobody with a nasty temper. Then he made some accurate predictions about political things, and wham, he was at the top of his game. That's when he got the money to buy the mine. The previous owner, a white guy, had died suddenly from a snakebite. Nagali snatched up the mine before anyone heard it was for sale. Mining copper is a sideline; being Amin's kingmaker is his main thing."

When Aiden left her house later after thanking her for a great meal, he made no uncomfortable advances. He was a polite, rough-cut gentleman. She wished him good luck and shut her door quickly, listening to his Harley roar down the hill on the dirt track, sure her neighbors would not be happy.

Feeling rattled by her realizations, Askara sat on a yoga

mat in her living room to try to calm down. She shut her eyes and tried to breathe deeply but choked on short, quick gasps. Her body shook; she cried uncontrollably. Gripped by anguish, she whimpered, "I need help. Please, someone, help me. I'm going mad. I'm scared."

The tightness in her chest loosened. Her thoughts slowed. In the darkness of her closed eyes, she perceived a glow that pulled her attention to a distant point, like a lighthouse beacon. She felt her body follow. Three words floated into her consciousness: *Magi, Magi, Magi*.

The Respected One appeared at the beacon. Askara walked toward him. She saw herself as a young child, and he as her adoptive father. She ran to embrace him. Askara and Asha became one in his embrace. In her clasped hands, she saw she held a small cup containing an oil wick flame. The Respected One spoke to her like a gentle breeze coming from a distant land.

"You have done well, child. You must move forward and accept your destiny. Leave despair behind. Join Dastur in India. Your lives will unfold in many ways as your bond determined long ago. Walk your paths to the best of your abilities. Remember who you are."

His image faded. A pink glow filled the room, and Askara felt at peace. She sat up straight, took a deep breath, and felt joy at the thought of leaving to join Darian in India and start their new life together…whatever it may hold.

THE END

Author's Note

Thank you for reading Cup of the Shining Sun. I have published others, but this effort, my first, is dear to me. It's also been the hardest to write because it's personal. Much of the detail comes from my travel journals from 1972-1974. The story grew in fits and starts in 2001, but I had less time to work on it when I became a full-time college professor of visual arts rather than associate faculty. The story percolated in my imagination and took shape over many years.

This book is unique to me because I lived much of it. After graduation from UC Berkeley, I hitchhiked through Europe, working when my money ran out and crossed through Yugoslavia (remember that name?) where I heard young people talk of revolution, and ended up in Greece. On Corfu, I worked taking tourists from England on horseback riding outings, part of a vacation package deal from London. One family group became pivotal to what I did next. A man who had served in the British Navy with Emperor Haile Selassie's nephew wrote me a letter of introduction should I find myself in Ethiopia. I had no set plans, but when the December rains came to Corfu, my job ended.

I traveled to see ancient sites. At the Oracle of Delhi, an Australian woman approached to say hello. It was fun to speak to someone in English, particularly someone with a witty sense of humor. Sarah and I became friends and hatched a plan while seeing the Temple of Knossos in Crete to fly to Cairo and go overland through Egypt, Sudan, and Ethiopia to Kenya for a safari. Hardest traveling ever! That trek imbued this fictional story with many factual details. (Try to guess which are true.) You may feel you're with us on the journey, in good times and bad.

The pivotal thing that happened, seeing Emperor Haile Selassie in his garden at Jubilee Palace, is accurate. My letter of introduction only got us inside the palace grounds. The Emperor's nephew was, as they say, out-of-station. He was in London at the time.

The Emperor stepped into the garden to bid someone goodbye, not forty feet from where we sat on a bench in the shade. He looked at us, studied us, without expression, but wow, what an impression Selassie made on me. He was a small man with a huge energy. Very neatly dressed in his military uniform and cap, he radiated the sense that here is a man who embraces his legacy, 3,000 year of it, as a descendant of the Queen of Sheba and King Solomon. He came to power in 1930 and ruled until the Marxist coup deposed him in 1974. He died in 1975.

We were there months before the coup, yet the civil war and famine were raging, although not formally known to the world. Emperor Selassie's face-saving approach prevented the world from realizing how bad the famine was and how much unrest existed until it was too much to hide.

Cup of the Shining Sun is book one in a trilogy. Those years of writing added up. Book two, buckle your seat belt, takes place in Madagascar!

I hope you enjoyed the story. Since I do not have a "big house" behind my efforts, I would appreciate your writing a review. I will learn a lot from your opinions, which is my goal. I may have been a professor for years, but first and foremost, I am a perennial student. I will learn from you!

Thank you! Enjoy the trip!

Made in the USA
Las Vegas, NV
23 November 2020